AWAKENINGS

Book 3 of the One True Child Series

Between the Lines Publishing
9 North River Road, Ste 248
Auburn ME 04210
btwnthelines.com

First Published: 2018
Original ISBN (Paperback) 978-1-7321723-9-5
Original ISBN (eBook) 978-1-7321723-8-8

Second edition:
ISBN: (Paperback) 978-1-950502-81-3
ISBN: (Ebook) 978-1-950502-83-7
ISBN: (Hardcover) 978-1-950502-82-0

AWAKENINGS

Book 3 of the One True Child Series

L.C. Conn

Also available from L.C. Conn

Realm of Dragons: Fight for the Crown

The One True Child Series

Sentinels (Book 1)
Domination (Book 2)

Praise for *Sentinels*:

"An excellent beginning to a fantasy epic. From page one, you'll be swept up into this battle of good and evil with all of creation at stake."
— **Jo Neiderhoff, San Francisco Book Review**

Praise for *Domination:*

"Once more, Conn weaves her spell, and we are immersed in Carling's spectacular world. Adventure, magic, and romance leave us hungry for more!"
— **Tamara Benson, San Francisco Book Review**

"Fantasy is alive and well and exerting its power to enchant and beguile in this novel of foretold destiny." — **Diane Donovan, US Review of Books**

Early praise for *Awakenings*:

"Once more, Conn gives the modern young female reader a heroine to look up to. Her prose is accessible, and her storytelling skills shine brightly, leaving us waiting for more in books to come." — **Manhattan Book Review**

Dedicated to my two children, Terry and Samantha. Thank you for putting up with the hours of plot discussions and character analyzations.

Chapter One

The first few stars of the evening were just starting to twinkle into existence as the last of the sunset's ruddy glow disappeared in the windows of the surrounding buildings. The bright reflections were soon replaced with the illumination of fluorescent lighting from within. Traffic below snaked through the narrow streets, honking, and revving as people tried to get home from their daily lives while the city started to wind up into its own nightlife. From somewhere in the distance Christmas music blared from a shop, competing with the *thump, thump, thump* beat coming from a nearby bar along with the noise of its patrons. It was the heartbeat and rhythm of the city, which brought out the best in some but the worst in others, reflecting the often grimy and gritty streets that surrounded them.

Above these streets and noise stood two teens looking down at the alley, which—from their perspective—looked like the Grand Canyon dividing two identical buildings. Claire leaned out over the abyss. Her hands rested on the low wall, the only barrier between a five-floor drop and the hard, dark pavement below. The large hand of Adam pulled her back to safety, and she shook him off.

"Come on, Claire. You're never going to be able to jump that!" he said to her. Adam pointed the camera that seemed to be permanently adhered to his hands at the gap before them.

He filmed the distance between buildings, and then pointed it back at Claire. "You're crazy! If you think you can make that, then you've gone bloody mental." Adam's face was knitted into a worried frown.

"Watch me," Claire said determinedly, plugging her earbuds in and cranking up the music to drown out the surrounding noise. She jogged to the opposite side of the roof and turned back to face Adam. A look of concentration settled on her face as she let out a couple of deep breaths and waited until a certain part of the song came up. Drums suddenly erupted in her ears, loud and fast, and Claire started her run-up. Determination exuded from her while her long blonde hair, caught up in a ponytail, flew behind; her large blue eyes fixed on the spot she knew she must leap from. Her heart thumped in time with her footsteps, and the heavy beat pounded away in her ears while her arms pumped at her sides. It was only a matter of seconds until she reached the point of no return, but to her, time stretched out and slowed.

Her foot reached for the invisible mark on the low wall, and she pushed off with all her strength. This was what she lived for, the feeling of flying, of nothing underneath her. The freedom of open air and not being tied to the ground always made her wish she was a bird and could continue to the horizon. Adrenalin pumped through her veins and heightened her senses. Her landing spot on the opposite roof was fixed firmly in her mind, and all too soon it came rushing up to meet her. First her right foot, then her left contacted the roof, and she went into a tumble to slow herself down. She came back up on her feet and raised both fists into the air in triumph as she danced around.

"Suck that, Adam! Told you I could do it!" she yelled at him and then danced around in a circle.

"You're a freak, Claire Brown!" He laughed and continued to film her celebration.

"Well, are you going to try it?" she called out to him, still breathing hard.

"Nuh-uh, not me! I'm not stupid enough to try that. This one is all yours." He bowed to her with an exaggerated flourish. "Meet you down on the street and we can go over the footage from tonight."

Claire nodded and then went looking for the fire escape at the back of the building.

Once on the street, Claire waited at the entrance to the alley. She was only seventeen and was fast gaining a reputation as being the best free runner in the city. Her best friend since childhood, Adam Ryder, was always her cameraman. He enjoyed free running as much as Claire but was the first to admit that he was nothing compared to her. He was her voice of reason in most of the stunts, making her stop and think about whether she could actually make a leap, what obstacles there could be in her way, and generally if it was a stupid idea. He was also the one who posted the clips online to share with the world. But most of all, he was her confidant.

A noise made her turn, and from behind a large bin a shadowy figure came running towards her. Adam soon reached her side, breathing heavily. His dark hair was plastered to his face with the early summer heat and the exercise. His green eyes were bright and shining, and they always made Claire smile.

"There's some amazing stuff here," Adam told her between breaths while they walked down the street together.

"You know, you need to exercise more. You're getting a bit out of shape. I know—next time *I'll* hold the camera and *you* can do the amazing, dangerous stunts!" Claire hit him in the stomach lightly and laughed at him.

"No way! I'm not as crazy as you are," he said as he held open the door to a coffee bar and waited for her to enter.

"Thank you, kind sir," she said mockingly. They ordered some food and drink, found a booth in the back, and sat down. "So, come on; let's see," Claire demanded, holding out her hand for the camera.

Adam passed it over and watched her face as she reviewed her performance. This was always the best part of the night, just the two of them together, laughing and appreciating each other's company. They would sit and enjoy a meal, talk, and sometimes when things were tough at school or at home, they would vent as well.

The waitress arrived with their food, a grilled sandwich and water for Adam and a large cheeseburger with fries and a large milkshake for Claire. "Where do you put it all, Claire?" He shook his head.

"I dunno! I'm a growing girl," she protested, taking a bite from the burger.

"Growing? Huh! The only growing you are going to be doing from now on is *out* if you keep eating that crap," he said, indicating the food in front of her.

"Who are you, my own personal fun police?"

"You keep eating like this and there will be no more jumps like that last one. I don't know how you do it; it's almost like you're flying." He grinned at her, and she blushed, feeling all fluttery inside.

"Oh my God! Are you blushing? Have to mark this date in the diary. The day I finally made Claire Brown blush."

"Shut up, you dick! I'm not blushing. It's only the exercise making the capillaries in my cheeks flush," Claire said as she put on a posh accent.

"Yeah, right! And pull the other one. It's got bells on!"

"Does it? Can I see?" She ducked under the table jokingly.

"Get up, you fool." He gave her a gentle swipe and pinched one of her chips.

They fell into a companionable silence as they ate their food, with Claire occasionally slapping Adam's hand whenever he tried to take one of her chips. They talked of school and the teachers they hated. Claire complained of the girls who were so catty that they needed to be declawed, and Adam sympathised and told her that they would be all clambering to be her friend when she was famous. The conversation turned to talk of their plans for the rest of the weekend.

"Hey, Jordan was talking about going to the new skate park. Is that still happening?" Claire asked him, popping the last chip into her mouth.

"Nah, he's been dragged away for the weekend by his olds. But I have something in mind," Adam said grandly.

"Do tell, please, Mr Ryder. What is this big announcement you have to make?" She held a pretend microphone under his nose and looked very seriously at him until she started to crack up.

"Can't you take anything seriously?" Adam shook his head at her, but the grin that spread across his face betrayed his true feelings.

"Yes, when I need to. Now what is it you have in mind, Adam?" She put her head in her hands and looked at him with a vapid smile on her face.

"I'm going to ignore that for now. Well, you know how you're always looking for a challenge?" She nodded, and he went on, "I think a great opportunity has come up. I've been talking to Dad about you and showing him the videos, and he wondered if you would be up for a bit of a game."

"You know you talk like him sometimes. What type of game?" she asked hesitantly, becoming serious. On the occasions that she had met Adam's father, she had not liked him. Marcus Ryder always came across as a bit standoffish and uninterested in whatever his son and his friends were doing, but his eyes had always followed her.

"Well, he's got this new building and it's just about finished. They've just put in a new state-of-the-art alarm system, and he was wondering if we would like to test it out. Dad said we could have full run of the place and he will pay us for each alarm we don't trip. It's so he can see if it needs to be beefed up or not. He wants to make sure he isn't being ripped off." He looked at her and smiled. "Come on, Claire. It'll be cool."

"So, he's just going to let us into this building so that we can run around, and pay us?"

"Yeah, but no. Sorry, I know that didn't help. No, we have to break into the building first and then try to get to the top floor, where he will be waiting for us with the money." He waited for her reply.

"We have to break in?" she asked, sitting back into her seat as she studied him. "I'm not sure about this, Adam. I've got a bad feeling about it."

"What's to feel bad about? He's giving us permission to break in, and he's going to pay us money for having fun. Honestly, there's nothing to worry about." He smiled at her and reached across the table, placing his hand over hers. "It's all legit. I promise."

At that moment a group of their friends joined them noisily at the table, and Claire didn't have a chance to give Adam an answer. She couldn't even say to herself why she was uneasy about the plan; it just didn't sit right with her. While trying to enjoy the rest of the evening, Claire mulled over the problem until it was time to leave.

Adam walked her home—or at least he walked while she jumped, tumbled, flipped, leapt, and scaled objects along the way. At times he would ask her to do a move again so that he could try a different camera angle, or he would suggest adding a twist or two. They kept this up until they finally reached her door.

"You didn't answer me in the café," Adam said while she fumbled with her keys.

"Can I give you an answer tomorrow? I want to sleep on it for now." She found her key and slipped it into the door.

Adam reached up as if to touch her hair and then dropped his hand down again. "Sorry," he apologised, looking slightly embarrassed.

"I promise I'll give you an answer in the morning, Adam. See ya." Claire pushed the door open, waved goodbye, then closed it, leaving him standing on the doorstep. She watched through the frosted glass as his shape moved down the steps and out of sight, then she turned to enter the living room.

It was a large, comfortable room with a masculine suite of green leather chairs and a couch with matching darker green cushions. Sitting in his favourite chair was a very long-legged man reading a book. He looked up at her over his glasses as she entered the room and rested the book on his knee.

"Good night?" he asked as he looked at his watch.

"Yes, thanks, and I am in well before curfew. It's not even nine thirty yet." She launched herself onto the couch and put her feet up.

"Claire, how many times have I got to tell you not to throw yourself onto the furniture or put your shoes on it?"

"Yes, Uncle Geoff." She swung her legs and kicked her shoes off onto the rug, then returned her feet to the couch.

Geoff Brown was Claire's guardian and great-uncle. She had come to live with him after a car accident claimed the lives of her parents when she was ten. Her parents had named him her godparent and guardian when she was born. She had been a timid girl at that age, and it took a while for her to warm to the uncle she had not seen very much.

"Uncle Geoff, you work for Marcus Ryder, don't you?" she asked as she played with the zip on her jacket.

"Yes, I do some legal work for him from time to time. Why do you ask?"

"What sort of company does he run?"

"It's really a bit of this and a bit of that. Everything from developing projects such as buildings to making boxes. Why the sudden interest in Mr Ryder's empire? Are you thinking of trying to wed his son for his inheritance?" Geoff said, trying to repress a smile.

"Oh, God, no. Adam and I are just good mates."

"Methinks the lady doth protest too much," he told her. "Come on, Kid. There is something you want to ask me, so out with it."

For as long as Claire could remember, he had always called her Kid. It never failed to make her feel secure when he did. "It's just...Adam told me his father wants to test a new security system in a building that is just about finished. The idea is to break into this building, make our way up to the top floor, and meet his father up there. He said that Mr Ryder is willing to pay us for every sensor and camera that we don't trip."

"Is that so? I'm pleased that you have come to me about it first. He hasn't mentioned anything to me. I take it you're a bit hesitant about doing it."

"I am. For a start, breaking in doesn't seem right to me. Why not just let us in and take it from there? I wouldn't have a clue how to break into a place like that," Claire added quickly.

"I am very glad to hear that, Kid. When do you have to let him know if you will or won't do it?"

"I told Adam that I would let him know tomorrow. We're meeting up at the park after lunch. I have to finish that English assignment for Miss Pollard in the morning," Claire said, making a face. "I swear she just gives us these assignments to torture us."

"Miss Pollard is a very nice woman. You should be happy to have such a caring teacher."

"It's only because she has the hots for you!" She giggled at the face he pulled.

"Let me make a phone call in the morning to check if this is all aboveboard, then you can have your answer by the time you leave for the park."

"Thanks, Uncle Geoff." She slid off the couch and bent down to kiss him on the forehead. "I'm going for a shower and then bed. Good night."

"Night, Kid. Have a good sleep." He watched her leave the room and picked his book up again, but he did not resume reading. A worried frown creased his face as he considered what Claire had told him.

The following morning Claire was finishing up her assignment, tapping away quickly at her keyboard, when Geoff walked in. He leaned up against the door frame and watched her work for a while. Concentration etched her face as she moved from laptop to paper and back again. It always surprised him how much she could retain from just a glance at a book. When she was younger, shortly after coming to live with him, he had made a game of it as a way of distracting her. He would give her a book and ask her to skim through it, then he would take it back and open it up to a random page and ask her what was on it.

Geoff entered the room and started to straighten up her bed and pick clothes up off the floor. "When are you going to clean this pigsty?"

"Yeah, I'll do it in a minute," Claire told him absently. "Busy now." Geoff sat on the bed and watched her work some more.

When she finally sat back after a single keystroke to print the assignment, she let out a sigh. "Thank God that's over." She turned in her seat and jumped when she saw Geoff sitting there. "When did you come in?"

"You don't remember? I talked to you about cleaning your room."

"Did you? Sorry." She stood and started to gather up her books and papers, pushing them into her backpack. "Was there something you wanted to talk to me about?"

"Yes. You came to me last night and asked me about Marcus Ryder."

"Oh, yeah. You said you would make a phone call to check it out."

"And I've done that. Marcus was a bit cagy, but he confirmed that he had asked Adam if you two would like the challenge. Claire, if you are not comfortable with doing it, then don't. You never have to do anything you don't want to do. Please remember that." Geoff grabbed Claire's hand and pulled her down to sit beside him. "The choices we make today affect our lives in the future. If by doing this you have fun and make a little money on the side, it is all well and good. But if you have reservations of even beginning this, then I say stick to your gut feeling. The choice is yours, Kid."

Claire kissed her uncle on the cheek. "I still haven't made up my mind but thank you for caring and for always helping me." She hugged him briefly and then stood again. "Now can

I please get you to leave so I can get dressed? I can't go out in my pj's."

Geoff did as he was asked, but he turned back just before she shut the door. "Can you at least put your dirty washing out? Your room is starting to stink worse than a teenage boy's." In answer, Claire shut the door in his face while poking out her tongue at him.

Within twenty minutes she was walking out the door, calling her good-byes to Geoff and running down the road to meet Adam. Along the way she ducked and dove around people on the footpath, jumping over rubbish bins and generally enjoying herself. She waited at the lights to cross the road to the park and spied Adam sitting on a swing. His head was down, looking at the camera screen in his hands. He looked up, spotted her straight away, and came to meet her as she crossed.

"Hey, Claire! How's it going?" He already had the camera up in her face.

"Will you put that thing away? I'm fine; finally finished that assignment for Pollard this morning. Agh! I hate her. '*So, Miss Brown, when are we going to see that handsome uncle of yours?*'" Claire imitated her teacher and then shuddered at the thought.

"You're free now so you can stop thinking about her. What do you want to do today—leap a tall building in a single bound? Climb up the side of the tallest tower downtown?" he asked then looked at her sideways. "Or we could break into Dad's new building?"

"About that...yeah, I'm still not sure. I just have this really bad feeling something's going to happen."

"What can happen? It's an empty building, we have permission to be there, and Dad's going to pay us money for doing it. You know how tight he is."

"Yeah, says the guy whose allowance is ten times more than mine!" She laughed.

"Hey, the least you could do is go look at it. You can make up your mind then." He smiled at her. For some reason she could not see any harm in just looking, and she agreed. "Sweet. You won't be disappointed. I promise."

They walked out of the park and headed downtown. The air was electric with sounds, smells, and sights. Their senses were so used to the noise and pollution of the large city, they usually didn't register any of it. But that afternoon Claire was on edge. A large truck blasted its horn as it sped past them, and she jumped at the sound. Adam noticed and laughed at her reaction. She smiled back, trying to make light of the moment, but she felt uneasy.

"There it is," Adam told her as they stopped on a street corner. He pointed at a new and shiny building across the road on the opposite corner. The walls were still white and had none of the grey grime that seemed to cling to its neighbours. The bottom-floor windows were covered up with signs announcing the shops that would soon be moving in.

"It's huge! How many floors is it?" she asked, looking up at its silhouette against the sky, the many panes of glass reflecting the moving clouds that marred the day.

"Dad said there are twenty floors with a penthouse up on top. The top three floors are going to be apartments and the rest are all offices." He looked at her and could see the curiosity starting to affect her. "Do you want to go in for a closer look?"

"It couldn't hurt to just look, I suppose." She glanced both ways and ran across the road. Adam had to dodge a few cars before he caught up with her.

"There's an alley that runs up the side and to the back of the building to a parking garage underneath," he told her. "See, he even told me the best way to get in."

"What about the alarms? Are you sure we won't get in trouble with the cops?"

"No, we won't. Dad told me that the alarm system is in, but it's not hooked up properly to any monitoring place yet. He has a computer set up in the penthouse that he has hooked into the system, so he can see if we trip the sensors and which cameras pick us up. It's all good."

"Look, Adam, I had Uncle Geoff ring your dad and ask about it. I hope you don't mind," Claire told him, still looking up at the tall structure.

"He told me this morning. This is going to be some serious fun, Claire. Can you imagine the hits we'll get off this one? It'll be off the charts!" he said, referring to their internet channel. "Of course, we don't have to mention that it's my dad's building."

His enthusiasm was infectious, and she began to be swayed to his side. Claire put up her hands in surrender. "Okay. All right. I give in. We'll do it. What time is this all supposed to happen?"

Adam started punching the air in his excitement. "Awesome! Claire, you won't regret this. I promise."

"Okay, Adam. Calm the hell down!" she said, looking around her to see if anyone was watching.

"Sorry. I guess I'm just a bit excited. When does it go down? About eight tonight. He said to stay away until then 'cos there may still be workers inside, and he has to get into place, so he can track our progress." He was talking fast and when he finally ran out of puff, he took a deep breath. "Sorry," he said sheepishly.

"No more coffee for you today," Claire admonished him. "Come on, I'm hungry. I haven't had lunch yet."

Claire dragged him down the street to a fast-food restaurant and pushed him inside when he started protesting about unhealthy food. They spent a good hour in the restaurant, making a plan of attack. The rest of the afternoon they spent in a similar way, planning, talking, and generally joking around.

Eight o'clock on the dot found the pair standing at the entrance of the alleyway attached to the building that towered above them. The streets were ablaze with light and bustling with people intent on having a good Saturday night. Flashing neon signs competed with LCD ones, and music spilled out from bars and clubs further up the road. Cars drove up and down looking for non-existent parking bays, honking their horns at other drivers and pedestrians in frustration. The wind swirled lazily around the buildings, bringing with it the smell of exhaust fumes, overflowing rubbish bins, and the salty hint of the harbour nearby. It was a thriving city, full of life, and it was the city Claire loved.

She had been born in this city, and it was her home. She knew every street, back alley, and abandoned building where a person who was obsessed with free running could get a thrill. Regardless of what she had said to her uncle, this was not the first time she had broken into a building, but this was the first new building and for her it still felt wrong.

Both Adam and Claire watched the shadowy alley. Bins full of discarded construction materials lined one side of it, and a light further in indicated the entrance to the underground car park. They looked at each other and started towards the beacon. Claire was slightly behind Adam when they reached the pool of light, and she stopped before truly entering it.

Adam made his way to the security door and turned back to her.

"Are you coming, or are you gonna wimp out on me?" He beckoned her over to him.

"Yeah, yeah. Calm the farm," she told him with a bit of bite to her voice that was not like her.

"It's okay. Everything is all squared up." He placed a hand on the door and then punched a number sequence on the keypad. They both heard the loud click of the lock opening. Adam pushed on the door, and it gave. He held it open for her, and as she brushed past him, he smiled down at her.

The lights in the corridor flickered on when the door was opened. The buzzing from the fluorescent lighting above seemed loud to her in the sudden quiet as the door shut behind them with a secure thump. She looked about her surroundings and took in the stairs leading up and down, and the white walls, bare except for the green exit signs and lock-release button beside the door. She did not see alarm sensors or cameras up on the ceilings or walls.

"Right, shall we get started?" Adam asked her as he made his way to the steps.

"Can you tell me how we're breaking in if you've got the code for the door in the first place?" She followed him up the steps, always keeping an eye out for the alarm traps he had told her about.

"I told you it was all squared up," Adam said, his voice hushed in the quiet of the building.

"Then why are we whispering?"

"I don't know. You started it." He carried on up the steps till they reached the first floor. He stood at the access door and waited for her to catch up.

"You don't really seem that worried about alarms, Adam. Why?"

Just then his phone started to buzz in his pocket, and Adam rushed to answer it. Holding it to his ear, he listened to the person on the other end.

"It's Dad," he told her, holding the phone so his father couldn't hear. "He caught me snooping around this morning with the security guy, trying to get inside information. He wants you to do your tricks to see if the cameras can pick up any dead spots."

"What does he want me to do?" Claire was looking around her at the large staircase. She leaned out over the rail and looked upwards as it snaked around and around, climbing higher.

"He says he can see us now. Try moving about a bit," Adam instructed her.

Claire moved to the wall and placed her back to it. Following it around, she kept an eye on Adam, who shook his head. "He can still see you."

Taking another look at the staircase, Claire climbed the railing and jumped up to the next level. Hauling herself over the metal balustrade with ease, she leaned on it to see his reaction.

"He couldn't see what you were doing," Adam called up to her with a grin.

With that in mind, Claire tried again and again, working her way up as Adam raced up the steps, trying to keep aligned with her, phone still pressed with one hand against an ear and camera in the other to capture her moves.

Working their way up the flights of stairs, Adam was puffing by the time they reached the third floor and Claire stopped so he could catch his breath. She did suggest taking the elevator, but he waved it away, saying that it was not part of the fun of the evening. So, they continued until they reached the tenth floor.

Claire stopped, and as she waited for him to catch up and gain control of his breathing once more, she pushed on the fire door to level ten. Her curiosity had once more got the better of her, and she wanted to have a look at what was behind these doors that they had passed on the way up. She stuck her head through the small gap. The hallway beyond it was lit up with wall lights that sent beams both towards the white ceiling and down to the grey tiled floor.

"What're you doing?" Adam whispered breathlessly in her ear, so close that it made her jump. The phone was back in his pocket, but the camera was still focused on her.

"Just looking. You said that these were going to be apartments?" Claire asked, returning her gaze to the hallway.

"Not on this floor; higher up," he indicated with his finger. "These are offices. You want to have a look? Some of them are just about finished." She nodded, and he pushed past her into the hallway. The door closed with a soft thud behind them, and they made their way down the short corridor.

A large, glossy black door stood out against the stark white of the walls at the end, and Adam pushed it open. The carpet under their feet masked their footsteps. Claire looked about her in wonder at the huge, open space. Along one wall stood glass cubicles all waiting for office furniture to fill them, and the expanse of ceiling-to-floor glass on the opposite opened to the world outside. Claire walked over to the window and looked down at the street below, watching the cars drive past. She smiled when she started to compare it to her uncle's small, pokey office, which looked like something out of the 1930s.

"Dad said you did a good job. He couldn't see you at all climbing the railings." He was still following her around, filming her every move and reaction. "This is nothing. The best part is the penthouse—wait till you see that one. It's got gold-plated taps in the bathroom," Adam told her, and he looked at his watch. "Are you finished looking around? Just we've got to go meet Dad."

He seemed nervous to Claire, but then again, she knew his relationship with his father was not a very good one and chalked it up to that. She followed him back out of the office, and they had just reached the fire escape door leading back to the stairs when the black door opened behind them, and a figure appeared. He was a large man in a dark suit, and he stopped dead in his tracks when he saw them.

"What are you kids doing in here?" he demanded and started to walk towards them.

Startled, Claire quickly reached for the door and pushed hard, sending it crashing against the wall, and sped through the opening with Adam on her heels. As she skipped stairs on her way down, she heard the man yell at her to stop, and a loud bang echoed down the concrete walls, making her ears ring.

"Don't bloody shoot her!" yelled someone else from farther up. To Claire's ringing ears, it almost sounded like Marcus, Adam's father.

"Run, Claire! Get out of here!" Adam urged her from somewhere behind, and she didn't need telling twice.

Taking the stairs two at a time seemed to be taking too long. Soon she was leaping over the railings to the level below her, making good use of every skill she had learned free running. By doing this, she outran not only the men pursuing her, but also Adam. She took a moment to look up and see if she could see him somewhere above her only to see his head being pulled back from the railing by a disembodied hand.

"Run!" he called to her in a desperate voice, and she did.

She kept up the pace until she reached the exit door and saw two men entering as she landed at the foot of the stairs.

Without thinking, she turned and headed down the stairs that led to the garage, both hot on her heels.

Once inside the dark, open space, she realised she had nowhere to go. She ran as fast as she could into the darkness to put a bit of distance between her and the men, then hid behind one of the large pillars that held the ceiling up. She waited for the two men to pass her, so she could double back and get out of there, but she could not hear them running. Slowly she calmed her breathing, and soon her heartbeat was no longer beating so hard in her ears. From her left came the soft scuff of a shoe on the ground. They were close and had split up.

Claire crouched down where she was and pulled herself into a ball, praying that they would not spot her in the dim light. Her head was on her knees, and she could hear their footfalls come closer and closer. She prayed harder, embracing her legs tightly in her arms, trying to make herself smaller. The seconds dragged on and on as she promised every god she could think of and even her parents that if she got out of there, she would never do such a thing again.

Footsteps farther away from her brought her head up. The two men had passed her. Thanking her luck, she stood up and carefully made her way back to the door. From behind her, she heard one of the men swear.

"She has to be here somewhere. Go back and look," one of them commanded.

It was at this point that Claire knew she had to get out of there quickly, and she started to run. Unfortunately, her pounding feet gave her away, and she could hear them call out and begin chasing her again. She made the door and slammed it behind her, leaping up the stairs two by two until she reached the entrance foyer and rushed to the door. She slammed her hand on the lock release button protruding from the wall and yanked the door open. Once outside in the back alley, she did not give the building a second look but continued to run.

If she thought she was home free, she was wrong. From behind her another shout came ripping through the air. She cast a quick look behind her and saw two figures giving chase. Claire did not know or even care if they were the same ones from the garage. She hit the end of the alley and turned right, running down the street and dodging the late-night revellers. She could hear the men behind her pushing people out of their way trying to get to her.

Up ahead and across the road, a building she knew well came into view. It was the old Regent Theatre. It had been abandoned for decades but was under the protection of the Historical Places. That did not stop the likes of Claire and her friends exploring the interior for themselves. She had found a network of walkways above the stage that had thrilled her, not to mention all the other good hiding spots.

Cutting in front of a car that came to a screeching halt with the blast of a horn, Claire crossed the road and made her way to the rear of the theatre. Behind her, more cars could be heard sounding their horns in protest as the two men followed. With a running leap, Claire launched herself at the chain-link fence, making the climb to the top with ease. She pushed off the other side and landed in a crouch, taking the opportunity to look for her pursuers. They were fast, but not as agile as she was, and she felt sure they did not know the place as well as she did.

Back up on her feet once more, she circled the large building until she came to the loading bay. Hauling herself up onto the large platform, she ran to the huge double doors that once accepted magnificent scenery for performances gone by. A smaller door was cut into the left-hand side, and she pulled on the handle. It opened easily with a creak that made her wince, and she slipped inside. Claire stood in the darkness, making her way unerringly to her right toward the back of the stage.

At first, the building seemed to be in total darkness, but as her eyes adjusted, she could see small shafts of light coming through the walls from the streetlights outside. The building was crumbling and in a bad state of repair, but it was quiet except for the soft cooing of the pigeons above that now made this once magnificent theatre home. Claire came out onto the stage and made her way down the side steps to the right. She had already decided to hide in the many rows of rotting seating that remained in the main auditorium. The boxes and the higher balconies had all been stripped bare years ago. She had considered hiding in the orchestra pit, but she knew what was down there.

Claire chose a row and slipped into it on her hands and knees with time to spare. A light shone out over the auditorium, and two voices were calling to each other. She did not want to risk looking up and made herself small again, trying with all her might to squeeze under the seat at her back.

"I swear she came in here," one said with a very deep, booming voice.

"I know. I saw, too," another answered, softer and gentler.

There was silence as the light moved around the stage and over the seats, its beam visible with the dust motes that it caught.

"You had better call him. Mr Ryder is not going to be happy about this."

"You're telling me. We're going to be in some shit for letting her get away," said Deep Voice.

"You might as well come out, girl. We know you are in there, and there are men all around the building now waiting for you," the other called out. Claire stayed where she was. If she could just hold out, maybe she could get away.

"Hey, Tony, Mr Ryder is sending someone. He said that this guy can find a needle in a haystack," Deep Voice called.

"Good luck to him. Keep your eyes peeled. We don't want her getting away again," Tony told his companion.

The minutes ticked by, but Claire didn't dare move even an inch to look at her watch. She wondered what had happened to Adam and why Mr Ryder's men had been there with guns. Questions went around and around in her head—questions she had no answers to, but when she got hold of Adam again, she was going to beat them out of him. She could feel herself start to shake with the cold that was seeping in under her clothing, and she hugged herself tighter.

The theatre fell quiet, and she could hear the wind whistling through the holes in the roof. Wings flapped somewhere above, and she wondered if one of the men had risked the walkways that crossed above the stage and auditorium. She risked a peek upwards, but it was lost in the darkness, so she remained as still as possible.

She could hear more footsteps coming from the stage area. Some were slow and measured, but others were hurried.

"She is out there somewhere," Tony spoke to the newcomer, and in her mind, she imagined him pointing out to the auditorium. A softer voice replied, but it was hard for Claire to pick out. She didn't even know if it was a man or a woman. She tried to make herself smaller and creep closer to the chairs.

Going up both aisles, they threaded their way through the block of seats Claire was hiding in. She could hear their footsteps. The torchlights shone up and down the rows of seats, and she prayed they would not see her. Her heart was thumping in her ears and her mouth had gone dry.

The footsteps had stopped. Claire tried to swallow. She had never known fear like this, not even when she had been told her parents had died and she wondered what was going to happen to her. Thoughts of her Uncle Geoff came into her head, and she wished she were home with him. It was at that moment she became aware of someone standing over her. When she pried her eyes open and looked, a dark figure loomed large, and she almost gave a cry of alarm.

The figure bent down, and a beam of light caught his features. Claire did not know what to make of what she saw. It was her uncle. He held out his hand to her, telling her to get up. She froze for a moment, her head spinning as she tried to make sense of it.

"Uncle Geoff?" Claire asked in a soft and confused voice.

"Come on, Kid. We don't have all night." He reached down and pulled her up into a standing position.

"We were told you were to take her to Mr Ryder immediately, Mr Brown," Deep Voice said, shining his light on the girl.

"I am aware of that," Geoff told him curtly. Then to Claire in a softer voice, he said, "I'm sorry, Kid."

Chapter Two

Claire watched her uncle's back as he led them out of the theatre. She was caught between the two men who had chased her, each gripping her upper arm to ensure she did not escape them again. When she struggled against the pair, they tightened their grip. She wanted to cry out for help; she wanted to protest what was happening, but her uncle's cold silence kept her quiet. She had never seen him like that before. The only time he had looked at her was when he had told her, *"Sorry, Kid."*

They reached the side-stage door and Geoff stood to one side as Tony managed to jimmy it open. He watched them push his niece out the door and followed. There was no need to scale any fence, as she saw they were now in front of it. She recognised Geoff's car next to the stairs. Like him, it was big, a sedan that was shiny and dark green. The car lights flickered for a moment as Geoff disarmed the alarm remotely.

"Put her in the front seat, please, Mr James," Geoff addressed the man Claire thought of as Deep Voice.

"Do you want us to come with you?" Mr James asked.

"No, I believe you have your own transportation that needs to be dealt with. I suggest you go do that as soon as we are away."

"Yes, sir," Mr James replied. Once he had settled Claire into her seat, he joined Tony and left the alley.

Geoff took off his overcoat and placed it carefully on the back seat of the car and then sat behind the steering wheel. He looked at her, put a finger to his lips to keep her quiet, and started the car. Carefully he backed down the alley, swung the car out onto the still busy street, and drove off. Claire sat waiting and wondering what was to befall her.

So lost in her thoughts was she that Claire was unaware of where they were heading. Coming back to herself, she looked around at the streets and buildings they were passing. For a start, they were not going in the direction of Marcus's building or his offices. She looked at her uncle and he shook his head, again motioning her to silence. She was beginning to be afraid.

Geoff continued to drive at a sedate pace with no fast lane changes or speeding. He was acting as if everything was all right and that they were going home. But one thing was different—they had just passed the turn that would have taken them to their street. Claire could see street signs directing them to the motorway. They were heading out of town. She sat back in her seat and rested her head while she waited for an explanation from her uncle. Claire was certain that he would eventually give her one and that there was some need to be patient.

The soft hum and motion of the car lulled her to sleep just after they entered the motorway heading north. The orange glow from overhead streetlights strobed over the car, and when Geoff looked at his niece, she was peacefully unaware of where they were going or why. There would be enough time to explain how he had found her, how he had always known where she was. The story was going to be a hard one for her to accept, but it was one she had better accept quickly.

About an hour out of the city, Geoff pulled into a service station to fill up. As the petrol pumped its way into the car, he opened the bonnet and had a good look. Satisfied that everything was in order, he closed it and then got on the ground to look under it. He reached underneath and stood up holding a small black box with a flashing light. Still not satisfied, he opened the car door and felt under the dashboard by the driver's seat. He found nothing and moved over to the passenger side.

When he opened the door, the cool night breeze passed through the car, waking Claire. She woke with a start and looked around her, starting to ask Geoff where they were. Once again, he motioned her to be quiet as he felt under the passenger-side dash. He pulled his hand out, and a small round device came with it.

He handed Claire the two devices and told her to wait while he went into the service station to pay for the petrol. He returned with some food, which he exchanged with Claire for what she was holding. Geoff placed both items on the ground and brought the heel of one of his very large shoes down on it with a crack. Bits of circuit board and wires scattered out underneath him, and he picked them up and placed them in the bin beside the petrol pumps.

"Well, that's done. Let's hope there are no more," he said as he settled himself into the driver's seat. He started the car and pulled back out onto the road. "I suppose you have some questions for me then, Kid," he stated and waited for her to speak.

"Umm, yes! For starters, where are we going? What were those things and what the hell happened back there? Those are just some that come to mind at the minute," she said.

"Very valid questions, I might add. Okay, to answer them in order. Where are we going? We are going home."

"Home is back that way, Uncle Geoff, or are you going senile on me?" Claire cut rudely over the top of him.

He sighed and tried to remain patient and calm. "No, Claire. That is not home. That is a place that we resided in. It is not the place we are from. Well, you were born in the city, but we're heading to where your parents and I grew up. It is a little town—more like a village than a town—and it is located about four hours out of the city, so we will be there in another three."

"What's the name of it?" she asked him.

"It doesn't really have a name. We just call it The Community. But the town nearby calls it Templeton. Our family goes back generations—back, in fact, to the founding of it. Now as to the 'what were those things' question, it was a tracking device and a listening device. I have suspected for quite some time now that I've been bugged—at home, at work, and in the car. Marcus likes to keep a firm eye on his employees, especially ones who keep his secrets."

"What secrets?" Claire asked, eyeing the food in her lap.

"Eat, Claire. You must be hungry by now." She ripped open the hot pie and took a large bite, burning her mouth in the process. "As to what happened back there, well...that's a long story that begins before you were born—even before I was born, if it comes to that."

"You said that it is going to take us three hours to get to where we're going, so I think we have time," she spoke between mouthfuls of drink and pie.

"Okay, here it is, and I would appreciate it if you left the questions until after I have related it to you." Claire assured him of her cooperation, and he continued. "The village was founded by people who came to New Zealand when they had to flee their homeland. They were exiled because others did not understand their special Talents." He halted as Claire made a sound. "You promised, remember? Right—where was I? Yes, special Talents. It is not known where these Talents come from. Our history was lost to time and our removal from the homeland. But our people have abilities that normal humans don't. Most of our people keep these Talents to themselves and only use them when it will benefit The Community—like healing, for instance, or strength. But unfortunately, there is always that one person who wants to use them for their own gain, and Marcus Ryder is one of them."

Claire opened a bottle of water for her uncle and passed it to him. He took a long gulp and handed it back to her. "Marcus has the Talent of Longevity, which means he will live for a very long time. He is currently around one hundred fifty-six years old."

"You are having me on!" Claire scoffed.

"No, I am not. I'm deadly serious, and this is something you need to know, so please listen carefully. Marcus is over a hundred and fifty years old and has the Talents of Longevity and Charm. He uses the Charm to get the deals he wants and has amassed a great fortune. He wishes to use that fortune for his own advancement to power, and he has been luring those with Talent for some time to help him."

"Did those two tonight have powers?"

"Mr James and Mr Benning? No, they are just normal humans. Marcus does have some who are Talented, but not as many as he wishes. You see, the Talent must be passed down certain bloodlines. Over the years, some of those bloodlines have died out or have been bred out as our people have married outside The Community. There has been a concerted effort in the last century to encourage this, and some people have been forbidden to marry. Your parents were among them." He waited for some sort of response from Claire, but there was none. When he looked over at her, she was still wide awake.

"When those who have come from families of Talent marry, their children can have stronger Talents. So, when your father was told he could not marry your mother, but another had been found for him, they eloped to the city. By the time they had been found by the watchers, they were already married, and you were on the way."

"You're trying to tell me something, Uncle Geoff, and I would appreciate it if you would just come out and say it," Claire said calmly, looking out the windscreen into the night.

"I am saying that you have a Talent, Claire. Two, actually, that I know of. I believe you have the beginnings of Flight and of Hide. If you were a child brought up properly in The Community, you would already have had an education in your Talents and would probably be proficient already."

"Flight and Hiding?"

"Have you never wondered how you can do all those amazing stunts that no one else seems to be able to do? And as for hiding, you would spend hours hiding from me when I first took guardianship of you."

"If I am so good at hiding, how come you found me tonight?"

"That is because I have the Talent of Seek. I always know where you are and can find you no matter how hard you try to elude me."

"You said children of those with Talent could inherit Talents, so does that mean Adam has a Talent? He is Marcus's son."

"I believe he has the Charm Talent. I've often felt it whenever I saw him."

Claire chewed on this information for a while. Her head was starting to hurt, and her eyes were starting to feel gritty. For a moment she wondered if she was dreaming all this and pinched herself just to be sure.

"Look, this is a lot to take in and process for you, Claire. Get some sleep and we will talk about it more in the morning." He reached over and placed a large hand over hers, giving it a squeeze. She pulled away, feeling that this man was not the uncle she knew. Her whole world had just been turned upside down.

Eventually, she slept. The quiet of the car soothed her back into dreams of chasing someone up ahead through a thick white mist. They were always out of her reach. She remembered having the same dream before, but no matter how hard she tried, she could not see who it was she was trying to catch up to.

The car pulled to a stop and Geoff gently shook her awake. Claire rubbed her eyes and looked around as she exited the car. They had parked up the driveway of an old two-story house. It had a pretty porch and veranda with seats attached to the front. A garden path wound its way to the front steps with immaculately trimmed hedges and flowering shrubs bordering it. She followed her uncle up the path and then jumped at the sound of a voice in the dark.

"You made it, finally." A thin, old woman stood up from a seat in the shadows. Beside her was a younger man in his late twenties.

"Mary, I told you on the phone that you didn't need to meet us," Geoff said as he climbed the steps, slightly angry.

"Of course, I did! Someone had to welcome you back and give you a few supplies for the morning." She indicated to the younger man to give Geoff a basket that was at their feet. He lifted it up and passed it on.

"Thank you, Jack. That was very thoughtful, Mary, but it is two-thirty in the morning. We can talk more later. I'd really like to get Claire settled in first," he told her pointedly.

"Of course, you do," Mary said, coming forward to stand in front of Claire. "Welcome home, Claire. I hope you will be happy here. There are so many people who are looking forward to meeting you." She grasped both of Claire's shoulders and looked deeply into her eyes. "Come along, Jack," Mary said finally, letting go of the girl. "We will say good night and we look forward to catching up with you, Geoff."

"Good night, Mary, Jack," Geoff said as he and Claire watched the odd pair go down the path and through the front gate. When they were out of sight, he fumbled with the keys and then opened the front door. Clare followed him in, and he turned on the light. The house had the smell of an unused building—a bit musty and dusty—and as she looked about her surroundings, she decided her uncle's preferred old-English-gentleman's-club style was stamped on everything.

"Upstairs with you—the door just to the right is your room," he informed, flicking the lights on to show her the way.

"Who were those people?" she asked as she started to mount the stairs.

"That was Mary Sheridan and her son Jack. She is an Elder of The Community, but we will talk more in the morning. Go, get some sleep."

Geoff watched her as she slowly climbed the stairs and entered the room he had directed her towards. Not for the first time in the last seven years did he wonder if he was doing the right thing by her. Ultimately, he decided, the decision to come here to protect her was the right one, and he would deal with the questions when he was more capable of answering them in the morning.

Chapter Three

Claire opened her eyes and lay there listening, but all she heard was birds. There was no traffic rushing past, no horns blaring—and it bothered her. She looked around the room she was in, and—although it was very similar to her room back home—it was not her room. She sat up, stretching, and brought her knees up to her chin, remembering the events of the previous night. The break-in, the escape, the story her uncle had told her; none of it made any sense. Why would Adam, her oldest friend, lie to her? Why would her uncle? And why did Marcus have his men chase her?

She decided she was not going to get any answers sitting on a bed in some backwater village, so she stood up. She was still wearing the clothes she had been wearing the night before, but she couldn't help that. Leaving the room untouched, she headed down the stairs and explored the house. Standing in the main hall by the front door, she first looked left and saw a closed door. And to the right, there was a short hallway ending in what clearly looked like a kitchen bench. The smell of bacon cooking lured her in that direction, her hunger driving her more than her curiosity. Peering into the very clean room, she spied her uncle sitting at a small table up against the far wall, plate in front of him, already empty, and a newspaper spread out in his hands. He looked up over the paper as she entered.

"Morning, Kid. Do you want some breakfast?"

Claire nodded and sat opposite him.

"You probably have plenty of questions for me, but they can wait until you are fed, clean, and freshly dressed," he said as he rose to make her something to eat.

"But I don't have any clothes with me," she protested.

"You have drawers full of them upstairs. Didn't you explore your room?"

"My room? Uncle Geoff, you're making no sense whatsoever! What do you mean, my room? What clothes?"

"Well, this is my house, and that room has always been your room. Well, that is to say, it is your room now. Look, eat first, then shower, because you reek. We will have all day to chat." He turned, refusing to answer any of her questions until she had done as he asked.

When Claire came down the stairs for the second time that day, she was freshly dressed in clothes very similar to the ones in her cupboards back home in the city. They were comfortable and practical, just the way she liked them. She had never been a girly girl—more a tomboy, which had brought her much grief at school.

"In here," Geoff called out from her left as she turned and found the door open. She looked in and found a spacious room, with bookshelves all around the walls. Opposite the door was an ornate, old-looking desk, complete with an obligatory green lamp, blotter pad, and an antique pen and ink set. The large chair her uncle sat in completed the look of the room; it was high-backed and leather with beautifully carved armrests in a dark stained wood. The windows were wide open, and the breeze moved the sheer net curtains, bringing with it the smell of the fresh country air and flowers from under the windowsill.

Geoff indicated the chair opposite him and invited her to sit. She did as she was told and sank into the deep, leather-clad cushions. They looked at each other for a moment.

"So, explanations are in order," he said, tidying away the paperwork he was going through. "This is my house. It is where I live when I visit the village. I had my sister-in-law pick up some clothes for you a while ago. We can go shopping later to get you anything else you might need."

"Your sister-in-law?"

"Yes, you have quite a bit of family in the village, and they are all eager to meet you."

"Why am I only hearing about them now?" Claire demanded.

Geoff moved uncomfortably in his seat and leaned back. "It has to do with not only your parents, but what happened after your parents' death. You see, their accident was no accident, Claire. They were murdered."

"Murdered? What...how...why was I not told of this before? Why have you been keeping this a secret from me?" Claire could feel anger building up inside her. He had been lying to her this whole time. She was starting to feel betrayed, and it hurt.

"I understand how you're feeling, as this must be quite a shock to you, but we all thought it would be best that you didn't know," Geoff carried on calmly.

"Who decided?"

"Your parents, myself, your grandparents, and the Elders at the time. They wanted me to infiltrate Marcus's operation and find out what his plans were. I didn't want to let you out of my sight after I had faithfully promised your parents that I would keep you safe. They thought you would have a better life in the city than here in the village, but they didn't understand Marcus's ultimate plan."

"What is this plan of his?" she asked, feeling like he was holding something back.

"Well, when you started to show your Talents, I let the Elders know. Somehow that information was then passed on to Marcus, but he had his suspicions before that, given who your parents were. He has his own Watchers, and he uses them very well."

"You used that word last night...what's a Watcher?"

"A Watcher is someone who is placed on a Talented one to—well, basically watch them. To let the Elders know if that person has used their Talent and what the reason is. Most of the time the watchers and Talented ones become friends, and there is never usually a need to report back. Marcus's watchers are to identify who is Talented, where they are living, who they marry, and whether they have any children. I believe he has been building up a nice dossier on everyone who has ever lived in the village and whether they are Talented."

Claire sat for a while, thinking about what her uncle had told her. This new view of Marcus fitted in with her feelings of mistrust towards him.

"You said Mum and Dad were murdered. By whom, and did they ever get caught?"

"No. They never were caught. The coroner ruled it accidental, but I know for a fact he was on Marcus's payroll. Marcus Ryder had your parents killed because they would not join him. They never liked your friendship with Adam. They always worried that it would lead to trouble."

"But I don't understand, Uncle Geoff. If he killed my parents, why did you agree to work for him?"

"That is a very good question, Claire. I worked for him because The Community needed me to. I never wanted to, and I've never enjoyed it. The things I had to do for him I know are unpardonable for some, but I did it to keep The Community safe."

"Again with *'The Community.'* What is this community and why must it be kept safe?"

"It's bigger than you think—we aren't just this tiny village, Claire. Our people are out in the world living their lives just as normal people do. They are not held captive here. They are encouraged to leave and see the world and they're welcomed back when they return. Each generation continually builds on our history. Some are actively seeking exactly that, trying to put together the pieces of where we come from. It is a support system. Each person knows that if they were to find themselves in trouble, they can reach out and someone from The Community will help them."

"Did my parents?" Claire asked quietly.

"Yes, they did. Before you were born, Marcus first made an initial contact with them. What he told them frightened both Jess and John, and they called the Elders for help. I was probably not the right person at the time, but I tried to protect you all." He fell silent and looked at his clenched hands, his fists white. He unfolded them, flexing his fingers.

"You said I have family here, so who are they?"

"Both are sets of grandparents, plus one uncle who lives in the area and another who lives in the city. They both have families...young boys, I think. Which reminds me, your grandparents will be here soon." He looked at his watch. "Grace couldn't wait, but I told them to let you get your feet under you first."

"I don't know about feet. And somehow, I don't feel like you have told me everything yet, Uncle Geoff, and I don't know if I believe what you've told me so far."

"That's understandable, Kid. If I were hearing it for the first time, I would have the same reservations. But there is one thing you can do for me. Can you please just keep an open mind about it until you learn more? Can you do that?" he asked with a raised eyebrow, which meant that expected her to do just as he asked.

"I'll try," she agreed, and he nodded his thanks.

An hour later, Claire was going through her room and reorganising everything. To be honest, there was not much to go through. She had ample clothing until she went back to the city, hopefully in a few days, and the dresses she found in the wardrobe she pushed way to the back. She did not wear dresses and she was not going to start now, especially the floaty, flouncy, floral ones residing in her wardrobe.

She looked around and thought there was really no point getting comfortable here. The bed was cosy, there was a shelf that held no books, a serviceable chest of drawers which held an assortment of clothing in colours she would not normally wear, a bedside cabinet with a lamp on top, and a desk that she would never use for schoolwork. *School. I have to hand in that final assignment for English,* she thought.

Rushing out of the room, Claire headed downstairs as the front door opened. Four people she had never seen before entered, causing her to stop in her tracks. They were old, but there were resemblances that caught her breath. Grandparents.

"Claire!" Geoff called out, spotting her on the landing. "Come down and say hello," he encouraged. The four unfamiliar, but somehow familiar, faces turned up to look at her, and she suddenly felt shy.

Slowly, she descended the stairs, and the two ladies turned to each other. "She looks just like Jess," the grey-headed lady said.

"But with John's eyes, I think," replied the bottle blonde.

When she reached the bottom, Geoff made the introductions. "Claire, this is your Grandmother Grace and Grandfather Malcolm Brown. Malcolm is my older brother." She went to shake hands with them, but Grace—the bottle blonde—pulled her into a tight embrace.

"I have waited so long to do that. Finally, it's happened." She shot an accusatory stare at Geoff. When Grace let her go, Claire shook the hand of her paternal grandfather.

"Nice to meet you, Claire. I hope we will get to know one another well," he said with a bit of embarrassment.

"Claire, this is your Grandmother Lynnette and Grandfather Robert Fuller," Geoff introduced her to her maternal grandparents. Lynnette searched her face for a moment before hugging her close as Grace had done. When Claire turned to Robert, he dutifully shook her hand and said to call him Bob.

Geoff ushered them into the living room with a mention of a cup of tea, to which Grace and Lynnette took over. In no short order they were bustling around the kitchen with dismay at the lack of food and congratulating themselves on forward thinking in bringing cakes and biscuits. Meanwhile in the lounge, Claire sat in silence with her great uncle and two grandfathers. She started to compare her Grandfather Malcolm to her Uncle Geoff, as they were both of the same height, were clean-shaven with some resemblance to each other, and both had the big ears and big nose—but Malcolm was portlier than his younger brother.

When Grace and Lynnette joined them with trays of tea and cakes, she could see why Malcolm was a bit more on the tubby side. The cakes were not just one-layered with a bit of icing, but huge, fancy edifices, and she found herself wondering how they were managing to stay upright. There was cream and jam between the layers, and the top was drizzled with a thin white glaze that dribbled down the sides. Biscuits the size of her hand with large chocolate chunks poking out of them sat on another plate, and she eyed them hungrily.

Lynnette passed her a cup of tea, and Claire helped herself to a biscuit as Grace asked what they had been talking about.

"We haven't been talking at all, Love," Malcolm told her. "We have been waiting for you to join us." He turned to Claire and asked, "Is there anything you'd like to know?"

The question took her unawares, and she nearly choked on the mouthful of chocolate chips she had just taken. She swallowed some hot tea and tried not to cough. Once she was able to talk, she asked, "Uncle Geoff mentioned some other uncles?"

At this point both grandmothers started to talk, but Grace's voice overrode the other. "Yes. We have another son, Benjamin. He's six years younger than your father, and he's married with two wonderful boys. They are twins. He has his own construction company—which is proving to be very successful," she said with pride.

"And his wife?" Claire asked.

"Charlotte. She is a doctor in the city and because of her work, we don't get to see them often," Grace revealed with just a bit of disappointment in her voice. Malcolm looked a little discomforted at his wife's view but remained silent.

Lynnette filled the void in the conversation. "You have another uncle from our side as well, Claire. David is his name, and he now runs the family farm. His wife's name is Elizabeth, but she prefers to be called Beth. They have two boys; Jasper is ten and Hunter is six." She turned to Grace. "The twins are the same age as Hunter, aren't they?"

"Yes, oh...they are such sweet boys. They talked to me the other day over the computer thingy! What's that program called?" she asked Malcolm, not waiting for an answer before continuing on. "They are doing so well at school, getting very good grades. I think they are very advanced for their age."

"How are you doing at school, Claire?" Bob asked when Grace finally stopped to take a breath.

"I'm doing all right...passing all my subjects," she said shyly.

"She is top of her class," Geoff told them proudly. "But I told you all this in my email last month." Claire looked up at her uncle in surprise. Yet another thing he had kept from her.

"Speaking of school, Uncle Geoff, I have to get that assignment in for English, as it is a big chunk of my grade," she said.

"School is going to have to wait, Claire. Don't worry about the assignment. I've made some arrangements already. I'll talk to you later about it," he replied, trying to reassure her.

Claire was not happy. She may not have enjoyed the social side of school much, but she did enjoy the work. Retreating into her own thoughts for a while, she did not realise that her grandparents were leaving—not until Geoff touched her on the shoulder. She lifted her head and looked blankly at him momentarily before realising what he was telling her. Jumping to her feet, Claire said a dutiful goodbye to the grandparents she had not known she had twenty-four hours ago.

At the door, Grace reminded Geoff not to be late and to make sure that Claire wore something pretty. He ushered them out and closed the door behind them with a deep sigh.

"I love my sister-in-law, but she can be a pain in the arse," he told Claire with an air of exasperation.

"What did she mean not to be late and that I have to wear something pretty?" Her eyebrow arched at that last word.

"You weren't listening, were you? There is a little get-together tonight—for you to meet your extended family. It was Grace's idea. Poor Malcolm, he hates parties. And apparently, she has bought you some dresses and she wants you to wear one." He almost managed to hide the smile that he was trying desperately to conceal.

"Have you seen those things? They're hideous! I am not going to be wearing one of those for anyone, let alone a grandmother I have only just met," Claire declared to her uncle.

"Don't shoot the messenger," he said, laughing openly. "Hey, you want to go out for a walk, see where it is you are living? We have to pick a few things up from the shop."

"Yes." Claire was still sulking over the prospect of wearing the dress as she followed her uncle out the door and down the path. "Uncle Geoff, you didn't lock up." She spun back to the house.

"It's okay, Claire. It's not like the city. There is a certain amount of safety here and we don't have to be as security-minded."

"But what if someone breaks in?"

"Then the neighbour next door will probably see who it is and let everyone know." Geoff waved to the man in the next yard, who was watering his garden. He looked up and waved back.

"Oh, okay," Claire said uncertainly. It felt weird not to double lock a door behind her.

They wandered down the road, and Claire really began to appreciate the quiet of the village. From somewhere, she could hear children playing in the summer sun and envied their growing up in such a place. She barely heard her uncle's patter as he told her about this house and that, until they reached the corner and turned towards the centre of the village.

It was such a small village, only a few streets in total surrounded the main cross-intersection. The houses all looked like they'd been built in the twenties and fifties—on large sections with beautifully maintained gardens. One thing she did pick up was that a lot of the houses were empty, and The Community maintained them so that the village didn't look like a ghost town. It was something that she could appreciate as she tried to picture in her mind what it might have looked like.

The main part of the village consisted of a crossroads, and on each corner stood a prominent building. One was a small café, which she wondered at, as there were apparently not many people living in the village. Another held the shop, their destination, and an old stone building, which Geoff told her was the village hall. The last building in the set of four was a petrol station. Even that was clean, with sparkling pumps and a garage that was well-organised and tidy. The mechanic was wiping his hands on a bright red rag. He gave a wave to Geoff, who answered with one of his own.

When they entered the shop, Claire saw a few heads look up and stare at her and her uncle. Geoff waved and greeted a few people as they went around the shelves gathering their supplies. For a man who had lived in the city for a long time, he knew a lot of people. She found herself thinking about that, but not for long. As they finished their shopping and Geoff paid for the goods, the manager welcomed Claire home. She blushed, walking quickly out of the shop.

"Don't worry, Kid...news travels fast in a small place like this." He handed her a chocolate ice block and she unwrapped it, carefully placing the rubbish in the bin on the corner.

They wandered back to Geoff's house and along the way, Claire had a few questions. "Uncle Geoff, there's been something bugging me."

"What's that?"

"About these powers."

"Talents, Claire, we call them Talents."

"Okay. Talents, then. You said that I had some, but how can you be so sure?" She licked a drip from the bottom of her ice block before it could run down her hand.

"Well, it started after you came to live with me. Remember you used to go and hide away? I always knew where you were, but sometimes when I found you, I'd have trouble seeing you."

"That's a contradiction in terms, Uncle Geoff. How can you find me, yet not see me?"

"Ah, well, one has to do with my own Talent and the other has to do with yours. You see, I can find you no matter where you are hiding and where you are in the world. But when you want to be hidden, your body goes through an unconscious change that makes it hard for people to actually see you—even if they are looking straight at you."

"But how?" Claire asked, still confused.

"We don't know how, but we will be getting you the knowledge you need to fully control that Talent as well as the Flight."

"That's the other one I don't understand. You said last night that it was because I could do things other people can't, like free running, and that made you suspect that I had this other Talent. But a lot of people all over the world can do what I do."

"Not quite. I've seen the videos you and Adam have posted online, you know. But there is also something else that has already confirmed it for me. You hover in your sleep," Geoff told her so simply, it was almost as if he were telling her that she snored.

"Wait, what?" Claire stopped in her tracks and stared at him, her ice block dripping away and finally falling on the ground at her feet. She looked down at it, a bit disappointed, and then back up to her uncle.

"I'm not giving you mine, if that is what you are thinking," he told her straight-faced, taking a bite of his own.

"Come again?"

"You are not having my ice block."

"No, not that! The bit about me hovering in my sleep?" Claire asked, dumbfounded.

"When you have had a particularly stressful day, you hover in your sleep. You know, up off your bed. The first time I saw you do it, I nearly had a heart attack. I thought you would be flying around the apartment in no time, but you never developed any further. So, I never told you. I figured what you didn't know couldn't hurt you."

"So, having these Talents is normal here?" she asked him.

"Not really. Most who develop Talents only have one. You're a Full Talent...which is rare. A Full Talent has two, but one is usually more dominant than the other. So, we will let you study both and find out which is which."

"Just like that?"

"It's no different from an athlete. They have one sport they are better at than another, but a footballer can run, and a runner could play football."

"You're rambling again, Uncle Geoff! You sure you're not going senile?" They had reached the front gate to Geoff's house and Claire opened it, holding it for her uncle to pass through.

"Don't worry, Kid, it will all become clear with time. Trust me." Geoff said with a note of condescension as he opened up the front door and they entered into the cooler shade.

Chapter Four

Checking her image in the mirror one last time, Claire finished dressing for a night out at the village hall. The dress she wore was—to her mind—the least offensive of the five that hung in her wardrobe. It was sleeveless, pale pink with darker pink rosebuds around the hem, complete with a silly sash and a skirt that billowed out a little with scratchy petticoats underneath. She had no idea why some girls thought that this was something comfortable to wear. The only thing she was happy about were the shoes she was wearing: flat ballet slippers.

Before she headed downstairs where Geoff was waiting for her, Claire checked her phone again. She had been hoping for a text or a call from Adam with an explanation for what had happened, but she was disappointed. Her phone was flat, and there was nothing but a blank screen and her own reflection staring back at her. She felt doubly disappointed when she remembered that the charger for the phone was back in her bedroom in the city, hours away.

In disgust, she threw it down onto her bed and grabbed a light cardigan. Pulling it on, she left her bedroom and headed down the stairs.

"Who are you and what have you done with Claire?" Geoff called out when he saw her.

"Nice one, Uncle Geoff," she replied with just a hint of sarcasm.

"You look lovely, Claire." He bent and kissed her cheek. "Shall we go?" He offered his arm as he opened the door and Claire swatted him away.

"If we must," she said, slipping through the door before him.

Geoff followed her out to the street and shut the gate behind them. They then walked down the road together. "Uncle Geoff?" Claire started.

"Yes, Claire."

"You don't have a charger here at this house that would fit my phone, would you? It's gone flat and I was hoping to hear from Adam."

"No... sorry, Kid. I don't, but we can organise one tomorrow or the next day if you want." He did not tell her that he secretly wished Adam would not have any contact with her at all. They continued to the hall in silence.

The closer they came to the hall, the more the butterflies decided it was time to party in her stomach, and she noticed that her uncle was walking more slowly than his normal long-legged lope. Claire looked up at him and could see a nervousness on his face that for some reason comforted her but did nothing to settle the butterflies. They increased even more when they entered the hall as people stopped talking to look. Claire tried to hide behind her large uncle, but she was soon swept away by her two grandmothers—who were bent on introducing her to everyone there.

Names and faces soon melded together and she could not have told anyone who was who: cousins, second cousins, cousins by marriage once removed. It seemed the whole village was related to each other in one way or another. *No wonder the young people are encouraged to marry outside the village,* she thought to herself. *Maybe that's how these powers developed originally*. Claire was pleased when her grandmothers guided her to a final table and made her sit between them.

But the introductions were not finished. At the table sat Mary and her son Jack, whom Grace introduced to her, completely ignoring the comments that they had already met. Across the table sat a younger couple and two boys. Lynnette introduced her to David and Beth and their two sons—Jasper and his younger brother Hunter, who looked like he just wanted to go play with the other children present. Also at the table were her two grandfathers, both nodding at her, and her Uncle Geoff, who gave her a small smile of encouragement.

Starting shortly after, dinner was a noisy affair. Everyone had contributed to the meal, and it was an enormous potluck dinner. Claire noted that there were a lot of sweet things such as cakes and puddings, all elaborately presented as if the makers were trying to outdo each other. She took little notice of the conversation that went on around her, but she became uncomfortable with the number of looks Jack kept sending her way.

During dinner, David made several attempts at conversation with Claire, but either Beth or someone else would interrupt. She felt as if he really was interested in what she had to say—and she was very keen to talk to him, to inquire about her mother growing up. After all, he was her brother, and who else was better to tell Claire what she was like?

After eating, there were many toasts and speeches from the Elders, including Mary, welcoming Geoff and Claire back. When Claire looked around, she could see the younger people getting fidgety, waiting for the boring part to be finished so they could start the music.

The tables and chairs were soon being moved back against the walls as dishes were cleared away. Music blared out of ancient-looking speakers that were hung from the rafters while Claire took herself off to one of the corners to try and be as inconspicuous as possible. Many times, she saw people look her way, and she hated feeling like she was exposed. She blushed to the roots of her blonde hair and only looked at her hands clasped in her lap.

Looking up, she took courage as she caught Geoff's eye. He started to move towards her but was waylaid by a very elderly gentleman. He gave her a small smile of apology, and they began to chat. Afterwards, Claire looked around and spotted David and Beth talking to her grandparents, Lynnette and Bob. Beth didn't look like she was enjoying herself and wore a fixed smile on her overly made-up face. She then saw Jack watching her and felt horrified when he started to walk towards her through the crowd on the dance floor.

"Good evening, Claire. I hope you are enjoying yourself this evening." Jack sat down beside her.

"Yes, I am. Thanks, Jack," she replied, moving slightly away from him.

"So, you live in the city. I've always wanted to live there, but someone has to look after Mother. Do you enjoy the city?"

"I do...I was born there, so I don't know what it's like to live anywhere else!"

"Of course you don't." Jack nodded in agreement with her. "And do you have many friends there?"

"Some," Claire replied, trying to remain polite. It was the same conversation she had had with many other people that night, but with Jack, it sounded almost like an interrogation.

"I would suspect a pretty girl like you has lots of friends. Boyfriends as well!" He tried to make it sound like a joke.

"No, I don't have a boyfriend, but I do have some very good friends and some of those are boys."

"See, I knew it was so." He slapped his thigh, as if he had won a bet. "And what do you and your friends do for fun?"

Claire got the feeling that he was odd the more he talked. "We hang out like most teenagers do."

"Oh...don't be so coy, Claire. I have seen the videos on the internet. You are very *talented*." Claire got the message loud and clear. He knew she had Talent. After Claire did not give him any reply, he went on. "You know, we will be getting to know one another well in a few days." Watching her reaction, he nodded while leaning in towards her and dropping his voice. "Yes. Mother has asked me to teach you how to use your Hide Talent. I am very much looking forward to it."

The news took her by surprise, and she responded with almost a whisper. "You have the Hide Talent?"

Jack nodded with a grin. While she tried to pick one question from many that were exploding in her mind, he stood up and held his hand out to her.

"Can I have the honour of this dance?" he asked politely.

And before Claire knew what was even happening, he had her in his arms and was twirling her around.

Claire blushed again when she saw people looking. She frantically tried to search for her uncle but could not see him anywhere. The constant swaying and spinning were making her feel uneasy, and she felt great relief when Geoff tapped Jack on the shoulder.

"May I cut in?" Geoff asked the younger man. Claire took a step back from Jack and waited for his answer.

"Of course, Geoff." Jack did not look happy as everyone looked on when he submitted Claire's hand to her uncle. Surprising Claire completely, Jack kissed the backs of her fingers and mumbled something about seeing her again soon.

He then backed away from the uncle and niece to re-join his mother.

"Uncle Geoff, can we please go home?" She lifted her pale face to him.

Concern written all over his own features, he agreed. They made their farewells to her grandparents and left the building for the short walk home in the fresh air. Music followed them down the street, along with chatter and laughter. One particularly shrill laugh could be heard over the top of everything else, and Geoff looked back towards the hall.

"Your Aunt Beth, I believe—trying to sound like she approves and is having fun," he said.

Claire shuddered and hugged herself tightly. "Does she not approve, then?"

"No, though that's a long story and one that can be told another night," he stated firmly. "I am very proud of how you carried yourself tonight, Claire."

"I didn't talk to anyone. They kept staring at me."

"You are new to The Community, so that is going to make you a bit of an oddity for a while."

"Cool, so now I'm odd." She pushed against him with a smile.

"No, that is not what I meant. You can be a bit frustrating, you know." Geoff pushed back.

"I know. Good, eh? I like to keep you on your toes...admit that it keeps you young."

"It's what is making me severely old before my time!" He laughed alongside her.

Remaining quiet for the rest of their walk, Claire said good night as soon as they were at the door and went directly to her room. Closing the door behind her, she gladly shed the frilly, impractical dress, pulled on her pyjamas, and climbed into bed.

While lying down and listening to the distant music coming from the hall, faces began to swim before her eyes. Her grandparents, David and Beth, Mary and Jack, even her cousins. So many people she didn't know existed yesterday, but now had such strong connection with her. Her brain was going into overdrive contemplating what Jack had told her, and she realised she had not told Uncle Geoff. She set it aside and promised herself that she would tell him in the morning, as her bed was far too comfortable to get out of just yet. But still, her thoughts would not stop bouncing from one thing to another until she rolled over onto her back and sighed deeply.

Claire tried to clear her mind, to make it empty and at peace. She remembered something she had read in a magazine about meditation being a good way to control not only the body, but the mind. The suggestions on how to create a meditative state had included some soothing music, comfortable positions, relaxing all the muscles in the body, and clearing the mind of everyday clutter and thoughts—finally concentrating on the heartbeat.

Music was altogether out as she remembered her phone was flat, but the rest she could do. She set about relaxing the muscles, flexing each in turn from the top of her head and down to her toes. All that did was just remind her that she had missed some exercise. Shaking her head, she tried again—this time with a better result. Her heart rate was steady and calm as she concentrated on the sound of it in her ears, hearing the *thump, thump, thump*.

An hour after Claire had gone to bed, Geoff headed to his own room to get some sleep. The day had seemed long and drawn out, and he was just a little angry with Grace and Lynnette for organising the welcome for Claire. He felt it was too soon and she was not ready for all the fuss. That was evidenced by how pale she was at the end of their evening.

As he usually did, he peeped in her bedroom to see if she was asleep and to check up on her. It had become a habit after he had taken her in, since he would hear her sobbing into her pillow—heartbroken at the loss of her parents. He would routinely comfort her. At first, she had resisted him, but she soon clung to him for the much-needed reassurance.

Inside Claire's room, he found what he expected. The stress of the day had been too much for her and now she floated a short way above the bed. Gently, he entered and carefully stroked her hair, making reassuring noises to settle her back down on the bed. Once he was sure she would sleep peacefully, he left her side and quietly slipped back out. He closed her door and headed to his own room. Tomorrow was another day that he was sure would cause her stress.

Chapter Five

Very early the next morning, Claire rose as the sun was not even up—only a soft glow illuminated the hills in the distance. The dawn chorus rang out in the tree outside her bedroom window, and she cursed it for waking her. In the city, it would have been the traffic of people heading to work in cars and buses, but here it was birds. She remembered that it was Monday, and she should have been getting ready for school, which reminded her to ask Uncle Geoff just how he was going to get her assignment in for her. She had worked hard on it and didn't want to get a fail.

Putting that aside, she started to reach for her phone, remembering once more that it was flat and adding that to her list of things to remind Geoff about. She got out of bed and started to stretch. Deciding she needed a run, she dressed quietly before grabbing her sneakers and opening her door. As she crept down the stairs—and winced each time she hit a creaky step—she was thankful there was no sign of her uncle anywhere. She waited for a moment to see if Geoff had been disturbed. Satisfied upon hearing no noise, she jumped the last lot of steps and landed as softly as a cat at the bottom.

Opening the door only just enough to let herself out, she made sure that there was no audible click or slam as it shut behind her. Once outside, she slipped her shoes on, then jogged down the driveway to avoid the squeaky gate. Turning left, she realised that she had no idea of where to go next, as the only places she had ever been to in the village were the hall and the shop, but she kept going. Instead of left to the centre of the village, she went right and picked up speed. To her, running was a refuge. Claire enjoyed it, as it calmed her. In a way, the release of energy set her free, and her spirits were rising the more distance she put between herself and the village.

The houses slowly disappeared, replaced by farmland, green fields, and crops. The smell in the air screamed country, which she remembered from a school trip when she was young. Sheep looked up from their early morning grazing to stare at her running past. They looked like white puffballs. Pasture after pasture flew by as she kept up her pace. Newly ploughed fields with neat rows smelled of freshly dug earth, and some fields were green with crops poking their shoots up out of the ground. It was simply peaceful. Lungful after lungful of fresh air filled her with a new exhilaration. She could run forever.

A new sight soon greeted her as she kept going. Hedges and shady trees in a field surrounded by a high wooden fence. A long, grey face leaned out over the high fence, looking at her as she neared, its ears flicking, shooing away a pesky fly. Claire slowed down to greet the horse as it huffed softly. She raised a hand and it accepted her touch, nudging her slightly as if it were expecting something. Steadying herself against the horse, Claire stroked its nose. The hair felt coarse, and large brown eyes regarded her quietly, without judgment.

The sun finally managed to haul itself over the edge of the hill, bathing the world around her in a soft golden glow as the air started to warm. Bugs lifted off their hiding spots, and a little brown bird with a long tail chased after them in the morning light. Claire was captivated by the sight, watching the aerial acrobatics as it swooped and soared, trying to catch its breakfast.

As Claire leaned against the warm neck of the horse and watched the bird in its erratic flight, she heard the unmistakable sound of running feet coming towards her. Taking a quick look around the long nose of the horse, she saw a man heading her way. Just as she was about to hide, he hailed her. It was David, her mother's brother.

"Good morning, Claire. I see you have met Janie." He walked over to her and patted the long face, slipping an apple from his pocket to give to the horse. "She's a good horse. I bought her for the boys to ride, but Beth won't let them, since she says they might fall and get hurt. You are some ways out of the village...Geoff told me you enjoyed running. By the way, I'm sorry about last night—not talking to you much and all—but Mum and Grace seemed to be occupying most of your time," David said, his sentences tumbling over each other with obvious embarrassment.

"They were a bit, Uncle David," Claire agreed, hesitant to try out the honorific on him.

"Claire, you don't need to call me uncle if you don't want to. It's fine by me," David said gently. "All this land around us is our family farm. This is where your mother grew up. Was she happy in the city? Were they both happy?" he asked her with a catch in his voice.

For just a moment, Claire thought about what to say and then told him plainly, "They were very happy, David. They were the best parents I could have ever hoped for...they laughed a lot and I know they loved me. I'm sorry they didn't include the family in our lives. I had no idea that you all existed." She hid her face in the horse's neck, trying to control the sudden surge of emotions that came to the surface.

David placed a hand on her shoulder. "Hey, I'm sorry. I didn't mean to make you cry," he said softly.

She shook her head, looking up at him as a single tear escaped and made its way down her cheek. David reached down to wipe it, but Claire moved away and dashed it on the sleeve of her hoodie, sniffing loudly. Between the two, there was a shared embarrassment.

"I only asked because your mother and I were close as kids—as close as twins could be."

"Twins?" Claire asked, turning around to look at him.

"You didn't know?" The hurt in his voice pained her. Not only had she not been told she had an uncle, but that the uncle was a twin to her mother. "I wonder why they didn't tell you," he said, more to himself than to Claire. "You know, I knew the moment she died. It felt like there was an empty space opening up inside me." He realised what he was telling her and blushed.

There was an awkward pause between them. Not knowing what to do with the information David had just given her, Claire tried valiantly to process it all. "What are you doing all the way out here on your own, anyway?" David asked, seeing the stress on her face.

Grateful he had found something else to talk about, she replied readily, "Blowing the cobwebs out with a run. I feel like I've been under a blanket for a good couple of days, so I needed to just get out."

"I have to pick up some bits from the shop in the village. I'll run with you." His offer sounded like an excuse, but she accepted.

"Won't Beth wonder where you are?" They started to walk back to the road.

"No, she and the boys left early this morning to travel back to their house just outside the city. The kids go to school there," he answered. "They come back on weekends and usually head back on Sunday afternoon—but we had the party last night and I thought it was important that they be introduced to their cousin."

"Oh, okay," she said as they started to run.

Claire didn't want to go too fast and outrun her uncle, but she found she was the slower one and sped up to match David's stride. All too soon the run became a sprint and Claire was enjoying herself immensely. The wind whipped her hair back as she pumped her arms. Her heartbeat matched the pounding of her footfalls, and she soon found herself smiling.

By the time they reached Geoff's door, the sun was up, and people were moving around the village. They then stopped at the gate and neither one was puffing hard, but Claire was laughing.

"I'll see you later, Claire. I enjoyed our run, we'll have to do it again sometime," David said, giving her a smile before turning back down the road towards the centre of the village.

She walked up the path, and the door opened before she even reached the steps to the porch. Her Uncle Geoff was standing there in his dressing gown. "You're up early!"

"I had to go for a run," she explained. "I ran into David while I was out." She picked up his paper from the doorstep and handed it to him, following him into the house. "Why didn't either you or my parents tell me about my family and the fact that David is Mum's twin?"

Her uncle looked unabashed and answered just as directly as she had asked. "I didn't tell you because your parents didn't tell you in the first place. The Elders and I decided that we should keep it that way."

"David knew when Mum died." Geoff looked very interested in that piece of news. She left him standing in the hall and went upstairs for a shower.

Freshly washed and dressed, Claire headed downstairs to the kitchen—where one elderly lady sat at the table with her uncle. Still dressed in his robe and sipping on a cup of coffee, Geoff looked none too pleased that the woman was there.

"Claire, I'd like you to meet The Communities records keeper. She's here to teach you about the history of our community and to help you gain information on your Talents." He placed his coffee cup down on the table with more force than normal and stood up. "I still think that it is too soon for Claire to be told."

She looked at him with disdain. "It isn't up to you to decide, and I really don't care what you think."

Geoff left the room and Claire could hear him climb the stairs, slamming his bedroom door shut moments later. Staring at the lady in shock, Claire had never before heard someone talk to her uncle in that manner.

"Would you like a cup of tea or coffee?" Claire offered, suspecting that her uncle had failed to offer her any.

The woman smiled. "Yes, thank you, Claire. I will have a cup of tea if you have it." Claire busied herself making the tea as the quiet seemed to hang between them. "Do you know who I am?" the woman asked.

"No, sorry, I don't," she said, placing the teapot and cups on the table.

The woman made a tutting noise. "Typical. Well, I am your Great Aunt Lilith—your grandfather Malcolm and I are twins. And your Uncle Geoff is our little brother."

"So, twins run on both sides of the family?" Claire asked.

"Yes. In fact, twins are very common in The Community. The reason I am here is because you've not been taught anything until now. A child of your age should have been given a thorough education in the history of The Community and the Talents when they first emerge. His keeping you in the city has not helped you at all," Lilith declared.

Claire sat opposite her, pouring the tea, and passing a cup to her.

"Were you at the hall last night?" Claire asked, knitting her brows together as she tried to remember whether she'd seen her there.

"No. I was not. On that one, I agreed with him, as it was far too early for you to be introduced to everyone like that." Lilith seemed to be all business. And if Claire thought she was going to get any real insight into the day-to-day workings of the village, she was sorely mistaken. "Right...shall we get on with it?" Lilith took a small sip from the cup, then passed three booklets to the girl across the table.

Claire picked them up and flicked through them. It was the opening Lilith needed, so she started to tell Claire her heritage.

The story she told was similar to the one she'd heard in the car from Geoff. The community was founded when New Zealand was first settled. The people came from a much older community, and they had been driven out by the locals who had discovered their secret. Of course, the secret was the Talents that some of the people had. The development of these Talents was lost in the mists of time, and nobody knew exactly where they'd come from—only that certain bloodlines were more likely to develop them. Lilith then indicated the blue book.

"This one contains the genealogy of your families and who is connected to whom. And the red one is a list of the Talents with a brief description for each that has been documented since the time of settlement."

Claire opened the red booklet and promised to read them. Her curiosity was rising when a sudden thought came to her, the question burning on her lips. "Am I really going to be taught how to Hide by the Elder's son?"

Lilith appeared a bit shocked by the statement and looked at her blankly for a while before she collected herself. "Where did you hear that piece of information, Claire?" she asked very carefully.

"Last night. Jack told me that Mary had asked that he teach me."

Lilith looked thoughtfully at Claire, nodding. "That would explain a lot of things." She suddenly looked as if she wanted to be somewhere else in a hurry. Pointing to another booklet, this time yellow, Lilith passed it to Claire.

"This one contains more of The Community's history and how it works today. If you have any questions, please come and see me. I'll try to answer them. Also, you will need instruction books on your Talents—which I have in the archives—ready when you are. I will see you soon, Claire." With that, she closed her bag with a loud click, picked it up, and left the house hurriedly.

Geoff re-entered the kitchen shortly after the front door slammed shut and looked at Claire. "What was the matter with Lilith? She left awfully fast!"

Claire shrugged. "All I asked was if it were true that Jack's going to be teaching me to Hide. She got all funny and left." He stared at her in the same way that Lilith had. It had baffled her when Lilith had done it, but it scared her when her uncle looked at her that way. "What's wrong?" she asked, getting herself some cereal, and sitting at the table to eat. He sat down as well and asked what the Elder's son had said to her. She then repeated it back to him word for word.

Geoff rubbed a large hand over his face and looked at her again. "He just announced it to you. Just like that?"

"Just like that," she reiterated between mouthfuls.

"It's no wonder she ran off like that. She is the one who's supposed to be informed when a child develops a Talent, so it can be recorded, and the bloodlines re-examined. If she had no idea of his having this Talent, then Mary has kept it quiet for a reason...and Lilith will be asking for those reasons very emphatically." He quickly hid his frown and smiled at her when Claire started to look confused. "Look, this is nothing for you to worry about."

But Claire felt there was something very necessary to worry about. She just couldn't quite grasp what it was.

Chapter Six

Dishes were not Claire's most favourite chore to do, but she did them anyway. As her uncle had quietly told her when she was younger, there were only the two of them and they both had to pull together to look after each other. She smiled at this thought—now knowing that he meant she would do the dishes if she wanted her allowance, because he had hired a housekeeper shortly after.

Somewhere in the house, Geoff's phone rang, and she turned on him. "How come *your* phone is charged?" He shrugged his shoulders at her and didn't say a thing as he left her to answer it.

His deep voice carried through the house, but Claire could not hear what he was saying, even when she stopped cleaning the dishes and deliberately tried to listen in. She finished what she was doing and as she was putting the last cup away, he rejoined her in the kitchen.

"Um, I have to go out for a while. The Elders have called a meeting. This has something to do with what you told Lilith this morning, no doubt." Geoff started to check his pockets. "Have you seen my glasses?"

"Uncle Geoff, I'm really starting to worry about you." She reached up and pulled them off the top of his head, handing them to him.

"What would I do without you, Kid?" He kissed her forehead. "Right, so there is plenty of food in the fridge. I don't know when I will be home. These things tend to be a bit long-winded."

Claire watched him leave and then returned to the table to look at the booklets. She picked the blue one up first. The gold lettering on the front declared it "Your Genealogy," and she turned to the first page. The paper was crisp and white, and the book felt new in her hands. The names of all the families were listed alphabetically on the first page with the page number you could find them on. Claire went straight to Brown, finding that the list of names went on—page after page—until she saw the following: "Stephen married Angela Brewer and had Lilith and Malcolm (twins) and Geoffrey. Lilith unwed. Malcolm married Grace Carter and had John and Benjamin. John married Jessica Fuller and had Claire. Benjamin married Charlotte Turner and had Oliver and Owen (twins). Geoffrey (widower)."

This word jumped out at Claire, again another fact that her Uncle Geoff had never mentioned to her, and she continued to flip through the book. The names and dates confused her, and it was just as bad on the Fuller side of the family.

She put it to one side, swearing that there had to be a better way to list the names than just writing them down. Hadn't these people heard of the ancestry sites that you could go on these days? Then she picked up the yellow book. "The Community's History" was the title of this one. It looked older and well-worn.

Again, she found the same thing; lists of dates and events that were significant for The Community, but no real substance to it. She began to wonder about the books Lilith had mentioned to her and wondered if they would provide the answers to the questions that were going around her head. Just the thought of all that information sitting there excited Claire, since she loved to find things out...to better understand how things work and how they came to be.

Jumping up from her seat, she went to her uncle's study. She felt a bit guilty entering the room without him being there, but she had not seen any paper or pens anywhere else in the house. Finding what she needed quickly, she went back to the kitchen table and the waiting booklets. Opening the yellow one again, she reread it through, making notes as she went. The questions became longer and more involved the further into the little book she read.

The red booklet was the one she had been really wanting to read, but had saved it till last, so she could appreciate it even more. "The Talents," it declared on the front cover in stylised gold lettering—standing out on the deep red. Claire opened it carefully, and again it looked well-thumbed through. She read the introduction, hungrily devouring the book within half an hour. More and more questions were written down—especially about her own Talents. But what surprised her most was the ones that were classed as harmless, such as music, art, and literature. How many people were out there who had these Talents that were related to The Community?

Hours passed before Claire realised she was hungry, and looking at the clock on the wall, she found that it was nearly two in the afternoon. She couldn't quite remember what time it was when her uncle had left that morning. Claire rose from her chair and stretched to get the kinks out of her neck and back, then went and made herself a sandwich.

Finishing off her lunch while reviewing reams of notes and questions, she heard the front door open and saw Geoff enter the kitchen. By the look on his face, Claire knew it was not the time to bombard him with them as he went straight to a high cupboard and pulled out a bottle of whisky. Pouring himself a glass and downing it quickly, he then poured himself another. Geoff turned around and looked at her with pity in his eyes.

"What happened at the meeting?" Claire asked, knowing it couldn't be good news, as she could not remember the last time she'd seen her uncle drink alcohol. He sat down, opened his mouth to speak, and then closed it again. Looking at her, Geoff downed the second drink. "It can't be all that bad, can it?" she asked.

Geoff shook his head, outlining what had happened at the meeting. "Well...it is true, Jack has the Hide Talent, but the best bit is that Mary has been using his Talent for years to confirm her Foresight visions. Get this: Mary had kept the secret of his Talent from The Community, because she had seen before he was born that it was necessary to do so. But she would not tell us why it was necessary. What she did say was that he would be teaching you, so that you'd become a useful tool in defeating Marcus."

"I am what?" Claire exploded as he nodded and poured himself yet another drink.

"That is what I said to Mary. According to her—you, my dear Niece, are apparently the one who defeats Marcus, and it is on your tender shoulders to save The Community." She sat in shock, and she watched him as he placed his glass on the table. The amber liquid settled, glinting in the sun that was streaming through the window. He leaned against the wall and pushed his long legs out in front of him, wiping his hands across his face wearily.

"I swear, Claire, had I known that you were to be used in this way, we would have run in the opposite direction—away from The Community—and kept you safe from harm, as I promised your parents I would do. But it is too late for that now. They are watching and waiting for Marcus to make his first move. They've been watching us equally...as they have already had watchers on us from the moment we arrived back into The Community."

She sat back in her chair and let out a long breath. The pen was still in her fingers as she slowly tapped it against the notepad, thinking about what he had told her. "Have they had watchers on me since my parents died?"

"Well, I was John and Jess's watcher, so yes; even before you were born...I've been reporting on you. If Mary had a vision about you, then the news that your mother was pregnant would have spurred her into action. The Elders don't leave things to chance." He looked at the pad she was tapping the pen on. "So, what have you been up to?"

Claire passed the list of questions for him to look at. Geoff leafed through the pages. "I don't know if I could even give you passable explanations to these. Lilith would be the one to answer them."

"I thought that might be the case. Oh, I wanted to ask you how you were going to get my final assignment to the school."

"I rang Maggie and told her that we had to leave on a family emergency and that you had an assignment due. She promised to get it to the school for you." Claire felt very touched that their housekeeper would do that for her, as she had always got on well with the older woman. "How did you manage with the genealogy book?" He smiled as he picked it up and flicked the pages.

"That book is giving me a headache. There has to be a better way than that to cross-reference all the family paths."

"Lilith is good at unravelling the knots, I'm sure she made a big sort of family tree at one point. I seem to remember lots of red string going back and forth on the wall connecting everyone." He stopped at a page, looking curiously at it. Geoff then tapped a finger on a name and pointed it out to her. The name was Jack, Mary's son.

"Yeah, so it's Jack. What is so puzzling about that?"

"Look for his father's name." There was no name associated with the Elder's son at all. Every other entry gave the names of both the mother and father, but his was missing.

"Who do you think his father is?" she asked.

He shrugged, tossing the booklet back on the table. "I have no idea, but it is a very curious thing that not only has Mary kept his Talent a secret, but she has also kept his father's name off the records." As he pondered this, he picked up his drink and took a sip.

Claire cleared the books and papers off the table, but not before making sure the whiskey bottle was back in its cupboard. She had not seen her uncle drink before, and his downing a couple of good-sized glasses of the amber liquid in quick succession made her feel nervous.

"What do you want for dinner?" she asked, hoping to break him out of the morose mood that he seemed to have slipped into.

"Anything, Claire...I don't care," he replied, still thinking.

In some ways, it felt like the most normal thing that she had done since she was forced to come here—slipping back into the role of child and guardian. If she could keep things as normal as possible, then she wouldn't have to think about the sudden turn of events that had taken over her life. All the ones that made her feel sick to her stomach. Since the age of ten, she had lived with her Uncle Geoff, and they had cohabitated in the same house for seven years. She felt she didn't really know the man who had taken responsibility for her life, but she also felt that he was as close as her father had been.

She knew he worried about her—knew that he cared—but the night he brought her here had shaken their relationship, and he was suddenly not the man she knew. Looking at him now, care-worn, and anxious over her, the feeling of closeness renewed. She did trust him, completely. It should be him she turned to for guidance always. She walked over to him and gave him a hug, kissing his forehead.

He smiled. "Somehow, it's going to be all right. Somehow, I will help you through this."

Claire smiled back at him and said, "I know you will."

Chapter Seven

The next day, Claire bundled her list of questions and booklets into a bag she found in her room. After getting directions from her Uncle Geoff, she set off at a run to Lilith's house to go over them. Upon seeing how they had reacted to each other the previous morning, she thought that it was better not to ask Lilith to her uncle's house. The run was not a long one, as her aunt lived only a few streets away in a pretty little one-story house. It had a cottage garden in the front, full of roses and daisies. Hardly panting, she waited for her aunt to answer her knocks. Lilith, dressed as impeccably as the day before, opened the door with a warm greeting and ushered her inside.

After making a cup of tea for Claire, she led the girl out into the back garden, which was just as full of flowering shrubs and plants as the front. Under the shade of a large, old weeping willow, they sat at a table and Claire retrieved the booklets and questions. Getting down to business, Lilith answered all her queries to the best of her ability as Claire took notes. Her knowledge seemed to have no bounds. The more Claire asked, the deeper the answers became. Her great-aunt didn't hold back any knowledge from her great-niece, and Claire began to wonder if that was because of the previous day's meeting that her Uncle Geoff had attended.

After they'd gone through the history of the community, Claire asked Lilith directly, "Did you attended the meeting yesterday?"

"I did," Lilith replied in such a manner as to make Claire believe that she was not going to hear many details of said meeting.

"Did you realise that Jack has no father's name listed?"

"Of course, I am aware. It's my job to be aware of these things...I am the archivist for The Community." Lilith became very defensive about the issue.

"I'm sorry. I didn't realise," Claire apologised to her aunt. She picked up the red booklet. "I haven't finished with this book yet. Can I hold on to it?"

"These books are yours to keep, Claire. Everyone—whether they are Talented or not—gets a copy of them on their thirteenth birthday. Or earlier...if their Talent develops before then. I also have another couple of books for you to read that might help you understand things a bit better." They went back inside and retrieved the books.

By the time she was finished with her aunt, it was almost lunchtime. She bade Lilith farewell and left to return to her Uncle Geoff's house. The air in the village was sweet and fresh—unlike the city—and the sun on her face felt wonderful. Enjoying the moment, she walked down the main street and soon became aware of someone walking behind her. Turning to see who it was, a wave of concern broke over her as she saw the Elder's son. Jack, seeing that she'd spotted him, put on a congenial smile, and called out for her to wait up. He appeared sweaty, as if he had hurried to catch her, and Claire groaned inwardly.

"Thanks for waiting for me," Jack said, slightly out of breath. "Would you like to join me for lunch at the café?"

Claire felt like she could not refuse him. Tongue-tied, she was unsure how to act towards him. "All right," she agreed as they walked together.

Not slowing her steps so he could catch his breath, she sped up slightly until Jack asked her if she'd slow down a bit. Walking in silence, they finally reached the café and entered. There was no one else in the small shop. After they placed their order, Jack seemed to deliberately guide Claire to a seat in the main window—almost as if he wanted to show off that he was with her. She put her bag down and looked at him.

"I suppose you're wondering why I wanted to talk to you."

"It did cross my mind." She nodded her assent. "If it's about you teaching me, then a phone call would've done."

He laughed at that, and she really did not know what to make of him. "No...it is not about that, but we do need to set up a time to start your training." He put on a concerned look and continued. "I just wanted to talk with you and find out about you. I wanted to find out how you are coping with the change of moving to the village. You must find there is a big difference from the city." He seemed to just ramble for the sake of talking to fill in the silences that she let creep in.

"I'm fine. Thank you, Jack." Claire decided to keep things polite. "It's a bit different, but I am adaptable, and we won't be here long anyway." She didn't offer any more than he had asked for. There was something about him that she distrusted.

She lost concentration as Jack rambled on, until he was suddenly talking about the area she had grown up in before her parents' death. It sounded as if he knew the place, so she stopped his talking with a question. "You've been there? Where I grew up?"

"Yes, you don't remember? I visited your parents when you were small at mother's bidding. She wanted them to come back to The Community and raise you amongst our own, and

I was sent to convince them. I remember seeing you—you were a beautiful child, just as you have grown to be a beautiful young lady."

Staring at him, she asked, "How is it I don't remember this? Why has Uncle Geoff not told me that this happened?"

"We met in secret. Geoff was not told of the meeting, even though he was their watcher." The sound of his voice was meant to imply information that may have been secret to her, but Claire already knew that.

They sat in silence, and she stared out the window, contemplating this new piece of news. He stared right back at her with an odd glint in his eye, which she caught slightly as she turned to look back at him. At that moment, their food and drinks arrived at the table, and she started to eat. She didn't realise how hungry she was until she took her first mouthful.

It was not until she was halfway through her food that she remembered to ask him, "So, do you know who your father is?"

This question seemed to throw him, and he choked on the mouthful that he had just taken. She waited patiently as he got himself settled and took a long gulp of his drink. She arched her eyebrow and waited for his reply.

"Why did you ask that question?"

"I was going through the genealogy book, and it just struck me odd that everyone's lineage is described in the booklet...except for yours."

"I actually don't know, and Mother has always refused to tell me." She took him at face value and thanked him for his reply.

"I think we should start your training soon. How about we start in a couple of days. Would that suit you? I think my home would be a nice quiet place. I know Mother will leave us be," he suggested.

"Well, I don't really know if I truly have any Talent, so is it wise to train for something you don't have?" Claire asked, feeling uneasy at his suggestion.

"From what Geoff has reported to the Elders, he believes you have the Talents, and you need to study and train to master them properly. Hide is the only one I can help you with. Mother has seen that you are the one who saves The Community. I just want to help you get there."

"I'll think about it, Jack." Claire grabbed her bag from the floor and stood up, looking down on him. "I'm sure Uncle Geoff will let you know when I'm ready to start training."

As she started to leave, he called out to her. "Well, don't take too long. Mother has had a vision. It showed her that everything will be over by the end of January, and we are already in December now." She left him and walked out the door.

When she arrived home, she found her uncle at his desk. She sat down on the chair opposite him and told him of the morning's events. He quizzed her on Jack's responses and questions and the fact that he had revealed that it was all supposed to happen so soon. She gave her answers as succinctly as possible—remembering how he looked at her and how he sat while talking. Her uncle seemed both interested and worried with some of the things that Jack had said.

"Have you had lunch yet?" Claire asked.

"Yes, thank you. I made myself a sandwich about an hour ago. Look, Claire, I want to apologise to you about how I acted when I got home yesterday...and for getting you into this situation."

"Don't worry about it, Uncle Geoff," she brushed his apology aside and got up to leave.

"Claire, have you been through my desk?"

"I took a pad and pen from there yesterday, but they were both sitting on top. I didn't touch anything else. I know better than that. Why?"

"Oh, nothing, it just feels like someone has been through my drawers and files. I'm not picking anything specific up. It's just a very odd feeling that some things have been moved slightly. Don't worry about it, Kid." Even though he told her not to, he looked worried himself.

"You are the Seeker...I thought you were supposed to be good at finding things out." She felt proud of herself for remembering the correct term.

"It doesn't work that way. I have to have a connection with the person I am searching for. The sense I have of you touching my desk is mixing up the signals and I can't find a lead. So, you've read the Talent booklet, then?"

"Yes, but I haven't really studied it yet. I'm going to get to that this afternoon. Lilith also gave me a few other books to study as well."

Chapter Eight

The next few days were full of study and grandmothers. They had decided that she'd had enough time to settle in and they wanted to get to know her more. Grace and Lynnette brought her more floaty summer dresses that—they assured her—her mother had liked, but she found a pain to move in, preferring her own shorts and running gear. They also decided that Geoff's house was totally unacceptable and set about setting it right—to their standards. Claire would spend evenings after they had left, putting it back to how she knew her uncle preferred things. One night he told her to stop because they would only change it again. She did as she was told and went back to studying the red booklet.

Geoff watched her reading, curled up on the couch, her eyebrows knitted together. He knew she was a very good student at school, but he also knew the concentration that she was putting in was extraordinary.

"Come on, then, tell me what you've learned, Kid." He put his own book down on the arm of his chair.

She looked up at him. "What...now?"

He laughed and nodded. "You have had your nose in those books for the last couple of days. I'm sure you have read them at least three or four times. It only took me half an hour to read all three books when they were given to me. So, tell me what you've learnt."

She took a deep breath, sighing as she put the booklet down. Claire knew his rules when revising. They had done this many a time over the last seven years as he helped her study for tests. She began to outline the theory of her own main Talent and how it usually meant that it would lead to flying. She then outlined how a person could hone their skill and slowly begin to hover. Once that skill was learnt, the movement into flying came to the fore.

"But I doubt that I'll even get to the hovering stage," she voiced her own nagging doubt.

"Well, we know that can't be true. For a start, the free running that you enjoy so much is you using flight unconsciously. And I've already told you that you can hover...I've seen you do it. So, I put the two together and that is how I determined that your free running was not just a great, normal human ability. After last night's party, you were hovering." He then asked her about her hiding Talent. "What do you know about it?"

"The book states: *The user of this Talent first shows the signs of being very good at games like hide-and-seek while still young and can develop very quickly into melting into the background and then on into invisibility.* The book then goes on to say that shrinking should not be attempted at all without proper training first."

"Good. I hope you take particular note of that, Kid," Geoff told her pointedly.

"Yes...I have," she assured him with a bit of boredom in her voice. "But all I ever try to do is to blend into the background, so no one takes much notice of me in social situations. Or when I just don't want to be bothered by people. What I don't understand is how the Talent can be turned in on itself and the 'user' can metamorphose to shrink themselves. I mean, you can't change the basic structure of matter. You can change its physical state like water into ice or steam—that's basic science—but the actual body matter cannot be made to shrink to such a size as the books suggests."

Listening to her, he considered a well-measured argument before responding. "The only way to be sure is to go and have lessons with Jack." When she rolled her eyes at that suggestion, he went on. "What exactly is it about Jack that you dislike so much?"

"It's just a feeling I get from him. The way he looks at me as if I was a possession to him. It creeps me out." It was the uncle's turn to knit his brows at her assessment of the man. Although at times she could be quite naïve in her judgment of people, this time her words troubled him.

"Is it rare for a person to have more than one Talent? I've been reading through the books Lilith gave me and it only hints in their contents that it has occurred before."

"Yes, it is rare. I have never really made a study of the Talents, except for my own. So, I think your best bet to understand them more would be to go back to your Aunt Lilith. And I may not have talked to her for a while, but I do know she would prefer you to call her aunt," he admitted.

"I will...I simply need more information, since there's not enough in this little book to tell me anything." She threw it at her feet in disgust.

"I think that it's time for you to go to bed. If I know you, you'll be up early again for a run. So, go get some sleep."

"Yes, Uncle Geoff. Good night," she said as she left the room.

Even though Claire had some misgivings about Jack, he was still the only one who could really train her properly in at least one of the Talents. Hide Talent, from what he'd recently read himself, was a tricky one and could be dangerous for the user. Geoff's worry for his niece just increased a little more.

The next day, Geoff was up before Claire left for her morning run. He watched her get ready. "Claire...about taking lessons with Jack, I really do think you should have them—even if you have misgivings of him."

"Okay, I will. But not at his place like he suggested. Somewhere more public, please," she agreed hurriedly, itching to be out on the road. "I'm off...I'll be back in about an hour."

"I'll have breakfast waiting for you," he called to her as she headed out the door.

With all the new information going around and around in her head, Claire didn't have any sense of where she was heading. It was only when she spied the grey horse Janie that she realised she was again at David's farm. She greeted the horse with a pat and promised that next time she was running this way she'd bring her an apple. The horse nickered back to her, pushing her shoulder.

Claire gave Janie one last pat and started to run again, but she did not head back to the village. She wanted to go a little farther—she was hoping to see the house where her mother grew up. The road narrowed a bit more and large drainage ditches deepened on either side as long grass grew in the hollows, almost making them invisible. While her mind was wandering, she was almost too late to react to a car that was coming up behind her.

The engine revved, and the sound took her by complete surprise as Claire turned to look at the noise. The corner of the car's bumper clipped her as it passed, and Claire found herself falling into the ditch she had just been looking at, landing hard. The tyres of the car screeched as it pulled away from her and headed down the road. She caught a glimpse of it as it sped off, but she could not have told anyone the type of car or the number plate—only that it was black or dark blue. She lay in the ditch panting, trying to get her bearings and checking to see if any part of her was damaged. Satisfied she was fine, she clambered up the side and looked to where the car had disappeared. There was no sign of it returning, but that didn't mean that it wouldn't come back.

The idea that it could come back at any moment took hold of her mind and fear gripped her. Panic started to set in as she felt the need to protect herself. Claire could feel herself slowly drawing her energy and directing it inwards. She'd read all the information, and she didn't need the Elder's son. She slowly imagined herself decreasing in size, trying to be as small as a mouse.

Staring at a single spot on the horizon, Claire pushed all her will into the thought of being small. The world seemed to melt around her, and when her eyes adjusted, she looked at her surroundings. Her heart beat faster in her chest as she realized that the long grass that towered and swayed over her now was only just brushing her ankles moments before. The depth of her breathing increased, and Claire started to panic again. Her mind couldn't cope with the comprehension of what she'd achieved. Suddenly the sensation of falling overcame her, and when she next had the nerve to open her eyes, she found herself lying on the ground—full-sized again. She lay still, trying to stop the world from spinning.

It was sometime later that she heard a car pull up beside her. Forcing herself to open her eyes and sit up, Claire readied herself to act. David came running around the back end of a white four-wheel drive and crouched down beside her to check her over, making sure nothing was broken or damaged—while calling her name.

"I'm fine," Claire revealed weakly. She didn't know how much he knew, or even how much he was involved.

"Geoff rang...a strange car had been seen in town, and he was worried about you," David said as he helped her up and into the car's front seat.

Flashes of light danced in front of her eyes, and Claire was beginning to feel dizzy once more as nausea went along with it. Placing her head in her hands to try to stop the sensation, she noticed a sticky, wet patch in her hair. When she pulled them away, she found that the left one was covered in blood. She looked up at David as he entered the driver's side.

"There was a car...it almost hit me...no, it did...it clipped me. I fell into the ditch as it drove away." Claire did not tell him about her mad experiment in shrinking and how she had been successful; how she felt sick to her stomach because she really did not know what she was doing. All she wanted at that moment was to go home, to talk to her Uncle Geoff. She was feeling fuzzy-headed, vaguely aware of David talking. She wasn't sure if he was talking to her or not. Suddenly, he was holding her up with his arm while desperately trying to keep control of the car, begging her anxiously not to go to sleep. The car came to a sudden, jolting stop, and she hoped that she was home, so she could crawl into bed. David opened the door and undid her seatbelt, slowly helping her out of the car and walking her up a path on legs that felt like they didn't belong to her.

Claire managed to lift her head and tried to focus on her surroundings, but all that managed to do was make her feel even worse. She was aware of David holding her and then, as if she were as light as a doll, he lifted her up and placed her onto a narrow bed. She heard him tell her it was going to be all right.

A light was shone in her eyes, and she could feel hands moving over her body, checking all the grazes as she whispered quietly, "My head."

Soon the hands were investigating where the blood was coming from. She heard someone say X-ray, and all the while David held her hand. Raised voices came crashing through her awareness, and soon Uncle Geoff was at her side as well. The doctor asked both men to stay in the waiting room until after she came back. At that moment, the world went black, and she heard no more.

Hushed was how Claire would describe the room when she next became aware of her surroundings. Then the sterile smell of a hospital assaulted her nose. She'd been in plenty in the past—aiding friends who had hurt themselves, just doing what came naturally to herself. She could feel her body screaming at her. Muscles, grazes, and contusions made themselves known to her consciousness, but worst of all was her head.

Beneath her eyelids, stars flashed, and she squeezed them shut. Her hand was caught up in a much larger one. A quiet voice told her to lie still, and she could hear someone else calling for the doctor. She recognised her Uncle Geoff's cologne and struggled to open her eyes to look at him. He asked her how she was, and she tried to sit up, but he gently pushed her back down and told her to wait for the doctor. Geoff then asked if she remembered what happened. She gave a slight nod and heard David say that he would go find the doctor. Claire found her voice to quickly tell her uncle everything, including trying to shrink herself. He told her to hush, that there was plenty of time for her to explain. She didn't see the wave of concern that crossed his face.

David soon returned with the doctor and nurse in tow. Geoff moved out of the way to make room for the medical staff, and the doctor shone a light in her eyes, making her squint and turn her head away. The doctor told them that she had a mild concussion and that they would like to keep her in overnight for observation. Moving restlessly, Claire felt so tired that she didn't care what was being said. They all exited the room and left her in peace, and she had the chance to look around. The room was white on white on white with grey, hard-wearing, highly polished floors. The window beside the bed was slightly open, making the net curtains blow lazily in the breeze. She watched it billowing out and falling slowly back into place, masking the blue sky outside with a misty look.

Claire did not know how long she lay there—not thinking, just being—but she became more aware when she heard hard-heeled shoes tap their way into her room. She moved her head and saw David's wife walk up beside the bed. The sour look she gave Claire sent a slight chill down her spine. Noticing Claire was awake, Beth sat in the chair her uncle had vacated and looked at her intensively. She settled herself in and placed her handbag squarely on her lap. She reminded Claire of someone out of the fifties. Her ginger hair was pinned up, and she wore a slimline skirt and high-collared white shirt with a lightweight blue cardigan over the top. A set of matching-sized pearls was strung around her neck. She waited for the woman to speak, but she just stared at Claire.

"Hi," Claire managed to croak.

"Oh, you're awake," Beth said primly. "Well, I have been ordered to come and sit with you, as if I hadn't had anything better to do. This is the sort of thing better suited for the grandparents and those who are not as busy as some people." She inspected her impeccably manicured nails, and they looked as if she had never done a day's work in her life. Claire started to tune her out as Beth was clearly talking more to herself than the girl, muttering things like people needed to be more careful and watch where they were going. The woman sat and looked at her as if she was seeing her for the first time.

"You look remarkably like your mother," Beth declared.

"Did you know Mum?" Claire asked.

"Yes. It was me who was supposed to marry John." Seeing the confusion in Claire's eyes, she nodded. She then took great pleasure in laying her own pain bare to Claire. "It had been determined by the Elders that we should make a good match, as the bloodlines would have been almost completely untainted with any children we might have had. But then he left with your mother. Left me here in the village humiliated and passed on like chattel to her brother. To be so related to that family and leaving my children's bloodlines so uncertain is abhorrent." Beth paused slightly to appraise Claire. "Look how you turned out. Tainted. So, it definitely runs in that bloodline. Fully tainted, too, from what I hear. Oh...they don't think I hear things—they don't tell me anything—so I have to find out for myself. I hear them talking and then they order me to come here and sit with you." She then sat tight-lipped.

Claire wasn't sure whether she was supposed to make some comment back about it. Her head hurt too much to really think about any injustices done to this woman sitting next to her, so she closed her eyes. She heard the woman make a disgusted noise, followed by the unmistakable sound of a magazine being opened and flicked through.

Sometime later—she was not sure how long—Claire woke up and looked around. Curtains now blocked the view outside, but Claire could see that it was dark out. Beth was nowhere to be seen but slumped in the chair was her Uncle Geoff. His head nodded on his chest as he dozed, and he made a soft snoring sound that seemed a little ridiculous considering the size of his nose. She smiled softly to herself, shifting in the bed. It felt like she had been hit by a train. Everything hurt. Her grunt of pain woke Geoff, and he lurched forward to make sure she was all right. Claire waved him off, even though that produced a new bout of muscle spasms in her shoulder. She assured him she was fine and lay back on the pillows. She asked if the bed could be moved up and he fumbled for the control, then slowly raised the head of the bed for her. She sighed in relief. He asked if she would like a drink or something to eat. The thought of food made her stomach lurch and not in a good way, but her mouth was as dry as a desert and she agreed to a glass of water.

After her thirst was slackened, he asked her to elaborate on what she had told him earlier about the accident. When she got to the part where she described her shrinking, he sat still and stared intently at her.

"You attempted something you don't know much about? Out in the middle of nowhere? With no one around to help you?" he asked succinctly after she had finished. He shook his head at her. "A very dumb thing to do, Kid."

She agreed. "I swear I'll ask for Jack's help before ever attempting to do it again. What did the doctor say?" Claire inquired, changing the subject.

"He said that you have a concussion and the best thing for you is to rest. He won't even consider using Healing, as there's not much to be done with a concussion. You'll be allowed home in the morning. The effort of shrinking is probably the cause of most of the pain you are experiencing and other than that—only a few cuts, bruises, and grazes. He thinks you should be back to normal in a couple of days, if you take it easy," he told her pointedly.

"Do I really need to stay here...can't you wrangle it, so I can come home with you?"

Geoff shook his head. "You don't get it. You could have seriously harmed or killed yourself attempting what you did this morning." Tears started in his eyes, and she heard the catch in his voice as he talked. "I have lost too many members of my family. I am not going to lose you as well."

She reached over and took his hand. "I'm sorry, Uncle Geoff." He patted her hand back, quickly dashing at his eyes to rid the tears.

Claire silently cursed herself for her foolishness and felt a lump growing in her own throat. She swallowed hard, looking away from her uncle to see Jack leaning against the doorway. He looked between the uncle and niece and had a surprised look on his face. He stepped quickly into the room, coming up to the bed.

"Did I hear you right? That Claire successfully managed to shrink herself?" Jack asked in an almost conspiratorial half whisper.

Geoff sat back in his chair, letting go of her hand and confirming the news to the intruder. Jack plopped down on the bed, causing pain to Claire as she speedily moved herself away to make room for him. He patted her leg and apologised.

"That was a very dangerous and foolish thing to attempt for the first time by yourself, Claire, and it's the reason behind all the pain you are experiencing. If you had waited for me to teach you properly, you would've been armed with the techniques that would have stopped the pain from occurring. I hope you have learned your lesson." He talked to Claire as if she were a naughty school child.

"Yes...I have, Jack," she agreed wholeheartedly.

"Well, I heard you had an accident, so I thought I would come out to make sure that you were okay. I can see that you are, so I won't annoy you too much." Once more he patted her leg, almost possessively and too high up her thigh for her comfort. "I hope to see you in a few days to start your proper training. Get better soon." With that, he left, and an awkward silence fell between uncle and niece.

To fill the void Jack's leaving had created, Claire broached the subject of Beth. Her Uncle Geoff nodded knowingly at her and confirmed what she had told Claire.

"It was a sad tale that has not ended well," he informed her. "David's a good man who deserves a better partner in life than that woman. Most of the year, Beth and their two children live away from The Community—near their expensive school. David only came back to The Community to run his parents' farm when Bob and Lynnette decided it was time to retire. David had a very good construction business going in the city. When he came back, he sold it to Benjamin.

"When your mother and father ran off together, they left a rather large mess behind. It almost ripped The Community apart with people taking sides. It was then—with great patience, understanding, and time—that Mary and I made the new match. Beth was feeling humiliated, and had gone to stay with relatives, but when she came back, she wanted to regain face, so she agreed to marry David. It was only after I started to report back that I thought you might have Talent, that Beth started to sour in the match, realising that—as she calls it—the tainted blood would be in any children that they had." Geoff paused and continued gravely. "You see, Claire, to some people...talented blood's much less desirable than untalented." He gave a little chuckle at that and then carried on. "But she would have married into a family that still had a touch of the taint. Look at me." They both chuckled at that thought.

Chapter Nine

Nestling herself onto the couch after getting home from the hospital, Claire heard a knock at the front door and then the sound of the handle being tried. She started to rise to answer it, but Geoff told her very firmly to stay put and headed to the hall. She heard her Aunt Lilith's voice as the door opened, asking why on earth it was locked. She couldn't quite hear what her uncle told her in his deep soft voice, but it sounded like *better safe than sorry*, and she knew he worried about the mysterious car. She heard them walking up the hallway, and Claire greeted her great-aunt as she entered the room.

"Oh, I am so happy to see you back home. I did pop into the hospital yesterday, but you were fast asleep, and I didn't want to disturb you." Lilith sat on the other end of the couch. "I have come bearing gifts—to be borrowed only and returned when you've finished with them." Out of her bag came several volumes of thin books, and she handed them to Claire. "Geoff visited me and told me that you'd like to know more about those with your Talents and also how those with more than one dealt with it."

Claire cradled them gently on her lap, carefully leafing through the top book. Small script ran across the pages, and the smell of old books assaulted her nose—reminding her of libraries.

"Thank you, Aunt Lilith, and you too, Uncle Geoff." Claire held the books close to her. She did not see the small, pleased smile Lilith gave when she heard the title *aunt* in front of her name.

"A little tea wouldn't go amiss, Geoff," Lilith demanded of her younger brother, pulling up a chair to sit by Claire as they started to pore over the books.

Geoff left them to it and soon returned with a pot of tea and cups for both. Lilith then waved him away as if he were dismissed. Claire looked at her great-aunt and wondered what had occurred between the two of them that could have caused such a rift. She almost asked her aunt, but courage left her, and she lost herself in the writings of those who had gone before, making a detailed study of the Talents.

Hours later, after Lilith had left and Claire had her head in one of the books, she glanced up at her Uncle Geoff. He had brought some of his work into the living room to keep her company—or so he had told her—but she suspected something else. She suspected that all through the night at the hospital she was not alone, that different people at different times had come in to check on her and make sure she was safe.

Geoff put down his paperwork and looked at her. "What?"

"Nothing," she said.

"Well, you keep looking up at me, so what is it?"

She placed the book on her chest and folded her arms over the top. "What exactly happened between you and Aunt Lilith?"

Sighing and shaking his head, Geoff replied, "You're determined to hunt out every secret this community has, aren't you?" Tidying his paperwork into a folder, he laid it on the table beside him. "If I'm going to tell you this tale, I'm going to have to have a stiff drink in hand."

Geoff got up and went into the kitchen. Claire could hear him pour the whiskey into a tumbler. As he came back into the room, she thought that this must be a bad story and started to regret her curiosity. He sat himself down again and took a sip.

"It began when we were younger. I think Lil and Mal were about twenty-four. Mal was already married by then and I was about fifteen. My sister loved a man, but I knew he was not suitable for her. I knew that he was bad to the core and would eventually destroy both himself and my sister if she married him. Both Mal and I told her that we objected to the match strongly, but even exposing how bad he was to her didn't change the way she felt about him. This man was eventually exiled from The Community for various things he had done, which I will not go into." He gave Claire a hard look, taking another sip and sitting quietly.

"Lil swore she'd never forgive me because of what I had done. With Mal, she was more tender-hearted, as she believed that it was all my doing anyway. But what was funny was that it was Mal who had warned me in the first place. I have borne the brunt of our sister's animosity all these years. She swore that no other man would be good enough for her and she's remained unmarried ever since."

Claire waited for him to be quiet for a while and then asked, "Why didn't Lilith follow him? I mean, if she was that in love with him, why did she stay?"

He took another sip. "Our parents ordered her to stay. Lilith was almost—but not quite—a prisoner of her family until word came to The Community from the watchers outside that he had died. Killed by an angry father. Lil was then told of what happened, and she never talked to our parents again. Mum died shortly after, and Lil refused to attend the funeral. Years later when Dad died, she did attend his, but spat on his grave. She was still adamant that she could've changed him.

We have avoided each other for years, and when I went to university and then left with my wife to live on the outside, the only news of her was through Mal—who is still deeply saddened with the rift in the family, but at a loss as how to mend it."

Through the silence, the clock on the mantelpiece ticked away the minutes and the shadows grew longer on the floor. Claire did not know how long they sat in the living room in the afternoon's quiet, but she felt ashamed she'd made him relive this awful part of his life. One piece of the tale caught her attention, and she puzzled on it for quite some time before speaking up.

"I didn't know you had been married. You've never mentioned her, and it's not in the genealogy book."

After slugging back the last dregs of his drink and swallowing, he chuckled. "You really are a ferret today, aren't you?" He placed his glass on top of his paperwork and laced his fingers together. "Okay, my little ferret. All the secrets must come out." He then related the tale of his wife.

"We were married when we were both young. Fortunately, the match that had been made for us was not only a good one, but a loving one. We adored each other. When the situation with my sister got worse, we decided that we should try to make it on the outside. I set up a small law firm by myself, and Katy helped in the office. We made a comfortable home for ourselves and got ready for children, but they never came." His voice caught in his throat and his eyes closed for a moment, before resuming his tale.

"The year before your mother and father ran away, Katy was diagnosed with a very aggressive cancer. So, we shut up shop and moved back to The Community, but she survived the move only by a couple of months. At her funeral, my sister spoke to me for the first time in years. She told me, *'Now you know what it is like to lose someone.'*

"I mourned my Katy hard. I took to drinking to numb the pain and hid myself away. Mal and Grace tried to make me see sense, but I could not get past the grief. It wasn't until well over a year later when your parents disappeared together, that I was summoned by the Elders. Mary said to me that my time of mourning was over and that I needed to re-join the community. She told me she had a job for me to do—that I was to go to the city and track down your parents. I argued with her, berating her for asking me to do this, but she just stood there and took it. Then she calmly told me that it was in a vision she had had, and the visions must be obeyed. She gave me some items that belonged to your mother and father. So, you see, if you're a ferret for secrets, then I am the bloodhound. I immediately knew where they were and went to find them. When I did, they were already married, so I left to report back to The Community. I then helped to deal with the Beth problem and thought I could live out my days in peace here in the village. But I was wrong.

"The Elders sent for me again, asking me to be your parent's Watcher. Mary told me that she was very concerned for the safety of them both and their future daughter. It was then she told me of Marcus; of his threat to the community and what he wished to do. So, I packed up and moved back to the city. I made myself known to my nephew first. I warned him of the possible danger Marcus posed to them both and that I was there to help." He paused.

"It was the proudest day of my life when they made me your godfather." He smiled to himself and touched his fingertips to his mouth, looking up at her. "Have I ever told you how proud I am of you; how proud I have always been of you? You and your parents were some of the most important people in my life. You helped me come back to myself. I almost lost it again when they died, but I had you to look after. Once again, I was preparing to move back to The Community when Mary contacted me herself and told me it was highly important that we stay in the city.

"So, I stayed where I was and prepared to bring you up. You used to hide from me, but I always found it easy to find you. Sometimes I sensed that you needed to be alone—to grieve in your own way so I would leave you, knowing you were safe. I somehow knew that you'd come to me when you were ready to have a father figure in your life again...and you did. For over a year, we lived together until you were ready for some guidance. And my heart sang the first time you put your hand in mine. We never talked about it. We just knew.

"So, some more secrets. I was told to make myself known to Marcus, and to make my services available to him. I was to let him know who I am and what I could do. He found me very useful, and I hated doing his bidding—especially knowing what he had done to your parents. Knowing he had taken from me the closest thing to a family as I'd ever come to having. But I hated him even more for leaving you alone in the world with a broken man as a guardian. It made me sick to my stomach working for him. I knew that he had managed to get his son close to you, but I was unaware of the trap Marcus had set. I had to act fast that night. I knew you were scared and in trouble, so I tracked you down to the theatre. I'm sorry that I scared you and caused you pain—thinking I'd betrayed you. But I was doing what I thought was best.

"When we came here, and Mary met us at the door, I could see the greed in her eyes, but chose to ignore it. I had no idea of what she had in mind for you. To use you in such a way. She is going to pit your untried Talents against those of Marcus Ryder. I keep telling them that they risk you recklessly. That

Marcus will kill you if you don't join him. For he sees you as a prize; a full Talent he can use as a broodmare to start his army of Talented ones." He closed his eyes, knowing he had caused her even more anxiety.

Claire felt sick to her stomach hearing these words—since she had never known exactly why she must fight Marcus—but now she felt her blood boil at the thought. The thought of being used in that way made her head spin.

Her Uncle Geoff stared at her as she attempted to process the information he had just given. He stood up and moved towards her, hugging her to him. "My little ferret, you have all my secrets. They cannot harm either you or me now. Arm yourself with them and survive."

He felt her nod into his shoulder. As he held her for a while, she spoke. "I prefer it when you call me Kid. I don't like ferrets."

Chapter Ten

Claire stood in the middle of the mostly deserted hall—apart from herself and the Elder's son, Jack. The sun streamed through the high windows and dust motes danced on the eddies of a draft; illuminating and sparkling in the shafts of light. The air was stuffy inside the hall, smelling slightly stale. At the stage end facing Claire, Jack stood and looked at her intently, making her feel uncomfortable. He was trying to get her to be aware of her surroundings—trying to get her to feel the wood beneath her feet and the stone in the walls. He had told her that he needed to know how much of her Talent had developed naturally.

She was confused about what he wanted, so Jack demonstrated the Talent. Claire had watched him carefully. First, to her eye, he became almost unimportant—like one of the chairs stacked up against the wall. She moved her sight from one side of him to the other, her eyes just skipping across him. The next thing she knew was that she could see right through him. The outline of his body was there, but the pattern on the wall was as plain as day when he stood stock-still. Jack kept fading until there was no sign of him at all, and she was impressed. He came back to himself and then moved slightly. She could see him getting visibly smaller. He walked towards her, gradually shrinking in size until he stood at her feet—as small as a mouse.

Claire bent down, and he walked onto her hand. She lifted him up. There was no distortion to his features. Jack was a perfect miniature of himself. Suddenly he began to feel very heavy in her hand, coming back to full size again and laughing at her surprise. He explained the three stages—that he could combine them and be invisible as well as small. He then told her that they'd start at the beginning. Small baby steps were what was required.

Jack took her through several techniques he had developed for himself, but ultimately it would be up to her as to how she'd get to where she needed to be. He asked her to show him her own technique and to pretend he was someone she didn't want to talk to. This part was easy for Claire, as she didn't have to pretend too much. Jack told her she was on the way, but to try it his way next. She did as he asked, and he nodded at the results.

"That's good. There was some noticeable difference to your shape that time. But I could still see you clearly. My eyes did not skim over you as they should," he informed. All morning they tried—until she sat down on the floor and put her hands on her splitting head.

"Okay, I think that is enough for today. With the concussion on top of what you've tried, I think it may have been a bit much for you." Jack grasped her hands and pulled her up off the floor.

"I think you might be right, Jack. Thanks for today." When Claire tried to release her hands from his sweaty ones, he held on for a moment longer than necessary. She felt uneasy having him stand so close to her, as she could see the look in his eye and tried not to shudder at it. As soon as she left the hall and Jack behind, she noticed how the tension in her body eased off.

When Claire got home, she jumped into bed and closed her eyes. She felt drained mentally and physically, but not tired enough to sleep. Picking up one of the books Lilith had brought her, she flipped to a page in the centre. She tried to concentrate on the script writing—puzzling out the words. This section of the book dealt with her other Talent, Flight. Claire had read these passages several times and found it hard to work out the technique it suggested. Her uncle had told her that it was only at night he'd seen her hovering, and only after a particularly stressful day. The way she was feeling right then, she'd place a bet that it would happen again that night. The feeling of Jack's hands in hers made her shudder again, and this time she did not suppress it.

Claire read the passage again out loud—going through it very slowly and trying to visualise what was supposed to happen. Using the technique of making the body lighter than air, she whispered the mantra the writer had suggested over and over. Concentrating hard on not stumbling over the words, Claire did not hear Geoff open her door to ask her if she was hungry; she only heard his loud gasp. The experience of falling quickly followed by the sudden landing on the bed with a bounce shocked her. Geoff's face said it all, and she didn't need for him to tell her that she'd achieved what she was trying to do.

"Well, you've been studying hard! Why don't you take a break and come downstairs for some lunch?" With that, he shut her door and walked down the stairs.

That was how Claire spent her days for the following week: morning lessons with Jack and afternoons spent training in the privacy of her own bedroom. Jack was very happy with her progression through his techniques, but she also studied others from the books provided by Lilith and added a few refinements of her own. Her hovering was going well. From the bed, she decided to progress to a sitting position on the floor. With her legs crossed under her, Claire would visualise and go through the mantra, as it had now gotten to the point where she could do this without looking at the book, but she still stared intently at a spot on the wall to focus on. She could feel herself lift off the floor—feel the breeze from the window waft under her as well as around. She could raise herself up higher and higher until one day she managed to hit her head on the ceiling, giving herself a fright and bringing her crashing back down onto the floor.

Geoff's running footsteps thundered through the house as he took the stairs two at a time and rushed into her room. Laughing to herself, Claire was on the floor. Her laughter doubled when she saw the look on his face.

"What happened? Are you hurt?" he asked urgently. This only made Claire laugh even more. And through her laughter, she explained what happened.

"That's it, then. I don't want you crashing through the floor into my study while I'm in there working. Time to get you a bigger space to practice in and maybe something softer to land on!"

The next afternoon, she found herself on David's farm—in a large unused barn—walking around an enormous mound of hay that had been heaped into the middle of the floor. Over the top of the hay was spread a large tarp, and a small ladder leaned up against it, so she could climb up on top. In the barn with her were her two uncles and Grandmother Lynnette, all watching as she circled the hay pile.

"That pile is a bit of overkill, but thanks." Claire gave the three a small smile.

As she was climbing up the ladder, Beth walked into the barn, tiptoeing in her high heels, demanding to know what was going on.

"Claire's going to be using the barn for some Flight practice, Beth," David replied.

Beth placed her hands on her hips and huffed. "This is outrageous. How dare you allow that girl here to practice such unnatural acts! I do not want her corrupting my children!" Beth screamed at him.

Going bright red at this tirade, David looked at his wife. "Firstly, this isn't your home, you hardly live here. Secondly, I will invite whomever I like here to do whatever they wish to do. Even if that means—as you so nicely put it—*unnatural acts*. And finally, you never let the boys anywhere near this barn, so they're unlikely to be corrupted." He paused. "Why are you here, anyway? Shouldn't you be down south with the kids?"

"They broke up from school yesterday for the summer holidays, or did you forget that next week is Christmas? And that this year we are spending it here on this godforsaken farm!" she seethed.

"No, I did not forget Christmas. How can I forget when you are always reminding me to do things for Christmas? Will I be allowed to play with my own children while they're home from school? Or will they be just as regimented here as you have them there? Better yet, maybe I won't pay for that fancy school next year and all their other activities. Maybe they can go to the local school like I did and actually learn what it is to be part of The Community." His face went from red to magenta as he spoke.

Beth was affronted by his words and stormed off, not caring what got on her shoes.

"Oh dear," Lynnette muttered under her breath, throwing her son a baleful look, and going after her daughter-in-law.

"It's about time you took a harder line with her. I'm sorry, David, for pushing the match on you. It was a bad one and I knew it," Geoff admitted.

"Forget it. That was nothing. That's just our way of communicating." David's colour was slowly returning to normal, and the two men turned their attention back to Claire, looking around to try and see just where she had gone.

They searched around the hay pile and David even looked in the loft, but it was only when Claire released her breath and unclenched her hold on herself that they could see her. Incredibly impressed, the pair looked at each other in awe.

"Well, she's making some progress, at least," David teased.

"Nice to know that Jack has actually taught her something," Geoff replied.

Claire climbed the ladder, looking down at them both. "I think I can manage on my own now." Taking on a superior tone, she then told them, "I do believe that you two will only make a nuisance of yourselves. You can go." She pointed to the double barn doors that stood wide open and waited for them to leave.

"Do you see what I have to put up with every day?" Geoff asked David.

"I can sympathise with you, my friend," David commiserated with the older man and placed an understanding hand on Geoff's shoulder. "I just can't seem to get away from demanding women. You know, her mother was *exactly* the same, so I can't say that I'm surprised."

"Was she really?" Geoff prodded.

They continued in this manner until they were both out of earshot and Claire sat down on the hay pile. "Men!"

Chapter Eleven

By the time Christmas rolled around the following week, Claire was trying to combine her Talents. With the help of Jack, she could now become invisible and small at the same time. She found she was still having some pain after the shrinking, but every day the pain eased a little more. After her lessons with Jack, she would go home and grab a bite to eat. Once she had checked in with Geoff, Claire would run to David's farm to stretch out the cramps. There she would practice her hovering—since now she was able to float slowly around the barn. During one windy day, Claire had discovered the trick to moving by accident when a sudden gust blew open the barn door and she moved across the room with it. Since then, she'd moved herself slowly sideways—trying not to let her excitement run away with her—before she had a full handle on the Talent. At least she learned her lesson there, as patience, practice, and concentration were what was required.

Claire was finishing up on Christmas Eve, softly settling herself on the ground, when she became aware of someone watching her. Scared of who it might be and without even thinking, she eased into invisibility—drawing it around her protectively like a cloak. Ever so slowly, she moved around the barn. As Claire tried to see just who it was that was spying on her, she came across one of her cousins, Jasper. She could see his confusion as he looked for her. Sneaking up behind him, she tapped him on the shoulder. Jasper jumped a couple of feet in the air and looked around wildly. She released her will and appeared in front of him.

"So, you can turn yourself invisible!" Jasper exclaimed excitedly.

Claire nodded. "Why are you spying on me? I thought you weren't allowed anywhere near the barn."

"I was curious, and I wanted to see what you could do. I heard Mum and Dad fighting about you. Mum really doesn't want you here."

Feeling concern for her young cousin, Claire asked, "Do they fight often?" She sat down on the hay as he shyly joined her.

"They always fight. Mum doesn't like it here—she much prefers it when we are closer to Nan and Poppa." Claire presumed that they were Beth's parents. "She told Hunter and me that we're not allowed to come to the barn, and we're *definitely* not allowed to talk to you."

"So, why're you disobeying your mother?"

"Because I like being on the farm, and I like being near Dad. When did you know you had a Talent?" The last question took Claire off guard, but she noticed he did not call it tainted.

"Only when I got here, and Uncle Geoff explained everything. I grew up in the city, and he never told me anything about The Community. But I always knew that I was better than anyone else at running and jumping things. Some things that other people wouldn't even attempt to do. Why do you ask?"

"Some boys in my class showed me one of your clips. You're wicked. When I went back the other week and told them that you were my cousin, they didn't believe me. Can you keep a secret?" Jasper's dark blue eyes were full of hope.

"Yes, I can keep a secret. Why?"

Jasper placed his hands together as if he were praying, then slowly cupped them. From between his fingers, a glow was escaping. When he finally pulled his hands apart, a small ball of light hovered on the palm of his hand. He looked up at her expectantly, and she was awed by her young cousin.

"I discovered that I can do that by accident," he said as he quickly extinguished the light. "I was locked in a dark cupboard at school by some boys. I'm afraid of the dark, and I clasped my hands together and felt a warm feeling growing between them. Once I pulled them apart, a small spark danced in my palm. I don't know how I managed to do it, but the more I make the little lights, the bigger and stronger they become. It is one of the Talents, isn't it, Claire?" Jasper asked eagerly.

"It is, Jasper. I read about it in the red booklet." Claire did not tell him that she had read that the light could also be used as a weapon. She decided then and there that David and Geoff needed to be told so he could get guidance on the matter and a little help dealing with not only his mother, but with being bullied at school.

It was while she was pondering this that she heard Beth calling Jasper's name. She told him to go out the back of the barn and not say a word of the Talent to his mother. She did not want the boy to be in trouble with Beth for talking to her. Just as Jasper left out the back, Beth entered through the main doors.

"Has Jasper been here?" Beth demanded.

"No, I haven't seen Jasper since the party. I thought you told him not to come near me," Claire said, more bravely than she felt.

Beth wasn't fully convinced by her answer and stood appraising Claire. "Ever since you arrived here, there has not been a moment's peace. David is at Geoff's beck and call, and everyone seems to be running around after you."

Claire looked at the woman and wondered exactly what it was that she wanted her to say. "I'm truly sorry if I have caused any trouble, but once the matter with Marcus Ryder is finished, I'll be leaving to go back to the city."

Beth's face flickered when she heard the name, and Claire could plainly see that there was something about Marcus that Beth was hiding. The woman in front of Claire regained her composure and tried to hide any trace of what she may have given away. "I suppose you will be coming to Christmas lunch tomorrow?"

"Sorry, Beth, but I really don't know. Uncle Geoff hasn't told me what's happening yet. To be honest, we don't really celebrate Christmas," Claire stated frankly.

"Don't celebrate Christmas? How ridiculous! How can you not celebrate Christmas?"

"Because that was when my parents died," Claire said softly.

The older woman had the good grace to look shocked, and once she regained her composure, she retorted with, "Well, you just stay away from my boys." Beth then stalked off.

On the run home, Beth's reaction kept running through Claire's mind, and she promised herself to let Geoff know about it as soon as possible. While running, she saw David up ahead—stroking the horse Janie and feeding her some apples. She pulled up to speak to him, unsure of how to broach the subject of his son Jasper having a Talent. She understood that he was very supportive of her, but his own offspring was another matter altogether.

"Hiya. I had a visitor at the barn today," Claire informed him as she slowed down to a walking pace.

"Did you now? And who would that be?"

"It was Jasper." Claire then decided it was better to be out with it than to make any sort of innuendo that might be mistaken. "He showed me that he can make Light between his hands."

Surprised by this news, David stood silent and tried to get a grasp on what his niece was telling him.

"Apparently he was being bullied at school and some boys locked him in a cupboard of some sort, and that's where he made the discovery that he could make Light."

David still stood staring, blinking at her for a little while. Claire got a bit nervous and then carried on talking. "Beth also came to the barn today—she was looking for Jasper—but I told him to go out the back way so that he didn't get in trouble with his mum. While Beth and I were talking, I mentioned Marcus and she had a really strange reaction to the name. You don't know if she's ever met him, do you?" Claire found herself rambling and slowly came to a stop, waiting with uncertainty for David to react.

"Jasper has a Talent?" he asked, and she nodded. "Well, I'll be. Her bloodline is not so pure after all!" David chuckled a little before collecting himself. "Thank you for telling me. I will make sure that Jasper gets all the help he needs, and I think it's about time I made good on my threat. I've been out of my boys' lives for far too long." He gave her a kiss on the forehead and told her he was going to set his house in order. David then walked down the road with his hands in his pockets, whistling a tuneless song.

That night, she related to Geoff the day's events over dinner, alternatively speaking and shoving food into her mouth as fast as she could. She found she was absolutely ravenous these days.

"Will you please slow down? The food will still be there in the next five minutes!" Geoff told her. Claire laughed, and the sound was music to his ears.

"Hey, I haven't told you the best bit," Claire said with a certain amount of glee. "Jasper came to talk to me today and showed me that he has a Talent. He can produce Light! He asked me to keep it a secret, but someone has to help him—especially with that mother of his. I bumped into David on the way home and I told him about Jasper. He was over the moon. But he didn't answer my other question."

"What question was that?" Geoff asked, bemused at her rambling.

"I asked him if Beth had ever met Marcus, because when we were talking, I mentioned his name and she went a bit funny on it. Or am I being a ferret again?"

Geoff wiped his mouth on a napkin and sat back in his chair. "In this case, I don't think you are being a ferret; not much of one, anyway. But it does sound as if she knows him. I wonder..." he trailed off as Claire could almost see the cogs in his brain turning. Suddenly standing, he asked her to clear the dishes up, and then he left. Geoff walked down to the hall and into his study, slamming the door shut loudly behind him. Stunned by his actions, Claire stood still for a long time before she started to clear the table.

By the time she'd finished the dishes, Geoff had emerged from his study with a look on his face that she hadn't seen since the night he'd found her in the abandoned theatre. The look scared her, and she wasn't sure what to make of it, let alone what to even ask her uncle. As she hung up the tea towel to dry, he flicked the jug on to boil.

"I am going to need a lot of coffee tonight." Geoff turned to look at her. "And I'm going to have to go back to the city for a couple of days."

"Cool. I'll go grab my stuff." Claire made to move out of the kitchen.

"No," he said firmly. "Stay here and continue with your studies. I also want you to go stay with your grandparents. Lynnette and Bob are expecting you tonight, I've already rung them, and they are very pleased to have you for a few days."

"But Uncle Geoff, it's Christmas! What about our traditional bad game of chess and our horrible frozen dinner?"

"Look at it this way, you get to spend time with family and finally have a real Christmas for a change—instead of being stuck with me and my bad cooking." He left her in the kitchen to go pack.

"But you're my family," she said quietly to herself. Claire was unhappy about this arrangement. Her grandparents were lovely people, and she knew they loved her very much, but they always fussed over her.

When he returned downstairs, he had a small bag and his overcoat with him. "Are you at least going to tell me what is going on and why you have to go to the city tonight?" Claire asked. His reply did not make her happy.

"I'll tell you everything when I get back. For now, it's probably safest that you know nothing." The jug finished boiling, and he hunted around the cupboards to find a thermos to make coffee in. Claire stood in the corner of the kitchen, watching him as she leaned up against the wall. He suddenly turned to her and pointed his finger at her. "And you can forget about turning invisible and hiding in the back of the car, young lady."

She looked shocked but then recovered, giving him a sly smile. "Me? Do that? It honestly never crossed my mind!" They laughed together as he gave her a bear hug.

"Please do as I ask. I don't want to have to worry about you as well. Look after yourself and keep your eyes open."

"I promise I will," she replied as they parted.

"Oh! I almost forgot!" he exclaimed, diving a hand into his bag." Merry Christmas." He handed Claire a small package that was wrapped in festive paper, with a sparkling red bow on top. She quickly tore into the paper and held up what was inside. "See, I remembered," he said smugly. In her hands, she held a phone charger.

She spent the next five minutes packing a few things into a bag to take to her grandparents' and within another five, they were in the car and dropping her off.

The door to her maternal grandparents' house opened to welcome them in. Geoff thanked them for taking her in on such short notice and gave Claire a kiss on the cheek, telling her to behave. Within moments, the noise of his car was lost in the summer night air and Claire was in the most heavily decorated room she'd ever seen. There were Christmas baubles and tinsel everywhere, but it wasn't the decorations that caught her notice. It was the photographs that nearly took up an entire wall. Photos of her mother and uncle together showed the progression of their lives as they grew up. Further along the same wall were photos of her mother with a baby— and of herself at special moments in her own life. Her grandmother saw what she was looking at and came to her side.

"Geoff would send us photos of your mother and you whenever he could. He sends me one for Christmas each year. He sends them to Grace and Malcolm as well, but Grace never puts them up. She finds it too hard still." She invited Claire to sit. "Did you know that your parents were thinking of coming home?" The girl shook her head. "Jess rang me, and we had only a short conversation, but she wanted to know if there were any houses available. Well, of course there are empty houses all over the village. That was the day before they died.

I was so hopeful about having you all come back to us," Lynnette finished wistfully.

Claire heard her grandfather *harrumph* in his large lounge chair. "That would've caused more problems if they did come home," he said, looking away quickly and mumbling under his breath. "They should have come home sooner, then nothing would have happened to them." Claire sensed that under that gruff exterior sat a man who still grieved the loss of his only daughter. Her heart went out to him, and she moved over to sit beside him.

"What was Mum like as a child, Grandad?" she asked. Luckily, her simple question was the opening that he needed.

"You are the very image of her, Claire, as well as your grandma at the same age. But your other grandmother got it wrong. You have your mother's eyes—not your father's." They spent the rest of the evening talking about her mother, recalling all the normal childhood mishaps and funny moments. And Claire felt comfortably close to her grandfather that night.

Chapter Twelve

Four days had passed and there was still not a word from Geoff. Christmas came and went, and Claire found the holiday to be an overload of her senses. And all revolved around food. The actual day was spent at David's farm—with both sets of grandparents, David, Beth, and the two boys.

Grace and Malcolm joined them because it was the year that Benjamin and Charlotte were to spend Christmas at her parents'. Claire tried to make herself useful, helping to prepare food and to clean up after, but she got the feeling from Beth that no matter what she did, it just wasn't good enough. Every time she tried to talk to her cousins, her aunt would invent a chore either for the boys or for her.

Keeping her promise to her uncle, Claire kept up with her studies. By night she'd read diaries and findings of those who had Talent in the past, and she had even gotten both her grandfathers interested in the subject—they would test her knowledge and listen for hours as she talked about it. She was switching between grandparents' houses as well—two nights at one and two nights at the other.

On the fourth night, Claire was sitting in Grace and Malcolm's living room. Reading a new book Lilith had dropped off for her, she suddenly had the urge to ask a question she thought her grandmother might know the answer to.

"Grandma, what do you know about Jack?" She didn't know why she asked, but the subject just popped into her head.

Her paternal grandmother raised her head from the tapestry she was stitching and looked over her glasses at her. "What on Earth made you ask about him?"

"I don't know really. Only I spend most of the morning with him training and I don't really know him at all. How old is he?"

"To be honest, I'm not really sure. Lilith is the best one to tell you—if you want to know his exact age—but I think he's in his late twenties now," her grandmother replied. "I remember when he was born. It caused a big stir. Mary had been away chasing a vision she had, and when she came back, she was heavily pregnant and wouldn't tell a soul who the father was. We all thought she was far too old to even get pregnant—having that child nearly killed her, you know. And not that I listen to gossip or anything, but some think that her visions have diminished since having him. But we would never have thought that she'd keep it secret that he had Talent. Now that is shocking. Because if anyone would've shouted it from the rooftops that their child had developed a Talent, it would have been her."

Grace put her tapestry down and went on, warming to the subject. "Jack gave her no end of heartache as he was growing up. Just when we all thought he would leave her and go out on his own, he suddenly became a devoted son—looking after her and making sure that she would want for nothing. Which was very odd, but everyone seemed to be pleased that he'd finally come to his senses and taken the responsibility of looking after his mother. But Jack has turned out to be an incredibly nice young man. Just look at the way he is helping you!"

The next day, Claire checked her phone for the umpteenth time, and there was still no message from her Uncle Geoff. She sent yet another message for him to call her, telling him that she was getting worried. Another worry was the fact that there was no message from Adam. He hadn't texted or left a voice message since she had left the city, and that was rather unusual for him.

After eating breakfast, Claire helped her grandmother with a few household jobs when Grace looked at the clock, reminding Claire that she had better go or she'd be late for training with Jack. Slowly gathering her things, she promised that she would be back at lunch time to collect her belongings to go to Lynnette and Bob's—before she went to the barn. She left in good time and dawdled to the village hall.

Making it to just outside the little shop and contemplating getting an ice cream before heading across the road, Claire saw someone cloaked in black and coming out of the door of the hall, rushing around to the back of the building. She hung back for a bit and automatically became invisible while she watched. A moment later, a black four-wheel drive sped out from the lane behind the stone building and turned onto the road—heading in her direction. She tried to see who was driving, but the windows were too darkly tinted to see through them properly. She directed her gaze back at the hall just as Jack appeared in the doorway, looking after the car. Hoping that he wouldn't notice her, Claire shrunk into the shadows right as he ducked back into the dim interior just as fast.

Something screamed in her mind, warning her it was wrong. She agreed with her gut instinct. It would not be a good idea to go to training that day. Sticking to the shadows where possible in the growing heat of the summer's day, Claire worked her way to her Uncle Geoff's house and let herself in via the back door, making sure to lock it behind her. The house stood in silence, but she didn't really know what she had been expecting to hear. Letting out a huge sigh of relief, she tried to think what to do next. *Report,* she thought as she headed to Geoff's study, dumping her backpack at the foot of the stairs.

Sitting at his desk reminded her of how much she missed him. His solid presence would've calmed her, and he would have asked her the right questions to get all the information he required to make a decision. Pen and paper were at the ready, so she began to write.

The first thing she wrote was the description of the man she'd seen coming out of the hall. Slim and tall with an athletic build, he was wearing a lightweight black hoodie. The hood had been pulled up to cover his features which was strange on such a hot summer day. He also wore matching long pants and trainers to boot. Claire even described the way he moved— how he took long, fluid strides before he disappeared around the back of the hall. She then described the car she had seen speeding away with its tinted windows, even the mag wheels that were on it. Closing her eyes, she tried using the visualisation technique she had read about in one of the books for those with Recall.

The image swam in front of her eyes for a moment before it came into focus. Even when she opened her eyes, it was still there. Adding a fuller description, Claire included the make, the model, the registration number, and even the fact that there was a slight dent along with a scratch mark on the passenger-side front bumper. Claire tried valiantly to see the driver, but again, the tinted windows were just too dark and hid his face.

Claire continued with the report, writing down how she had observed Jack's expression as he'd searched the street before going back into the hall. She noted the time and day this all happened, grabbing her phone from her pocket to send another message to Geoff. But just as she was about to hit send, she thought better of it and rewrote the message. Instead of telling him what had happened and that she'd left a message on his desk for him, she decided to put it a different way. The message now read: *I have made up the shopping list...I left it for you on your desk.* She hoped that he'd understand that something had happened and would come home soon, as she had never made up a shopping list in all the time she'd lived with him.

The decision to code the message was something that had come to her the previous night. As she lay worrying over Geoff's silence, her thoughts had led to the dark suspicion that their phones might have been hacked in some way. Claire hoped that she was wrong.

Leaning against the high-backed chair, Claire pondered what to do next. She knew she didn't want to go anywhere near the hall just now, and she wasn't sure about going to David's barn for training either. For some reason, the sight of the unknown man in the village had unsettled her. The way he walked reminded her of someone, and she couldn't quite place him. She knew the piece of information would come to her eventually. Trying to force it wouldn't help her now. Putting the desk back into order, she then went to the stairs and picked up her bag. Even the thought of going back to her grandparents' house was not appealing to her right now, knowing all the questions they would ask. She climbed the stairs to her room, thinking that she had plenty of time left in the day to decide.

The room was stuffy and hot, having been shut up for four days. When she opened the window, a warm breeze wafted in to compete with the heat. Sitting on her bed, she grabbed a book out of her bag and started to flick through it. She knew it by heart, and it didn't take her long to find the passage she sought. Rereading the passage on Recall and the techniques for bringing forth complete and detailed images, she couldn't believe that she had managed to do it downstairs so easily. Claire couldn't remember any mention in the red booklet—or even in the books Lilith had loaned her—of anyone taking techniques from one Talent and using them to help with another. She wasn't even sure herself how she'd managed to use it. While she was musing and trying to find any reference in one of the books, she heard the back-door rattling.

Sitting still, she listened, waiting to hear if she'd just imagined it or if there was actually someone there. The door rattled again, and then she heard the unmistakable squeak as it opened. She gathered her books back into her bag and quietly shut the door to her bedroom. Claire thought about shrinking herself—maybe making herself invisible—but she knew if it was Jack, he would know what to look for. He still didn't know that she had managed to move while hovering, as the thought of shrinking herself to the size of sparrow and flying out of the window came to her. Not having the time to go through all the necessary steps to do both things, she moved quickly. She heard the noise of a creaky step as someone put their weight on it. She went to the ledge, pushed the window open to its fullest, and climbed up just as the door flew open.

Taking one look behind her, she was shocked to see Adam, wearing a black tracksuit, framed in the doorway.

"Adam!" she gasped.

He put his hand out to try and stop her. "That jump is too high even for you, Claire. Why don't you come back inside? We'll talk." She could feel the waves of his Charm offensive crashing over her, telling her everything was okay, reassuring her that she was safe.

She shook her head. "You'll never know what I can do now, Adam, and it's no use trying to use your Charm on me! It won't work anymore."

With that, Claire did four things simultaneously. Throwing herself out of the window, she shrunk herself while drawing on a cloak of invisibility, and then flew away. The sensation took her breath away and she knew that she would pay later for the hurriedness of it. She made straight for the large tree in the backyard, landing softly on one of the broader branches. Looking back up to her bedroom window, she saw Adam leaning out, trying to find any trace of her. He slammed down her window and within minutes, she saw him leave through the back door and around the house. She stayed where she was—her heart hammering in her chest—and cursed her bad luck. Of course, he was the one she'd seen earlier, but why? And was it him who had tried to run her down?

Claire paced up and down the branch, trying to think things through. Adam was the son of Marcus. She knew his father had told him to get close to her to bring her into his fold, but why try to run her down? The only reason was to try to possibly hurt her, so he could take her back to the city without anyone knowing. But why had he left her there? Unless the car that tried to hit her was not Adam's but someone else's? She stopped pacing the branch.

More questions piled on top of one another. What was Adam doing at the hall with Jack? What were they talking about? Was Jack part of this or was he just asked for information? If that was the case, was Marcus getting desperate? Did he know that her uncle was away from home and that she was on her own? Did he have spies in the village? Were there people sympathetic to his cause? In that case, who could she trust? She decided that she didn't want to put her grandparents in danger, so going back to either one was not an option.

Sitting down cross-legged on the branch, Claire placed her hands on her knees and attempted to do some calming techniques. She simply had to get her brain in order. She had to start thinking clearly without jumping to conclusions and making up wild theories. Firstly, she lowered her heart rate and then her breathing. She concentrated on the vision of a single flame in her mind and started to think logically. The most pressing thing she had to do was find a place to hide. Uncle Geoff's house was no longer a safe haven, and neither was her grandparents'. David's barn came to mind. The nights were still warm, and there were plenty of places to hide—both inside and out—if Adam ever came looking again.

Still shrouded in invisibility, Claire floated down from the tree and across the lawn to the back door, making herself large again before entering. Quickly, she rummaged through the kitchen for supplies—eating as she went—then raced upstairs to grab a set of clothes and a couple of blankets she'd seen in the hall's cupboard. She ran down the stairs, throwing everything into her backpack as she headed for the door. Once outside, she concentrated for a moment and felt herself raise up. In all this, she was still not sure how far she could go before she lost energy.

As she lifted into the air, Claire watched the village become small beneath her. Getting her bearings, she propelled herself forward. While up in the air, she concentrated on the landmarks she knew well down below. She found the wind a challenge as she worked arduously to keep herself on track.

By the time Claire reached the barn, sweat was pouring from her skin with the effort of keeping herself both afloat and invisible. As she came to land, she noticed that she'd lost a lot more height than she had thought and stumbled when her feet hit the ground. Quietly, she entered the barn from the back and immediately climbed the ladder that led to the loft, collapsing on the hay that lay there. Her muscles were all still tensed, and she tried to loosen them up, knowing that if she didn't do it now then she'd pay for it later with screaming pain. It seemed to take forever to do her exercises to release the tension. Finally feeling able to move more freely, she set up an area, so she could hide from anyone trying to find her.

Once she had settled herself in, Claire pulled out her phone once more. There was still no contact from Geoff, and she chewed on a nail while she thought. She sent him a quick, cryptic message asking, *when you get back, can we fly somewhere warm and remote?* She hoped that he would understand where she was and come find her. Turning the phone off to conserve the battery, Claire settled back on the makeshift bed, shutting her eyes, and deciding she'd check it every couple of hours.

She didn't know how long she'd dozed in the warm air of the barn, but the noise of a car pulling up outside woke her. Claire lay still, straining to hear who it might be. Outside the main doors of the barn, she could hear David's voice telling someone that they could have a look if they liked, but he hadn't seen Claire all day. One of the giant doors was pushed to one side and fresh air cut through the barn from front to back, escaping out of the open windows. She could hear people moving around downstairs—peering in the corners.

"What's up there?" the unmistakable voice of the Elder's son, Jack, called out loudly through the large space. Claire held her breath, waiting to hear whether he mounted the steep stair to the loft.

"Just some old hay. We don't use it anymore because the floorboards are rotten. I warned Claire and I will warn you, Jack, not to go up there. It's too dangerous. This whole barn is going to be pulled down when Claire is finished with it. I don't think you're going to find her up there," David called from the entrance and waited for Jack to move away from the ladder. "So, you say she didn't turn up for training and Mum and Dad haven't seen her? Any other ideas where she is?"

"No, none. Being her uncle, I thought you might know. Our sessions have been going really well and Claire's coming along in leaps and bounds—pardon the pun." He let out a little laugh at his feeble attempt at a joke. When he didn't get the same response from David, he fell silent and asked, "How's the practice for Flight going?"

"When Claire comes, she lets me know she's here, but I just leave her to it. The books she has been studying have been very helpful, but not as helpful as actually having someone who knows *exactly* what they are doing and can help her see what she needs to do. But she loves to study, anyway. I wish my own kids were as dedicated to their studies as Claire is." He laughed at that point, but it died when Jack did not partake in the chuckle.

"Well, I can see she isn't here. Will you let me know if she turns up? I'm just a bit concerned, as I heard that an unknown car was seen near the village again today. You haven't seen anything?" Jack asked.

"No, I haven't really seen anyone today. I've been too busy with ploughing to notice anything, and we don't get too many cars out this way. I'll let you know the moment Claire turns up. She's probably running somewhere. She has been working very hard lately," David replied. "Now, if you don't mind, the fields won't plough themselves!"

The massive door slammed shut with a loud bang. Claire heard her uncle farewell Jack as a car started up and drove away. She lay still just a moment more before hearing the car disappear into the distance. Claire then waited to hear whether David had left as well.

It wasn't long until she heard a voice say, "I thought you were up here. You *really* have to work on making your breathing a bit quieter."

Leaping into the air and automatically switching on not only the invisibility but the Shrink Talent as well, Claire looked up from her hiding place and saw David standing there in massive proportions. Now she understood why mice ran away from humans; she, too, would run from giants.

"Don't worry, he's gone. I promise. I watched him go. Come out, Claire! You're safe." Slowly, she released her mind to flow back into her normal self. "That's better. Now, are you going to tell me why you've run away and hidden up here?" He sat himself down on one of the hay bales and looked at her expectantly.

She sat down herself, gathering her thoughts. "How come I didn't hear you creep up on me?"

David chuckled. "Your mother always wanted to know how I did it, too. Think back to your red book." He waited for her to remember the Talent he alluded to.

"So, you have a Talent, too? David, have you got Stealth?"

He nodded his assent. "I used to make your mother hide somewhere and I'd creep up on her—it drove her crazy." He laughed at the memory. "Now are you going to tell me what is going on, or do you want me to call Jack back?"

"No," she said emphatically. "I was in the village, just about to cross the road, when I saw a man come out of the hall and walk around the back. A black car came from out of the alley and sped past. I'd made myself disappear, so they didn't see me. Jack came out of the hall about a minute later and looked around. I got this feeling that I shouldn't go into the hall, so I went to Uncle Geoff's house and wrote him a note to tell him what I saw—then went upstairs. Not long after, I heard someone break in the back door and come up the stairs. So, I used my Talents to fly out the window and made my way here."

Claire didn't understand why she had left out the part that the *someone* was Adam. Part of her didn't want to believe it herself. All the while, David was nodding. It had felt different talking to him than to Geoff, as he didn't interrupt with questions and waited until the end of her talking before saying anything.

"Well, in the meantime, you're welcome to stay here. I think it'll be safer than Geoff's place. Have you got food and blankets?"

"Yeah. I do, thanks. Have you heard from Uncle Geoff?" she asked.

"No, I haven't. Sorry, Claire. But I do know a way to get in touch with him. I'll try tonight for you. I promise. Geoff knows what he's doing, so I wouldn't worry about him not contacting you back."

David rose and turned to go when Claire quickly stopped him. "Can you not tell anyone where I am, please?"

"Even your grandparents?"

"Yes. Everyone."

"Okay, I won't. I'll come check on you tomorrow."

"Thank you, Uncle David," Claire said as he started to descend the ladder. He looked up quickly and gave her a small smile.

Even though it was summer, the air that night was chilly from the southerly squall that had blustered in through the mouth of the harbor earlier that day. Dark clouds raced over the sky, their rain long since dumped on the city below, leaving the streets slick and wet. Puddles reflected the streetlights in dancing patterns, lending a glittering effect to the dimness of the night, and belying the grubbiness that seemed to be oozing from every back ally.

Geoff Brown walked with purpose down the road from his house. It had seemed so empty and quiet without the presence of his niece to fill the void. It didn't feel like home. He pulled the collar of his long overcoat up to guard against the sharp wind that was still blowing after the storm. He was on a mission. A contact had insisted they meet, saying he had important news that could only be delivered in person, and Geoff was hoping it was the news he had come to the city for.

The original reason for his mad drive back on Christmas Eve had already been confirmed. Beth was indeed the mother of Adam. He had confronted her aunt himself and she had broken down when she retold the tale. Jody had been used by Marcus and was now only a shadow of her former self.

Even though the hour was late, and the weather was so inclement, there was still a great deal of traffic around. The city never really slept, and it always seemed to be perpetually awake during the holiday season. He stood at the edge of the main road, waiting impatiently for the traffic lights to change so he could cross. Cars roared past, spraying water from under their tyres, but for once he did not take any notice of how dirty it was making his coat. He was trying to focus.

The light changed and the cross signal flashed green. Geoff stepped off the curb and quickly crossed, illuminated in the dark night by the headlights of the cars that had stopped. Just as he reached the other side, the lights changed again, and the cars sped off, their occupants not thinking of the lone pedestrian again. Quickly he walked along the road until he reached the park on the waterfront. He turned onto the path that led to the interior and made it to the rendezvous point. There was no one there.

Standing behind a large tree to get out of the wind, he looked around him. Seasonal revelers were walking through, sometimes in large groups of young friends. Their laughter and shouts were drowning out the nearby traffic while couples taking a romantic walk in the dark kept their talk to just themselves. Noise was all around him, and he strained to hear the telltale sign of someone walking towards him. Then it came.

Geoff stepped out from behind the tree, ready and waiting for his contact, but it was not who he thought it would be. Walking slowly and deliberately towards him was Marcus Ryder. The very man who he was hoping not to see. Marcus flashed a grin at Geoff and stopped. Quickly Geoff looked around for his bodyguards, but there was no one else near them.

"Good evening, Geoffrey," Marcus addressed him "I hope this evening is treating you well."

"Marcus." Geoff replied curtly. There was a wave of geniality coming from the man and he tried to ignore it. "It's turning out to be a bit of a surprise, to be honest."

"I bet it is," Marcus said with a grin that held no humour to it. "I had heard you were back in town. You left so suddenly, and with Claire too. Adam was extremely disappointed she wasn't here for Christmas. Will you tell her we can't wait to see her when she comes back?"

"I will pass the message on, but I don't think she will be back in a hurry," Geoff replied, silently deciding not to tell Claire.

"Maybe we could join you. I can't remember the last time Adam and I had a holiday together."

"Claire is dealing with a lot at the moment. She has just been reunited with her grandparents and extended family," Geoff told him, now feeling the full effects of Marcus' charm offensive. He had felt it before, but this time it was overt, and Marcus was not trying to disguise it.

"That would be a lot to deal with. You really should have introduced them a long time ago, you know," Marcus said with mock seriousness.

Silence descended between them. Geoff was trying to keep his anger under control. If Marcus had not killed her parents, then she would have lived a normal life where he didn't have to protect her the way he had.

"There was another matter I wished to discuss with you," Marcus spoke up, breaking the tension.

"And what might that be?" Geoff asked with a little hesitation.

"My plans for the future."

"And what does that have to do with me?"

"You have served me well over the last seven years. Your work has been exemplary and rarely have you disappointed me. So, I wish to reward you."

"In what way?"

"I want to make you a partner in my new venture. An equal partner." Still Marcus was exuding his charm, but this time Geoff could see he was expending his energy in trying to win him over.

"I have seen some of your ventures and your dodgy dealings. I have even executed some of them on your behalf," Geoff said, finally breaking free of the Charm and feeling it fall to pieces around the man before him. "I don't think I want to be part of that life anymore, Marcus."

"You think it is just that simple?" Marcus almost growled, trying to get his anger under control.

"Think of this as me tendering my resignation."

"There have been others who have thought they could get free. But I never let those go whom I deem useful."

"I know, your grandson is one," Geoff said deliberately and watched as Marcus inadvertently betrayed his feelings for once. The subject of his grandson was a touchy one, for both parties.

"Despite what he thinks, he is still in the fold and is still useful to me. He knows his place," Marcus told him shortly.

"I no longer wish to work for you or any of your companies, Marcus. My conscious will be better served if we part ways," Geoff replied firmly to which Marcus gave a short snort of laughter.

"Your conscience. That is a joke. What of Claire's inheritance? Do you still keep the terms of her parents will from her? In that matter we are still tied."

"Her inheritance and the terms have nothing to do with you at all, Marcus, and you well know it. You have no claim on her there," Geoff spat back.

"And yet you still keep her in the dark about it," Marcus gloated.

"I think we are done here," Geoff replied and started to turn away.

"We are done when I say we are," Marcus shouted at him.

From out of the shadows a little way off, a man stepped into the light which illuminated a path that led to the street. Geoff could only see one man but knew there would be more around them.

"I know you have snaked your claws into my organisation with your little spies. But can you really be that confident that they have passed on correct information to you. You know what I am capable of. You know of the extent of my Watchers. You and your niece cannot hide from me, no matter where you go in the world. You already know how special she is and what she will become. Why not make it easy on yourself and just let her go?" Marcus hissed at him.

"I will never let you have her," he growled in return, his anger building once more.

"I am coming for her. If you value your life and those in that pathetic village, you will not stand in my way."

Geoff heard him walk away and knew that the threat was very real. He slowly came to the realisation that he had underestimated Marcus and had been blinded by his own ego that he could have kept things from the man. He stared at Marcus as he walked through the park as if he didn't have a care in the world, while collecting his shadows along the way. Dread started to seep into Geoff's mind, and he felt it weigh heavily on him. He knew he was still being watched.

Pulling out his phone quickly, he scrolled through his contacts before hitting the call button. It rang for some time, and when it was answered the noise in the background was loud and raucous.

"Mr Brown, how can I help you?" a rough voice answered.

"I need to call that favour in," Geoff replied, still scouring the park for possible Watchers.

"Which one? I think I owe you a few by now?" the man laughed.

"Just one for now. I need a place to hide for a few days, and an escape from the city."

"You know where I am, come on over. We'll sink a few beers and talk about the mess you seem to have found yourself in."

"I'm going to need help getting there." Geoff was certain there were at least two Watchers in the shadows. "I'm exposed at the moment, in the waterfront park."

"Help is on the way, don't worry mate. We'll get you out of there," the man told him, with all sense of humour drained from his tone.

Chapter Thirteen

Claire spent a very uncomfortable night in the loft of the barn, and for a place she had thought deserted, it was in fact crawling with occupants. Sleep seemed to elude her, as she flinched and jumped at every sound the residents made. She soon discovered that a small family of owls had made their home in the rafters. The loud, insistent calls from the nearly grown owlets to their parents woke her in the morning's early hours. But before that she was visited by a dozen mosquitos—all of whom enjoyed her company far more than she enjoyed theirs. The last intrusion into her sleep was a couple of mice. Having already experienced what it was like to feel that small and well aware that there were predators above, Claire took pity on the tiny creatures and let them stay. Besides, she'd never had the aversion to rodents that some other girls did.

When the sun forced its way into the barn, Claire awoke from the rays and immediately shielded her sore, gritty eyes. Bites covered her arms and legs, and she reminded herself to ask David for some bug spray when she next saw him. The hay underneath her poked through the blanket she slept on as she was trying to pull it up around her chin. The morning was cold, and Claire was beginning to dislike the thought of too many more days staying in these conditions. But stay she did.

Unfortunately for Claire, she ran out of reading material within the first day. The next few days were spent practicing her Talents—exercising her muscles as well as her brain—and when she ran out of things to do, she snuggled up in her blankets, trying diligently not to let the questions get the better of her. Every couple of hours, she'd turn her phone on to check for messages from her Uncle Geoff, but there were none. She hoped that David had made good on his promise to get word to Geoff, but when he would come to check on her, David told her there was still no word. It became her habit to go for a run at night, as it helped to clear her head and beat out her frustrations.

Into the third day of her hiding from her spot in the loft, Claire became aware of car tyres crunching on the gravel road outside, slowly pulling up to the barn. She peered through a gap in the wall to see if it was David. He had promised the day before to bring her more supplies, as hers were nearly depleted. But it wasn't his car that pulled up. Instead, it was a black four-wheel drive with tinted windows—the same one that she'd seen in the village. Claire gasped a little and then immediately sprang into action, scrambling around and gathering all her possessions. Meagre as they were, she shoved them into her bag. Hearing the main barn door open, Claire froze at the sound until a shout from outside ripped through the air.

"Hey! What are you doing?" David's voice rang loud and clear. Again, he shouted, closer now along with the sound of his feet hitting the ground at a run. "What do you think you're doing? You're trespassing."

"The lady at the house gave me permission to look inside," a very familiar voice replied calmly.

"Exactly why do you want to look in my barn? And it was not her place to give you permission." Her uncle's voice was firm and demanding.

Adam chuckled. Claire could tell that he was starting to build his Charm to use on David, and she made good on the chance that her uncle had given her. She shrugged her backpack on and carefully made her way to the open window. Within minutes, she had left the barn and perched herself on a nearby tree, watching through the green leaves as David led Adam into the barn.

Their voices became muted as they entered the large building, and Claire longed to know what was being said. Along with her uncle's face, Adam's appeared at the loft window, and she could hear him tell Adam that his boys were always playing in the barn. She was relieved he had thought of that lie, as she knew how hard it was to keep anything from Adam. Waiting on the branch for them to emerge from the barn, Claire watched them carefully when they did.

"Well, thanks for letting me look, guess I'll be going now," Adam said robotically. They didn't shake hands, but David stood while Adam climbed back into his car and drove off down the road. He looked around, looking for something, but then shrugged and went back to work.

Claire spent the rest of the day in that tree. Twice she had to fend off birds who mistook her for something tasty to eat, as she had not bothered with making herself invisible— smartly wanting to conserve her energy. A breeze kicked up, and she felt the branch sway under her feet. It was an eerie feeling, much like an earthquake. When she looked to the horizon, she saw dark clouds billowing over the hills and decided that it probably wasn't a good idea to spend the night in a tree during a summer storm. Cloaking herself in invisibility, she fought against the rising wind to go back to the barn. Slipping in through the window, she leapt down to the floor of the loft and made herself a little burrow in the hay.

Claire thought that being small was still the preferable way to go, as she was scared that the place was being watched.

It was quite comfortable lying back in the hay at this size, and she let her mind wander as much as she allowed it—while remaining hidden. The barn began to creak as the wind picked up; loose boards flapped about, making a rhythmic banging. Through the noise of the increasing storm, another sound came from within the barn. She crept out of her burrow and went to investigate. Peering over the edge of the loft, Claire saw Beth with a large red plastic can in her hand. It took Claire a moment to realise that Beth was splashing the liquid contents everywhere, bringing with it the distinctive smell of petrol.

A loud crash rent the air as the barn door collided with the old, rusty tractor that was stored there.

"Beth! What the hell are you doing?" David demanded while entering the barn.

Putting the can down, Beth then yanked an oversized box of matches out of her pocket. "This farm will no longer welcome *your* niece. That girl is the cause of all the problems that have come to the community in recent months, and I am taking matters into my own hands!"

Before he had time to reach her, Beth struck a match and dropped it into the petrol-soaked hay. With a great roar, a wall of flame suddenly erupted in front of Beth, scaring her. Stumbling back, she fell over the can she had just dropped. David rushed to her side as the flames now leapt high into the air and consumed all that was around them. He picked her up without hesitation and carried her out of the barn.

Claire stood transfixed at the sight of the fire as the bright orange and yellow flames spread fast and soon engulfed most of the bottom floor. Thick, dark, choking smoke billowed up and was caught under the old iron of the roof, making her cough. That was the cue for her to leave. She sped back to where she had burrowed into the hay, finding that her bag had gone back to its normal size. Laying a hand on it, the backpack shrank before her eyes. Claire snatched it up and leapt out of the window. Flying as fast as her Talent could carry her against the building storm, she landed back in the tree safely with an enormous effort. She looked about her and located her aunt and uncle while she clung to the swaying branch. He had his arms around her protectively as they stood watching the barn burn, their hair and clothing whipping around them in the increasing wind.

David let her go and turned to his wife. "What the hell made you want to burn down the barn, Beth?"

Beth had the good grace to look shamefaced. "Claire is to blame for bringing that man to the farm earlier. It is all her fault that Marcus is targeting us!"

David shook his head, trying to comprehend what she was saying. "I still don't understand. What has this got to do with Claire?"

"Marcus suspects that Claire's at the farm and sent his man out to search for her. That man threatened me! He threatened our family! Marcus knows a secret of mine and if it gets out…" She put her hand over her mouth as she began to sob.

"Geoff is right. It's the secrets of this community that will be the death of it." He ran his hands through his hair and walked away from his wife. The rain started to pelt down, leaving great dents in the dust at their feet. "Get in the car, there's nothing we can do about the barn now. But we're going to have a very long talk back home."

David drove off, and Claire was soon following. She could not believe how she managed to keep pace with the vehicle below her as she moved from tree to tree. Or how she managed to dodge the extremely large raindrops that were falling steadily faster and heavier. She still was only a moment behind them as they pulled up outside the old farmhouse.

Finding an open window, Claire slipped through it and found her aunt and uncle in the kitchen. She perched on top of the fridge and watched them as they sat at the table.

"Okay, Beth," he said with a patient voice. "I want you to tell me everything and don't leave anything out."

Beth took in a deep breath as she prepared herself to tell her husband the whole story. "After your sister ran away with John, I was so devastated that my parents thought it would be a good idea for me to go visit my aunt in the city. While I was there, Aunty Jody found me an office job and I started to build a life for myself. I soon found myself falling in love—or so I thought. He was older and very handsome, and he was the owner of the business. It was Marcus Ryder. I had no idea who he was, and my parents had never mentioned him to me or my sister. And as we didn't have Talents, I suppose they thought he had no relevance to us. I now wish to God that they'd taken the time to educate us properly, because none of this would be happening."

Taking a deep breath, Beth then spoke very slowly and softly. "It was during this relationship with Marcus that I fell pregnant."

Letting out a breath that he was not aware he was holding, David sat back in the chair. "You had a child with Marcus? Where's the child now?"

"Just wait, I'm getting there," she said impatiently, continuing her story. "When I first found out I was pregnant, I went to John. I waited for Jess to leave their house one day and then just knocked on the door. I had found out where they lived when I first moved to the city, but I never had the courage before to go there. John was so surprised to see me, but when I told him what had happened, he told me he couldn't help. He said I needed to either go back to the Community—to my parents—or ask my aunt for help. He told me that he had his own little family to be concerned about and he told me that Jess was pregnant."

Pausing her storytelling, she got up and poured a glass of water for herself and one for David. She set the drinks down and resumed her seat. David remained quiet the whole time.

"What did you do?" he asked her finally.

"I did think of coming back here, but the thought of facing my parents pregnant was something I could not bear. My parents would've been ashamed and disappointed. So, I told my Aunt Jody what was happening and begged her not to tell my parents. She was furious at me, telling me that she would get the blame for what had happened after all she had done for me. After a few days of my aunt doing nothing but yell at me, she finally calmed down and formed a plan. She told me that she had found an adoption agency that would take the baby and that this was the best option, as I was so young. She told me in no uncertain terms that abortion was out of the question and that if I even contemplated it, she would call my parents.

"So, I went along with the plan. The pregnancy was an easy one and so was the birth. But as soon as the baby was born, he was taken from me. I never got to hold my baby. They would only tell me that I had a son." She put her head in her hands, sobbing quietly.

David stared at his wife as if he were seeing her for the first time. He saw how vulnerable she was and how the emotion was still raw to her. He left his seat opposite, came to kneel by her side, and put his arms around her. She cried into his shoulder and clung to him, the sobs wracking her body.

"Why didn't you tell me this before?" he asked her gently, stroking her hair. "Did you think that I would disapprove? That I wouldn't marry you?"

She could only shake her head at him, as her voice was too constricted for words. Eventually her sobbing eased, and she moved her head away from his shoulder, wiping her eyes and smudging her impeccable makeup. He reached over to the bench and grabbed the kitchen paper towels, handing them to her. Beth pulled off a couple and thanked him, then wiped her tears away and blew her nose.

"I felt so ashamed. When I came home with my tail between my legs—even more humiliated than when I left—that was when I found out about Marcus. I would have agreed to just about anything my parents proposed for me at that moment, and they told me of the possible match with you. I know how stupid I am for not really giving our marriage any sort of chance. But in my own way, I do love you. I love how you are with the boys, and that's why I insisted they go to their school for most of the year, because I feel so jealous that I don't have the same relationship with them." The sobs had stopped, and she hung her head.

David drew her to him again and held her for quite some time. Claire started to feel like she was spying on her aunt and uncle but didn't know where else to go. She sat cross-legged and pulled off her backpack, hugging it close to her. She missed Uncle Geoff so much and she just wanted him home. She did not know what to do with all this information.

When David thought his wife could answer more questions, he carried on. "What happened today, then? What happened to make you take such drastic action?"

"When Marcus's thug came knocking on the door, I didn't want to help him find Claire, but he was so charming and so soft-spoken. I felt that if he found her, she'd be safe with him." Beth shook her head at this and then continued. "He had driven away toward the barn, and I thought that that was the end of it, but he came back. This time when he talked, he was a bit angrier and more forceful. He told me that we had better find Claire soon and that…and that if we didn't, Marcus would let the world know my secret. I told him to leave and that we didn't know where Claire was. When he sped off down the drive, I felt myself get so angry. That Claire was going to take away from me everything I held dear, including you." She looked into his eyes. "I'm sorry for what I've done, but for some reason, that barn seemed like a symbol of Claire taking over everyone—and everything—in the village. She hadn't been here for days, and I was so tired of everyone asking if Claire had been seen on the farm, so I snapped and decided to burn it down." She blew her nose gently again, looking at her husband. He'd resumed his seat but had moved it closer to her.

Leaning forward in his chair, David's elbows rested on his knees as his hands were clasped together, pressed against his mouth—all the while listening to this last bit of her story. He looked at her from over those knuckles.

"But she's been seen on the farm. She was in the barn when you set fire to it." He watched for her reaction, but it wasn't the one that he had predicted she'd give.

Her face turned as white as a sheet, and she covered her mouth with a trembling hand as she let out a gasp. "No! That is not possible…no one was there! I even checked the loft!" Beth said, shaking her head.

David took her trembling hands in his own and held them.

"I am certain that she would have gotten herself out before it burnt down."

"How can you be so sure?"

"She's a very resourceful girl and has the Talents to get herself out of any situation."

Claire fervently hoped that was the case.

Chapter Fourteen

To Claire, sitting on top of a fridge wasn't very comfortable. There was a vibration running through her, and the metal underneath was very cold despite the warm, humid day. Wind and rain continued to rage outside, and the light had faded considerably with the onset of the storm. But Beth and David were completely unaware of the tempest raging outside.

Her aunt was still pale at the thought that Claire might have perished in the fire, and Claire was surprised when Beth started to speak again.

"We cannot let Marcus anywhere near her. I know what he's like and if he has changed, the world would have stopped in its tracks." Looking at her husband, she shook her head. "Don't ask."

Beth got up and started to busy herself around the kitchen, tidying up non-existent messes. Finally, she turned to face him. "She can still stay here, because it's better we know where she is than if she's just out there...where God knows what can happen to her. Where is Geoff? Why hasn't he come back yet?"

"I don't know. I've tried contacting him using all the ways we had set up, but he's just gone dark. I wish I knew what he was looking for in the city. All these damn secrets!" David thumped the table beside him, making Beth and Claire both jump. It was only the second time that she'd seen him angry. He was usually so easy-going and calm. "As for Claire—from what Geoff has told me—she's probably in this kitchen right now, listening in on our conversation."

Beth furtively looked around the kitchen, trying to catch sight of the girl. Claire knew it was time to make herself known, and she prepared herself. But instead of just leaping from the fridge and appearing in front of them, she first flew to the doorway and changed form there, as if she was just walking in, still hugging her backpack to her chest. Beth gave a start of surprise, but David didn't seem the least bit fazed by her sudden appearance.

"How long have you been spying on us?" Beth rounded on Claire when she had recovered from the shock.

"I followed you home and I've been here the whole time," Claire explained truthfully.

Beth then put her hand to her mouth, turning her back on the pair of them. David told Claire to sit down, and she pulled out one of the chairs.

"Uncle David is right, Aunt Beth. Secrets are the biggest obstacle in this community," Claire said very quietly.

To her credit, Beth held her tongue, returning to the table as Claire went on. "It's only because of secrets that Marcus has been able to do the things he has; he markets in them. I don't pretend to even understand what happened all those years ago when he was exiled, but it started then. The community was divided by those who still wished to have the Talents and those who thought they were otherwise. Through the years—it seems to me—it's become a bit of an 'us and them' situation." She paused and looked between the two adults.

David nodded, encouraging her to go on. She searched her mind, trying to get the thoughts organised. "It's only by everyone being open and honest that the pain can be avoided. It's the keeping of secrets that pains people. I'm sorry, Uncle David, that I asked you to keep my secret and I'm pleased that it's out, though I've a feeling that I've put everyone in danger." David was about to say something when Claire cut it. "Thank you for your support and the offer of staying with you, Beth, but it would be better if I found somewhere else to hide out until Uncle Geoff comes back. Somewhere nobody knows." She emphasised the last words to both her aunt and uncle. "The last thing I want to do is put any of my family in danger. Especially Jasper and Hunter. Can you please keep trying Uncle Geoff for me, Uncle David? It's really important that I talk to him."

David nodded his assent and before he could reply, Beth chimed in. "You are not going anywhere, young lady...until you have had a decent meal and a good bath." This surprised both David and Claire. Beth stood up and straightened her skirt, looking expectantly at Claire. "Upstairs with you. David, get her a towel out of the cupboard, please. When you get back down here, there will be a hot meal waiting for you," she said and dismissed them both.

When Claire came back down the stairs—clean and with a fresh set of clothes on—she headed back to the kitchen. Before she entered the room, she stopped and listened to her aunt and uncle talking. Amid the clatter of plates and cutlery being moved, she heard Beth's voice speaking quietly. "Why didn't you yell and scream at me when I told you my secret?"

Equally quiet and very tenderly, David replied to her question. "Why would I yell at you for something that happened in your past—something that happened well before we were married? You should know me better than that by now, Beth. I'm not that petty or vindictive...or even jealous. Your past is exactly that: in the past. I can't change it any more than you can, but you can change how it affects you today. I have always loved you, even when we were all kids."

There was silence at that point, and when Claire thought enough time had passed, she entered the kitchen. Becoming aware of her presence, Beth and David released each other with a little embarrassment. Beth invited Claire to sit and eat, all while a departing David mumbled something about trying to reach Geoff again. The plate that was placed in front of her was piled high with toast, eggs, and bacon. The smell rising from it made her mouth water. Claire descended on it, complementing Beth on the food through mouthfuls, and eating until she could fit no more in. It felt like it had been days since she had last eaten so well.

"Well, I must say, I can't see where you put it, Claire." Beth laughed a little in amazement at how much the girl had consumed.

"I have a theory on why I eat so much. I think it has to do with the energy it takes to firstly use my Talents and then to maintain it for long periods of time. I think I use up the stored resources that my body has and when I'm finished, I get crazy hungry, so I have to replenish them. If that makes sense?"

For a moment, Beth stared at the girl with her mouth slightly ajar. "I had better prepare a proper basket of food to take with you, then."

"Thank you, Aunty Beth."

Just then, David stepped into the room. "I've tried Geoff again, but there's still no word from him." He sat down and started to pick at the toast that was left over on the table.

Claire suddenly remembered that she had not checked her phone all afternoon and pulled it out of her backpack at her feet. She switched it on, and within seconds came the unmistakable beep of a message coming in. She fumbled with the phone before she managed to open the message up.

"It's from Uncle Geoff." Still staring at the screen, she went on, "It says that he's on his way home and that he'll be here in a few hours." She looked at her aunt and uncle. "I want to be there when he gets home. Please."

"I'll drive you," David offered.

"No, I'll be fine. I can run."

"Don't be silly, Claire, it is pouring out there!" Beth indicated the windows. "We're going to Lynnette and Bob's anyway for New Year's Eve," she reminded David. "How about we all go, and we can wait with you there until Geoff gets back? There is safety in numbers, after all." Beth looked expectantly between them, and they could not fault her logic.

Claire still did not like the fact that she'd be putting her family in danger. Then she thought of Jasper and how much he would be in danger if his Talent were to be widely known. Taking their silence as agreement, Beth became busy with tidying herself up while Claire and David cleaned the kitchen.

"Uncle David, have you told Beth that Jasper has a Talent?" Claire asked her uncle.

"No, I don't have a clue how to tell her. But I will, soon," he promised.

Half an hour later, the three of them pulled up outside David's parents' house. Claire had already hidden herself and flew out of the car silently and entered the house without—she hoped—anyone noticing. It was only when the door was securely closed that she revealed herself. Her grandparents Lynnette and Bob were beside themselves when they saw her, both hugging and telling her off for disappearing without telling anyone. David filled them in on what had happened in the last few days.

During David's account, Lynnette told them she had some news of her own, calling Jasper forward. She encouraged him to show his parents what he could do. At the same moment, both Claire and David cried out to stop him. Beth and Lynnette were both confused for very different reasons.

David turned to his wife and quietly asked her to sit down, taking her hands in his. "I'm sorry that I didn't say anything earlier. I really didn't know how to approach the subject with you. But Jasper has developed the Light Talent."

Beth looked at her husband and then at her eldest son, beckoning him to her. Jasper walked with tentative steps and stood before her with a look of trepidation. Beth bundled her son to her and pulled him onto her knee as she had not done in years. "I am so proud of you, Jasper," she whispered, kissing him on the forehead.

"Mum!" Jasper giggled as he tried to get away from her grip, but then he relented and hugged her back.

Claire noticed that her eyes were not the only ones glistening in the Christmas lights that were still up. This change in Beth seemed so remarkable to Claire. She remembered lying in the hospital bed as Beth had said how disgusting it was to have a Talent. It made her wonder.

They all crammed into the small living room. Lynnette and Beth busied themselves making coffee and dishing out the cake while Jasper entertained Hunter, David, and Bob with some of the tricks he had learned. Claire sat on her hands, trying not to notice the slow ticking of the clock on the mantle and how the hands seemed to have stopped working. She was feeling anxious and impatient. She wanted her uncle now. He had always made her feel so safe in the past, but could he protect her now?

Bob leaned over and nudged her. "Sit still, girl, you look like you have ants in your pants!" He winked.

A loud and heavy knock came from the door. Everyone froze except for Jasper and Hunter playing cards in the corner of the room. David looked at Claire as he moved to the door and Claire made herself small, hiding under the couch she'd just been sitting on. She heard the voices of her other set of grandparents and relaxed a little. But as David came back into the room with them, he motioned for her to stay hidden. Pointing nonchalantly at the couch, he let Malcolm and Grace know where she was.

"Happy New Year, Malcolm. That storm was a doozy, wasn't it?" Bob said, shaking his friend's hand.

"It was a good one. We haven't had a decent storm like that for quite some time! Mary must have been concerned about some of the elderly residents. We've just seen Jack outside in the street. Or it could've been that black car we saw driving around as we made our way here."

"Dad, I think that storm may have damaged the shed out back. The last time I was in there I thought the roof looked a bit dodgy, so I'll just go check on it," David informed his father and then left the room quickly.

Staying put, Claire leaned up against the leg of the couch and waited for him to come back while watching her grandparents settle in and start talking. Unable to help herself, Grace tried to spy on her granddaughter as she kept looking down to the edge of the couch.

It was a moment too late when Claire realised there was someone behind her. Turning slowly, she knew full well that she would find Jack standing there.

"Happy New Year, Claire. I've been most concerned about you. I'm so pleased to find you safe and well." He walked closer, leaning on the couch leg facing her. "So where have you been? You've missed quite a few of our sessions."

Claire's mind raced. She knew that she could get away — that she could fly out of danger — but she wanted to know a few things first.

"I've been around, Jack," she replied, trying to sound casual. "How do you know Adam?" She was pleased she had surprised him with the question and could see him trying to figure out how she knew. He was not good at hiding what he was thinking. It was written all over his face.

"Who?"

Claire laughed a little, happy to have the upper hand for once. "Oh, Jack, there's no point in lying to me. I saw him coming out of the hall the day that I disappeared, and I saw you come out after." Moving away from the leg of the couch, she turned back to face him. Peering from under the edge were two large faces of boys watching. Smiling at Jasper and Hunter, Claire motioned them to be quiet and then focused back on Jack—thankful he had been too distracted with her comment to notice.

"Why was Adam there? Are you working for Marcus? And if you are, why?" The questions tumbled out of her. Her curiosity was gaining. He scuffed his foot on the floorboards, moving the dust around. He didn't look at Claire, and she knew he was hiding things from her.

Finally, he spoke. "I'm to take you to him," he revealed.

"Why?"

"Because that's what I was told to do. To teach you how to use your Talent and then bring you to him when you were ready. I figured you are ready now. I believe you have mastered your other Talent as well. Am I wrong?"

"Yes, I have. But you know that from Adam. He was at my home when I finally put the two Talents together." She felt there was no point in lying at that moment. "What have you been offered, Jack? A place in the 'new world' that Marcus wants to build? Money?" She crossed her arms and stared at him intently, trying to figure him out like a puzzle.

"All of that and more. You could have it too, you know. You just have to join us!"

She laughed at this. "I know what my role will be in this new world. Do you really think that the world will seriously accept people like us? Look at this village. They're already divided between those who have Talent and those who don't. It wouldn't work. For a start, the government will come in and capture people like us and experiment—all to figure out how we have these Talents. This community will be raided and anyone displaying any sort of difference will be hauled away."

"He wouldn't let them. And you've been watching way too many superhero movies." He chuckled at this last bit, but Claire didn't find it funny.

"You're willing to sacrifice all these people for Marcus's cause? Including your own mother?"

"My mother?" he retorted with a snort. "My mother's part of this! There's a secret you haven't found out."

Claire had always had the sneaking suspicion that she and her Uncle Geoff had been spied upon, but she decided to play along. "Your mother is part of this?"

"Of course...she has Talent, I have Talent. Why would we seriously want to breed it out—as if it could? Families are still giving birth to children with Talents. They will never go away. And it's about time that we stood up and made a difference in the world."

"What sort of difference are you talking about? Do you want to be heroes? Because I don't think that's what Marcus has in mind. I think he wants to be rich and powerful, and he will use anyone and everyone he can to get there."

"No, that's not true, he told me himself. He promised that we would be helping the world, making peace, and working behind the scenes to make this country great."

"I think you were lied to, Jack." She could see his face get angry, knowing that she had hit a nerve.

"My father wouldn't lie to me!" That information shocked her. No wonder Mary had never wanted anyone to know who the father of her child was. "My mother was so pleased when you came here, and so happy that I was going to be teaching you. She told me that we would make a lovely couple—that she'd seen it. My father told me the same. He told me that you and I were destined to be together." Claire took a step back from him.

Jasper's large face saw that Claire was frightened of the little man who was talking to her, so he decided to do something about it. He had been practicing his Talent without his parents knowing and thought he knew how to go about what he planned to do.

Placing his hands together, Jasper concentrated hard and squeezed his eyes tight. A small ball of light appeared between his hands, and he lowered it gently onto the palm of his right hand. He bent all his will on the light and blew on it. Slowly, it started to move and then it left his hand, moving around the leg of the couch to where Jack was standing. The ball pushed at him from behind until Jack was surrounded by the bright glow. Claire stood in fascination, watching the light consume his body—then jumped into action.

In one quick motion, she was invisible and moving. Flying from under the couch, she looked for a way out. The door to the kitchen was open and she dove through it. The back door was closed, and she hovered—looking at the closed windows—wondering how Jack had got in. It was at that moment that David opened the door. Taking the opportunity that had been presented to her, Claire swooped out into the backyard, just as she heard Jasper calling for his father.

Her only thought was to get away; get somewhere safe. She thought of the attic at her Uncle Geoff's house and remembered her uncle complaining about a hole that had appeared due to rotting boards, so she made her way there. As she flew past the houses, her head spun with the news that she'd just received. So, Mary and Jack were working for

Marcus. More to the point, Jack was Marcus's son. Things started to fit together in her brain, but she didn't want to think of them yet, as she needed to get somewhere safe first.

Flying to where she knew there was a small gap, Claire pushed her way in. It was a tight fit, but she managed. Landing on one of the rafters and sitting still, she listened to the world outside. Even though she was in the attic space, she felt relieved to be home. She desperately wanted to call Uncle Geoff, but she had to go back to normal size to do it and at the moment, that didn't seem like such a good idea. Pacing up and down the rough wood of the roof trusses, she tried to figure out what to do. She decided that her uncle was more likely to come back there first, so she needed to leave him a note—at least to tell him that she was okay. But getting into the actual house would be a problem.

In the dim light of the roof space, she saw the air-conditioning unit and the ducting that snaked around, feeding the upstairs rooms. Claire made her way over to the tube—which was made up of a shiny material—and pushed on the side. It moved with the pressure she placed on it. Doubting that a hole could be easily made by her current size, she looked at the connections. Claire discovered one of the ducts was loose and there was a small gap. She hovered in front of it and then managed to get between the metal rim and the unit, pushing it wider to allow her to pass through the space. Inside was pitch black, and she wished she had one of her cousin's light balls to shine the way for her. Keeping one hand on the side of the ducting, she headed off. It seemed to take an age until she could see any source of light, as it was dim—but it was enough to see where the ducting bent and fed into a vent.

Making her way out of the vent, she glided downstairs and into her uncle's study. On the desk was her previous note, and the pen lay beside the pad where she'd left it. She landed on his desk and tried to pick the pen up. However, it was so heavy and bulky that she wasn't sure if she could write like this. Claire was beginning to think that she would have to return to her normal size when a cage descended over her. The mesh that encased her was so small she could only just get her hand through and when she looked past the wire, she saw the face of Adam looking down on her.

"Hey there, Claire! Aren't you so cute. I think we need to catch up."

Chapter Fifteen

With a smug expression on his face, Adam sat back in her uncle's desk chair as Claire stared at him through the bars of her cage. "So, what are we waiting for?" she demanded.

Leaning forward, he cupped his ear. "What was that, Claire? Your tiny, squeaky voice just doesn't carry to me. You are going to have to speak up." Adam chuckled.

Claire looked around, unsure of what to do. The cage was much too heavy for her to lift and the mesh too small to fit through. She kicked at it, berating herself for not staying in the attic until Uncle Geoff arrived home. Gathering her energy, Claire set about to project her voice and hoped it would work—as she had never even thought of it before.

"What are you going to do with me?"

"That's better. I can hear you now. What am I going to do with you? I'm going to take you to my father of course. But before I can do that I have to wait for Jack. That useless twit promised he could get you to come with us. But just as well I had a hunch that it'd all go tits up and that you'd come running back here." He stood up and looked out the window. "Where the hell is he?"

"Last I saw, he was my cousin's new toy." She didn't want to tell him about Jasper. "He distracted him for me. I don't think he'll be coming anytime soon." Claire sat down cross-legged on the desk, putting her head in her hand. She hoped that she could delay him long enough so that her uncle could make it home and looked at her watch. *It can't be too much longer until he gets here*, she thought.

Adam sat back down. "Geoff isn't going to be home soon, so we have time to wait for my idiot brother." He leaned on the desk, hands palm down and chin resting on them. "Jack told you he's my half-brother? I can tell by the way you didn't react to the news when I said it. So that was his great plan to get you to go with him. Dad was stupid to allow him to even try, he should've just left it to me. I know you like the back of my hand, and I could always anticipate what your next move would be, Claire. What did you once tell me? That I was the closest thing to a *brother* that you had ever had! Did you ever stop to think that I wanted to be more than just your brother? We could be good together. With our Talents combined, could you imagine what the possibilities would be for any kids we had? Because that is what Dad has in mind."

Claire made a face at that thought, turning away from him. "You sicken me. The both of you. As if I'd have anything to do with either one of you now." She stood up and faced him, clinging to the cage. "Nothing you ever said to me has been real, has it? Not once did you warn me or try to talk to me about it. Instead, you strung me along and tried to get me to your father in such a sneaky way. You betrayed me, Adam. Of course, I was going to run away! And as for your brother, you better talk to him about what he thinks is going to happen, because I think your dad is playing you against each other." She pushed on the cage with all her might, but it didn't budge.

"Calm down there, Claire...you're going to hurt yourself. Jack's been told lots of things to keep him and his old hag of a mother sweet and on our side. I can handle them—they're like putty in my hands. I can talk the birds out of the trees if I have to. No, you know I can, so don't look at me that way. I charmed you for years, but all I'm getting now is a blank wall. How are you blocking me?" He sounded as if he genuinely wanted to know.

Claire moved around the cage and finally came to rest on the pen that was captured with her. "Did your father never give you the red booklet? He never taught you about your Talent?"

"He taught me what I needed," he said defensively. "I never got a red booklet. What are you talking about?"

"It's only one of the most important books that people like us should read before we are trained in our Talents. Oh, so that means you don't know how to properly use your Talent! I wonder why your father never taught you all the tricks. I'm sorry, Adam, sorry that your daddy didn't trust you enough with all the info you should've had!" Her voice dripped with sarcasm as she tried to bait his temper. "I wonder if he squashed any other Talents you may have developed." She could see the look in his eye, and she pressed on. "You probably don't know your genealogy either."

"What are you talking about? I got my Talent from Dad."

"That is so funny, considering how it's more likely to come from the female line than the male. You see, I've been making a study of it since I came here. Who was your mother?" she asked, suspecting the truth.

He turned away from her. In all the years that she had known Adam, he'd never mentioned his mother at all. She'd always had the feeling that it was a taboo subject and had left him alone to deal with it himself. Now she was connecting the dots. Bits of information she'd recently received slipped together like the tumbler lock on a safe.

"I know who your mother is. Actually, I'm almost certain of it." She started to walk around the cage. "It all fits nicely into place. The timing would be right—especially as we're the same age and you *do* have a certain look about you that reminds me of her. You have the same colour eyes as her."

"What are you talking about? You're not making any sense at all! My mother abandoned me the first second she could, leaving me with my dad to raise on his own." In his agitated state, he pushed away from the desk and stalked out of the room.

Claire wondered if she had pushed him too far, but she was almost certain she had pieced together who his mother was. Her leg brushed up against the nib of the pen, and she looked down at the large line it had left on the training pants she wore. She reached out and touched the nib, and an idea formed as she looked at the ink it had left on her finger. She smeared more of the blue gel onto her hand and then knelt to the blotter pad she was standing on. As she finished what she had to do, Adam walked back into the study.

"Are you ready to hear what I have to say?" she asked, not wanting to miss a moment. Knowing he had a temper on him, she wanted him to react to her words. "Because if you want to know who it is, she's in this very village right now—just down the road, in fact." She leaned against the bars. Her voice was starting to feel very tired from all the yelling she was doing.

"Okay, smart arse, who is it? Who's the woman who wanted nothing to do with me?" His arms were crossed against his chest, defensive-like. If Adam knew her like the back of his hand, then Claire knew him just as well and knew exactly which buttons to push.

"Her name is Elizabeth and you've already met her. You met her this morning when you went to that farm to look for me."

"Her! You're telling me that that woman is my mother? You're having a laugh! She looks like the sort who won't even have it off with her own husband."

"I believe it's true. The timeline all fits. She found out she was pregnant with you around the same time my parents found out I was on the way. It was her aunt she was living with who introduced her to Marcus, and it was her aunt who organised the adoption. But I believe there was no adoption. I think that her aunt handed you straight over to Marcus. And that was the secret you threatened her with." Claire laughed at this.

"How do you know all this?" he asked angrily.

"Uncle Geoff calls me a ferret for secrets. They just seem to come out around me. I heard it from her when she told her husband the truth at last." She paused and looked up at him. "When secrets come out, they can't hurt people anymore. Your threat this morning is the reason she came out with it, so that your daddy dearest wouldn't have any hold over her. What hold does he have on you? Does he not tell you the truth about your mother deliberately to keep you at his side?" Her voice dropped a bit at the next question. "Does he even *really* love you as a father should?" The room fell silent, and she could hear the clock ticking in the living room as Adam sat in her uncle's chair lost in thought.

Wanting the minutes to tick by faster, Claire hoped that he would stay there until her uncle got home. But she'd be disappointed. Suddenly sitting up, Adam pulled a piece of flat metal out of his pocket, starting to slide it into the cage.

"You had better get on, or you're gonna lose your legs."

Taking his advice, Claire jumped onto the cage's temporary floor. Hopes of her uncle arriving in time were fading fast until she heard a car pull up the driveway. Adam rushed to the window, saying that it had to be Jack—but he swore when he saw that it was Geoff. He snatched up the cage and Claire went flying off her feet, landing heavily against the mesh bars and the floor—knocking the wind out of her. She slid around the cage until she managed to grab hold of one of the sides and hung on for dear life, too occupied with stopping herself from getting hurt to concentrate on trying to help herself escape.

Out the back door they flew as Adam ran, leaping over the fence into a back yard she knew was part of a closed-up house. They raced to the garage, and he flung open the door, climbing into the driver's seat of his black four-wheel drive. After putting her down in the passenger seat, he gunned the engine and took off. Claire went flying again, hitting her head hard on the metal of the mesh cage, and all went black.

When Claire came to, she became aware she was in a sitting position on a soft surface rather than hard metal. Slowly opening her eyes, she found that the cage was gone, and she was once more her normal size. As she lifted her head up from where it rested, pain seared through it—making her wince. Groaning with the ache, Claire opened her eyes again. The world outside was dark, and she realised the car was stationary. Looking to her right, she found Adam sitting in the driver's seat with his hands gripping the wheel.

"Where are we?" she asked him, her voice shaky.

He jumped at the sound of her voice. "Are you okay?" he inquired with care.

"Apart from the thumping head and possibly the second concussion in a month, you mean? I suppose I'm fine. What happened?"

"We're about an hour out of the village. You started to go back to your normal size as we were driving, so I pulled over and let you out. I didn't want to hurt you, Claire. I *never* wanted to hurt you."

"You're not really doing a good job of that!" She tested the sore spot on her head and was pleased to find that there was no blood. "Why have we stopped? I thought you were taking me to your father."

"I was. But with an hour to think about what you said, I just had to pull over. Is what you told me back there true?" He turned to look at her. It was so dark she could barely see his face.

"Yes. Every word I said is the truth. And I do think that Beth's your mum because there are just too many coincidences for it not to be true. Look, you don't have to believe me if you don't want to, but I've never lied to you, Adam. In all the years that we've known each other, it was only you I've ever been completely honest and open with." She left it up to him to decide whether what she said was true.

Without trying to raise his suspicions, she quietly tried the door. But it was locked. Claire knew that she could have the door open in no time and fly out into the darkness, but something made her stop. The way he was acting was not the way she had thought he would. If he truly believed in what his father was trying to do, they would still be on the road—not sitting beside it in the dark in the middle of nowhere. She leaned her head back against the headrest, waiting for him to mull over what she had said. Aching as she realised she'd done none of the techniques to come out of shrinking properly, Claire wasn't looking forward to being sore for a day or two because of it.

"Adam was it you who tried to run me over?" Claire asked quietly, dreading the answer.

"No, it wasn't. Dad was really mad when he heard you'd been hurt. The guy who *did* do it...well, he got dealt with," Adam revealed before falling silent again. The door lock thumped open and Claire looked at Adam. "Get out," he ordered.

"What about your dad? Isn't he going to be mad knowing you had me and then just let me go?"

"I can handle my father," he said, spitting out the word as if it were something disgusting.

"Adam, come back with me. I'm sure Uncle Geoff can keep you safe."

Adam pushed his face toward her, and she could see the pain etched around his eyes. "Your uncle couldn't even keep *you* safe, Claire, and I'm surprised that he made it home. Don't you see? I have to go confront my father."

"If you need help, call me. Please, Adam, please call me," she begged him, grabbing hold of his hand and squeezing it. She would not go without getting his agreement that he'd call her if he needed to. Adam nodded slowly but said nothing. As she opened the door to get out of the car, he grabbed her arm.

"Claire, I know I haven't been the greatest friend—as I should've been—but it wasn't friendship I was wanting, anyway. I care about you deeply. I want you to know that. I've always cared for you. I'm sorry for what happened. I didn't know that he had men with guns there. I didn't know what he was going to do, I swear. I wouldn't have agreed to his stupid idea if I'd have known." He let go of her arm and sat back in his seat before starting the car with a roar. "Now get out and go home."

Claire sat still for a moment. "I care about you too, Adam. Stay safe." With that, she slipped out of the car, and he sped off into the night before she even had a chance to close the door.

Watching his taillights fade into the distance, Claire wondered at the change in him. He was more sombre and worried than she had ever known him to be, and that concerned her. Claire stared after him for a moment longer, eventually walking back the way she presumed they'd come.

But she had no idea where she was and stopped dead in her tracks. Feeling her head start to swim with dizziness, she sat down and pulled her phone out of her pocket. She dialled Geoff's number, praying he'd answer.

It rang once before she heard his voice. "Claire! Stay where you are. I'm coming."

"Hurry...please." It was at that moment the phone decided to die. Claire remembered that it'd been a few days since she had the opportunity to charge it.

She hoped the brief connection would be enough for her uncle to find her as she put the now useless phone back into her pocket. The night air was cool, and she was beginning to feel the effects of her concussion. Her head swam, and her stomach clenched, but she got up. Stumbling to a bush nearby, she started to dry heave. There was nothing in her stomach to bring up, as she'd not eaten anything since leaving David and Beth's house. Looking at her watch, Claire calculated that it was a good six hours before. As she looked around, she wished her uncle would hurry.

In the distance, she saw a light turn onto the road. Her head split at the sight as the points of illumination pierced her eyes. With her muddled thinking, Claire knew it wasn't intelligent to just simply be standing out in the open. *These lights that are hurtling toward me could be anybody*, Claire thought as she stumbled back, moving away from the road. Feeling she didn't have the energy or the means to concentrate and fully hide from whoever was speeding towards her, Claire hid behind a bush and watched the two headlights approaching her position. With the roar of the engine growing louder and louder, the car then sped by. She let out the breath she did not realise she was holding and started to relax her limbs when the car came to a sudden, screeching stop. The rear lights lit up like a Christmas tree and the tyres squealed on the dark bitumen of the road with the force the driver was putting on the car to back up fast.

Coming to an immediate stop opposite where Claire was crouching, she prepared herself to try to Hide, to get away from whoever was in the car. It was only when she heard the deep and reassuring voice call out her name that she realised it was her uncle. He had come for her—of course he had, she thought to herself. Her brain had momentarily refused to make the right connections in her confusion. Slowly leaving her hiding spot, she started to clamber back to the road. Her uncle ran around the car and caught her up in a warm and comforting embrace.

"I told you I can always find you!" he mumbled into her hair as he held her close. "I promised to keep you safe, and I mean to keep that promise."

Moving her to the car, Geoff gently helped her into the passenger seat. She fumbled with the seatbelt and managed to clip it in as her uncle slipped into his seat. He turned the car around and drove back to the village, taking a corner a little too fast. Claire suddenly told him to stop the car and Geoff slammed on the brakes, coming to yet another sudden, screeching stop. Claire only just managed to open the door and lean out as far as the seat belt would allow, again dry retching on the road.

Concern rang through his voice. "Are you okay? What did they do to you?"

She wiped her mouth as she leaned back against the seat. "I hit my head again."

"I'll go slower. Man, I really think we need to get you to the hospital." Geoff started to drive again.

"No, please. I just want to go home." Tears streamed from her eyes. "Please, Uncle Geoff, please don't take me to the hospital. I just wanna go home."

"All right. We'll go home." His concern for her overruled his common sense.

"Thank you," she said weakly, her tears still flowing freely until she drifted off to sleep.

When Geoff realised Claire was unconscious, he pulled over and made a quick phone call—then continued. He was kicking himself for putting her in this position, for leaving her on her own and in danger.

Geoff drove back to the house as he had promised and gently woke her up when they arrived outside. Dazed and confused, Claire started to panic but calmed when she saw her uncle's familiar and concerned face. He helped her out of the car and up the steps to the front door, fumbling with the keys for a moment and letting them into the dark house. Flicking on the lights, he then shut and locked the door behind them. There was something about this act that she thought she should tell her uncle about, but Claire couldn't quite remember what it was. Her head was feeling fuzzy, and the pain was still rolling around it. He guided her up the stairs and into her bedroom, placing her on the bed and slipping her shoes off her feet. Geoff stood and shut the curtains after he'd made sure that the window was secured and locked—then turned and pulled a blanket over her. His worried expression continued as he pulled out his phone and called someone.

"We're home, can you come right away?" There was a pause as he listened to the person's reply. "I'm not sure. She's asleep again." There was another short wait on the other end. "Good. I'll see you in a couple of minutes." Sitting at the end of her bed watching her sleep, he knew she probably shouldn't do so at the moment, but she looked peaceful, and he didn't want to disturb her just yet.

Moments later, he heard footsteps on the porch, and somebody knocked loudly on the door. Leaving Claire's room and going down the stairs, Geoff unlocked and opened the door. A couple stood looking at him expectantly. He greeted them warmly with a hug for each and made sure to lock the door again. After Geoff told the couple that Claire was upstairs, the three of them then ascended. Coming up last, Geoff followed closely behind into Claire's room. The man handed the woman a black case and she opened it quickly, pulling out a light and stethoscope.

As the woman lifted one of Claire's eyelids, Claire flinched and woke with a start. Geoff was at her side telling her it was all right—that Charlotte just wanted to make sure she was okay. Claire felt foolish at this, realising that her uncle would never put her in danger.

The woman named Charlotte smiled. "Can we try this again?"

Claire nodded as the woman began to examine her. It was while she was taking her pulse that Claire noticed the man in the room. He looked familiar to her, but she was not sure why. Maybe she'd seen him in a picture somewhere, but there was something in the way he was watching.

Charlotte finished examining the wound area on the back of Claire's skull and declared that the girl was indeed suffering from a concussion. "She needs to be in a hospital."

"Is that truly necessary? Can't she just stay here? I promise I'll keep an eye on her through the night?" Geoff asked.

Charlotte reluctantly agreed only after the man said that he'd help. "You had better get back to the kids, they'll only play up for Mum and Dad," he told her.

"It is very nice to finally meet you, Claire. I hope that we can become friends." Her smile was radiant and reassuring. She then turned back to the man, and they walked out of the room together. Claire could hear them at the door saying their farewells so quietly that it was but a murmur to her ears.

"Who are they?" she asked turning back to her uncle.

"Sorry...they are Benjamin and Charlotte," Geoff replied distractedly as he tried to find a pair of pyjamas for Claire to change into.

She was about to ask who Benjamin and Charlotte were when the man himself walked back into her room.

"I'm your uncle. I'm John's younger brother," he said, smiling and shaking his head in disbelief. "You look just like your mother. Oh, and Charlotte's my wife. I wish we were meeting under different circumstances, but..." he trailed off.

Just then, Geoff placed pyjamas on the bed and suggested she might like to get a bit more comfortable, telling her that they'd just be outside if she needed any help.

As they left the room and the door closed, Claire smiled. "As if I needed the help of an uncle I barely know," she mumbled to herself picking up the pyjamas Geoff had left for her. "And an uncle who has the worst idea of comfy pj's."

The ones he had laid out for her were winter fleecy pyjamas—with large red roses all over them. Knowing it was definitely not something she would have picked out for herself, Claire had the feeling her grandmothers had a hand in choosing them. Getting up from the bed, she went to her drawers and pulled out a T-shirt and a pair of soft shorts. Once she was changed, Claire climbed into bed and announced that she was ready.

Geoff re-entered the room, carrying a large comfy chair and a rug that she knew lived in his room. He placed it in the corner.

"You aren't seriously going to sleep in here, are you?" she asked him.

"Of course, I am! That's what I promised Charlie. There is no possible way I'm letting you out of my sight, young lady—

not with all the worry you've given everyone lately," he replied

Claire managed to look a bit ashamed at the admonishment and lay down, pulling the covers up over her. She enjoyed the feeling of being in her own bed. Shortly after, Benjamin entered the room and handed a cup of coffee to Geoff. Her great-uncle then told Benjamin that the spare room was made up and to make use of it. He bade them good night and left them to it. Geoff turned off the main light and let the golden light of hallway spill in through the open door.

Claire lay there thinking how nice it was to be home, remembering thinking almost the same thing earlier in the day. She then bolted upright only to have another wave of pain and nausea course through her. Once she'd stopped dry retching into the small rubbish bin that her uncle had managed to get to her in time, she told him about the back door—that it was the point of entry Adam had made. The noise from the room had brought Benjamin running, half dressed in a borrowed pair of his uncle's pyjamas that were far too big for him. Geoff asked him to go and check the back door while he tried to calm Claire down. He came back a short time later.

"It's been forced at some stage, but I jimmied one of the kitchen chairs up against it for the night. I'll fix it in the morning," he told them.

"Thanks, Ben," Geoff said with a yawn. Ben then bade them good night again and left them alone.

Once she was sure the spare room's door was shut, Claire told her uncle about Adam using the closed-up house behind them. He promised that they'd make every effort in the morning to investigate. He tucked her in—just like he had when she was younger—and then settled himself in his chair for the night, drinking his coffee as he watched her fall asleep.

A few hours later, Claire woke in a cold sweat. She'd been running after someone, but she didn't exactly know who. A recurring dream she had had since she was young. As her heart started to calm itself, she looked over at her uncle only to find that it was not Geoff with his long legs sprawled out before him, but Benjamin. He smiled at her when he realised that she was awake.

"It seemed like a nasty dream. Are you okay?" he asked with some concern.

She nodded, sitting up. "I'm thirsty," she said through a mouth that felt like it was full of cotton wool.

Heading downstairs, Benjamin was back in a minute with a glass of water.

"Just sip it," he instructed as she took the glass from his hand. Her stomach still felt wobbly, and the last thing she wanted to do was vomit in front of him. She put the glass on her bedside table and then looked at her newly introduced uncle.

"Benjamin, how much younger than my father are you?" Claire asked as Ben raised his eyebrows.

"I'm six years younger than your dad. And please, call me Ben."

"So, you didn't *really* grow up together, then?" It was more of a statement than question she posed to Ben.

"No," he agreed. "We didn't grow up together—not really. I was the pesky younger brother who always followed him around. I idolised your father, Claire. He was my hero, and not once did he ever tell me to go away and leave him alone! He always seemed to include me in the mischief he concocted up." Ben smiled, remembering his older brother.

"Until he ran off with my mother..."

"Yes, until he ran off with Jess." He nodded at that. "What a fuss that caused. I remember our dad being very angry, but

Mum didn't seem to think that it was so dreadful. I think she preferred Jess to Beth. I know that Lynnette and Mum were always good friends. We were always over at each other's houses. David and John were best friends, and I think that when they eloped, he felt it more because of that."

Claire found it nice to hear about her dad from someone who was so close to him. She thought that David had only ever talked about his sister. And she wondered if he still resented John for taking his sister away from him. She only realised that she'd spoken that aloud when Ben answered her.

"I don't think he resents John anymore. It's more that he and Jess were so close—as only twins can be. I know my boys are close. So close that they even have their own language. Oh, you don't know that you have two little cousins! Owen and Oliver are six." He got up and fumbled with his wallet, pulling out a picture and showing Claire the young family. The small boys were like two peas in a pod and so blond they almost appeared to have white hair. She complimented the photo and handed it back to him. He seemed as proud as any parent, and Claire couldn't help but wonder if her own parents had shown photos of her as a child to other people with the same enthusiasm.

"Grandma told me all about them. What sorts of things did he get up to when you were younger?" Claire asked her Uncle Ben, settling back down in her bed while he resumed his seat.

He chuckled a little. "I don't know where to start." He then regaled her with adventure after adventure of her father and she smiled as she was lulled to sleep by the sound of her uncle's voice—a voice that echoed in her mind—and one that was much like her father's.

Chapter Sixteen

It sounded as if an aviary had been set up in her room. Claire would gratefully have traded all the birds outside her window for a thousand cars speeding by. She opened her eyes slightly to the world, snuggling deeper into her bed. As her body finally caught up with her mind, she felt the pressing need for two things: getting something to eat, and more urgently, relieving her bladder. She swung her legs from under the covers and sat up. *So far so good. No nauseous feeling and only a slight dull ache in my head!* Claire thought to herself.

Taking a quick look at the sleeping form of Ben snoring away on the chair, she tried standing. Wobbling a little, she held onto the bedside table until the world righted itself. As she took her first step, she could feel the tightness and pain in her muscles—screaming at her for not going through the proper techniques for shrinking and stretching again. She made it to her door frame and held onto it as she turned the corner to the bathroom.

Once finished with the most pressing need, Claire came out and stood at the top of the stairs. It suddenly looked like a very long way down, and they seemed to have gotten steeper, too. She closed her eyes a moment, and then when she opened them up again, Geoff was standing at the bottom holding a tray.

"What on earth are you doing out of bed?" he demanded as he started to ascend the stairs. Claire turned to go back to her room, but the action was too quick for her stiffened and cramped muscles to work properly, and she stumbled against the door frame, landing heavily at the feet of Ben. He bent down and scooped her up, depositing her on the single bed gently. Geoff came into the room and put the tray down on the desk in the corner.

Just then, a knock could be heard from the front door. Ben looked up and then back at Claire.

"You're lucky that Charlie wasn't here when you pulled that stunt." He grinned at her before answering the door. Geoff made sure she was properly covered up and then handed her a cup of tea and some still-warm toast on a plate.

"None of us mess with Charlie," Geoff said as he swiped a piece of toast and then turned to greet Charlotte.

Claire peered around him as the couple walked into her room and she finally got a good look at Charlotte. She was as tall as her husband and lithe. Her long, chestnut hair was caught up in a ponytail and she was dressed immaculately in what looked like casual clothes, but on her, they looked stylish. She once more carried a bag with her, placing it down on the bed as she greeted Claire.

"Happy New Year, Claire. Did you have a good night's sleep?" Charlotte asked.

Claire nodded, having a mouthful of toast, and suddenly feeling very awkward beside this glamourous woman.

"Good, Ben didn't snore too loudly, then!" Charlie smiled as Ben mimed behind her back that he didn't snore and that his wife did. But Claire—having heard his efforts for herself—just smiled. Charlie was looking at her with a cheeky gleam in her eye. "He's trying to deny it, isn't he?" Claire nodded back to her, and Charlie returned with a beaming smile. "Never mind his antics. Let's have a look at you."

Going through the same motions as the night prior, she once again examined Claire and declared that she was on her way to recovery. "But I'd like her to stay in bed for the rest of the day," Charlie informed them. "You can get up tomorrow, but remember, Claire, no stress and also no noise—or any overactivity for the next week—especially since it's been just a few weeks since you've recovered from a previous concussion."

Charlie started putting her instruments back into her bag and then spoke to Ben. "I've tried to tell your mother that she should leave it for a day or two before she came to see Claire, but she is insisting that she and Lynnette come over and make sure she's being properly looked after. Sorry, Uncle Geoff." She gave the older gentleman a small smile. "But you know how she is. I thought looking after the boys would keep her occupied, but she has arranged for Malcolm and Bob to look after them. She said that they'd be here around ten."

"Mum means well, Charlie."

"I know, honey, but sometimes she gets my back up."

"Coffee?" Geoff offered, handing her a cup. She sat on the end of Claire's bed as the girl continued to eat, finishing off the toast. Claire grabbed her cup of tea and gulped it down, as if it were going to be taken away from her.

"Hey, slow down there, Kid. It's not going to run away," her uncle told her.

"Sorry, I'm hungry. I haven't eaten anything since yesterday afternoon and using the Talent takes a lot of energy."

"Okay, I get the message. I'll go make you some more toast." He left the room and the silence became awkward.

These were two people she had only briefly heard about and had not met until last night.

Charlie broke the silence. "So, are you going to stay here all day?" she asked her husband.

"I have to fix Uncle Geoff's back door. It's been forced at some stage. Other than that, was there something you wanted me to do?"

She shook her head. "Not really—only it'd be nice to spend some time with you." Claire could detect an undercurrent of pent-up feelings and she wished they would continue their discussion elsewhere. Anywhere away from her.

"Well, the door should only take an hour tops and then I am all yours. We can take the boys to David's farm and see if we can do a bit of horse riding if you like. I know he has some ponies that would be suitable for the boys."

Charlie smiled at the idea and agreed to it. "As long as your mother isn't there!" She looked at Claire with a raised eyebrow. "I'm sorry, Claire, but sometimes I do not see eye to eye with your grandmother—especially when she's dishing out advice on how to raise our sons."

They were quiet once more until Geoff came back into the room with a plate of toast and fresh cup of tea for Claire. Ben and Charlie took the opportunity to take their leave, again reminding Geoff of Grace and Lynnette's impending visit and to make sure that Claire had a quiet day.

"I hereby promise that I'll do everything in my power to make sure that Claire's confined to quarters. She won't sneak out to chase bad people today!" He promised with a stiff salute to Charlotte.

They chuckled at that and left Claire in peace. She started to eat the toast and polished it off with her second cup of tea. Feeling better, she leaned back on her pillows and closed her eyes—finally feeling safe and cared for. Her mind was now unburdened from worry, and she felt only peace.

Sometime later, Claire awoke to voices whispering in her room. She recognised her Uncle Geoff's voice first.

"She's still asleep. Maybe you could come back later?" He sounded a little hopeful.

"It's not good for her to sleep so much after a concussion. She should be kept awake," one feminine voice said, trying hard to whisper.

"I agree, and this room needs an airing. Fresh air will do her a world of good!" another woman's voice agreed with the first as Claire then heard her window being opened.

The two voices belonged to Grace and Lynnette. Their impending visit had arrived, so it must be around ten o'clock. She sensed someone sitting on the end of her bed and heard her grandmother Grace speak.

"She looks so peaceful asleep, she really does look like your Jess, Lynnie—almost a carbon copy."

"Yes, she does," her grandmother Lynnette said with pride and a touch of wistfulness in her voice.

"But her eyes are definitely John's. So kind and caring," Grace said firmly.

"You think so?" Lynnette asked as Claire remembered something Bob had said.

"Geoff, be a dear and make us a cup of tea, would you? I have been run off my feet this morning looking after those boys." Grace sighed dramatically.

Geoff assented, and Claire could hear him head downstairs.

"He's such a good man. It's a pity that he never remarried," Lynnette said.

"I know, but it wasn't from lack of our trying. He so loved his Katherine and her death hit him very hard." There was a nod of agreement from her other grandmother, and they fell silent for a time.

"You know Charlotte works long hours. She hardly gets to see the boys and it's a shame. So much of their childhood will be lost to her."

"But she's a doctor and a good one, Grace. It's something she has worked hard for."

"Oh, I know that, but it pains me that they have to hire a nanny to look after them. Ben is so busy with his company, and you would think that he's bringing in enough for her to stay at home and be a proper mother to those children."

"Grace!" Lynnette exclaimed. "You cannot mean that! You know she loves what she's doing and being a young doctor is all about hard work and long hours. Once she has established herself in that hospital, she can cut back. She has told you this herself. Why do you have to be so stern with her? If I had a daughter-in-law like Charlie, I'd be as proud as punch. Look what I have!" The last part was said in a conspiratorial whisper.

"Beth is a bit uptight, but she means well, and at least she cooks for the family. Anyway, she wasn't so bad yesterday. There was something that was different, and it almost seemed that David and Beth were a proper couple."

"Yes, there has definitely been some sort of thawing between them—which I hope lasts." They sat quietly until Geoff returned with a pot of tea for them both.

It was at this time that she decided she had better let them get the visit over and done with, as she didn't feel like hearing her grandmothers' opinions on each family member or everyone in the village. She stirred and opened her eyes, hoping that she looked convincing enough.

"Good, you're awake. Happy New Year, dear." Grace kissed her in greeting.

"Happy New Year to you too, Claire! I hope this one is better than the last one was for you," Lynnette said warmly.

"You really shouldn't sleep so much after a concussion, it is not good for you," Grace repeated.

"Charlie told me to get a lot of rest. She said that it was the best way to heal," Claire replied, wanting to defend her newfound aunt in some way.

"Oh," her grandmother said, her lips tightening slightly before taking a sip of her tea.

"Want a cup, Claire?" Geoff asked brightly, trying to steer the conversation away from and impending argument.

"Sure. Why not?" she answered as he then busied himself pouring it and passing it to her.

"What happened yesterday, Claire? One minute you were there and then the next you were gone. Jasper had some story about a little man and you disappearing," Lynnette said.

Claire glanced at her uncle and then back at her two grandmothers. She didn't know where to start, and to be honest, some of the details were still a bit fuzzy. Sitting up straighter in bed, she told them what had happened in the easiest terms she could. She glossed over some points like Jasper's role in her escape, and she was still not sure how David was dealing with that matter, so she didn't mention the note she left on Uncle Geoff's desk, either. She wanted to tell him these things in private. She had grown to love her grandmothers, but she didn't feel they needed to know everything just yet.

By the time she had finished her telling, she felt tired and rested her head back on the pillows. Geoff stood up straight from his position of leaning on the doorframe and quietly said to them, "I think it might be time for you to go. Claire is exhausted, and she needs to rest. If Charlie finds out that I have allowed her to overdo things, she'll have my hide." Grace and Lynnette agreed with him and kissed their granddaughter goodbye, promising to come back in a day or two. Geoff escorted them down the stairs and out the door. He returned to make sure she was okay.

"I'm fine, Uncle Geoff." But she didn't sound like it. He came and sat on the bed.

"There is more, isn't there? What is it that you didn't say in front of Lynnette and Grace?"

Claire sighed deeply and pushed herself further down the bed, finally ready to tell her uncle everything.

"You know that Jasper has developed Light Talent," she said, watching him carefully. He nodded his knowledge of this. "Well, he helped a lot last night. I was hiding under the couch when Jack found me. Jasper and Hunter were watching, and Jasper used the light to hold Jack while I got away."

"Well, that'll be the reason David wants to talk to me so urgently. He rang first thing this morning," he informed her. "What happened after you got away?"

"I flew back here and got in through the roof and air ducts." Claire shifted slightly. Her eyes were starting to droop a little. "I went straight to your desk and wrote you a note about what Jack told me. Both he and his mother are working with Marcus, so you can't trust them, Uncle Geoff. He told me that Marcus is his father—which would explain why his father's name isn't listed on the genealogy." She ran a weary hand across her eyes and let out a great yawn. At last, the events of the last couple of days had caught up with her.

"I think that's enough for today," Geoff said with some concern. "Get some more rest, Kid. We can talk later." He looked at her one more time before leaving her room. She was pale, and he noticed she was visibly thinner. Not for the first time in the last twenty-four hours, he cursed himself for leaving her alone—for leaving her in danger.

Geoff walked down to his study and found the note she had left for him about Jack meeting with Adam. He read her clear and concise description of the man she'd seen and the car he had driven, as well as how Jack had followed him out of the hall and looked around. He felt he was there witnessing it with her. The other message he found on the blotter, he could see her tiny, smeared handprints spelling, *Mary Jack no trust*. He admired her tenacity and thinking on her feet.

They had to act soon, or he did not know what was going to happen to the girl upstairs. Not just a great-niece and his charge, but the closest thing to a daughter he would ever likely have and—not for the first time since she had come to live with him—wished she was his own. He picked up the phone and started to dial.

Chapter Seventeen

The days seemed to have only two phases to Claire: awake and hungry or asleep and wracked with dreams. And it was always the same dream. A faceless man would either be stalking her, or she'd be chasing him through a white mist with people telling her to run. Uncle Geoff, Beth, David, Bob, Malcolm, and at her side—always and constant—was Adam. He'd reach out to her, soundlessly trying to tell her something. She could see him call her name over and over, and when she woke, Claire would be in a sweat, shaking and scared. She didn't understand what he was trying to tell her, but she knew it was important.

After what seemed like the thousandth time she'd dreamed the same dream, she pulled out her books and started to flick through them frantically. Geoff walked through her door and watched her discard book after book, getting more and more distressed. He carefully stepped to her side and took the books away from her.

"Claire, what's wrong?"

"I don't know! It's got to be in here somewhere!" she replied frantically, with tears streaming down her face.

"What is? Claire, talk to me!"

"The answer; the answer is in the books, but I don't know what I'm looking for!" Claire continued to manically search through the books.

He tried to calm her down by grabbing her hands, fearing she may do damage to herself.

"Tell me what started this frantic search. What was the catalyst? Take a deep breath and tell me slowly," he pleaded.

His questions were enough to break through to her and Claire did as she was told. She calmed down and breathed slowly, relaying to him the dream she kept having.

"But I am sure what Adam is trying to say is important. I can just feel it. I have to find out what it is, Uncle Geoff! I remember reading something in one of these books about dreams and being able to send messages through them, so I'm sure it's one of the Talents that can do this. If I can find the right one, then I could figure out his message—if only I can find the right passage." She began her search once more.

"Okay, okay. I understand." He pulled the books from her. "Let me get Lilith here to help, since she knows these books inside and out. Just keep calm till she gets here, or I'll have to tell Charlie to give you something to calm down. Got me, Kid?" He looked into her eyes as she nodded her head and promised.

Geoff helped her back into bed, pulling out his cell phone. As he waited for Lilith to answer, he watched Claire pick up one of the books and slowly thumb through it. On the other end of the line, he heard his older sister's crisp voice.

"Lilith speaking."

"Lil, its Geoff. Claire needs your help. I'm not sure what she's searching for, so I'll put her on." He handed the phone to Claire without waiting for Lilith to reply. Geoff stood with his arms crossed, wishing he knew exactly what she wanted—a phrase she had remembered, something he could use to help with her search—after all, that was what his Talent was for. He concentrated on the books with the word *dream* forward in his mind. He got that tingly feeling from several of the books but nothing definite. He came back to himself when he heard Claire call his name. She was holding out his phone to him.

"She's on her way. She knows exactly which Talent I mean, and she's going to be bringing more books with her." Claire noticed he was in deep thought. "Are you okay? You look funny."

"I feel disappointed I can't help. I mean, I should be able to help you, but I feel hobbled. All I'm getting are vague hints."

"At least that's more than I've got. Which books are you getting the feeling from?" she asked, laying them all out on her bed.

Geoff placed a hand over the top of the books and reached down to the strongest one. He picked it up and handed it to her. She carefully flipped through the book and came to a passage that looked promising. She looked back up to her uncle.

"Any others?" she asked.

Coming closer, he picked up a couple more books, gave her one, and looking at the other. He flicked straight to the page he was looking for and passed it to her, then taking the other from her hands and finding the passage that had spoken to him. She was busy reading the first passage; her finger carefully underlined each word to make sure she didn't misread the messy script writing. Geoff read the passage he had just found and could not make heads nor tails of what the author was trying to convey. The talk of dreams seemed to go round in circles, and he was soon getting a headache from it. He was pleased when there was a knock at the door so he could put the book down to answer it.

Geoff ushered Lilith into Claire's room and pulled the big comfy chair up for her to sit on. He muttered something about tea and left the room. Lilith tutted at his sudden leaving and then produced more books from her bag, giving them to Claire.

They started to discuss the passages that Geoff had helped to find for Claire, and they were soon making notes on a scrap of paper about Dream Messaging. Claire was referring back to the red booklet when Geoff came into the room bearing a tray with tea and biscuits. He put it down on the bedside table and poured a cup each.

"Is there anything else you need?" he asked the pair of them.

"Yes, can we perhaps have a proper notebook or pad we can write on, that would be wonderful, Geoff." The tone of Lilith's voice took Claire by surprise, and she looked at her uncle. He didn't seem to notice that there was far less ice in his sister's voice than normal, and she smiled at that.

Geoff hurried away and returned with two pads and a supply of pens, just in case one didn't work. He suddenly had a very strong pull towards one of the books at the bottom of the pile on Claire's bed and in his haste to get to it, he knocked them all onto the floor.

"You bumbling fool, what on earth are you trying to do?" Lilith yelled.

"I'm sorry, but this one might have the answers you're looking for. Try page thirty-two." Geoff pressed the book into Lilith's hands. He then left them alone to clean up after him and reorganise the books. Lilith opened the book he had handed her and let out a little exclamation.

"Oh, I had forgotten this woman. Look here, these are the musings of Anne Crimble—she and her twin brother both had Mind Touch and could talk to each other in their thoughts. But Anne also developed a way to talk to other people in their dreams. Look, she describes the technique to do so. This is gold!"

"And Uncle Geoff found it," Claire exclaimed.

"He did," Lilith replied with a hint of a smile.

They spent the rest of the morning and some of the afternoon poring over all the books, cross-referencing each one with the other until they had built up a full picture. Their main study was Anne Crimble's diary, as the other references all seemed to back up what she had discovered. Claire read the last passage to Lilith out loud.

"'It is such a pity that most of the old lore of our people has been lost. I hope that by writing these attempts and final techniques down, that they might help someone in the future.' That's where the book ends. The rest is just blank pages." She thumbed through the remainder of the book.

"Amen to that," Lilith replied.

When Claire rubbed her head at the onset of another headache, her great-aunt put a stop to the research.

"But I want to try some of these techniques! I want to be prepared for the dream again," Claire protested.

"Not today, young lady. I will come back tomorrow, and we shall go over what we've found out and start slow." She picked up all the books and the notepads, bundling them up into her arms. "I'll be back here at ten o'clock sharp tomorrow."

"You're not taking them with you, are you?" Claire asked.

"I think it'd be best to keep temptation out of reach for the rest of today and tonight. And I do not want you trying to attempt to contact Adam tonight. It could be dangerous in more ways than one. Make sure you keep your distance for now." She placed a caring hand on the girl's cheek. "Get some rest, Claire. Remember, you're still healing. There is plenty of time tomorrow." With that, she turned from the girl and walked out the door.

Claire could hear her aunt and uncle talking downstairs and crept out of her room, trying to hear what they were discussing.

"She's going to do some permanent damage if she doesn't look after herself."

"I know that," her uncle retorted. "I'm doing my best to keep people away and Claire calm, but when the girl wakes shouting every couple of hours, it's very hard to calm her down. Sometimes I swear she's still asleep while I am trying to reassure her."

"I know you are doing your best. You look so tired. Do you need a break?" Lilith asked.

"No, I'll be all right. I sleep when I can—usually when she's asleep."

"Well, look after yourself. You're no good to her if you're run down as well."

"Thank you, Lil. I will try," Geoff responded.

She could hear them walking to the door and scooted back into her room and into bed. She was pleased that their attitude towards each other was warming.

Claire was not ready to give up for the day just yet. Recall exercises had worked well when she needed more information on the car that Adam drove, and she was determined to try it on the dream. Settling herself back into the soft pillows, she stared up at the ceiling, closing her eyes and concentrating on recalling the dream. The images that she wanted to see started to fade in, but they remained fuzzy and indistinct to her sight. Her headache was interfering with the Recall, as it wouldn't let her see clearly and her concentration kept slipping. Claire wanted desperately to help Adam—for she was sure that these were true Dream Messages—but she was unsure how he was achieving it, or if he even *knew* he was doing it.

Calming her breathing again, she decided she'd have to wait until her aunt visited the next day. It seemed a long time to wait, but if what her uncle had told Lilith was true, then it was imperative that Claire wait to do the exercises without a headache pressing on her. Sometime after this, she fell into a deep and dreamless sleep.

When Claire woke, she felt rested—calm and at ease—as the dream had not come to her. She sat up and looked out her window. It was dark out and she looked at her watch. Her aunt had left her about three in the afternoon and she had fallen asleep shortly after. Now it was eight. She had slept through five hours. Sitting up and swinging her legs out of the bed, Claire stood. For the first time in three days, there was no lurching of the ground under her feet. She grabbed her dressing gown from off its hook on the back of the door and wrapped it around her, then went downstairs.

At the bottom the stairs, she discovered the only light on in the house was coming from her uncle's study. Quietly, she pushed on the door and made Geoff jump at her appearance.

"Wow...look at you, Kid!" he exclaimed, once he had gotten over the surprise. "I take it you're feeling better?"

"Yeah, I am." She sat in the chair opposite him.

"How's the head? Do you need any more painkillers?"

"No, there's no headache. I feel so much better. I slept like a log."

"Yes, you did. There's some dinner for you in the fridge. I didn't want to wake you. For once you were sleeping peacefully."

"Thanks. I didn't have the dream either. It's so weird. I've been having that dream for the past few days and now nothing."

"Really? Can you tell me something? Did Lilith touch your head at any point this afternoon?" he asked. His eyes squinted a little as they always did when he was suspicious of something.

"I think so. Before she left, she put her hand on my cheek and told me to get some rest and that I was still healing. She also told me that there was plenty of time tomorrow."

"That sly cow!" Geoff said slowly.

"Uncle Geoff!"

"No, you don't understand. I wasn't insulting her. She has the Talent of Mind Touch, but she doesn't use it very often and it was part of the problem we had when she stopped talking to me. She thought she could Mind Touch the man she loved and change him. I told her that that was not fair to him and that her Talent shouldn't be used in that way." He sighed deeply. "She must've used it on you so that you'd get some peaceful sleep — enough sleep to help you heal. These dreams have not been letting you get the rest you needed. If Adam is somehow trying to Dream Message you, then he has been doing you no favours. Come on, let's get some food into you." Geoff stood and at the mention of food, Claire's stomach started to growl as she followed him to the kitchen. On the way out of the study, she spotted the pile of books Lilith had left there.

Once again, she wolfed down her food as if it was going to run away.

"Well, one thing is for certain, your body's still trying to gain back the reserves you spent." He got up and dished her a large bowl of ice cream, slicing a banana into it and pouring chocolate sauce all over. "Do you want sprinkles like you used to?" he asked jokingly.

"Of course. It wouldn't be one of your specials without them!" she replied with a smile.

He laughed and pulled out of the cupboard a large container of multi-coloured sprinkles and poured a generous amount over the ice cream. He placed it down in front of her.

"God bless your belly, Kid."

"I thought you didn't believe in God?" Claire said before shovelling a large spoonful of dessert into her mouth

"I don't. It's just something you say, really. Hey, do you remember the first time I made you one of these?"

"Yeah, Mum and Dad never really let me have ice cream or sugary things—they said it made me too hyper." He watched her polish off the dessert and push the bowl away from her. "I'm so full!" Claire complained.

"About bloody time!" her uncle exclaimed back at her. "I thought you were going to eat me out of house and home!"

"Well, I gave it a damned good try." She picked up the bowl and took it over to the sink. "How come you never told me that Aunt Lilith had a Talent?" She turned and leaned against the bench.

"Probably because she hasn't used it in years. Well, not to my knowledge anyway. That particular Talent is not very well-liked, even among the Talented. It scares people that someone can have control over your thoughts, feelings, and ultimately, your actions. I am pleased, however, that she used it on you today."

"She's talking a lot nicer to you, too. I did notice that."

"Yes, that was a surprise. But I didn't want to mention it to her, just in case she had a relapse. I'm hoping that it wasn't a one-off."

"Me too. I don't like tension around me. I noticed there was a bit between Ben and Charlie," Claire said, coming to sit back down at the table.

"Yes, unfortunately it increases when they come to visit Grace and Malcolm. Charlie is well aware of how Grace feels about her working such long hours, and part of that is because she feels it herself. She knows that she's missing out on the milestones that most other parents take for granted and tries to be there for her boys, but they love her regardless. Ben is lucky that he has built up a very good construction business and has got to the point in his career that he can afford to leave it for a few days at a time to look after the boys and work from home. Unfortunately, Charlie still has a few more years until she can do the same, so she really relishes the time they come here, but she gets frustrated when Grace takes the boys off her hands and spoils them rotten. Was there anyone else you'd like to discuss tonight?" Geoff asked with a bit of a grin.

"No. I think I have had my fill of ferreting." She laughed, then remembered something. "Hang on, what's happened with Mary and Jack?" She asked, placing her chin in her hand.

"Well, Jack has been made safe and secure, thanks to Jasper's help. Apparently, the light he surrounded Jack with held on long enough for David to capture him and put him somewhere safe. Mary—as you can imagine—is quite concerned about Jack's whereabouts and started to ask around about that night. Someone told her that they'd seen him in the company of a young man in a large black car heading out of town."

"Really?"

"Yup. I've been waiting to confront her, but I wanted you a lot better before I did."

"Maybe we can get Aunt Lilith to use her Mind Touch on Mary," Claire suggested.

"Believe me, I have thought about it. It would solve a lot of problems, but I think your aunt would have some severe objections to it. Now back to bed with you, Kid. Your aunt's suggestion will probably only last until morning, so make the most of it."

"Yes, Uncle Geoff." She got up and started to leave the room, then turned and looked at her uncle she had come to see as a surrogate father. "Thank you for everything you've done for me. I know some of it hasn't been easy, and I certainly have not been the easiest of kids to look after. I love you."

Claire turned back to the hallway and went to bed, not knowing that she'd left her uncle sitting at the table with tears in his eyes.

Chapter Eighteen

Lilith's suggestion did only last until the next day, and the following night, Claire was wracked with the same dream again. The message now sounded muted—like he was speaking underwater—but as she tried to focus her will, it seemed to slip away like sand through her fingers while she slept. The next morning, she woke feeling tired and frustrated. The only bright spot was being allowed to do light exercise downstairs.

After one particularly frustrating morning training with her aunt, Claire decided to just chill out in the backyard. Grabbing a rug, she spread it out on the lawn under the large tree and lay on her back. The quietness of the village made it easy for her to just clear all her thoughts as she stared up at the sky through the leaves. Watching them dance slowly in the light breeze that disturbed them, the lazy dappled light played across her face, inducing her to close her eyes. It was in this relaxed state that she once again tried the Recall exercises—this time with a lot more success.

The dream came sharply into focus in her mind, and she discarded the parts she didn't want, concentrating only on Adam. The muted sound was again playing, and she tried hard to follow what he was saying, but to no avail. It was only in frustration that she accidentally sped up the dream. Then his voice came through a little clearer. It was just like a recording. She could speed up, slow down, and rewind at will. Again, she sped the playback up faster than the last time and his message came through as clear as a bell. Quickly she dismissed the vision and stood up to find her uncle.

Claire rushed into his office and grabbed a pen and paper to scribble down Adam's message.

"Well excuse me, young lady, but I am working here," Geoff protested.

Claire only made a sound of assent as she kept writing. She handed the paper to her uncle when she'd finished and collapsed into the chair opposite him.

"Is this what I think it is?" he asked after reading it. Claire nodded to her uncle. "How? I thought you were still having problems with the Dream Message!"

"I tried a different method—a Recall one. I'd read about it and used it when trying to recall the details of Adam coming out of the hall for you."

"How many Talents have you got, Kid?" he asked her in amazement. Two was rare—especially in modern times—but even before the breeding out started, it was still considered unusual. The girl sitting in front of him seemed to have developed a third Talent. He did not know how to respond to that and decided quietly to have a good talk with Lilith on the matter.

"I don't know. I read about the Talents and sometimes the techniques just sort of click into place in my mind. But getting back to Adam's message, do you think it is a true Dream Message, or is it just something my scrambled brain cooked up?"

Geoff knew the answer she desperately wanted to hear, and he could not in all honesty give it to her.

"I just don't know, but if it's a real Dream Message, then we need to act soon. I've already taken steps in anticipation of taking action, but it's not ready yet. I still need to get some things lined up in the city."

It was this mention of the city that reminded Claire she hadn't asked what it was that had taken him there in the first place and why no one could contact him. She asked the question and waited for his reply.

Geoff straightened the papers on his desk and placed his pen down neatly beside them. He took a deep breath and began his tale. It didn't take him long to retell, and Claire was almost certain he had left things out to protect her.

"Finally, a message got through from David and I risked using my phone to receive your messages. What I heard frightened me, Claire. I left the city at once and raced home. I rang David's cell first as I entered the village and he quickly told me what had happened. I then came here, but there was no sign of you. I didn't even remember you had left me a note. I was getting frantic at that point, and once I had calmed myself, I tried to find you. I could feel you moving away from me fast. I knew in which general direction, so I jumped in my car and came after. You have no idea the relief I felt when you rang me. Even that briefest contact was enough to let me know exactly where you were.

"So now you know everything. Except that Mary now knows that something's going on, and that her precious Jack isn't in the city with his half-brother." At her quizzical look, he told her that he had a message from someone in the city.

"Oh, and it wasn't Adam who tried to run me down, but some other dude. Adam told me," Claire said.

"I hope you can trust him on that. Now go put the jug on, we'll be having company very soon!" He picked up his cell phone and typed a short message before sending it out.

Geoff wasn't joking about the company, but Claire didn't realise that it would entail her entire family. Her grandmothers soon shooed her out of the kitchen and told her to go sit down. They made short work of making coffee and tea, all the while telling the younger boys to go outside and climb the tree, while both Beth and Charlie told them that they had better not. With the children outside, they all squeezed into the living room and Geoff made a start.

He explained that Claire had been having a recurring nightmare, always ending in Adam trying to tell her something. That she and Lilith had been working together to try and unlock what the message might be, because they both believed that it was a Dream Message. He then revealed that Claire had managed to decode the message.

"On your own?!" Lilith exclaimed.

"I'll explain later," Claire replied.

Geoff carried on. "The message that Claire managed to decode is…" He pulled the piece of paper out of his pocket and read. "'Claire, he knows and he's angry.'"

"Who's Adam?" David asked.

"He's Marcus's son. He was also my best friend growing up," Claire said, looking at Beth.

"I didn't know he had a son," Ben added.

"Yes. Two, it seems, and it sounds like Adam is in trouble. Are you sure he can be trusted now, Claire? He was working for his father." Geoff voiced the concern that was still going around in her own head.

"I am sure. I told him to call me if he needed help. I believe he has had a change of heart."

"How old is he?" Beth asked quietly.

"I don't think that matters at the moment, Beth," David said, grabbing her hand and holding it.

"Yes, it does. It means a lot, actually. Is he the same age as you, Claire?" Beth asked her.

"Yes, Aunt Beth—he is the same age." She didn't want to meet her aunt's eyes, but she made herself.

"Is he...?"

"I don't think that matters at the moment. We can talk about it later," David repeated, trying to reassure her.

"You know what I want to know, Claire," Beth persisted, ignoring her husband.

"Yes, Aunt Beth...he is, and I told him myself."

"What is this all about, Beth...Claire?" Lynnette asked.

Beth took a deep breath and bravely started to speak. "Before I came back from the city to marry David, I had a child. With Marcus. That child seems to be Adam. My aunt told me that she had arranged an adoption for the baby, and I let her organise everything. She must have just handed the baby straight to Marcus, all the while not telling me a thing." A tear streaked down her cheek. David put his arm around his wife and pulled her close.

"Well, I never!" Grace exclaimed.

"Don't you dare, Mum," Ben admonished his mother.

"I wasn't going to say anything, thank you very much. So, what do we know about the boy? Has he got a Talent?" Grace asked.

"He has Charm and I think the Dream Message part of the Mind Touch. Though I'm not sure if he has the full Talent," Claire responded to her grandmother.

"He would've got the Charm Talent from his father— sometimes these can be hereditary, but usually from the mother's side," Lilith said as she gave Beth a look. "Marcus has both Charm and Longevity Talents." She fell silent when she realised everyone was looking at her.

"Go on, Lil," Geoff encouraged his older sister gently.

"Well, we know that Claire can deflect the Charm Talent, she has already managed it with Adam. What we need to now figure out is how to defeat the Longevity. Unfortunately, those with that Talent are not so easy to deal with. Even a direct hit to the heart cannot harm someone with Longevity, as their cells are very quick to heal, and they hardly get sick. Let me look through some of the books and see if I can come up with something."

"Let me help you," Geoff offered. "After all, I do have a knack for finding things, so if you could tell me exactly what it is I'm looking for, then together we could come up with something." Without hesitation, she agreed.

It was decided that there was little more they could do at that point, and Claire was asked to go put the jug back on for more coffee. As she headed to the kitchen, she found Jasper just outside the door to the lounge. She jumped a little and told him he had scared her. As she passed him, he followed her to the kitchen.

"Claire, I think I might know how to get that man you were talking about," Jasper whispered as she stopped in her tracks.

"What?"

"That man you were talking about—the bad one—I think you called him Marcus," Jasper carried on, whispering.

"Yeah, I know who you mean. But you're not supposed to know. How long were you standing there listening?"

"The whole time." He managed to look sheepish when he said it.

"So, you heard everything?"

He nodded. "I heard that I have an older brother who has two Talents like you, but of course not the same ones."

"No, not the same. Are you okay with this news?"

"Yeah, well, I mean...I'm a bit surprised, but it happened before Mum married Dad—so it's really nothing to do with me except that he's my half-brother, I suppose," he rambled thoughtfully before shaking his head and getting back to his original train of thought. "Anyway, I was trying to tell you how we can stop that man."

At that point, Charlie and Beth came into the room, stopping the conversation between the cousins.

"We thought you could use a hand," Charlie offered.

"Jasper dear, can you take some of those biscuits and give them out to the other boys?" Beth passed a plate to her son.

"Yes, Mum," he said as he grabbed two handfuls before heading out the back door.

"I hope he wasn't pestering you too much," Beth said, turning back to Claire.

"No, he's a good boy. Just asking questions is all," Claire replied.

They busied themselves with making the drinks and then helped to carry them into the living room. There was no chance during the rest of the afternoon to talk privately to either David or Geoff about what Jasper had tried to tell her. But she did manage to pull out her red booklet for a moment to consult about Longevity. It only gave the most basic of information about the Talent, but it did give one hint.

Studies of those with Longevity have found that they have sought out one with Light Talent to end their lives, but this must only be done with a Healer, a Recaller, and a Mind Touch present.

While she was there, she flipped to the Light Talent. Again, only the briefest of description was available—except that she reread one specific sentence with more interest.

Those with this particular Talent can also use it to restore life but also to take it.

But there was no more about that Talent in the small text. *Just another thing to look up,* she thought to herself.

Hours later, after everyone had left, Claire was found in her uncle's study—poring over the books that were stored there. She sat on the floor with her legs crossed and piles surrounding her. Her great-aunt and great-uncle stood in the doorway watching.

"What on earth are you searching for now?" Geoff's voice made her jump as she clutched the book she was immersed in to her chest.

"Sorry, I…" She looked at the mess on the floor around her. "I'll pick them up right away." As she jumped up, she managed to knock a pile over and it went sprawling, hitting another pile in its path. Claire quickly looked at Lilith and again apologised.

"Never mind that. Come on, you can tell us what you were looking for while we help you pick them up." They came into the room and Claire explained how Jasper had desperately wanted to tell her about something he had learned about his Talent.

"What was it?" Geoff asked.

"That's the thing—I've no idea. We were interrupted by Beth and Charlie. I've spent all afternoon trying to figure it out. But I can only find little hints on the Talent—nothing really in depth. They all seem to mention the ability to both restore and take life, but there's been no further mention of it or even how to carry out the Talent."

"That will be because of all the Talents, this has the most destructive force. The killing force. If a person with the Light Talent was deemed to be someone who could not be trusted with the ability to kill, then they were simply never given the opportunity to learn how to do it," Lilith told her.

The room was put to rights, and they sat down in the chairs at the desk. Claire noticed that Geoff had made a small pile beside him and asked what they were for.

"These are the ones that my Talent has told me might have information we are looking for on Longevity and how they can be dealt with."

"But isn't that in the red booklet already?" Claire rummaged around in her pocket and pulled out her now very battered copy, turning to the last page. "There it is. '*Studies of those with Longevity have found that they have sought out one with Light Talent to end their lives, but this must only be done with a Healer, a Recaller, and a Mind Touch present.*' I remembered that I had read it when I first got the book—I was curious about Marcus's Longevity Talent. But I thought nothing of it until now."

"That's because the more you use a Talent, the more it becomes part of you. Such as Geoff here picked out those books and put them aside as he was cleaning up. You're maturing in your Talents quite quickly and becoming proficient in so many." Lilith listed them off on her fingers. "Hiding, Flying, and Recall—not to mention the fact you can use two of those at the same time and are also receiving Dream Messages." She gave a speculative look at her great-niece and said to Geoff, "I think we may have a Chameleon on our hands."

"No, she's just a quick study, that's all," Geoff replied with a scoff as he placed a stack of books on his desk.

"To have two Physical Talents and combine them together is one thing, but to also have a Mental Talent mixed in there as well? I think she is. Oh, I wish we had time to explore this thought more!" She looked wistful as she spoke the last words.

"But aren't Chameleons extremely rare? And isn't it hard to identify one?" Geoff asked his sister.

Claire wasn't so sure whether they were talking about her or not. The Chameleon Talent had fascinated her when she first read the booklet—someone who had the ability to learn and become proficient and sometimes excel at other Talents. A Talented all-rounder was how she had first thought of it. She came out of her thoughts and found they were both looking at her.

"Look, I don't know if I'm a Chameleon or not—all I know is that passage in the red booklet tells me something. That Marcus can die, and unfortunately, it's up to one with the Light Talent to do it—in the presence of a Healer and a Recaller and Mind Touch. Is there a Healer we can call on? Because I know I can do the Recall, but I'll be damned if I'd let anyone use Jasper to kill Marcus."

They both looked shocked at her statement and then realised that she was right. Jasper had the Light Talent.

"No, I wouldn't ever dream of sending that boy into such a dangerous situation and use his Talent like that—he's only ten!" Geoff exclaimed. "But if you were to study the Light Talent, maybe you could…" He trailed away, outraging Lilith.

"Don't you dare suggest this young girl use that Talent in such a way! She's only seventeen, for heaven's sake! And you're supposed to be her guardian? God help us!"

"I'll do it," Claire said in a small voice. "It's the only way. First, it's me he wants, so I can get close to him…and second, he doesn't know that I have all these other Talents. So, he won't be suspecting it. It's perfect."

"No, Claire! I won't let you! This isn't like learning different tricks for your free running. Lilith is right. Your parents entrusted me with their only child, and I cannot shirk that responsibility. I *have* to protect you." She opened her mouth to object, but he put his hand up to stop her. "No arguments, Kid. That is my final call on the matter. We will find another way."

Claire slumped back in her seat, but her mind was already working.

Chapter Nineteen

Claire rose early the next morning. After getting dressed, she quietly left the house to go for a run. The need was urgent for her slackened muscles to be stretched and to just run free— to feel the wind in her hair and the blood pump through her body. The light exercise Charlie had allowed her to do wasn't cutting it anymore. And she was looking forward to a bit of solitude. The house had been so busy lately with everyone coming and going, including training with Lilith, all culminating in yesterday's meeting. The thought of being able to just take a breath without someone asking if she was okay seemed like a luxury, and Claire was wanting to wallow in it.

Turning from the front door where she'd carefully tried to make no noise, she headed down the porch steps. When she looked up to the gate, Claire stopped in her tracks. Leaning on it and stretching were not just one of her uncles, but two. Ben and David waved and smiled at her as she heard a window open from above. She turned to look up in time to see Geoff's face leaning out.

"Did you really think you could pull a fast one on me, Kid? Shame on you! Have a nice run," he called out, cheerily waving and then retreating back into the house.

Turning back to her uncles on the street, she shook her head. "I hope you old guys can keep up!" She exited through the gate David was holding open for her.

"I know I can run all day, but I don't know about the city slicker over there." David pointed at Ben casually with a thumb.

"Don't worry about me, old man. I can hold my own," Ben replied good naturedly.

They set off down the street at a fair pace and Claire realised how much she'd missed this simple pleasure. Up ahead she could see a sizable brick fence. It had towering pillars that teased and beckoned Claire.

"Don't freak out!" she yelled at her two escorts as she ran ahead.

With her words loud in the still of the morning, Claire launched herself into a series of forward somersaults twisting in mid-air to backwards tucks—then into cartwheels and side flips until she came to that brick fence. She launched herself up off the footpath and landed on the top of the first pillar. Without missing a beat, she leapt from one pillar to the other—performing perfect somersaults in between and culminating at the end in a double somersault with a twist—landing perfectly on her toes.

Claire felt exhilarated. It was the first time since she'd been brought to the village that she had done even the smallest bit of free running. She turned, flung her arms in the air, and pirouetted on the spot, letting out a yell of delight. Stunned, her uncles watched their niece demonstrate her great skill.

"That felt great!" she exclaimed.

"Shh, you will wake the whole neighbourhood," David said.

"I don't think she really cares," Ben opined with a smile on his face.

The pair of uncles took off after her as she sprinted to the end of the street, turning onto the road that led to David's house.

Running at an almost sprint all the way, Claire was impressed that Ben had enough stamina to keep up. Aware that David's Talent could let him run all day and night, if necessary, she knew she could go faster, but she was enjoying herself too much. Her muscles were working in perfect harmony, and she could feel them loosen and reawaken to her every demand. She decided that having a Talent was all very well and good, but nothing could beat true physical exertion—bending her body to her will and the reward of it replying and obeying. They turned into the driveway that led to David's farmhouse and she picked up speed, beating them both to the front door. She stood there panting, waiting for them to join her. Laughing as they came to a stop, Ben leaned down with his hands on his knees, puffing away.

The door opened behind them, and Claire turned to see her aunt come out of the house in a dressing gown. Claire decided she preferred Beth without makeup and the severe hairdo. Her naturally dark ginger hair fell loosely around her shoulders in long, lazy curls.

"What on earth is going on?" Beth demanded.

"I'm sorry, Aunt Beth, I didn't mean to be so loud," Claire apologised.

"That's all right, Claire, I just wasn't expecting you and your entourage so early," she said, looking pointedly at her husband.

"I left you a note," David reminded his wife.

"Yes, I know you did—thank you—but you told me last night." She blushed slightly at the mention of the note. "Well, you had all better come inside. I'll put some coffee on." She held the door open for them and watched them move into the house. "Good morning, Benjamin. I see Geoff roped you into this as well."

"That he did, Beth. And please, call me Ben."

Beth made them a hearty breakfast as David regaled her with the story of Claire's free running demonstration. On more than one occasion, she had to remind both Ben and David that the boys were still asleep, only to turn around and find them standing in the doorway, both bleary-eyed and in their pyjamas. Space was made for them, and they all sat together. It was now the turn of Jasper and Hunter to hear the story as they ate. At the end, both boys looked at Claire and asked if she could show them what she could do.

"There will be no such demonstration until both of you have helped with the dishes, washed up, dressed, and brushed your teeth properly," Beth told them, and they set to their tasks at the greatest of speed.

Claire wondered if this was what it was like in most households: noisy and full of chatter. She tried to remember what it was like before her parents had died. But only vague recollections came to mind.

"Claire, are you all right?" her aunt asked gently from beside her.

She looked at Beth and nodded. "I was just trying to remember what it was like before Mum and Dad..." She trailed off. A silence descended on the room, and she could feel tears start in her eyes.

"What I remember of your mother was that she always tried to pinch my bacon!" David said cheerfully. "And she never shut up!" This made Claire laugh a little and the tension was broken.

"John was always trying to pull one over on Dad. I don't know why he thought he could get away with it," Ben said. "It seemed to become a game between them. I know that it didn't stop when you all lived in the city. Funny things would suddenly turn up in the mail for Dad."

"You know, you still have family who love you very much. You are always welcome here, Claire." This last statement was from Beth, and it took the girl by surprise.

It was at that moment that Jasper and Hunter made an appearance, claiming their cousin's attention.

"All right, you lot—outside. But as soon as Claire has finished, I want you back up to your rooms to clean them and then get on with your other jobs."

A chorus of "Yes, Mum" came back at her as they were pulling Claire out of the back door by both hands.

The performance didn't disappoint the pair as she tumbled and leapt around the yard. Claire performed backflips and somersaults, flinging herself up into the oak tree in the corner and then almost flying to the swing set. *Ooh*ing and *ahh*ing, they clapped and called out to her as she ran straight to the wall of the house—almost running up the side and pushing off with her right toes, she pulled up with her arms, bringing her left knee up to drive the spin and tucking her arms in. With speed, she performed a 360 backflip with a double twist and landed on her toes with legs bent to cushion the landing.

Straight back into a run, she leaped into another side spin and butterfly motion and a set of cartwheels. The movements were so fluid that it was hard to tell where one movement finished, and another began. But the trick the boys liked best was the Kong vault, where she'd leap over obstacles like an ape in motion.

Claire was puffing when she had finally made her last landing and called it quits, saying that she still had to run home. They begged her to continue—to do some more tricks—but their mother appeared at the door and told them that that was enough. The boys both thanked Claire and then trooped into the house to get on with their chores.

When Claire joined Ben, Beth and David back in the house, David had changed for his day's work on the farm.

"I guess I had better get going, Uncle Geoff will be wondering where I am. Thank you for breakfast, Beth. It was wonderful," Claire said.

"I'm surprised you weren't sick after eating so much and then tumbling around out back." Beth laughed.

"I can give you a lift, if you like," David offered.

"That's all right. I still feel like running. It feels like ages since I used my muscles properly." A small groan came from Ben's direction as he heaved himself off his chair. "It's all right, Uncle Ben. I can make it back myself. I do know the way."

"Not if I want to live. Uncle Geoff would have my hide. He still scares me."

"Uncle Geoff? He's a pussycat!" Claire said, laughing a little.

"I'll tell him you said that," Ben said with an evil smile.

"Not if I get there first." On their way out, she gave her aunt and uncle a quick kiss and left Ben in her wake.

As they ran home, she felt a bit disappointed that she had not managed to do what she went there for. Claire had decided the night before to try and talk to Jasper and ask him exactly what it was that he wanted to tell her. She thought that he had been trying to say he'd discovered the same thing that she had—that his Talent could be used as a weapon—but a little confirmation would have been good. The plan she had decided on only needed her to study more—to learn how to perform the Light Talent as Geoff had started to suggest—but she didn't want to ask Lilith for the book she needed. Over and over in her mind, in time to the pounding of her feet on the road was, *I must get that book.*

While they jogged back, a question came to her mind that maybe Ben could help her with. "I was wondering—how can someone get hold of the plans for a building?"

Unlike her, Ben was puffing hard, and it took him a while to answer. "Why?"

"I was just curious." Again, she waited and then realised he had stopped. She turned back to him and waited for him to catch his breath.

"I know why you're asking and I'm not going to tell you."

"But Ben…"

"No. I will not help you with this insane idea you have."

"What idea?" she asked as innocently as possible.

"Don't lie to me. I know something has been concocting in that brain of yours! Look, we may have only just met, and you may look like your mother—but you have the scheming of your father. So, don't ask me to do what it is that I think you want me to do, and I won't mention this conversation to Uncle Geoff." She nodded and then started to run again, leaving Ben to catch up.

They reached Geoff's house and Ben said his breathless goodbyes, continuing down the road to Malcolm and Grace's house. She waved him off and entered the house, calling out that she was home.

"Do you want something to eat?" Geoff asked.

"No thanks. I ate at David and Beth's house," she said as she walked into the kitchen and then stopped. Mary was sitting at the kitchen table with a cup cradled in her hands, not looking happy.

"There you go, Mary, you can ask her yourself. Excuse me. I must go get dressed." Claire hadn't even noticed that he was still in his dressing gown and as he passed, he squeezed her shoulder. "Mary has a couple of questions for you."

Claire went to the fridge and took out a bottle of water from it. "What can I do for you, Ms Sheridan?" she asked as she twisted the cap off. She sat opposite the older woman in the seat her uncle had just vacated.

"I'd like to know where my son is, please. The day he went missing, he told me that he was going out to find you, but he never came home. Do you know where he is?"

"No, I don't, sorry." Claire sipped the water.

"I just find it remarkable that the day he goes missing is the same day that you turn back up from your mysterious disappearance. What do you have to say to that?" Mary asked, her eyebrows raising while placing her cup on the table.

"I'm sorry Jack is missing, but I really don't know what's happened to him." While Claire was telling her this, all she could think about was throwing it back in her face and demanding to know why she was working with Marcus. And why she had told no one that Jack was Marcus's son. Instead, she remained calm and waited for Mary to reply.

"I don't believe you!" she almost spat at the girl. "There's something fishy going on here and I am going to get to the bottom of it."

Just then, Claire had a thought. "I heard that there was a black car spotted in the village, maybe that had something to do with Jack's disappearance."

Claire watched the older woman's face blanch at the thought, and she spotted a slight twitch to Mary's right eye. She could see the Elder was having a hard time keeping her emotions under control, as her jaw was clenched tightly, and her breathing had deepened.

"Yes, I have already been told about the unknown car lurking about that day. I shall make my inquires elsewhere," she said through gritted teeth while standing up from the table. Mary made to move towards the door when she stopped and turned back to the girl. "How are your studies progressing?"

"Really good. I think I'm pretty much getting a handle on both Talents now. I did think that Jack was being fussy over our lessons, though. He kept saying that I needed more time under his instruction."

Mary's mouth started to work, but no words came out. "Tell your uncle thank you for the tea and the conversation. Goodbye." With that, she stalked down the hall and out of the front door. Geoff re-entered the kitchen shortly after.

"Thank God she's gone. She insisted on staying until she had spoken with you."

"I didn't tell her much. I did allude to the black car, and her reaction was priceless. She didn't want to show me that the car was significant. Anyway, I don't think I asked you where you're keeping Jack."

"The less you know the better, Kid. Now hit the shower. You stink, you grotty teenager!" He laughed and pushed her to the door.

Later that night, after she had gone to bed, Claire made sure that the room was as dark as she could make it then sat cross-legged on her bed and put her hands together, like she was praying. She tried to apply the same techniques of concentration for shrinking into trying to produce a light—no matter how small. Small beads of sweat sprung from her forehead as she bent her will to the task, but no matter how much concentration was put in, she couldn't produce even the smallest of sparks. Claire got up and started to pace her room, shaking her hands.

"Come on, Claire! How hard can it be?"

Once again, she sat down, resuming her efforts. She tried placing her hands in different positions, palm to palm, fingertips and heel of the hand together, fingers apart, but still there was no result.

Claire looked at her watch and sighed in frustration. She'd been trying for two hours and was almost ready to give up for the night—she hoped to get a quiet word with Jasper in the morning. The thought came to her that Geoff would have most likely retired for the night by now. She opened her door just a crack and peeped out into the hallway. All seemed dark upstairs. She opened it up further and crept out onto the landing, moving slowly to the head of the stairs. Satisfied that Geoff was now in bed and there were no lights on downstairs, she started to descend. Halfway down, the stairs tried to give her away when her foot hit the squeaky step. She paused and waited to hear if she had disturbed Geoff, but there was nothing—just the quiet of the night.

Just in case she had woken him up, Claire made her way to the kitchen and ostentatiously got a drink of water for herself. She leaned against the counter—waiting for her uncle to put in an appearance—but again, there was nothing. Leaving the glass upended on the drying board, she tiptoed to the study. The door was shut, and she couldn't see any light from under it, so she carefully pulled the handle down. Pushing it open and entering, Claire just as carefully closed it behind her. She made her way blindly to the desk and felt her way to turn on the lamp that sat there. The click might as well have been a gun shot, giving away her intentions. She waited again, but as there were still no sounds from upstairs, she went to the pile of books.

Wishing she had her uncle's Talent, she started to discount the books she knew the contents of and pulled out others that she didn't know. She moved to Geoff's desk and sat down, pulling the first book off the pile, and opening it. The musty smell of old books no longer bothered her, as she had read too many of them now. Book after book was discounted and moved to one side, and when it seemed her eyes couldn't read any more since they felt tired and sore, Claire opened a small book clad in green. There on the first page in a cursive, stylised hand was written, *The Light*.

"Finally!" she spoke into the dim room.

Leaning back in the chair and pulling her legs up underneath her, Claire settled herself in to read. It was all laid out in a clear and concise hand, as the writer had even glued in an index at the front of the book. It would be a shame to not start at the beginning and read the whole thing, because to do otherwise would—she felt—be an insult to the writer. So, she began.

"What on earth are you doing in here?" Geoff's voice broke into Claire's consciousness. She clasped the book she had been reading into her chest tightly. Sleepily, she looked up at her uncle and stared at him as it slowly dawned on her that the sun was up, and the new day had begun. She untangled her legs from underneath her body and stretched out.

"What time is it?" she asked, yawning loudly.

"It's seven o'clock and you still haven't answered my question."

"I'm sorry. I couldn't sleep last night, so I thought I'd come down here and read." He walked over to her and held out his hand. She passed him the book and he opened it.

"I thought we'd agreed that you wouldn't be dealing with Marcus, so there was no need to read up on the Light Talent!"

"No, you told me that you didn't want me to. I never agreed to anything. You dragged me here and encouraged me in my Talents and now you suddenly want me to just stop?" Her voice grew louder as Claire flared up, the frustration she had been feeling started to spill out of her. She hadn't yelled at Geoff for a long time, but now it was all coming out.

"Claire, please. I love you and want to make sure you're safe," he placated.

"That's crap! You forced me to this little village and introduced me to the Talents. And now you wanna wrap me up in cotton wool! I thought you wanted me to be part of this."

"I did—I *do*—but things have changed. It has become more dangerous than I thought. We've discovered that there have been moles in The Community. They are trying to bend things to their will, and ultimately, it is you they wish to use the most," he retorted.

"Why can't you just trust me? That I can be of use to The Community?"

"You can. But we just have to think things through a bit more."

"I'm sick of waiting. And I'm tired of thinking. I want to act!" She pushed past him and ran upstairs, slamming the door behind her. She flung off her pyjamas and threw on a shirt and shorts, pulling on her sneakers and running back down the stairs. She yanked open the front door and raced down the path, jumping over the gate to get to the street. From behind her, she could hear Geoff pleading for her to come back, but she took off on a run.

Hearing her heart beating in her ears, Claire's anger was still not spent as she sped up—the air pumping in and out of her lungs in time to her pounding feet. The measured stride ate up the ground, putting more distance between her and her uncle. Trying to exhaust herself, she continued to run, only stopping when she realised tears were streaming down her face. Her breathing slowed, and she just stood, not really seeing what was about her. She dashed her hands across her face, clearing the tears from her eyes.

From behind her, she could hear a car and she knew—without even looking—that it was Geoff. She stepped to the side of the road and waited for him to pull up.

"Do you feel better now?" he asked in anger.

"No." Claire realised she sounded like an irrational, petulant child. "I'm sorry I yelled," she apologised.

"Get in the car, Kid. Let's go home and get some breakfast." She nodded, climbed into his car, and he drove off. "You know, you really shouldn't pull this kind of stunt on me before I've had my coffee." He smiled at her. "And definitely *not* before I'm dressed." It was at that point she noticed Geoff was still in his pyjamas. She apologised again, but this time with amusement in her voice.

Back at home, they sat together at the table. The remains of their breakfast lay between them as they each held onto a cup of coffee.

"Do you want to go first or shall I?" Geoff asked when the tension between them was palpable.

"I don't know why, but it's important to me, Uncle Geoff. I understand that you love and care for me—that you're worried about me. But I have this drive inside telling me that this is something I have to do." She sat back and waited for his reply.

"I can't pretend to understand what you're feeling, Claire." He almost seemed at a loss for words. "Sometimes it feels like I've been making it up as I go along, and now I find myself at a point where I either hold you back or release you to your full potential. But do you realise that what you plan on doing is murder? No matter how you twist or turn it—or even try to justify it—it is still murder."

"I understand that, Uncle Geoff. I really do. I know what needs to be done can't be undone and it'll change me forever. But I see it so clearly that I can see each move that I have to make, just like when I'm planning a power move. No, it is not something I have been obsessing on every waking moment; it's just there." Trying to make her uncle understand where she was coming from raised the feelings of frustration, and she fought hard to suppress them.

They fell silent for a while as he processed what she had told him. He didn't quite know what to make of it. Feeling at a loss as to what to do, he reached across the table and put his large hand over hers.

"I need to think. This doesn't mean I don't value what you've told me. I've heard you. What it means is that—simply—I need some time to think."

"Okay. Thanks for listening."

"You can go back to that book," he replied, and Claire looked surprised at that. "You're going to find a way to read it anyway, so you might as well have my blessing for it. Now go on, Kid," he dismissed her. Leaving the room, she went straight to the study to retrieve the book.

Chapter Twenty

No matter how hard Claire tried, she just couldn't get the technique down for creating even the smallest and briefest of Light. Day and night, she pored over the books, garnering what she could from them. Every possible hint she found was studied and committed to memory. In desperation, she even tried techniques from other Talents, but nothing worked, and her frustration levels increased.

This frustration did not help the fact that her nightmares had started up again. Adam was becoming more and more insistent in his calls as she tried to reach out to him through the dream and talk. Each morning Claire would wake restless and tired, until one bright morning a few days later she woke with a smile believing that she had finally managed to return a message to him.

But it was the lack of progress of producing even the smallest of sparks that Claire was still worried about. And the fact that her uncle hadn't said a word to her about doing something about Marcus. The need to learn Light was so urgent that it pulled at her every day—like an itch that had to be scratched but never subsided. And she determined that speaking with Jasper was the only way she could get started on the road she'd decided to take.

Claire then went to Lynnette and Bob's with the hope of trying to organise some time with the boys. Her hope turned into a reality when she saw Jasper and Hunter running around the front yard of their grandparents' home. Quickly, they rounded on her. The boys wanted to see more tricks and somersaults, to which Claire readily agreed—in return for a favour from both. She ran and jumped, performing her best for the pair of boys as her antics made them squeal with delight. Hunter jumped up and down—so much so that it brought Lynnette out of the house to see what all the noise was about.

Breathlessly, Claire greeted her grandmother as the boys begged her for more. "Let me have a rest first!" she said, laughing at them.

"Come inside and have a drink. I've just made a jug of lemonade. You know, we have had the biggest crop of lemons this year and I'm running out of ideas on how to use them all," Lynnette said as she ushered everyone into the kitchen and handed them full glasses of homemade lemonade with ice cubes.

Claire took a sip. "Mmm, this is good. Thank you, Grandma. How about I take these two outside to sit under the tree while we drink it?"

"Oh, would you, Claire? I have so much to do this afternoon, and the boys get under my feet."

"No probs. Come on, you two, let's go." She led them out the back door and into the beautifully kept garden.

Sitting at the garden table, they drank their cold drinks while Hunter chatted away about all the fun games they'd played that day—including one game that Jasper had invented called Chase the Light. Claire asked him more about the game.

"Well, Jasper makes one of his light thingies and sends it out to hide somewhere in the garden, and I have to go chase it. It is so much fun, but last time, he sent it behind those flowers over there and they have lots of pointy things, which hurt." He pointed towards the rose garden in the corner and then showed Claire the scratches on his arm.

"Jasper! That wasn't a very nice thing to do to your little brother," Claire told him. "How do you make the light, anyway?"

"It's easy, Claire. All you have to do is put your hands together and then think hard on Light." Then Jasper did just that, and a small ball of light bounced on his hand until he sent it out into the garden—with Hunter in hot pursuit.

"Can you teach me?"

"Why do you want to learn how to create Light?" Jasper asked her.

"You wouldn't understand. You're too young."

"Everyone tells me that. When I ask Mum and Dad what's happening and why there are so many meetings and whispered conversations, they tell me that there's nothing for me or Hunter to worry about. They always make us go outside and play. I'm tired of it! I was the one who caught Jack and let you get away, so if I can do that, then why can't I know what's happening?"

Claire realised that Jasper seemed older than his ten years and that maybe he could handle some of the truth.

"Okay," she started hesitantly. "I'll give you the gist of it, but if you let anything slip, you did not—I repeat—did *not* hear it from me, all right?" He nodded in agreement. "Good. Have you heard of a man called Marcus?"

"Yes. At the meeting at Mr Brown's house—when I was listening in."

"Well, Marcus is a very bad man."

"Claire, I'm not five. You can talk to me in more grown-up terms."

"I'm sorry. Let me try again. Marcus wants to bend the world to suit his means. He wants to use those with the Talent to make himself richer and to influence governments. At the moment, we know he has some Talented working with him—such as Jack—but we aren't sure exactly how many. He's going against everything that The Community stands for."

"But if we have these Talents, why can't we use them to get rich?"

"Have you discussed your Talent with your father at all?"

"No, not really. He gave me a couple of books to read, but none of it made any sense."

"Okay, well, it has to do with the history of The Community. When it was first established here, it was because our people had been exiled from our homeland. We were cast out because of jealousy and fear from those who didn't have Talent. From what I understand from the Blue Booklet, there was one family who had decided that sharing their abilities for the betterment of others wasn't good enough. They wanted it all for themselves. So, for the safety of those others, they were all driven from the area that they had lived in for many years."

"Where did we come from originally? I read in the booklet that we're descended from a much older race of people."

"Yes, it does say that. But there's no answer I can give that could in any way tell you. It is simply lost in time."

"Wouldn't it be cool if there was a time travel Talent?" Jasper said eagerly.

"Yes, very cool," she agreed with a grin.

"So, what are we gonna do about Marcus?" he asked bashfully.

"For a start, the 'we' does not include you. But it has been decided that we have to stop him."

"How?"

"I don't think that matters right now, Jasper. All you need to know is that I intend to stop him."

Jasper looked at his older cousin very seriously. "You're going to kill him. Aren't you?"

After a brief reflection, she replied. "Yes."

"And by you learning the use of my Talent, you hope to kill him?"

"That's the plan."

"How are you going to use my Light?" he asked, confused.

"Have you been allowed to read up on your Talent?"

"No. Dad read me the passage in the Red Booklet, but I wasn't allowed to read it for myself. I could tell he was hiding something."

"I think he was trying to protect you on this one. You are going to have to take it up with your dad," Claire said, coming to realise she may have told him too much.

"What is it about my Talent that you won't tell me?"

"Some uses for it can be dangerous, so you're going to have to be taught how to control it carefully."

"I already can make it grow larger or smaller. And just the other day, I discovered that I can make it hotter!" His eyes widened. "Are you going to burn him?"

"No! Definitely not! There is another way to use it. But I'm not going into it right now. It may only ever be wishful thinking, anyway—if I can't even manage to master it enough to create a spark."

Claire and Jasper put their heads together as he tried to teach her how to make a small light. Again, and again, he made lights and sent them out into the garden until it looked like they had been visited by fairies—while Hunter tried to catch them all. The afternoon wore on until they finally gave up when Beth came to the back door and called them in.

Believing that she might have enough to keep going with, Claire said goodbye to them all and made her way home as she kept thinking about the information Jasper had told her.

Just after Claire had finished the dishes in the early evening, a pounding knock came from the front door. Peeking through the curtain to see who it was, she was surprised to see an unhappy-looking David standing there. She opened the door for him and even before she had a chance to open her mouth, he was inside and shouting at her.

"What the bloody hell did you say to my son this afternoon?" His face was red, and he was breathing hard.

"He wanted to know what was going on and I told him the truth! I told him that Marcus was a bad man and that we hoped to stop him."

"I don't want you anywhere near my son, do you understand me? It is not for you to decide what Jasper should know, as that's up to Beth and me and we will decide when he's ready to hear it!" He stared at her and attempted to get his anger under control. "You are too much like your father—so reckless. If it weren't for him, my sister would still be alive."

He then stormed out of the house, slamming the door behind him. Claire was in too much shock at his words to move. She didn't even notice that Geoff had come to her side and put his arms around her. With that simple comforting gesture, Claire burst into tears and turned into his embrace.

"David's just mad. And I'm sure he didn't mean it, Claire. It wasn't John's fault. He's only trying to protect his own family. The one truly to blame is Marcus."

With the dreadful words David had said to her the night before still rolling around in her mind, Claire was at a loss on how she could fix things the next morning. Her hands went to her head, and she just wanted to crawl out of her skin and hide. She berated herself for being so selfish, for not thinking of what other people might think or feel. How did she get to this point that she could be so conceited in her thinking? Just how could she believe that she knew best? These thoughts and feelings were starting to make her feel sick to her stomach. And one idea kept coming to her. *Run.*

Out the door she went, and she ran as fast as she could. But with every step she took, words kept haunting her. What had she done? Had she ruined her chances to know her family? Would David set them all against her? Was Uncle Geoff right? Should she not get herself too involved? Constant questions cornered her. Simply wanting peace, Claire's racing mind—and body—just couldn't calm down for one second.

On and on Claire ran until she didn't recognize her surroundings. Pulling up out of the sprint pace she had set herself in, Claire headed to the side of the road and leaned against the fence. Her breath came in huge gasps as she tried to fill her lungs with oxygen. Small black spots floated in front of her eyes, and she rubbed them, but they were still there and getting bigger. Soon, everything was black, and the world tipped on its head.

When Claire came to, she found herself on the ground—crumpled up in a ball. As she stood, her head swam with a wave of dizziness—but not in the same way as it had with the concussions. Fighting the feeling off, she immediately started to run for home as dread turned her stomach to knots. Heading the same way as she had come, Claire hoped that she could find her way even if she had no idea where she was.

"Claire!" a voice shrieked from afar as Claire looked around for the source. "Claire, I'm sorry I got you in trouble," Jasper yelled, suddenly appearing on the other side of a fence.

"Not now, Jasper. I have to get home."

"I just want to apologise. I didn't think Dad would get so mad."

"It's okay. I just can't talk now. I have to see Uncle Geoff. It's really important."

"Is there anything I can do?" Jasper asked.

As she was running away, she replied to him over her shoulder. "Tell your dad to get to Uncle Geoff's right now!" She sped off down the road, not stopping until she reached the front door.

The door slammed against the wall as she burst through it. Calling Geoff's name while running from room to room looking for him, Claire saw that he wasn't home. Panic started to rise in her gut as she picked up the phone to call his mobile, but there was no answer. She tried Lilith next, thinking he may have gone there.

"No, Claire, I haven't seen him today, but he may be with Malcolm and Grace," Lilith informed her.

As she hung up, a car pulled up with a screech and she saw David running up the path as she met him at the still-open door.

"What's wrong? Jasper said you looked like you had seen a ghost!"

"Maybe I have."

"That doesn't make sense, Claire. Where's Geoff?" David demanded.

"I don't know. When I left, he was here in the study, but he isn't here now and he's not answering his phone. I just rang Aunt Lilith, and she hasn't seen him, either. I just need to talk to him right away."

"Okay, calm down. Tell me everything and then we'll both go looking for him." He followed her into the kitchen as she got herself a drink of water.

"I'm not sure what happened. One minute I was leaning against a fence, taking a break before the run home, and the next, I was waking up on the ground. But I had a dream. I'm sure it's a Dream Message. Adam told me that Marcus is on his way here. He said Mary had told him that we had Jack and knew everything. And he was coming to deal with it himself. I got the feeling of pain and panic from him." She was still panting and drinking water.

"Both you and Geoff are sure these are true Dream Messages? I mean, you couldn't still be affected by the concussions?"

"I'm sure of what I am seeing, David. I've been trying to communicate back—with only a little bit of success. But I am totally sure," she said with conviction.

"Right." He was pacing the room with a look of uncertainty on his face. "Right. This is what we are going to do. You, young lady, are going to go upstairs and lock yourself in your room and hide. You are only to come out if you hear either Geoff or myself on the other side of your door. Got me? And don't argue with me, as I'm still upset about yesterday." He cut her off before she could speak. "I'll go look for Geoff, and we're going to have to sit down and discuss this and come up with a plan. Quickly," he added. "Go. I'll be back shortly." He ushered her out of the kitchen and steered her towards the stairs.

At that moment, Geoff appeared in the frame of the open door. "What the…Look, David, if you're still upset about yesterday, I'm sorry."

"No, Uncle Geoff, it's not about yesterday," Claire broke in. "Where have you been? I've been calling you and you didn't answer!"

Geoff looked at his great-niece's frightened face. "What's happened? Are you all right? Did you hurt yourself again?"

"No, I'm fine, but I do have something to tell you. I've had another Dream Message."

"When?" They all walked into the lounge and sat down.

Claire sipped her water and retold Geoff what she'd been told in the Dream Message. After she had finished, David spoke up.

"Can we be truly sure that what Adam's telling Claire is the truth? Could he be working for his father still?"

"I believe him!" Claire protested. "I'm sure that he's trying to warn us. I've known him most of my life." She groaned in frustration and stood up from her chair. "The night he let me go, there was a look in his eye. He was feeling sickened with what he had done to me, and the thought that his father was the one who had told him to do it made it worse. That's why he let me go. I told him if he ever needed me to call, and he has found a way to do that, via Dream Message. The only way for someone to do that is to first have a very good bond with the person they're trying to reach. Adam and I have that bond." She saw that her Uncle Geoff had a speculative look in his eye. "No, Uncle Geoff, not that kind of bond. The kind that's built on friendship—made by two kids in similar situations—and having lost a parent or parents, in my case. We understood each other's moods and supported each other through them. But this is getting us nowhere!" She threw her hands up in the air and thumped back down into the chair.

"Please don't throw yourself into the chairs, Claire. And you're right. This is not getting us anywhere. I believe that it's time. Time to get organised and plan this. I'm going to go make a few calls to confirm that Marcus has left the city and is on his way here. David, can you call Ben and Charlie, as well as Lilith, Malcolm, and your father? They are the only ones I trust at the moment."

"What about Mum and Grace?"

"Not yet. Not that I don't trust them," he said quickly. "But I need clear heads, and well, Grace can be a bit—you know…"

"I know." David nodded back. "On it." He pulled out his phone and started dialling. Geoff went straight to his study, shutting the door. Claire looked between the two. "Close your mouth, Claire, you'll catch flies." David then started talking on the phone to Ben.

Half an hour later, the group had assembled in the living room at Geoff's. Geoff was standing by the window looking at them all and took a deep breath before he started.

"Okay, so here's how it stands. Claire has had another Dream Message from Adam. She's certain it is one, but just to be on the safe side, Charlie can you check her over?" Claire started to protest but he talked over her. "I am just covering all bases, Claire, and as Charlie can tell you, the symptoms of a concussion can still affect you for weeks afterwards."

"Come on, Claire. Let's get this out of the way," Charlie said as she stood. They went to the kitchen, where it was quieter.

"All right. Let's have a look at you." She started with the light in the eyes. "Have you had any more headaches?"

"No."

"Any pains?"

"No."

"Any blackouts?"

"No, except for this morning when I received the Dream Message." Charlie took a step back and folded her arms.

"How long were you out for?"

"I'm not sure. I don't think it was for very long."

"To get to the first REM stage when you are asleep can take up to ninety minutes."

"That's why I'm so sure that this was a Dream Message and not just an ordinary dream. I'm sure I was only out for ten minutes—at the most." Charlie moved closer, starting to manipulate Claire's neck and head.

"I'm still not happy. I'd like to get you into the hospital to get another scan done. You didn't have one after that last concussion and I'm worried that you may have some damage."

"Can't we do that another day? I really wanna be here for this." She gestured towards the lounge.

"Claire, I'm only trying to look after you. If there is something wrong and I did nothing, your uncle would have my guts for garters. He scares me, you know."

Claire laughed a little. "He said the same thing about you!"

"Did he? Then good. But that doesn't change the fact that I want to get you checked properly. We'll go now and can be back in an hour, as they'll still surely be arguing about what to do. Please, let me look after you."

"What if there's something wrong?" Claire asked with worry in her voice.

"Then we can act on it. I'm not a doctor for nothing, you know." She raised an eyebrow at the girl.

"You're a Healer?" Claire asked and Charlie nodded. "Do you use your Talent in the city?"

"Oh, hell, no. No, I use regular medicine in the city—the normal methods of treating people. I only use the Healing here in the village and only on those I can truly help."

"But if there is something wrong in my head…"

"Then we will look at it—see if it's something that will heal itself or needs assistance."

"What if the injury is allowing me to receive Adam's messages? They only started after the last concussion."

"And it was because of him that you had that concussion. Claire, you can *what-if* me all you like, but I am still insisting on taking you to the hospital and getting a scan."

"Can't you just use your Talent here and scan my head?"

"Take it as me being as thorough as I can. Why go poking around in there when I can get a machine to pinpoint any problem and then go straight there? Now, are we finished capitulating?" She picked her bag up and waited for Claire to leave the kitchen before her. As they passed the lounge, Charlie let everyone know that she was taking Claire for a scan and not to worry.

The wait at the hospital was excruciating for Claire. Never before had she found it so hard to lie still on the uncomfortable bed while the machine hummed around her. Every time she thought that Charlie was about to take her home, her aunt would tell her, "One more second." Although they were not seconds to Claire—it felt like hours.

Having finally received word that there was nothing wrong with her brain in any way, shape or form, Charlie drove her home. When they returned, they found everyone still arguing about the best way to deal with Marcus and anyone else he may bring with him. Charlie gave her an *I told you so* look and went to join the argument. Around and around the argument went, each time someone coming up with a flaw.

It was at this point that Claire tried to make known the plan she'd been formulating for the last week. She first tried to tell Geoff, but he waved her away.

"Not now, Claire," he said distractedly.

David gave a similar response when asked. They just would not listen to her. And then she spotted Lilith—the woman who held the keys to the knowledge she needed.

"Aunt Lilith, can I talk to you?" she inquired.

"Does it have to be right now, Claire? We're all busy here."

"Yes, it does. Please, Aunt Lilith. Everyone else won't listen to me!" Claire pleaded.

"All right. What is it you want to talk about?" Her aunt turned her full attention on Claire.

"I have a plan, and it's a good one, but I need more info to pull it off."

"What's the plan, Claire? And don't think it'll be you who does anything..."

"The plan is that I use the Light to kill Marcus. But to do that, I first must learn how to produce the Light. I need more information. The books upstairs just don't go into as much detail as I'd like. Can you give me the books I need?" Hope was written all over her face as she looked at her great-aunt.

Lilith was shocked. "I can't believe you'd even contemplate such a plan, Claire. The use of the Light in that way is strictly controlled and only those deemed to have mastery of the Talent are chosen to study further."

"I know that Aunt Lilith. But it is the only way to stop Marcus. He has Longevity, and the only way a person with Longevity can die is at the hands of a Light Talent—with a Healer, a Recaller and Mind Touch present!" Claire's voice rose in frustration, and she soon realised that everyone was looking at her as she was yelling at her great-aunt. "I'm sorry for yelling at you, Aunt Lilith. But it is the only way."

David looked more shocked than anyone else in the room, realising that it was the Talent of his son that was the only way. "Is that why you wanted to talk to Jasper?" he demanded.

"Yes, but only to learn how to create the Light. I would never dream of asking him to do this. He is too young. But I'm having trouble even creating a tiny spark. I just can't get it." She turned back to Lilith. "I need that book—please."

"We haven't agreed to anything yet, Claire," her uncle's measured voice spoke through the crowd. "But just in case, I can't see the harm in letting her have the book, Lilith."

"You are impossible, Geoff! She's just a child. Do you really want her murdering someone? Because that's what it is at the end of the day. We're here arguing about the best way to murder someone and whether or not it is a good idea for a teenage girl to do the deed."

"Yes, Lilith—that is what we are doing—and I think everyone in this room realises that," Geoff replied gravely to his older sister.

"We aren't taking this lightly, Lil." Malcolm spoke up to his twin. "We are as concerned for her welfare as you are—and she is my granddaughter, after all." Everybody agreed.

"We are all family—connected by this girl—and for one reason or another, it has fallen to us to decide how to protect The Community from this threat. And don't forget, Marcus was the one who started murdering people—my daughter and your nephew being two of them," Bob spoke up.

"An eye for an eye, is it?" Lilith demanded.

"I reckon so," Bob responded in his gruff voice. "He has been out there charming his way into riches, threatening and murdering those who won't join him for over a century. It is about time The Community stood up for itself and put a stop to him." The rest of the room nodded.

"All right. She can have the blasted book," Lilith said, finally giving in. "But I still don't think it should be her who carries it out."

They went back to their conversations, discussing the merits and pitfalls of Claire's plan. Lilith left and returned later with the book in her hands.

"Now, you think long and hard on this, Claire. What you are proposing is very dangerous for yourself, and I don't want to have to be there to pick up the pieces after you have fallen apart over it." She saw Claire's stunned look. "I have read the book, you know—I am a Mind Touch, after all. I know that a person with Mind Touch must be present along with a Healer and a Recaller when one with the Light Talent uses their Talent on a person with Longevity. So, you see, Claire, it will not only be you there, but Charlie and I will have to be there as well. Read the book and make your decision." She handed the book to Claire and walked away, leaving a bitter taste in Claire's mouth.

Chapter Twenty-One

All that afternoon she studied and practiced until she was exhausted. But still no spark. She read the book from cover to cover, desperately trying to find that one clue she may have missed—that one hint that would make it all click into place. Claire now felt that frustration was her newest pet hate, and she crumpled herself up into a ball on the floor. Feeling as if she would explode, she tried to do some calming techniques to find some peace. Looking at her watch, she believed that if Marcus was on his way, he would have arrived by now. She remembered when she had met him when she and Adam were children. He always seemed so nice—if not a bit standoffish. But now, knowing what she did, it made her skin crawl.

At some point during the afternoon, it was decided that Mary needed to be dealt with. Geoff and the others were still not telling Claire where they were holding Jack. Lynnette and Grace were called in to help and everyone had to endure the tirade—not just from Grace, but from the usually calm and easy-going Lynnette as well. They'd been kept out of the loop. Apologies were profusely given from all round, and the women agreed to go get Mary. Claire hadn't heard about what happened when they did find her, but now she was curious.

Deciding to take a break, she left her room and went downstairs. Everyone had left—except Geoff, who was sitting at his desk.

"So, have you decided on anything yet?" she asked him curiously as she sat opposite him.

"No, except for putting Mary out of harm's way."

"Is that what we are calling it? I thought we were incarcerating her for passing information and manipulating The Community?" she said authoritatively.

"If Marcus decides that Mary is of no further use, then he'll get rid of her, just as easily as he did your parents," Geoff said quietly. Claire sat in silence, knowing she had been rebuked. "How goes the studies?"

"Not good. I can't even get one little spark going. I don't know what I'm doing wrong." She covered her face with her hands. "I'm following all the instructions. I'm using the meditation technique it tells me to use, and I get myself into a centred state and then nothing!"

"Maybe that's the problem. You're trying too hard. Or maybe, you simply don't have that Talent." He looked at her sternly, his elbows resting on the desk and his fingertips pressed together. Claire chose to ignore that statement.

"How do you get to that point when you know you're ready to search for something?" She hadn't realised until she asked the question that she'd never talked to him properly about his own Talent.

"It's something I've been doing for over fifty years, Claire. It's a part of me and I just do it. If I had to analyse it, I'd say that it's not something I consciously do. I just think of the person or object and then sorta send out feelers for want of a better word. When they touch on what or who I am seeking, I get a sort of tugging or tingling feeling—like someone's pulling a string—and I head off in that direction. To get me to that state before searching, the first thing I do is take in a deep breath and then let it out slowly. These things come with time and practice, Kid. What you are capable of, we have no idea, and frankly, it scares me sometimes. If you are a Chameleon—like Lil thinks you are—then it's up to you to find out what your skills are. Not all Chameleons can take on all Talents. If it comes down to it, a person who practices two Talents can be described as a Chameleon." He leaned back in his chair and waited for her response. When it came, it was not the one he was expecting.

"I'm scared, Uncle Geoff. I'm scared of confronting Marcus. I'm scared of failing and letting you and everyone down. I'm scared of what Adam's going to say, but most of all, I'm scared of losing everybody." A fat tear tracked down her cheek and dripped off her chin, and she dashed away the trail it had left with the back of her hand and gave a small sniff.

"Claire, it's fine to be scared. I'd be very surprised if you weren't—hell, I would be terrified if you weren't!" He got up and walked round his desk and knelt beside her, taking her into his arms. "I can't tell you that it'll be all right. I honestly don't know that it will. But what I can tell you is this: use that fear to your advantage. Keep *trying*. I am so proud of you, and I know your parents would be as well. We all love you, Claire, and we are here to support you."

They were interrupted by a knock at the door. Geoff got up to answer it while Claire dried her eyes and composed herself. She heard David's voice and got up to see not only David, but Jasper enter the hallway. Geoff closed and locked the door behind them and invited them into the living room.

"I can't stay," David declared without even taking a step towards the offered room. "I was just dropping Jasper off. He wants to try to help Claire learn how to produce a Light." He looked at Claire. "And I wanted to apologise for the other day again, Claire. I said a few nasty things that I didn't mean. I was only trying to protect my family."

"I know that, Uncle David, so you don't have to apologise."

"Good," he replied simply. "I'll pick him up later. I've just dropped Beth and Hunter off at my parents', and I am first up on patrol tonight, so I better be going. You behave yourself, young man. Do as you are told."

"Yes, Dad. And anyway, Claire's the one who has to do as she's told," he said with a cheeky grin plastered across his face. His father gently cuffed him around the ear and said his goodbyes.

"Right, you two, how about you go into the living room and make a start? I'll let you know when dinner's ready." Geoff left them.

"So, was it you or was it your Dad who made this suggestion?" Claire asked.

"It was me. And I'm sorry too—for getting you into trouble. But I had so many questions and sometimes, I just blurt things out without really thinking first," Jasper replied.

"That's okay. He was bound to find out, anyway. Let's get to work, shall we?"

They worked together for an hour before they were interrupted by Geoff calling them in for dinner. There was still no progress, and Claire was about to call it quits completely when Jasper passed a small ball of light to her by accident. It sat there bobbing in her hands, twinkling slightly as she stared at it, when Geoff walked into the room.

"You did it!" he exclaimed.

"I didn't, Jasper passed it to me." She sounded both disappointed and in awe of the tiny light in her hand.

"See if you can move it!" Jasper encouraged.

Claire knew the theory on how to make the light move, as it was similar to her own Flight theory. She bent her will to the action and it bobbed a bit more on her hand, so she tried again. This time it flew to her fingertips, teetering at the very edge.

"You've got to allow it to go, Claire. Give it permission to fly," Jasper told her. And she did. With just a point of her finger, the spark flew around the room, dancing lightly in the air. Just for the fun of it, she made the light circle around her uncle's head and laughed as he tried to bat it away. Jasper was on the ground at this point, laughing so hard at Geoff's efforts.

"Come on, Claire, that is enough. Dinner is ready. You can come back and play with the light a bit more after." He spoke to her like she was the same age as Jasper. Reluctantly, she brought the light back to the palm of her hand.

"How do we extinguish it, Jasper?"

"Oh, that's easy. I just squeeze it very tightly in my hand, and it goes out pretty soon."

Claire tried doing just that, but it felt like a small marble in her fist. The tiny ball of light resisted and no matter how hard she tried, she couldn't do it. "It's no good. It just doesn't want to go."

"Here, give it to me," Jasper said as he took the light ball from Claire. Within seconds of him taking it back, the light was gone.

As they walked to the kitchen for dinner, she spoke her thoughts. "Maybe it's because you created it—that you have the ultimate power to extinguish it."

"I don't know. Miss Brown has only given me the beginner's book to learn from." Claire was pleased to hear that someone was giving him access to the information he needed.

After dinner, they practiced some more. By the end of the evening, Claire could make the light change colour and shape and could even make it sparkle like a firework. She practiced making it go hot and then cold, but she still couldn't produce the light herself. Every time, she had to hand it back to Jasper for him to extinguish.

"How about you try again?" Jasper asked. "I'm sure you can make one. Here, I'll place my hands over yours and we'll try together," the boy suggested.

Claire sat on the floor cross-legged, with her cousin sitting opposite her. As she raised her hands up like she was praying, he placed his slightly smaller hands over the top of hers. Claire concentrated once more and went through the steps that Jasper had suggested. But there was still no light.

"I know what you're doing wrong!" Jasper cried out with some excitement. "You have to pull the energy from within you, not from around us. Try it again."

Claire nodded and took a deep breath. This time she did as he suggested and sought within her the energy to bring a little spark to life. She could feel the palms of her hands begin to warm and as she slowly pulled them apart in anticipation, her cousin told her to wait, pressing her hands back together. It felt like ages, as her hands were becoming very hot.

"Okay now. Slowly," Jasper whispered while removing his hands from hers.

Pulling her hands into a cupping position—one on top of the other—dim pulses of light could be seen between her fingers as she took in a deep breath and let it out slowly. When she pulled her hands apart, she saw a small golden light sitting on her palm—barely there and flickering as if it'd go out.

"Put a bit more energy into it," Jasper said softly. She tried to do so, and she thought it was growing in intensity, but it sort of hiccupped and then went out. Claire stared at her hand.

"Was that you producing it in my hand or was that me?" she asked finally.

"That was all you. I just tried to add my energy to yours to encourage it to grow. I've tried to make one inside Hunter's hands, but it wouldn't work. I thought that if you could give it a go and I could feed my energy into yours, that you might be able to create the Light," he replied.

Claire was about to say something else when there was a loud knock at the door. They heard it open and then heard David's voice in the hall. "I've come to pick up Jasper."

Jasper walked out to meet his father and Claire trailed along behind.

"How'd it go?" David asked them.

"It went all right. I think I'm making progress," Claire told him.

"Keep practicing, Claire," Jasper encouraged earnestly.

"Yes, sir!" she said with a stiff salute. He smiled back as they left.

Claire practiced for the rest of the night in her bedroom. She recalled the feeling when Jasper helped her produce her first spark and kept that in the forefront of her mind as she tried to recreate it. It was not only the way her energy from within had flowed into the point of light, but also how her mind had willed it into existence that mattered. By the time she was finally exhausted from all the attempts and the earlier work with Jasper, Claire had managed to produce only one more Light. Again, it was a tiny flickering thing that lay flat on her hand. She gave up on the rest of the night and collapsed into bed. Her eyes closed, and she was asleep just as fast.

She remembered mist. Swirling and curling around her, reaching out and clawing at her. Her hair was lifted like it was blowing in a strong wind, but she could feel no wind around her. She was following something: an indistinct figure in black. She desperately wanted to catch up to him—to turn him around and find out who he was. Then from out of nowhere, Adam stood before her. She could see him clearly. His bright green eyes, his olive skin and dark hair. She could see that he was calling out her name, and unlike other dreams, she could hear him. It was faint, but it was there.

"Claire, Claire, can you hear me?" She nodded, indicating with her fingers that she could a little. "He's angry. He thinks you have Mary and Jack."

"Are you here in the village?" she asked as no sound came from her mouth. He shook his head and pointed to his ear. She gathered her will and tried again, concentrating on making him hear her. "Are you here in the village?" she repeated slowly and carefully.

His eyes widened. "We were. Been and gone. He has a cabin nearby. We are there." She nodded her understanding.

"Are you okay?" she asked, taking a step closer to him.

"Fine. And you?" His voice became softer and she saw concern in his eyes. Her breath caught in her throat and she was thankful this was just a dream.

"I'm fine."

"Good. He's going to see your uncle tomorrow. Don't be there." They were standing close to each other now and with every step, their voices became louder. "Take care, Claire. He's dangerous."

With that, he was suddenly gone and the man in black was closer—watching her. She stood, frozen to the spot as he stared at her. His face was unmasked, and she screamed.

It was a scream that could have woken the dead, echoing through the darkened house as her door crashed open. Standing in the door frame was her uncle. She knew it was her uncle, but he was silhouetted by the soft light coming from the landing and she screamed again. He raced to her side and tried to calm the girl.

Once her sobs and heartrate had calmed and she was fully aware of where she was, Claire related the dream to Geoff. She told him about the man in black she'd seen—but she couldn't remember the face. She only knew it and was scared. He settled her back down, staying in the room until she was asleep again.

The next morning, Claire got up still feeling tired—not only from the dream, but from the exertion of the afternoon before. She headed to the kitchen and made herself a very large breakfast.

"You don't have to worry about me today, Uncle Geoff. I'll be going to spend the day with Jasper while he's in the village. So, I won't be around when...or *if*...Marcus comes here."

"I think that's a very sensible idea, Claire. I was thinking the same thing," her uncle admitted.

True to her word to both Adam and Geoff, Claire left the house and walked the short distance to Lynnette and Bob's house. When the door opened, Hunter exploded out of it and into her arms, begging her to show him more tricks and asking if she could teach him how to do them. David pulled his youngest son off his niece and welcomed her inside.

"You, young man, are still in your pj's. Go get dressed, you monkey!" With that Hunter began to make monkey noises and ran to the room he was sharing with his brother.

"Would you like a cup of tea, Claire?" Lynnette asked her as she entered the kitchen. They were still having breakfast and the table was covered in mugs, plates, and bits of toast. Claire could clearly see where Hunter had been sitting and angled for a different seat.

"I'm fine, Grandma, I've just had breakfast. Before I forget, Uncle Geoff wants me to tell you that I had another Dream Message from Adam last night." Claire related the dream to them as Beth started to clear away the mess, her face a stoic mask at the mention of both Adam and Marcus. "Uncle David, is there a cabin around here that you know of?"

"There are lots of cabins in the hills around here. But there's only one that I know of that is let out to people." He turned to his father. "It's the one on Saddle Hill. You know the one, Dad."

"I do. That belongs to the Trumans from over in the next town. They rent it out every now and then to people from the city. Hang on, I'll give Tom a call and see if it's occupied now." He picked up the phone and wandered into the lounge with it.

"So, I believe Jasper helped you a lot last night, Claire?" Beth asked. Claire was not sure if Beth was proud of her son or whether the idea of her son having a Talent was still disgusting.

"He did. He helped me a great deal." She turned to Jasper. "I managed to create one by myself last night."

"Wonderful," Jasper enthused. "It took me a while to get the hang of it."

Bob came back into the kitchen. "Yep. Tom said he got a phone call yesterday from some guy in town wanting to stay at his cabin for a few days. Apparently, it's not the first time this guy has hired the cabin, either. Tom is only too happy to rent to him because he usually pays him more than what is normally charged. But he wouldn't tell me the man's name— told me he liked to keep that kind of thing confidential, as if he expects superstars to hire it out."

"I can go take a look, if you like," David offered.

"Might pay, Son. I'll let Geoff know what's happening."

"Can I come too?" Claire asked hopefully.

"I don't think that's such a great idea, Claire. Your uncle would kill me if anything should happen."

"You have to stay here and practice anyway," Jasper chimed in. The look on his face was deadly serious, and Claire appreciated how much he was enjoying being part of everything, even if it was only teaching her how to produce the Light.

"When are you going, Uncle David?"

"I have to go check on the farm this morning, then do a few rounds of the village, so it probably won't be until later on this afternoon."

"So, if we put in some solid work this morning with training, then can I come with you later? Please? By then, I'll be climbing the walls wanting to get some exercise."

"I'll think about it, Claire," David said seriously.

"Which means you're going to be talking with Uncle Geoff to make sure that it's all right." She stood up and tugged at Jasper's arm. "Come on, Jasper. Let's get some work done!" He stood up and followed her out.

"She's a determined one, that one," Lynnette said to her son.

"She has a lot of courage, that is for sure," Beth chimed in.

"So, I take it you're now okay with her talking to—and training—with your son?" Lynnette asked her daughter-in-law.

"I must admit I was hesitant at first, but I believe that my hatred of the Talent stemmed from events before Jasper was born. If what you're all saying about Mary is true—that she was more determined to create more Talent than suppress it— there is nothing I can do about it, is there? I can't make my son hide his Talent and never use it! That'd be denying a part of himself, and I would ultimately become the loser and lose him forever. No. I have learned my lesson, but it'll still take me a little while to fully accept it."

Lynnette gave Beth a big hug and kissed the top of her head. "Baby steps, Beth. We don't expect you to change overnight, but we're loving the change so far." Beth blushed to her red roots as David squeezed her hand and kissed her.

Chapter Twenty-Two

The morning warmed up quickly, and soon the summer insects started to make themselves known with a cacophony of sound. Hunter moved among the bushes to see if he could catch some. He loved bugs, both slimy and crawly. The only thing he didn't like was spiders, and he'd come out screaming—wanting either Claire or Jasper to take the web off him. In turn, they would laugh as he jumped up and down yelling.

"Icky, icky...get it off me!" he kept repeating.

When they weren't being interrupted by Hunter, Claire was making very good progress with the help of Jasper, as she grew ever more confident in producing stronger and stronger light balls. They both delighted Hunter, entertaining him with a little luminous display that he would jump and chase after. Tiny fireworks leapt from their hands and burst into small stars in all different shades of the rainbow. They sent them zooming around the backyard, playing tag and piggy in the middle with Hunter, as the cat came prancing into the backyard.

Their grandmother's cat was an overindulged, pampered pet who usually took off when the children were around. Jasper sent one of his lights to buzz around the cat's head and it tried to swipe it out of the air. Hunter sat between Jasper and

Claire, clapping and squealing with laughter—giving Jasper instructions on what to do next.

In the middle of the afternoon, Claire and Jasper were both lying on their stomachs. Threading their respective lights through the rose bushes, they attempted to avoid touching the thorns when David called her from the back door. Telling her cousin they'd continue later, Claire quickly recalled her light and extinguished it as she went running.

"I've talked to Geoff and he's agreed to let you go with me, but—and there is a big *but*—you are to remain hidden and under no circumstances are you to make yourself visible at all." She nodded her agreement, and they left the house in his Ute.

They drove for half an hour up into the hills until David pulled off onto a dirt track, then they bumped their way through the trees until he pulled up in a siding.

"Right. We run from here. Well, I run—you do whatever it is you do."

"You mean this?" With an unnecessary flourish of her hand, Claire became small and hovered all in one go.

"You forgot to go invisible," he mentioned.

"Oh, all right," her voice projected as she vanished from sight.

"I hope you can keep up!" From his left shoulder, he heard her reply and a little laugh.

"You just worry about yourself—at least I won't be seen!"

With that, they took off. David set a steady pace through the trees. To Claire's eyes there was no sign of a trail anywhere in sight, but David led her on. The chase and speed were exhilarating to Claire as the fresh air pumped in her lungs and she enjoyed the freedom of being outdoors. She hadn't realised how much of this summer had been spent inside, closeted away with books. If she were still in the city, she would've been out every day—leaping and running amongst the buildings, trying for more and more dangerous stunts.

As David began to slow, Claire realised he wasn't making any noise whatsoever. The only sounds around were the birds in the trees, the odd scuffling noise in the tree litter on the sloping ground, and a small tinkle of water coming from the right. David stopped by a large tree and then hauled himself up into the branches as Claire followed him and tried to see what it was he was wanting to get a good view of.

Quietly, she asked him in a voice that would only carry to his left ear, "What is it?"

"The cabin's just ahead. I wanted to get higher to see if I can see into the property." David inched his way forward on the branch, pulling aside some leaves. "There...can you see?" He pointed through the small gap.

Claire looked and could see a green corrugated iron roof sloping down. Beside the cabin stood two large black SUVs, similar to the one Adam had been driving.

"They are there. I can see the cars," she told him.

"Geoff hasn't rung yet to let us know that they've arrived. So, we will just have to wait them out." He made himself comfortable on the branch and Claire drifted away to another. Standing watch on a thinner one, Claire looked back at her uncle. His eyes were closed. She shook her head in wonder, returning to keep watch.

After a while of just sitting and staring at the cabin that held no movement whatsoever that she could see, Claire became bored. To amuse herself she began leaping from one branch to another and peering into birds' nests along the way, until she came to the top of the tree. She looked out over the valley below and could make out the village in the distance. The sun sparkled off the little river that ran down the middle of the valley. It looked so beautiful—like a painting—and the many colours of the fields below were spread out like a patchwork quilt. Animals that she knew were huge looked like tiny ants from this distance, and she congratulated herself when she picked out David's horse, Janie, in her paddock.

As she was marvelling at the birds swooping and diving in the summer's clear blue sky, the sound of voices nearby caught her attention. Quickly descending the tree, she found her uncle awake and alert, and as she landed lightly on his shoulder, he flinched ever so slightly at the weight of her.

"They're leaving?" she questioned.

"Shhhh!" David replied.

She took off again and went closer to the edge of the leaves. Peering through a small gap, she saw three men get into one of the SUVs. One was unmistakably Marcus, but she did not recognise the others. That would mean that Adam was still inside the cabin. When the car took off down the drive, Claire returned to her uncle.

"Marcus and two others have left. I think Adam's still inside. Do you want me to have a look?" she asked hopefully.

"Not yet. Just wait," he replied with a shake of his head. They waited for another five minutes, but it seemed like a lifetime.

"I can be down there and back in no time. They won't see me."

"I'm still not sure Adam is being truthful. He caught you once..."

"That was because I wasn't expecting it! Please—I can do this," Clare argued.

"All right...anything to stop you buzzing in my ear like a mosquito. Be quick and do not drop your invisibility for any reason. Come straight back and report to me."

"Okay. I'll be right back."

Claire pushed off from his shoulder and flew through the outer branches and leaves. Once at the cabin, she started with the second floor. Quietly, she peered into each window. Finding bags open and an unmade bed in one of the bedrooms, she saw that the others were as neat as a pin. Everything in its place. There was no one upstairs, but she could tell that there were definitely more than just three men staying in the cabin. She flew down to the first floor and peered into the kitchen window. Yet again, everything was orderly—with no sign of anyone around—and there was no noise coming from inside, either. Moving around the cabin, Claire made sure to check each room until she came to the large living room area. Landing lightly on the outer sill, she looked in.

Stretched out on the couch was Adam. With one book lying idle on his chest, he stared out the window. Watching, she wanted to go to him. And she thought of doing just that until a large shadow moved across from behind her.

Claire pressed herself up against the wall of the cabin and then remembered she was invisible. A large, barrel-chested man had walked right past her and entered through a set of open French doors.

"All quiet out there," he reported.

"Of course, it is, we're in the country," Adam replied unenthusiastically. "So, he left you here to be my jailer, did he?"

"Wouldn't exactly call it a jailer."

"Well, I'm too old for a babysitter."

"I'm definitely not one of those either. You want a coffee?" the man asked, walking to the kitchen.

"No, I've had one of your so-called coffees. I'll make it." Adam pulled himself off the couch and headed to the kitchen.

"Cheers, Adam! That would be really nice."

"Don't mention it," Adam replied sarcastically.

"You know why your dad left you here."

"It's because I stuffed up last time, I know. I'm sick of hearing it, Richard."

"Also, he doesn't want you seeing that girl just yet."

"That girl has a name, and it's Claire."

"I know what her name is. For heaven's sake, I grew up with her dad," Richard replied.

"Well, there's a new tale," Adam said as he came back into the living room carrying two mugs. He passed one to the older man and resumed his seat on the couch. "Tell me more. I'm so bored that even one of your stories will be entertaining."

Richard took a sip of his coffee. "Well, it's as I said, I grew up with John Brown. He was a cocky sort of bloke."

"Sounds like his daughter." Adam gave a little laugh.

"Never met her. Others were put on to watch her. Met the mum a few times, though. What a looker!"

"Obviously before my wonderful father had her killed." Adam watched the other man carefully over the rim of his mug.

"I wouldn't know about that," Richard replied a little too quickly, moving uncomfortably in his seat.

"No—no one seems knows about it."

Claire felt she'd been there too long and didn't want to hear any more. So, she took off to the tree where she had left David. He was on the ground at this point, crouching closer to the house. She landed on his left shoulder and reported to him all she had seen and heard.

"Only one other?" David asked when she'd finished.

"Yes. I think the man in there had something to do with Mum and Dad's death. He just seemed to be a bit shifty when Adam mentioned it." David only nodded in response as Claire continued. "I think we need to get back and let Uncle Geoff know what's happening here."

There was still no response from David as he kept staring intently at the cabin, his face was a blank mask.

"Uncle David!" She raised her voice, breaking through his reverie.

"Okay, let's go. I want to be well away and back in the village before Marcus comes back." He turned around and crept quietly for some distance.

It was eerie how he managed to make no sound, breaking nothing—not a single stick nor even slightly rustling the fallen leaves that littered the ground. As soon as he judged they were a good distance away from the cabin, he broke into a gentle lope and they made it back to the Ute in very short time. He opened the door and Claire flew onto the passage seat. She was just about to come back to size when David told her not to.

"I don't want you seen at all in the car on the way back. For me, it's nothing to be seen in the area. I'm always out and about, but you're a completely different matter at the moment."

"I'll come back to size but remain invisible." He nodded as he started the Ute and pulled it back onto the track.

They were silent the whole trip back, both lost in their own respective thoughts. Claire focused on Adam and David on his sister. She was determined to try to reach Adam tonight in their Dream Messaging—to let him know she had seen him— or was that a bad idea? Worry and doubt ate away at her. Why would he try to reach her in such a way? Why warn them if he wasn't on their side? This was his father, after all, the only family he thought he had left—that was, until Claire had told him about Elizabeth. She wanted an honest, proper conversation with him, laying all the cards out on the table and seeing how they would fall. Why did life have to be so complicated?

As they were about to enter the village, David's phone rang. Pulling over, he took the call. When he had finished, he said quietly and through lips that barely moved, "Change of plan. I'm taking you home."

"Have they left already?" she asked, concerned at his tone.

"Yep. Let's go see what your uncle has to say. I think you'd better keep your disguise up," he suggested.

David pulled his Ute back onto the road and started to drive. Nearing the corner of Geoff's street, a big, black SUV pulled out and headed towards them as he heard his niece beside him gasp.

"That's him," Claire whispered.

As the two vehicles came closer to each other, the black car swerved and pulled up, blocking the road. David slammed on his brakes and stared at the car. A man in his middle years with black hair and olive skin stepped out of the vehicle and came around to the Ute's driver door, tapping on the window.

"That's Marcus," Claire warned her uncle before he wound down the window to talk.

"Is there some sort of problem?" he asked politely.

"David Fuller, isn't it?" Marcus asked.

If Claire thought in terms of Adam's Charm being like waves, then she would've described Marcus's like a huge, multistory tsunami. It didn't necessary break over them— more like crashed. It took all their awareness and energy to fight it off.

"Yes, and I think I can guess who you are," David said, tight-lipped, as Claire noticed sweat starting to stand out on his forehead.

"Yes, it is I. Now, David—it's all right for me to call you David, isn't it?" He didn't wait for her uncle to reply. "David, Geoff wouldn't see reason, so I am hoping as a family man you can see a bit more sense. I would very much like to talk to

Claire. I believe that I can offer her a future that this tatty old village cannot, and I would humbly request that you help me find her."

"If you think threatening me and my family is a way to get what you want, then you are sadly mistaken. Claire is part of my family, and we will protect her from you," he said through almost gritted teeth.

"Really? That kind of talk's not necessary, David. I am just requesting your help, so I don't think I've threatened you in any way." Marcus flashed a big, white-toothed smile.

"Then I'm sorry if I have offended you, Mr Ryder, but I cannot help you. I have no idea where she is and as you can see, she isn't with me. So, if you don't mind, I'd like to be on my way." There was now a vein popping out of David's neck, and Claire could see how hard it was for him to keep his emotions in check.

"Of course, I am sorry to have delayed you." Stepping away from the Ute, Marcus walked back to his car. When he was just about to get back into the large vehicle, he turned. "Oh! By the way, I was sorry to hear about your sister and her husband—they were such a lovely couple. My condolences." The smile he gave David was pure malice.

The Ute's engine revved and it was moving before Claire knew it, heading straight for Marcus.

"David, no!" she cried out, gripping the dashboard.

Swerving before hitting them, David drove off the road to get around the obstacle and sped away. Claire looked back as they passed the street they should have turned into, to see Marcus still watching them and appearing to laugh. They headed further into the village before David appeared to come back to his senses. He took the next left-hand corner a bit too fast, and the tyres screeched in protest as they skidded around it, and then again when they came to a sudden halt.

Claire stared at her uncle. His face was red and angry, and his hands clenched the steering wheel so hard his knuckles glowed white. Feeling scared for the first time in his presence, Claire was glad she was disguised. He sat silently, seething for quite a while before Claire built enough courage to talk to him.

"Can we go home now, Uncle David?" Her voice was small as she reached out a hand to gently touch his arm, making him jump.

"I'm sorry, Claire, I didn't mean to frighten you." David placed his own larger hand over hers. "Let's get you home."

They drove around the block and pulled up the driveway of Geoff's house. By the time David got out of the Ute, Claire had shrunk herself down and was sitting on his shoulder again, staying put until he was in the house. As soon as the door closed, she reappeared and startled Geoff.

"Sorry, Uncle Geoff. I didn't know if anyone was still around."

"That's all right, just give me a bit of warning next time—it's a little bit disconcerting." Then he noticed their demeanour, Claire pale and David's angry face still red. "I think we all have stories to tell."

"Yes, and I think I need a good shot of that whiskey of yours!" David replied while heading towards the kitchen.

"You first, Uncle Geoff. So, what happened? What'd he say?" Claire asked.

Geoff followed David and went straight to the top cupboard, pouring a couple of drinks for David and himself. Claire grabbed a bottle of water and some food from the fridge. Suddenly feeling ravenous, she quickly proceeded to make herself a sandwich.

"Well, he was ever so polite and courteous. He told me that he knew I knew who Jack really was—who his father was, and that Mary was working for him. He also asked very politely if

I knew where Mary and Jack were. To which I replied very courteously and politely that I had no idea where they were. I just reiterated the story of what had been seen, and of course, he didn't buy it." He took a long gulp of his whiskey and put the glass down. "You'll be glad to hear that he asked after you, Claire."

"I'm touched that he remembered me," she said sarcastically through a mouthful of her ham and cheese sandwich.

"He wanted to know if you were still living with me and to tell you that Adam missed you terribly. I didn't confirm whether you were here or not. I could feel his Talent battering me. That's the only pitfall with Charm. It eventually wears thin and a person can see right through it." He turned to David. "I want you to get your wife and kids somewhere safe. I'm sorry, but I did give him one piece of information. I told him I knew who Adam's mother was and that she was still here in the village."

"I came to the same conclusion not five minutes ago," David agreed, nodding before knocking back his drink in one motion.

"I think you'd better tell me your news," Geoff said, eyeing David.

"Just after you rang, we were stopped by Marcus—he blocked the road," Claire started before David could and continued to relay all that had occurred between the two men, until David cut over the top before she could finish.

"He gave me his condolences for Jess and John passing," David added. He gripped the glass so tightly that it suddenly shattered, sending glass shards all over the table and blood dripped from his fingers. Geoff grabbed a tea towel to wrap around David's hand while David apologised.

"There's honestly no need, David. Now I want you to do as I suggested and get your family to safety. I know Bob and Lynnette will probably refuse, but I think it's more important to get Beth and the boys out of harm's way. Can you do that?" Geoff asked in a calming tone, gripping David's shoulder.

"Right! I'd better get moving. Is Claire going to be safe here?" he asked as he held onto his injured hand.

"I think so. As safe here as anywhere else in the village, anyway," Geoff reassured him.

"Okay. I'll get Beth and the boys safely away from the village and come straight back. I'll stay here tonight if that is all right with you."

"Sure. I was hoping you would say that. We'll see you soon. Make sure you get that hand seen to as well," Geoff suggested.

David nodded while turning to Claire. "You do as you're told, young lady. Stay safe."

"I will, Uncle David!" she said as he left them.

"What about the other guys who were with him? You only mentioned Marcus," she asked, turning back to her uncle.

"What other guys?" Geoff asked while cleaning the glass off the table.

"There was the one who was driving and another. I saw them leave the cabin. Marcus was in the back seat and the other two were in the front. It was the same as when we met just now." Geoff immediately went to the back door and made sure it was locked.

"There was only Marcus when the car pulled up to the house. I saw no one else."

"Want me to do a quick sweep around the house?" she asked, getting ready to change.

"No. I want you where I can keep an eye on you," he replied firmly.

"Uncle Geoff, I can do this. Please, just for peace of mind? It helped at the cabin." Claire watched as he thought about it for a moment and then agreed.

"Be back as quick as you can and don't take any stupid risks."

Claire once again transformed as Geoff let her out of the window and waited there until she came back. Flying up high enough so that she could look out over the house, Claire made a circle around it. There was no one moving, no one around at all. She came down slowly and peered in all the nooks and crannies she couldn't see from above. Satisfied that there was no one hiding around the property, she remembered that Adam had used the empty house to the rear of her uncle's. She made a quick sweep of that house and found a man staring out a rear window that overlooked Geoff's backyard. Coming in through the window, she flew back to her uncle as he closed it quickly, locking it behind her. Claire came to her full state again and reported what she'd seen.

"So, he has set a watch on us. He's going to be very uncomfortable." He stopped and stared at her. "I have an idea, but I want to see it first before I put it into action."

"What is it?" she asked curiously.

"How is the Light coming along?" Geoff asked with a grin.

"Very well, thank you. And I think I've just worked out your plan." She grinned back at him.

Chapter Twenty-Three

After a little practice and fine tuning, they decided that the plan would work and settled in for the rest of the night, as Claire did her best not to be seen in any of the windows. Geoff's reasoning was that if Marcus had placed a watcher on the rear of the house, then he could have easily set one on the front as well. It was hard for Claire, especially when she had the sudden urge to lift the curtains and make funny faces out the windows.

The time came to set the plan into motion. It started out small enough. Claire had once more gone incognito and flown out the back door when Geoff opened it—to ostentatiously put the rubbish out. Cautiously, she made her way to the house at the rear and located every vent into the building she could. Making a small light in her hands, she sent it off into the first vent and set her energy to make it explode into a shower of sparks as soon as it entered the main rooms. From there, she moved to the next one and then the next, sending similar lights into each. Claire could hear them starting to go off outside along with the sound of curious footsteps running toward her. That was her opportunity to enter the house via a small open window and set the next piece of the plan into motion. Once it was done, she crawled into a corner and sent up another firework light.

True to form, the man came running into the room but stopped dead in his tracks. His face went as white as a sheet, and he started to back away from the apparition that faced him. Claire had carefully constructed several balls of light of different sizes—all twinkling different colours at different times—and had fixed them together in the shape of a human form. Bending them to her will, she made the figure take a step towards the man as he turned and fled. Claire leapt into the air, following him out the door and down the street. As they had expected, he ran straight up to a house opposite to her uncle's and pounded on the door. It was answered, and she could hear raised voices. The man was ushered inside, and she went back to the abandoned house to set everything right again.

Back at her uncle's place, she knocked on the window.

"Did you see which house?" she asked as he let her in.

"Yes. I wish I'd seen it."

"He turned a hundred shades whiter than when he started." She giggled. "So, do you want me to do the same over there?"

"Give them an hour for him to calm down. I don't know if they'll send someone else back to that house or not, but we will watch the watchers and see what they do for a change."

There was no movement from the house across the street, and Geoff sent Claire off to create the same effect. This time, however, she found it harder to gain entrance to the house. She was about to give up when she spotted a small cat door at the rear of the property. Carefully, she tried it. It was old and worn and she found the plastic was brittle enough for her to break, making a small hole to allow her to get in. Flying around the house, she set her sparks off again—timing them well.

From a room in the front, she could hear one of the men shouting.

"This is how it started!" he cried out, his voice trembling.

She sent a few coloured lights to float around the rooms and to pester the men, moving quickly when she heard their running footsteps heading toward the back door. Claire watched them yank the door open and jostle each other to be the first one out, amusingly reminding her of something straight out of a cartoon. Finally spilling themselves out the door, they ran to their car and jumped in, taking off at great speed while forgetting to turn their headlights on in the rush.

Laughing her head off, Claire quickly rushed back to Geoff's house. He let her in, and she collapsed on the floor. Once she had calmed down, she asked her uncle what the next step was.

"Bed. I don't think they're going to be back tonight, but I do believe that they'll be in the morning. So, no early morning exercise for you. I think you've done enough tonight."

"Speaking of which, I'm starving. I'll just get a sandwich first."

"I swear, you have hollow legs," Geoff said, shaking his head and laughing.

"I have been working on a theory. I only get hungry like this after I have used one or more of my Talents," she replied, rummaging around in the fridge.

"But I don't get hungry after I've used mine."

"That's because yours, Uncle dear, is one of the Mental Talents—whereas the ones I have used tonight are all Physical. I believe that it takes not only mental strength but also physical mass to use the Talents in conjunction with one another."

"Well, listen to you, Kid. Did you swallow a dictionary while I wasn't looking?" He smiled at her.

"I pay attention at school when it matters." She flicked her long, blond ponytail and set to make herself a very large sandwich.

After she'd demolished the sandwich, they sat at the table with cups of tea in their hands. Completely comfortable, Claire leaned back in her chair and sighed.

"So, you never told me what happened at the cabin," Geoff prompted her.

"There was only Adam and one other guy there. I think Adam called him Richard. Yes, definitely Richard. He said he grew up with Dad and that he had met Mum."

"Richard? I don't think I remember a Richard, but then again, that was when I was living in the city with Katy."

"This Richard guy got all bristly when Adam mentioned that Marcus had Mum and Dad killed. He said he didn't know anything about it, but I got the feeling he did. I told Uncle David all this as well when I got back."

"You told David that you thought this guy was responsible for their deaths?" Geoff asked slowly.

"Yes. He wanted to know everything. So, I told him."

"He should've been back by now. He said he'd come right back here." He checked his watch and then got a faraway look in his eye as he turned in his chair. "He's sitting in a tree in the woods."

"I know the one," Claire said, jumping up.

"It's dark. We can't go crashing around in the forest in the middle of the night, we'll be heard."

"I'll get him—I promise."

Leaving the house, they quickly clambered into his car and began to drive up into the hills. He stopped by the narrow track Claire and David had turned down earlier in the day.

"I can't drive my car on that, it's not a four-wheel drive," Geoff protested.

"It's fine, Uncle Geoff. Pull in somewhere up here. I can find him," Claire replied, already unfastening her seatbelt.

"Are you sure?"

"I am sure. Just once, please trust me without arguing." He pulled up on the side of the road as Claire jumped out, immediately transforming, and taking off down the track.

"If your theory is right, this is going to cost me a fortune in food," Geoff mumbled to himself.

Claire kept close to the ground and created a small speck of light to illuminate her way. It felt forever until she came across David's Ute pulled up on the side, and she may have missed it if it were not for the reflection of her light in the chrome. She headed off in the direction of the tree and unerringly found it in the dark. Extinguishing the light, Claire made her way up the trunk until she spotted him on a large branch.

"What are you doing here?" Claire asked, enlarging her voice slightly so only he could hear.

He jumped and had the good grace to look slightly guilty. "I only came to keep watch," he murmured softly.

"No, you didn't. Revenge can wait, Uncle David. It has waited this long; it can wait a little bit longer. I feel it too. They were my parents—not just your sister." She landed on his shoulder and sat down.

"They are so close. I could be in and out in no time."

"But you can't kill Marcus. There's only one way to do that and it is something I have to do." The waft of alcohol on David's breath assaulted her senses. "Have you been drinking?"

"Not much," he replied.

"That isn't going to solve anything!"

"Call it Dutch courage, then."

"You aren't thinking straight. What would happen to Beth and the boys if something happened to you? They need you. Please, we need to leave now," she begged.

"That man in there deserves it and I want it to be me who makes him pay," he said, a little too forcefully for Claire's liking.

"I didn't think that you were this—how did you put it? 'Petty and vengeful'?"

"Don't you dare throw those words back in my face, Claire! Those were words I spoke to my wife over an action that did not include murder. He needs to be punished for what he did. He killed a part of me that day!"

"He will. We will make sure he does, Uncle David. Please— if not for me, then for the boys." When that argument didn't work, Claire decided on another tactic. "What would Mum say if she saw you acting like this?"

This got David's attention as he looked at the small Claire perched on his shoulder.

"How would you know what she'd say?" he spat at her.

"Exactly why I'm asking you! You were her twin—you knew her better than anyone else. So, tell me, what would Jess say at this moment—what would she tell you?"

David hung his head to his chest and sighed. "She would tell me that I am being a bloody idiot and to get the hell out of here," he said quietly.

"Right! Are you going to take her advice?" Claire was feeling bolshie and stamped her foot when she asked the question.

"Yes."

"Good. Now, can you manage to get down the tree without making too much noise?"

"I could do it in my sleep, Claire. This Talent of mine is second nature." Not a scrape or a rustle of leaves was made as he descended the large tree.

Back on the ground, he crouched one more time while looking back at the cabin, shaking his head. Turning he then made his way silently through the forest. The hike back to his car was slow, but they made it without any sort of detection from those they had been spying on.

David was about to get behind the wheel of the Ute when Claire spoke up. "How much have you had to drink?"

"Not much," he replied while fumbling with the keys.

"Yeah, right." She made herself large again and held out her hand to him. "Give them to me!" she demanded.

"You can't drive!"

"I can a little. I just don't have my licence yet," she told him. "But I will not stand here and let you drive drunk—are you really going to be that stupid?"

"I beg your pardon! Are you calling me stupid?" David asked, a little shocked.

"If the name fits," she said, staring at him coldly.

"Your problem is that you are too much like your mother!"

"I really wish you'd make up your mind, Uncle David. The other day you accused me of being just like Dad and now you say I'm like Mum?"

David looked at her with a bewildered look and then burst out laughing.

"You have me there, Claire." He tossed her the keys over the bonnet of the car. "I'll teach you as we go." David went around the Ute and got into the passenger seat.

The drive back to the road and to Geoff was very nerve-wracking for Claire. Not once had she been behind the wheel of a car before, regardless of what she'd told David. Thankfully the car was an automatic—the thought of mashing through gears did not appeal to Claire—and she only had to concentrate on steering and the brake.

"You can go a bit faster, Claire," David urged her.

"I can't!" she shouted, feeling near hysterical as a tree jumped out in front of her from the darkness.

Finally, Claire made it back to the paved road, and she brought the Ute to a spluttering stop and a jerk beside Geoff's car.

"What the hell are you doing driving?" Geoff called out as he wound down his window.

"I'm sorry, Geoff, but I have had just a little too much to drink and this kind young lady has agreed to drive me home. Isn't she sweet?" David said while hanging his head out of the window.

"But you don't even have your learner's, Claire. You can't drive!"

"I know, Uncle Geoff, but we can't risk leaving the Ute out here, it might be spotted. If I follow you carefully, I'm sure I can make it back. I've played enough car racing games with Adam to sort of know what I am doing."

"There is a big difference between racing games and actually driving, Claire. For one: when you have an accident, you could legitimately get hurt!" Geoff retorted.

"What else are we going to do, then? We can't leave the Ute here. It'll be suspicious."

"Geoff, I'm not as drunk as Claire thinks I am, but I am too drunk to drive—she was right on that count. I'll make sure she does everything I tell her," David assured the older man.

"I am trusting you on this, David. I don't like it, but I see no alternative. Right, Kid, you had better listen to David and do exactly as he says. I'll be in front, so don't you dare run up the back of me." He pointed his finger at his niece and then to David. "You and I are going to have a very long talk when we get back."

David managed to look contrite as Geoff wound up his window with some force while starting up his car and then pulling onto the road just ahead of them.

The drive back was both thrilling and scary for Claire. She listened to David's advice on driving and concentrated on Geoff's rear lights just ahead. This, she decided, took more concentration than her Talents.

When they arrived back home, Claire stopped the Ute and hopped out as Geoff parked the vehicle. She stared at the house across the way but couldn't spot any movement.

Once inside, Claire and Geoff filled David in on their own adventure that night, and Claire had them in stitches with her mimicry of the watchers' reactions to her light "men." Geoff called it a night and sent Claire to bed but held David back for that promised talk.

Chapter Twenty-Four

"Where have you been?" Adam sounded upset and anxious. "I've been calling you, but I haven't been able to break through."

"I'm here now. It's been a very long night," Claire replied. "How come you managed to get through to me the other day when I was awake and not now?"

"I couldn't tell you, Claire, I think that I was more scared then. That might have something to do with it."

"You really need more training," Claire said with a bit of a laugh.

"I was worried. Dad set watchers on your house—one in the back and one in the front."

"We know. They've been dealt with already." She didn't tell him how they had got rid of them.

"That's a relief. There is just Dad and three others here in the cabin." He stepped closer to her, so close they could almost touch. She would have reached out for him if it weren't for the dark figure watching them from the side of the swirling mist. "I wish I could sneak out and see you," he told her quietly. "I need to talk to you in person."

Adam looked deeply into Claire's eyes, and she could see concern in their green depths, but when he reached out his hand to touch her arm, everything went black as she felt like she was falling. Her arms and legs began to flail about, and it soon felt like she was being tied up. She awoke with a jolt as she landed back on her bed with the bedsheets twisted around her. She rolled off the bed and landed with a thump, untangling herself. She sat like that for a long time—knees tucked up under her chin—rocking back and forth. The dark man had broken the connection somehow. She felt as if he didn't want the contact between Adam and herself.

Once her heart had stopped hammering in her chest and she calmed down, she pulled a book off her bedside table. She turned the light on and climbed back onto her bed. She opened the book and read a few pages, nodding her head in understanding. The book was on Mind Touch, and the passage she'd just read was about Dream Messaging. It told her that if a person using the Talent were to touch their receiver, the bond would become complete, and they would have access to the receiver's mind at any time—whether the receiver was awake or asleep. Somehow the man in black had saved her. The thought that someone could use that on her made her feel very uncomfortable. She put the book back in place and decided that she needed to talk to Lilith about it some more.

She rubbed her eyes, feeling like lumps of gravel were grating on her eyeballs. She didn't want to go back to sleep. She didn't want Adam there in her dreams with her. Claire sighed. A couple of nights before, she had wanted the contact with Adam. Even the previous afternoon she would have welcomed it, but now she wasn't so sure. Why had he wanted to strengthen the bond now? Was he fully a Mind Touch or did he only have the ability of Dream Message, and was that even possible? The internal questions just kept coming until she drifted back to sleep.

When she woke again, she wondered how the bedcovers got on the floor. She sat up and rubbed her gritty eyes, swinging her legs off the bed. She looked at her watch—it was still early—and the sun was only just starting to make itself known behind the hills in the distance. Her brain felt foggy, and she had a headache. As she rubbed her temples, it came back to her. The Dream Message, the man in black, and the passage she had read in the middle of the night.

"Got to talk to Lilith," she whispered to herself.

Claire left her room and headed down the stairs. Despite feeling groggy and slightly ill, her body still craved food. Her stomach rumbled as she entered the kitchen and started to cook some eggs and toast. The jug boiled as she made herself a cup of coffee and sat at the table to eat. Her uncle Geoff then entered with a raised eyebrow. "Do you know what time it is?"

"Yup," she said through a mouthful of dripping egg. Geoff sat beside her.

"You do realise it was about two this morning when you went to bed and that it's now…" He squinted at his large watch. "Nine minutes past six?"

Claire nodded as she took another large mouthful, waiting until she'd swallowed before answering him. "I had another bad dream last night…"

"Dream or message?"

"A bit of both." She took up her coffee and drank heavily from it before launching into her retelling and what she had learned from the book.

"What do you mean?" Geoff asked, his eyebrows knitted together as he had tried to follow her explanation.

"The person who is sending the messages—in this case Adam—would have full access to me, day or night."

"Day or night?" Geoff asked. She nodded again with her mouth full. "That does not sound good! And you say this dark man in your dreams stopped Adam from touching you?"

"Yup. I don't know what to make of him. He's there in my dreams—more sharply in recent days. But if I cast my memory back, I think he has always been there, well, for a very long time, anyway!" She shrugged it off. "I thought I might talk to Aunt Lilith about this one. After all, Dream Messaging is part of her Talent, and she might have some insight into it that I can't find in the books."

"I think that's a good idea, but I think you should wait a few hours before you call her. I've also done some thinking."

"I hope this is good thinking and not any 'need to lock Claire up' type thinking." Claire gave him a cheeky grin as she mopped up her plate with her last piece of toast.

"It's good thinking if that's how you want to look at it. But I don't think we should lock you up. Let them see you around the village—let's see who comes out of the darkness, shall we?"

"That sounds ominous," David said from the doorway, making both Geoff and Claire jump.

"Good morning, Uncle David, would you like some coffee or breakfast? I can make you some eggs and bacon."

"Are you not full yet?" Geoff asked, astonished.

"I'm fine!" she retorted.

"No, just a coffee at the moment, thanks," David replied, taking a seat at the table as Claire left it to make more coffee.

"So, we're trying to lure them out now with Claire being the bait?" David inquired.

"I think that might be wise," Geoff responded. "We hopefully got rid of two of Marcus's goons last night, and we know there's at least two—possibly three—up in that cabin with him and Adam. If there are more in the village, I want to know about it."

"Can't you just search for them with your Talent?" David asked before taking a sip of the coffee that Claire had just brought him.

"It doesn't work that way. I need to know the person or have something of theirs. How about you?"

"I need a trail," David replied with a sigh.

They all sat in silence, each pondering the limitations of their Talents. The thought of Talents brought the previous night to mind for Claire and she smiled.

"Why do you look so smug, Kid?" Geoff asked her.

"Just remembering last night. That was so much fun!"

"Oh my God, I've created a monster," Geoff said mockingly. "I would've dearly loved to have seen their faces when you pulled those pranks."

"I know I'd love to see the prank!" David joined in as Claire readily agreed.

For the next hour, Claire entertained her two uncles with her light show. She first created the human-shaped figure that had scared the men off, and then gave them a fireworks display. By the time she was finished, she was hungry again and looking around for something to eat. Geoff handed her an apple and told her there were plenty more in the bowl.

Later that morning, Claire found herself sitting in Lilith's work room, having a very intense discussion on Mind Touch— and especially Dream Messaging. Surrounding them were shelves of books that held the histories and descriptions of the Talents of The Community. Lilith was extending Claire's knowledge on the Talent with her own findings and how she had used it in the past.

"It is certainly not something that I've actually tried," Lilith admitted to Claire when the discussion came to Dream Messaging. "I have always tried to maintain an 'If it isn't broken, don't fix it' attitude with my Talent. I only use it if I *really* have to."

"Like the day you used it on me, so I would get some uninterrupted sleep?"

"Yes. But in my defence, you were so exhausted! The dreams were not letting you rest. I occasionally help Charlie as well...when she needs it," Lilith told her.

"I've been able to communicate more clearly with Adam in the past few days. I can now hear him and, in turn, can make myself be heard. The books you've already given me have been a help in that. But last night, something happened that scared me." Claire paused. "Adam tried to touch me and then the whole dream went black, and it felt like I was falling."

"It sounds like you aren't telling me everything, Claire. I can't help you if you hold back all the information." The older woman sat patiently, waiting for Claire to sort through her thoughts.

"A couple of nights ago, I had a dream that I was following someone. He was dressed all in black with a hood over his head. Then Adam was there sending me a message. When Adam had finished, the man in black was facing me and his hood was pushed back so I could see his face. I woke up screaming, but I can't remember the face. I've tried doing a recall on the dream, but every time I look at that part, it all goes black. Then when Adam reached out to touch me last night, I felt fear just before it all turned dark. But the fear wasn't coming from me, it was coming from the man in black. He stopped Adam from touching me and I'm happy he did after reading what that touch could've done."

"Have you had other dreams about this man in black?"

"Yes, I have. I realise that he has been there in my dreams for a long time—always in the background and never interfering. It's only been the last few nights that he has become prominent in them."

"I see." Lilith stood up and went straight to a bookshelf, pulling open a book. Muttering to herself as she flipped through it, she put it back in its rightful place before choosing another. Lilith did this several times before she found what she was looking for.

"Can you go make us a cup of tea, Claire, while I study this for a moment?"

"Sure," Claire agreed, leaving her great-aunt to it.

When she returned, Lilith was closing a book and pondering. Claire was amazed to see the same expression that Geoff always got when he was working on something. She poured the tea from the old China teapot and handed a cup and saucer to her aunt.

"Thank you," she said absently. Claire drank from her own cup and waited for Lilith to speak.

Putting her untouched cup down, she looked up at Claire.

"What I want to do is to look inside the part of your brain that deals with the subconscious. Now, I promise that I won't touch anything, imprint anything, or change anything that is there. I only want to observe. Do you trust me? Because this will not work if you don't."

"I trust you, Aunty Lilith," Claire said sombrely.

Lilith placed her two hands on either side of her head. Claire could feel a slight pressure in her mind as she closed her eyes and waited for her aunt to finish.

"Ah, there it is," she said with some satisfaction before her tone changed. "That is odd." For a while, they sat this way until Lilith slowly removed her hands and looked at her great-niece.

"Well, that was interesting!" She picked up her teacup and sipped the cooled liquid. "I could see Adam's footprints all over that part of your mind. He's a trampler, that one. The bond you share is a deep one. I can see that. But I would still be wary of making it more permanent at this stage—or at any time for that matter. As for the other presence, I could feel him there, but it wasn't until I moved to your subconscious that I could see him."

"So, he is just a figment of my subconscious, then?" Claire asked, hopeful.

"No, I wouldn't say that. This entity has come from an external source—it is not quite an imprint like a suggestion would be. No, this is something more substantial, and I'm going to have to investigate it a bit more. I seem to remember reading something a few years ago in one of these musty old books." She trailed off as she looked around her.

"Could you get a sense of who he is?" Claire asked in a slight voice.

"I couldn't." Lilith suddenly realised that Claire sounded scared. "But I get the feeling that he isn't someone you have to worry about...that, I definitely got the sense of. He's been with you for some time and has been watching over you. That is evident from last night's dream. He protected you when you were at your most vulnerable. By the way, I can see why you like this Adam so much. He is a very good-looking young man." Claire blushed. "First loves are hard to get over, Claire, so just be careful not to give your heart too soon!"

Claire did not push her aunt on this point. She knew the older woman was only trying to protect her and she didn't want to let on that she knew so much of Lilith's own painful past.

"Now, I have some reading to do, and it is best done while I'm on my own."

"I'll leave you to it. I said I would go see my grandparents, so I'd better do that now," Claire told her, getting up from her chair.

"How are you getting there, do you need a lift?"

"No, thank you, Aunt Lilith. I have my own personal bodyguard waiting for me. Uncle Geoff wants to see who's curious about me in the village."

"Is that Geoff-speak for *he wants to flush out the spies*?" Lilith asked, arching an eyebrow.

"Yes, but I think it's a good idea as well."

"Of course you do," Lilith said with an eye roll. "You have been under his influence for far too long. You're as bad as each other!"

Claire gave her great-aunt a kiss on the cheek. "Thank you, Aunt Lilith."

"You're welcome, dear. Stay safe."

"I will," Claire said with a grin.

With that, she left her aunt's to walk down the street to Grace and Malcolm's house. She knew that David was behind her, lurking in the bushes while going from house to house. But she could not hear him. She looked around, hoping to not make it obvious that she was searching for someone—anyone who might be following her—when she spotted a large black car coming down the street towards her.

As it passed, she tried to see inside, but the glass was darkly tinted. She could see figures, but no distinguishing features of the two occupants. Claire quickened her step and made for the safety of her grandparents'—all the while expecting the car to pull up beside her, but it didn't. As she closed the gate behind her, David stepped out from the hedge.

"I saw them," he said as he followed her to the front door.

It opened even before she knocked, and Grace pulled her into a hug.

"Come in... come in, the pair of you! Mind the mess. The boys haven't picked up after themselves again." She ushered them in and then led them to her homely kitchen. "It has been wonderful to have them here for the holidays and I will be sad to see them go." She then grabbed Claire's hand. "I wish we'd had the opportunity to have you here as well. But…well, you know." She gave it a squeeze and then let it drop, busying herself making lunch for them all.

As she worked, Grace chatted about how Benjamin and Charlotte had gone back to the city for a few days to check on the business and for Charlotte to check on her patients. She finished with her normal wish that they'd take more time to be with their boys. Claire rolled her eyes behind her grandmother's back at David as he gave a small smirk. It was at that moment that Malcolm came in the back door with two blond-haired boys hanging off him.

"I have two limpets that tell me they are extremely hungry here, Grandma."

"Sit down, then. We'll have some lunch. Claire and David are here as well, Malcolm." He turned towards them and gave Claire a big hug.

"How's the farm going?" he asked David, shaking his hand.

"Good, thanks. I think it's going to be a good crop this year; fingers crossed."

"You always have good crops," Malcolm said. "Are your boys doing anything this afternoon? Thought we could get them all together and go for a fish in the river."

"Sorry, but Beth has taken them to see her parents for a few days before school starts," David lied. Claire couldn't decide whether this was because he didn't want Grace to know what was going on, or simply didn't want to worry the couple.

Lunch was a noisy affair with the two six-year-olds. They were so full of energy, Grace was having a hard time keeping them in check. With lunch out of the way, Malcolm asked David for his advice on car trouble he was having, and they both disappeared into the garage. Claire helped Grace clean up after the meal and then helped to tidy the boys' things up. But as fast as they cleaned, the boys were making more messes elsewhere in the house. It got to the point where Grace went to the back door and yelled towards the garage.

"Are you taking these boys fishing or not?"

"Coming!" a reply came from the garage.

After Malcolm and the twins had left and the house was in peace for the first time in days, Grace settled herself in her large, comfy chair and let out a very big sigh.

"I am getting too old for this. Those two are terrors. It's times like these that I miss John. He would've taken those boys into hand. Benjamin and Charlotte are both too busy to raise them properly."

Claire didn't like to mention that Grace spoiled them rotten and that they knew they could run roughshod over her and take advantage of her kind heart.

"You have brought your two up properly—so polite and quiet," Grace complimented David.

"That's Beth's doing. If I'd had my way, they would be free-range kids who got into everything." David laughed slightly.

"Do you regret letting them go away to school?"

"A little, but that is going to change this year. Beth and I have agreed that they'll be going to school here this coming term. They can ride their bikes to school and be kids while they can." Claire thought he was going to say, *and they can learn to fit into The Community* as well, but he fell silent.

As the clock ticked the seconds past in the silence of the room, Claire had the sudden urge to leave, and she didn't know why. The compulsion to act was growing and she decided she couldn't ignore it.

"We'll leave you in peace, Grandma. Enjoy it while you can." She stood and stopped to give Grace a kiss on the cheek.

"You don't have to go already, do you? I get to see you so rarely these days." Claire bit her tongue on the fact that it was only a matter of a couple of months since they'd first met— realising that she herself could have done more about that.

"I'll come and see you tomorrow," she promised instead.

"Grace means well, Claire. She just talks before she thinks," David said once they were alone and walking down the street.

"I know. When this is all over, I'll spend more time with both sets of my grandparents."

"You're a good kid, Claire."

They turned the corner into the street on which she lived and saw the same large black car parked opposite Geoff's house. Claire and David slowed their walking slightly, trying to see what the car would do—but it just stayed parked, watching ominously.

"I bet you..." David started to say slowly, "...that I can make it to the house before you, and that you can transform and see who is in that car without being seen."

"I will take that bet," she said determinedly.

"Okay. On three, we start running. I'll open the door and you do your little bit of magic. Be sure to float back out before I shut it. I'll let you back in via the kitchen window."

"Sounds good to me."

"Right. One, two, three." They took off and matched each other's speed.

By the time they reached the house, neither was breathing hard. David opened the door as planned and Claire entered before disappearing. He closed the door behind him as she floated towards the waiting car. It hadn't moved an inch while they had been running, remaining in its place. Claire edge closer and closer to the vehicle and circled around it—to come up to it from behind. The windows were down slightly, and she could hear two men talking inside as she crept closer to one of the windows and peered in.

In the driver's seat was Richard, his seat reclined all the way back and his hands clasped behind his head. In the passenger seat sat Adam, and her heart did a little jump.

"What do you think that was about?" Richard asked.

"Knowing Claire, competition," he said. Claire couldn't tell from his voice what he was really feeling, since it sounded so deadpan.

"Very competitive, is she?"

"Yes."

"You're talkative today. What's up your butt?" Richard asked without looking at Adam, but steadfastly at the house across the street.

"Nothing. Do we have to talk constantly?"

"Sometimes it helps to pass the time."

"Well, not today," Adam replied with a sigh.

Richard spoke again after they were silent for a bit. "What do you think made Mark and Peter disappear?"

"I have no idea. But Dad's not happy about it. We have to stay here tonight and then he'll send Tony and Carl down from the cabin to relieve us early tomorrow morning. He can't get anymore up here until the day after."

"Those two are just as useless as the ones they're replacing. Can't you just do your—you know—Jedi mind trick on the girl, then we can all go home?"

"It doesn't work like that, Richard. And it isn't a Jedi mind trick."

This last remark gave Claire great concern. The fact that it was common knowledge that he had Mind Touch scared her a little and made her more determined to try to defend herself at night from his messaging. She'd heard enough, flying away from the car and back to the house.

The kitchen window was open, and she flew in, uncloaking herself while looking for David and Geoff, as well as grabbing an apple on the way.

"Right. Well, that decides it," Geoff said, pacing the room. "We have to act tonight. He's bringing in more of his men and I don't think the same tricks will work on them as the others last night."

"No, not tonight. Let them get settled in—see how boring it is—lull them into a sense that they have the upper hand and that it is us who're in hiding," David suggested. "We can take them out tomorrow night. I can lure the goon…" He looked at Claire at this point.

"Richard," she supplied.

"Yeah, Richard. I can take him out and then Claire can go in to deal with Marcus."

"You're forgetting Adam," Claire said calmly.

"I thought he wasn't a problem?" David asked her quickly.

"I'm not so sure. He tried to cement the bond last night, and it seems to be well-known with his dad's muscle that he has Mind Touch."

"Are you able to make sure tonight?" Geoff asked, concerned.

"I was going to try and avoid the connection tonight, if possible."

"We have to know, Claire, if he's with or against us. If he is against us, then we're going to have to try and eliminate him." David's voice was low and deep; Claire could see the revenge in his eyes and was scared for him.

"Okay," she agreed. "I'll try to find out."

"Claire, I know you've almost mastered the Light as a trick, but what about as a weapon?" Geoff asked. "It'll come down to whether you're able to use it in that way."

"I can make it hot and cold, and I can expand it. I haven't experimented with using it as a binding—and definitely not for killing."

"Practice on me," David requested. "I've seen what the results are when used for binding and it doesn't hurt. Remember, Jasper bound Jack."

"Only if you're sure. I wouldn't want to hurt you."

"Claire, you could never hurt me as much as they have already hurt me," David told her stoically.

For the next hour, they practiced in the living room with cushions littering the floor in case David fell. She practiced slowly at first, building up the strength of her light—making it impossible for David to escape it when she bound it to him. All the while he encouraged her, telling her that she may need to use it on Adam. This spurred her on more. She did not want to use it on him if she could help it. She didn't want to think of her friend betraying her, but he already had. It was Adam who enticed her into that building in the first place—an act that was designed to test her skill. This thought just made her madder.

"Whoa! Hey!" David cried out as she released him. "What the hell was that?"

"I'm sorry, did I hurt you?" Claire asked, quickly putting out the light bands.

"You almost burnt me!" David looked at his bare arms and the red marks the bands had left there.

"We need a break." She stumbled to a chair and plopped her head down in her hands.

"Are you okay, Kid?" David surprised her with the name Geoff usually called her.

"I was getting angry. I'm sorry—I lost control there for a bit. The Light must've been reacting to the anger and making the binding hotter."

"It's nice to know you can do that, but what was the anger directed at?"

"Adam," she answered simply. Tears welled up in her eyes, falling heavily down her cheeks.

David came to her side and knelt.

"Hey, it's okay. You have a right to be angry. You didn't ask for all this—these Talents and the betrayals. But remember, you have people who love you. You have family, and you aren't alone." Claire leaned into him as David put his arm around her when all the pent-up frustration and anger came pouring out. Geoff came into the room and raised an eyebrow at David. He shook his head and just kept hugging the girl.

When she'd finally cried herself out, Claire wiped her eyes and apologised for being so emotional.

"I'd be worried if you weren't, Kid," David told her.

"Come and get something to eat. Have a break for a bit," Geoff said gently to the two of them.

"I think you have definitely got the hang of binding, Claire," David stated as they went to the kitchen.

At the table, Claire picked at the food in front of her. A bleakness seemed to have come over her, and the two uncles exchanged worried looks over her head.

A knock sounded at the door, and David went to answer it. Following him back into the kitchen was Lilith, and in her hands were books. Claire looked up from her chair and smiled at her great-aunt.

"I come bearing news," Lilith declared.

"About the dreams?" Claire asked.

"Yes."

"Would you like some dinner, Lil?" Geoff asked.

"Yes, thank you, Geoff. I would love some dinner. You know, I think I forgot to eat lunch today. I became so engrossed in study." She sat down opposite Claire and pushed the books across to her. "I thought you might find these interesting." Claire looked at them. "They're on Dream Messaging and how to control it—not only from the perspective of the user, but I found an interesting notation from a receiver." She indicated a smaller book that was bound in red leather.

"Thank you, Aunt Lilith." Claire opened the book and started to pore over it. Subconsciously, she started to eat with more enthusiasm than just a few moments before.

"Thank you," Geoff mouthed to his older sister as she looked at him quizzically.

They ate, and Claire took no notice of the conversation that was going on around her. She studied the passages that Lilith had highlighted and committed them to memory. It was while she was reading these texts that she promised herself she would write her own diary—so in the future, people would understand a Chameleon as much as any of the other Talents. It was while she was musing on the Talents that something came to mind.

"Uncle Geoff?" she asked suddenly, emerging from the pages of the book.

"Yes, Claire?"

"Do we have any lamb roast in the freezer?"

"You can't still be hungry!" he exclaimed with a laugh.

"Not for me. I was thinking that I could use it to try out the Killing Light. I have to practice it and I thought that a raw roast would be the best to try it out on."

He got up, went to the fridge, and opened the freezer door. In the back on one of the shelves was a small, rolled beef.

"Will this do?" he asked her.

"It should do. I need to know if I can pass a Light through it. The next thing, I think, is to change the properties of it so that it leaves no mark but stops the heart." She saw her relatives shudder at the thought. "Believe me, I feel the same," she said in a quiet voice.

When Claire returned from collecting the book on Light from upstairs, she found the kitchen deserted. She backed up and looked into the living room. The three of them were sitting there calmly, drinking tea or coffee—she couldn't tell which.

"So, no moral support?" Claire asked with a raised eyebrow.

"You've done well mostly on your own so far, Kid. Why stop something that works?" Geoff grinned at her.

"Impossible." She sighed and went back to the kitchen.

Carefully, she found the page she needed in the book, read the passage, and reread it over and over. As she did so, she played with a small ball of Light in her hands, the colours transitioning through the rainbow. She stood up and walked over to the bench. The theory stuck in her mind as she went over it step-by-step. The ball of Light flickered and took on a steady golden colour. This was the moment she was dreading—how would it feel to push it into flesh?

"Don't think about it," Claire advised herself. "Just do it!"

With that thought, she placed the Light on the raw flesh of the beef roast and pushed down on it. She could feel the Light change at her command, encompassing the interior of the red meat and almost billowing out while quickly shrinking to a small sharp point, only then to vanish. She took her hand away from the meat and looked at it. There was not a single mark on its surface.

Claire wasn't sure that she'd performed it right, so she went back to the book and read it again. Talking it over to herself slowly—although she had it imprinted in her brain, and it would be impossible to forget it now—she still went step-by-step. She performed that act again, albeit slightly different this time, but she could not tell anyone how she knew this. When she finished up, she grabbed a knife and cut the meat into two pieces, separating it right where she had sent the Light—smack square in the centre. But there was nothing. Not a single mark could be seen to say the Light had been there, but Claire could tell that it had worked. It was like a bell ringing on the right note. She stepped back and shuddered.

The thought of what she had to do was becoming real to her now. The thought of taking a person's life and then standing there watching it ebb away was a visual she did not relish. Her brain rebelled at the thought as she started to breathe heavily. Her heart raced as she broke out in a cold sweat. Leaning against the bench, she could feel the world around her slip slightly to the right, then the floor rushed up to meet her and it all went black.

He was standing there again.

"Who are you?" she demanded. "Why're you in my dreams?"

"You know who I am." His voice was deep and raspy.

"I don't. I don't know who you are!" she protested.

"I've shown you once."

"But I couldn't remember when I woke up. I can't even see you under Recall."

"That is because you are not trying hard enough." From a distance, she could hear her name being called, and she turned about to find where it was coming from. When she turned back to the man in black, he was walking away from her.

"Come back!" she called to him, continuing to call out until she realised she was on the floor of the kitchen with three very concerned-looking faces peering down at her.

"She's awake. Thank God," Lilith said.

Ever so gently, David hoisted her to her feet and then lifted her into his arms. He walked her to the living room and deposited her on the couch.

"What happened?" Geoff asked while handing her a glass of water.

"I...I think I performed it," she said, sipping the drink. "No, I did do it. It was afterwards—I felt like I couldn't breathe. Did I just faint?" She looked at them and the question seemed so out of sorts with what she'd been saying that they laughed a little.

"Yes. I think you did," Lilith told her. "When you were coming round, you kept calling out. Who were you telling to come back?"

"It was the man in black. He wouldn't tell me who he was. He just said that I already knew."

"You probably do, in your subconscious. But I wouldn't worry about that. Right now, you need rest and quiet. Don't dwell on things that will remain hidden until you are ready. I'm going to say good night and leave you in peace." She kissed the top of Claire's head as Geoff escorted her to the door.

Claire could hear them talking softly and knew they were discussing her. She sipped her drink again and looked over at David.

"Do you think I'm barking mad as well?"

"No. I think you're a brave young lady who is taking on way too much for her years. But that's just my opinion."

"So, you don't think I should do this?"

"If there were another way, I would suggest it, but there isn't. The only other person who could do this is my ten-year-old boy and there is no way I am going to let him do that. So sorry, Kid, I'm throwing you under the bus on this one," he said with a slight smile. She rubbed her eyes with the heel of her free hand.

"I think I'll go to bed." She stood up, wobbling a bit.

"Do you want a hand up the stairs?"

"No thanks, I'll manage. Night, Uncle David."

"Night, Claire. Sleep well."

She walked into the hallway towards the stairs as Geoff headed back to the living room.

"Good night, Uncle Geoff." He pecked her on the cheek and then watched as she climbed the stairs.

Chapter Twenty-Five

The white fog was all-encompassing, pressing in and filling all of Claire's senses while dulling them. It was so thick that it resisted her as she tried to move through it. Claire could feel it unwillingly give way to her pressure. It clung to her legs and arms, trying to immobilise her. From deep within, panic started to rise as it pressed on her while the primal fear of suffocation condensed in her mind. And so, she fought—lashing out—attempting to make room to breathe. She tried calling out, but her voice sounded muted to her ears. Yet she screamed over and over. Her hands pulled and pushed the fog, trying to get it to move.

Finally, her energy waned, and she stopped, refusing to let the panic fill her being. Calming her breathing and racing heart took time. She then tried to clear her mind—for she knew that this fog was only in her dream. With her eyes closed, she reached out and felt no resistance to her touch, clearing a space around her and reopening her eyes.

The man in black was now there, just on the outskirts of the area she had cleared.

"Not a good idea, Claire," he said, shaking his head at her.

"I couldn't breathe."

"Yes, you could. I know what it is you are really doing, and it isn't a good idea," he repeated.

"I know now not to let him touch me. I have to know what's going on." She didn't try to deny it. "I have to know if I can truly trust him."

"He is Marcus's son. He will be loyal to his father."

"But we don't know that for sure. He didn't need to tell us that they were coming to the village."

"He only told you what you wanted to hear."

"That may be so, but I want to ask more. He was my best friend. I don't want to lose that." The man in black said nothing more, but she did get the feeling of compassion from him—the understanding of her feelings.

"Adam!" Claire cried out into the fogginess. "Adam are you there?"

There was no answer—just stillness. The fog hung on, still persistent and resistant to her touch. She spun around herself and pushed out, making the circle around her larger and larger. The man in black was now clearly visible, except for his head. In some ways, his presence was a comfort, as she was not alone.

Again, Claire called out. This time she heard a soft reply, muffled as if under a lot of blankets. She followed the sound, but it kept moving. Again, and again, she called out to expand the space until she could see a murky figure in the fog. She cleared the last of the fog away and stepped backwards.

"There you are. I've been searching for you, but all I kept getting was this fog...what is this?" Adam asked, trying to remove the last tendrils of the fog from his arms.

"I have my suspicions. But I've found you," Claire said from where she stood. Adam stepped towards her, but she held up a hand. "That's close enough, Adam." She could see the confusion in his eyes.

He took another step but suddenly the man in black was standing between them. "Why don't you want me to touch you?"

"It's dangerous. It's something we cannot do here," she said, speaking around her protector.

"I don't understand..."

"Who taught you to Mind Touch?" Claire asked quickly.

"No one. Dad gave me a book and told me I had to study on my own. What's going on, Claire? I wanted to warn you that there are watchers on you again."

"We know." She got the feeling that he was surprised about that.

"I'm in the house behind yours. Please, can we meet?" She could hear a certain note of desperation in his voice, and she took a while to answer him back.

"Yes," she said hesitantly.

"Come now—to the back fence!" he called as he backed away, disappearing into the solid white wall that surrounded her.

The man in black turned to her. "This is a stupid decision, Claire. You are letting your heart rule your head. I know how you feel about him, but he's not good for you."

"You don't know that," Claire said to herself as the dream world faded away.

Claire leapt out of bed and dressed quickly. As quietly as she could, she crept downstairs—carefully avoiding the creaky stair—and then stopping at the back door. She looked out the window towards the back fence and saw a head pop up. Her heart started to thump, and butterflies decided her stomach was a good place to dance. She knew this could be a trap, but she went anyway. Opening the window, Claire quickly disguised herself. She flew out into the cool night air and cautiously made her way to the fence. Once there, she could see Adam clearer. He was desperately searching over the fence for her.

"I'm here, Adam."

"Where? I can't see you." Searching for her, Adam's head poked up above the fence.

"That's the whole point. If you can't see me, then you can't *catch* me," Claire replied.

"Why would I want to do that? I...I...couldn't ever hurt you."

"You did before, Adam. Why did you let me go?"

"I let you go because it was the right thing to do. I've already told you this. You're my very best friend. You are my...you are my world, Claire. I couldn't take you to him. He makes all sorts of promises, but I can't remember the last time he actually kept one." Claire was silent for a while. "Are you still there?" he asked while looking around.

"I am," she said quietly.

"The day that I caught you, I went to see Jack. He told me what Dad had promised him and his mother. Then you told me about my mother still being alive and all his lies unravelled before me. I don't even know if he has ever truly loved me as his son—or only for what I can do for him with my Talents."

There was a catch in Adam's voice that tugged at Claire's heart for a moment, but she steeled herself against it. She was taking too many risks. She wanted to believe him, and she wanted that open and easy friendship back, but she knew that her next words would shatter that relationship into tiny pieces—never to be put back together again.

"You know what we have planned?" she asked him in a small voice.

"No, I have no idea."

"The only way to stop him is to eliminate him. And there's only one way to eliminate someone with Longevity," Claire told him slowly.

"You want to eliminate him? You mean, you wanna kill him?" The shock in his voice was real. "How? I don't understand, Claire. What do you mean that there is only one way?"

"A pulse of Light to the heart," Claire revealed.

Adam took a step backwards from the fence. She could hear his breathing increase.

"They are going to use the Light on him?" he asked incredulously.

"Not *they*," Claire said softly to herself.

"Claire, I know he has done some bad things—I got it all out of Richard—but do they have to kill him? Surely there is another way? There is always another way!"

"I'm sorry, but there isn't. A person with Longevity will outlast those who imprison them. He's already shown that he can't change or won't change. He has had over a hundred and fifty years to prove that."

"You're the one who's changed, Claire. You're not the girl I grew up with anymore." He backed away and left her in the dark.

His words stung her, and she cried as she made her way back to the house. Once back inside, she shut and locked the window. Just as she was about to head back upstairs, a voice spoke behind her in the dark.

"Did that help?"

She spun on the spot and saw David sitting at the table.

"Uncle David, I..."

"I know what you were doing, Claire. I heard every word."

"How? I made sure that my voice wouldn't carry."

"Ahh, but you forget my Talent. Great hearing can be a curse sometimes. I stood at the window and trained my hearing on you. So once again, did meeting Adam face-to-face and talking to him help?"

"I don't know. I don't know at all." She finally faced him, unable to bring to words what she was thinking.

"Right now is probably not the best time to talk about it. Shall we leave it until the morning?" he asked gently as he came towards her, and she nodded in the dark.

"I think I may have made things worse," she told him.

He smoothed her hair from her face. "You may have, Claire, but we won't know anything more until morning. Go back to bed and get some real sleep." He watched her go and then went back to the kitchen table, pulling Geoff's whiskey bottle toward him and pouring another drink. He knocked it back in one shot and then went back to bed himself.

Bleary-eyed and sullen was Claire's mood the next morning while she sat at the table. Her stomach was churning in regret and fear. And the more she stared at the cereal in her bowl, the more it looked unappealing. Finally, she pushed it away from her, spilling the milk onto the table.

Geoff entered the room and took one look at her before turning the jug on.

"You didn't get a good night's sleep, did you?" he asked, pulling a cup out of the cupboard.

"No. And can you *please* tell Lilith to stop putting suggestions on me that I do not want?" The venom in her voice stopped him in his tracks.

"I suggest that you tell your aunt yourself," he replied sternly as he sat down. "Why do I get the feeling that this is about more than just a suggestion from your aunt?" He waited for her reply. She sighed and put her head in her hands.

"I'm sorry. I'm not angry at you or Aunt Lilith. Just myself. I did something stupid last night."

"Do you want to tell me about it?" She gave him a small nod. "I'm all ears."

Claire sat waiting for the right words to come—afraid of how angry he would get. She lifted her face and just blurted it out.

"I met with Adam last night, face-to-face."

"You did what?" He placed his cup onto the table with a bit more force than he'd really intended.

"I am really sorry, but I *had* to talk to him," she admitted, defending herself.

"Claire, anything could have happened. You could have been taken!" The sudden anger had dissipated from his voice and was replaced with concern.

"I took every precaution, Uncle Geoff. I made sure that we were alone and that he couldn't get to me—I promise."

"Well, you had better tell me everything. How did you arrange to meet?"

"I broke through Aunt Lilith's suggestion and Dream Messaged with him," Claire began, and continued on with her tale.

Geoff listened carefully as she related the conversation she had with Adam. "And what was the feeling you got from him?" he asked when she had finished.

"I honestly don't know. He was shocked, but I don't know if what I told him is gonna help us or make it worse."

"Do you think he's aware? Aware that it is you who's going to do this?"

"I didn't tell him. I've never let on to him that I can do more than the Flight and Hiding Talents."

"Good. Let's keep it that way." He sat in silence, and Claire could almost see the cogs turning in his mind.

Just then, David entered the kitchen and looked at them. He poured himself a cup of coffee and then leaned against the bench.

"I take it you've told him about your little adventure last night?" David asked as Claire nodded, still watching her Uncle Geoff.

"All right. We know a few more things. They were unaware of our plan, that Marcus had promised something to Jack and Mary, and that Adam is—or should I say *was*—on our side," Geoff said, finally speaking up.

"I want to know what Jack and Mary were really offered," David said as he sat at the table.

"So do I. But so far, they aren't talking," Geoff told them.

"What if Aunt Lilith did her Mind Touch on them?" Claire asked.

"I don't think she'd be very keen to do that. She only likes to use it when she deems it necessary—like last night," he said pointedly.

"She said that yesterday when I went to talk to her about the dreams."

"Surely it can't hurt to ask her," David added.

Geoff thought for a moment. "I'll go and see her in person. This isn't something you can ask over the phone."

"What about the watchers?" Claire questioned. "I could bind them up for a while if you want. That way, they're out of harm's way and they can't contact Marcus."

"I can't see the harm in that. Can you, David?"

"I think that's an excellent idea—just be careful," David warned her as Claire rose from the table and started to head upstairs.

"Hang on, Kid, don't you wanna eat some more?" Geoff asked her.

"I'm not hungry," she replied, already halfway down the hallway.

"I think she's pining," David said at last.

"Pining? For what?"

"Not for what, Geoff, for whom!"

"Adam?"

"You've never noticed how she acts when she's talking about him?" Geoff shook his head. "Jess acted the same way about John when they first started dating. She is her mother's daughter." He laughed a little over that and drained the rest of his cup.

"But Claire is only seventeen," Geoff protested.

Thirty minutes later, Claire was ready. She stood in the hall beside her Uncle David, who was about to open the door slightly for her. He checked outside first to make sure the coast was clear and then stopped.

"A black car has just pulled up across the street," he reported. "There is one guy getting out—he's entering the house." He paused his commentary while the butterflies piled up in Claire's stomach. "Another guy is coming out and getting into the car. Now he's driving off, and the street is clear." He turned to Claire and looked at her expectantly. She gave him a single curt nod and as he opened the door, she disappeared through the crack.

Flying across the street, it felt great to Claire to be doing something. Talking was all well and good, but action was what she was craving. She thought to herself that that was due to the lack of exercise lately. Circling the house—first from above and then from the side—she could find no other access point other than the slightly broken cat door flap. She squeezed her way in and hid in the corner for a moment, getting her bearings.

The layout was very similar to her uncle's house, which was in her favour. Claire rose to the ceiling and hugged the walls as she made her way through the house until she reached the living room in the front. There was not a stick of furniture in most of the house and it smelt of old musty mould, but in the living room was an outdoor lounge chair and a camping cot alongside a cooler, which was doubling as a side table for the chair.

A tall man stood at the window and faced out, looking directly at Geoff's house across the street. He wore casual clothes, and his hands were clasped behind his back. He rocked slowly onto the balls of his feet and then back down onto his heels. Claire could recognise someone who didn't like the thought of being cooped up all day, doing nothing but watching. But she also recognised the man as the one she had dubbed Deep Voice from the theatre. His name came back to her in a flash—Mr James. The momentary jolt of empathy she had felt for him evaporated, and she relished the idea of getting a bit of revenge. Claire settled down onto the floor in the farthest corner from the man.

Cupping her hands in front of her, she pulled from inside a small light. Gently holding it, she took off again and shielded it from his view. Waiting until she was above his head, Claire quickly let go of the light and directed it to balloon out and take the shape of a donut. Before the man even knew what had hit him, the light tightened his arms to his sides and then started to extend, becoming tube-like. It now covered and bound Mr James from his shoulders to his knees.

With a wave of her hand, Claire lifted him off his feet and transported him into a lying position on the cot. She watched him struggle, trying to free himself from the constraint.

"Hello, Mr James. If you struggle, it'll only get tighter and hotter," she whispered into his ear.

Mr James looked around him to find just where the voice had come from and went as white as a sheet, lying still as he'd been told.

Zooming out of the house and back out into the fresh air, Claire filled her lungs as she moved across the street and over the roof of Geoff's house. Now down the other side of the apex and into the back yard, she paused at the fence and then gave herself a little shake as she passed over it, and entered the house via one of the vents she had found the other night. Inside, she went very carefully.

Flittering from one high ceiling corner to the other, Claire made her way through the house—searching for the other watcher she knew was in there—until she heard a toilet flush from the back of the house. A figure made his way down the long hallway and into the living room, where it had almost identical furniture to the previous house. *Very imaginative,* Claire thought to herself. The person stood in a pool of light that came from the side window as a wave of relief swept over her. He was not Adam, but he was the counterpart to Mr James, and she had to reach deep down to remember that he was called Mr Benning.

Quickly gathering herself, she performed the same task as she had before. And within a few moments, the second watcher was bound and lying on the cot. She gave him the same message as the first and laughed this time at his reaction. Swooping out of the house, Claire gave herself time to have a bit of fun before returning home through the kitchen window.

"Done. But I think we only have a few hours to work with," she told them.

"We'd better get moving, then." Geoff picked up a bag by the front door and they then left the house.

The sedate pace that Geoff drove started to grate on Claire's nerves. She thought she could have run to Lilith's faster. After the car had pulled up, Geoff told them to stay put and exited. She watched him walk to the front door that was draped in pretty pink roses. But before he could knock, it opened, and Geoff went inside. Sometime later, the green door opened again, and he came out, followed by an unhappy-looking Lilith. Slamming the door behind her, she stalked to the car with Geoff chasing along behind. Claire guessed that her uncle had done some fast talking to get Lilith to agree.

The short distance to the hall seemed laughable, with the three of them arriving only a minute after leaving Lilith's. Geoff's need for speed and secrecy seemed impossibly stupid, considering most people in the village only used their cars if they were going outside the village bounds—otherwise they would walk or bicycle. He parked the car in the rear of the hall and then led them to the back door with the bag in hand.

Inside, the light was cascading in through the high windows, sending it splashing on the old wooden floors. But it was not the main hall that Geoff was wanting. He went to the lighting board and opened the panel up. Underneath was a little switch, tucked away and almost unnoticeable. He flicked it and a panel moved in the wall, showing a steep spiral staircase going down. Claire raised her eyebrows.

The stairs were dimly lit, and it took a lot of patience to manage them, but down they all trooped—with Geoff in the rear to trip the panel back into place. At the bottom was a corridor and a single light, and off this space were two solid-looking doors. Producing a set of keys from his pocket, Geoff stood in front of the first one and opened it.

As the door was pushed aside, Claire could see Mary, sitting on a comfy chair with a book in her hands and feet up on a footstool. The elderly lady looked at them over the rim of her glasses. She stood up when she saw that more people than just Geoff had come to visit.

"Don't just stand there, you had all better come in!" Mary told them, shutting her book, and placing it on the arm of her chair.

Geoff entered first and placed the bag he had brought with him onto a small table. David and Lilith entered after him with Claire bringing up the rear, looking around the room. It was a small space that had been divided into different living areas to make it more comfortable for the only occupant.

"Well, I must say that it is about time you got here. You're late," she said with an officious tone to Geoff.

"Yes, sorry about that, Mary, something came up. But we are here now, and your supplies have been delivered." Geoff patted the bag.

"I hope you got the coffee I told you to get, and not that other muck you gave me before." She went to the bag and started to lift things out, studying each one before putting it away. Once she was done, she offered Lilith the only other comfy chair and sat down in the one she'd previously vacated. "So, to what do I owe the pleasure of so many visitors today?" Mary asked as she looked around at them all.

"Same as always, Mary—information," Geoff said.

"I have told you all I am going to tell you, Geoff, so you are wasting your time. Once Marcus finds out where you're holding Jack and me, we'll be out of here in a flash."

"We have been very patient with you, but you see, things are moving along rather quickly outside this room, and we cannot wait any longer now. We need to know exactly what it is that Marcus is going to do," Geoff said, but Mary kept silent and refused to talk.

"Mary, you know me! We were in the same year at school together. You know my Talent," Lilith told her as she moved in her chair, sitting forward.

Mary began to look increasingly nervous. "Yes, I do know you and I know that you would never use your Talent in such a way. It'd be abhorrent to you."

"The thought of doing this is abhorrent," Lilith agreed. "I don't want to be messing with your mind any more than you want me to. But we need to act soon or the lives of people I love are going to be in danger."

"You know the rules. You have no Recaller here. You cannot do this without one," she said triumphantly. "Not even the word of three Talented ones is good enough."

"You are wrong, Mary. There is a Recaller here in our midst," Lilith stated calmly.

Mary shifted slightly in her seat and looked at the other three. Her eyes finally alighted on Claire.

"Her? No, her only Talents are Flight and Hiding. You would've told me if she had any others—you being such a stickler for protocol."

"I am going to let you in on a little secret, Mary. Claire's a Chameleon, and an adept one at that. So far, we haven't found a Talent that she cannot turn a hand to. So, she'll act as our Recaller." Lilith's voice rang with pride for her great-niece as she gave Claire a beaming smile.

"A Chameleon? No, I don't believe you."

At that moment, Claire produced three Lights and started to juggle them while levitating.

"You see, she can even use them simultaneously. Show-off," Geoff said with pride. Extinguishing the Lights, Claire blushed at the praise of her aunt and uncle.

Mary leaned back in her chair. Her face had gone white, and her hands shook.

"You hadn't seen any of this, had you, Mary?" David asked.

"I have not had a true vision for some time," she admitted to them with some distress.

"For how long?" Geoff pressed.

"About a year, maybe two."

"How long have you been in contact with Marcus?"

"For over forty years. He sought me out, wanting to know what his future held. And wanting to know if he would succeed with his plan. He wrapped me around his little finger. He was so charming as he swept me off my feet. I was naive and didn't know how to resist his Charm." She was silent for a while. "Well, if I'm going to tell you the story, we had better have something to drink."

"I'll make it," Claire offered, feeling awkward in the situation. She took their preferences and went to the tiny kitchenette to make it while Mary resumed telling her story.

"I told him what he wanted to hear... that he'd be a successful man in business, and he would have sons and that he would be very old when he died. At that, he told me that he had no intention of dying. He's an extremely arrogant man—beautiful to look at, yes—but very arrogant." She paused. "I enjoyed our time together. I was a bit silly back then. He'd visit me every now and then and we'd meet in secret. I ran away from the village when he left to go back to the city. No one knew that he was here—he had been expelled from the community for a long time at that stage. I ran straight to him, and at first, he was happy to see me, but then I think I was a little too clingy. He soon became standoffish. Especially when I told him I was pregnant. Thank you, dear." She said as Claire gave her a mug. She took a sip and held it in her hands delicately as if she were holding a bone China teacup.

"I returned to the village with my tail between my legs, realising that he hadn't loved me and could not love me. He has no concept of the term—except for himself. When I gave birth to Jack, I let him know he was born and that he was a boy. I got a small package in the mail, and inside was some baby clothes and congratulations in the form of a bank statement with five thousand dollars on it. I was so ashamed. That is the reason I told no one who the father was. It had nothing to do with Marcus not wanting anyone to know. I just didn't want my boy being tarred with his brush." The defiance was back in her voice as she spoke.

"I had thought that he would leave us alone, but again, I was naïve. He somehow found out that Jack had a Talent. I don't know how—I had told Jack to tell no one of his ability and I certainly didn't say anything. But he found out and he decided that this was a good thing. He wants an army—that's how he put it. He wants an army of Talents to be at his beck and call, so he could use them to further his greed. I would let him know who had developed Talent and he'd handpick them for his cause. Some he could not, like your parents," she said, looking directly at Claire.

"My parents had Talents?" Claire asked, suddenly amazed that she had not been told by anyone that they had.

"Yes. You mean you haven't told her? Amazing." She turned back to Claire. "Your mother had Mind Touch and your father was a Recaller. I really cannot believe you kept this secret from her!" She laughed and shook her head at the thought.

"We'll talk about it later, Claire," Geoff said quietly. Everyone in the room was now looking at Mary, waiting for her to resume.

"Where was I? Oh, yes. Those he could not persuade over to him, he eliminated. I was so sad when Jess and John died. If they'd had more children—well, who knows what Talents could've been produced." She looked speculatively at Claire. "I had a vision of you, young lady. My vision was unclear, but

I could see greatness surrounding you with a shadow behind. At first, I thought that meant you had great people around you, but now I think the greatness might just be from you." She took another sip of her drink, pausing for effect to make her mysticism seem great.

"I told him about you, but he'd already had you in his sights and told me to leave you alone, but to keep you, Geoff, in check. Yes, he knew you were working for the other side, and it amused him to use you the way he did. He let information leak to you. He fed it to you and you had no idea. The high and mighty Geoffrey Brown—who thought he knew what was best for everyone—was just a lackey like the rest of us." She felt smug at this point and chuckled. "Then news came that he was going to be testing your Talents, Claire. He wanted you back here, so my Jack could teach you how to Hide. Jack wasn't happy about it at first, so I faked a vision to get him onside. Even as a child, he was always trouble. I told him that it was his destiny to teach you and through his teaching, he would come to know you and you'd be together— which made him happy, and he accepted. Especially after he saw you that first night. What I didn't know was that he'd reached out to his father. I couldn't tell you when it happened, but he was telling me that his father had agreed to the match. I think Marcus only told him that so that he would do his will. My poor Jack.

"So that's that. I don't know any more. Marcus only ever sent missives or watchers to me when he wanted something done and I could be of use to him. The plans we told you at the meeting, Geoff, have some truth to them. He *does* want Claire to start his army, but exactly who the sire will be? I have no idea." She sat quietly in the chair and sipped her coffee.

They were all quiet for a while until Geoff broke the silence. "Thank you, Mary. We appreciate your candour."

"Only because you threatened me with her." She nodded in Lilith's direction.

"Claire, can you please clean up the cups? I wouldn't want to put Mary out any more than I have to," Lilith stated, holding out a cup to her.

"Yes, Aunt Lilith." Claire collected the cups and took them to the sink, rinsing them all out and putting them on the draining board to dry. When she turned back, Lilith was standing beside Mary, and she had a strained look on her face. Geoff and David both looked sheepish and uncomfortable.

"Right, we'll be off now, Mary. Thank you for the coffee," Geoff said sincerely.

"Anytime, Geoff, it is always good to see you. And you as well, Lilith. Pass on my regards to your parents, David. Please tell your mother that I expect her next week for our usual card game."

Claire was startled at the change in Mary and put two and two together to get a whopping answer.

Mary spotted Claire as the girl moved towards the door. "Oh, you are so pretty, just like your mother. I do hope you are taking proper care of her, Geoff!"

"I am, Mary. Well, we really must be going." He opened the door and ushered them out.

"Please come again. I love having visitors," Mary bade them, waving them goodbye from where she stood.

When the door closed, Claire was about to say something, but Lilith spoke quietly. "Shh. We'll talk later."

Geoff had already locked Mary's door and had started towards the other as Claire stood still.

"I don't know if I can face him," she confessed to her uncle.

"I need you to. His bindings are wearing away and I do not want to ask Jasper to do it again." He flicked his eyes to David with a guilty look.

After a small nod of her head, Geoff opened the door. When Claire walked in, she saw that Jack was lying on the bed. The light that surrounded part of the room and encompassed him was dull and flickering. He sat up when they entered, smiling when he saw Claire.

"Can you do it now?" Geoff asked her quietly as she nodded.

She produced a light and sent it out towards Jack. The new light encompassed the space he resided in as the old flickered and died, shredding like confetti before blinking out.

"Why? How?" Jack stared at Claire, his face a mask of confusion.

"You know why, Jack," Geoff said, stepping up to the edge of the light.

"It won't change anything, you know. Father will be here soon to get me and then Claire and I can be together."

Jack looked her up and down suggestively. Claire shuddered at the thought as she noticed David stepping in front to shield her.

"That isn't going to happen, Jack. We've just had a nice chat with your mother, and she told us that this whole fantasy of yours is all her fault. She simply gave you a false vision so that you'd comply with your father's wishes," Geoff unveiled.

Alienated, Jack sat on the bed and looked at Geoff. "No, you are lying. Mother wouldn't have said that. Her visions *always* come true."

"Not for the last year, Jack. She hasn't had a true vision for over a year," Lilith told him.

"I don't believe you," he said, shaking his head. Claire was surprised at the calmness he was showing as she really expected him to rile and shout at the news.

While the three adults were talking to Jack, an idea was forming in Claire's mind. After witnessing Mary's transformation at the hands of Lilith, Claire wondered if it would work on Jack. She mulled it over as she leaned up against the door, going over all the books she had read and committed to memory—trying to find a kernel of hope for her theory.

Jack was still being defiant and unwilling to talk, refusing to believe what he was being told. Claire took the opportunity to pull Lilith aside and quickly whisper her theory to her. Her aunt listened carefully to what she was saying and wasn't sure if it was even possible. She started to argue that she'd need to do some more reading on the matter.

"We don't have time. I need to know if we can do it!" Claire said while looking pointedly at Jack.

"You are as bad as your uncle. This is unnecessary and unwarranted," Lilith told the young girl.

"But I think it's necessary and warranted. The Light will only inhibit him so long, then he's free to use his Talent. I've looked around this room and can see one, maybe two places where he could escape. By doing this, it'll save on us having to renew the bonds. If you are worried about it not working, then I'll happily bind him again and again and again."

Lilith waited a while before she spoke. "When we do this, it is going to have to be fast. I need to reach him before he realises he is free and can escape."

"I think I can do that." Claire nodded, clearly relieved she didn't have to argue anymore.

"You know," Jack began. "Whispering while other people are present is very rude."

Claire looked up and Lilith jumped. A small smile crept over his face.

"Secrets and lies. That is all you have brought me today. Secrets and lies."

Claire moved closer to the barrier, feeling very nervous and steeling herself for what must be done.

"Why would we lie to you, Jack?" she asked him, trying to sound casual.

"Because my pretty, pretty girl, you are against my father. You've been brainwashed by these people to think that what he wants is wrong. But it isn't. We were blessed with these powers to use them for our own good—for our people."

"Is that what Marcus told you? That he's doing this for The Community?"

"Of course, why else?" He got up and moved towards her. "He told me that we'll all live in luxury and will want for nothing and that we will all be happy together—not hiding from the world."

At that moment, she could see the little fatherless boy he must have been growing up, desperately wanting the acceptance and love of a father—one he knew deep inside did not want him.

Claire stepped towards the light and stood right on the edge. He came to face her, looking down with hungry eyes that made her want to run screaming in the opposite direction. It was all a blur—the light came down and with a speed Claire didn't know existed, Lilith leapt forward, reaching out to Jack. Claire was pulled out of the way by David as he shielded her with his body. Geoff started in shock and cried out. But it was done. Lilith crumpled to the floor—her face was pale and waxen, and her breathing came in short, sharp pants. David pushed Claire towards Geoff, turning and scooping Lilith up while also moving her closer to the door. Claire flew to the only exit she could see in the wall and hovered to watch Jack.

"Will someone please tell me what the hell is going on?" Geoff yelled and his voice echoed around the stone chamber.

Jack stared at him with a look of confusion and then quickly realised he could get away. Claire could see him attempting to escape, repeatedly trying to shrink and hide, but each time failing.

"What have you done to me?" he asked urgently.

"It is for your own good, Jack. Marcus was using you, just as he uses everyone. This idea of a utopia where we can use our Talents openly and live together in harmony was just rubbish he spun you to get you on his side. He was never going to let you have me," Claire said sadly as she lowered herself back to the ground.

"What did you do to me?" his voice whined at Lilith, who was leaning against the door.

"I burned your Talents away," Lilith blurted out between breaths. "I took them away, so you cannot harm Claire."

"You old witch! You give them back!" he exclaimed while stepping towards her.

David stood between them and stared Jack down. "I wouldn't do that if I were you," he warned Jack.

"I don't think there's any more we can find out here. Time to go," Geoff said, still slightly shaken at what had happened.

As they filed out of the room, Claire turned and set a barrier of light around the room once more.

"Just in case," she said to Jack before leaving him all alone.

Chapter Twenty-Six

"I need a drink!" Geoff said as he stalked back up the stairs, taking two at a time, with the others following at a slower pace. David helped Lilith, and Claire brought up the rear. He waited for them at the top, his hands on his hips impatiently. "What happened down there?" he demanded, his voice echoing through the hall. When they were all up, he triggered the switch and the wall slid back into place.

"It was my idea," Claire told him.

"Really? Well, you could've let me in on it. You scared me to death and back!"

They left the hall and drove back to the house. Lilith was still weak, and David made sure she was comfortable on the couch.

"Okay, we're home now, and I'd like a full report of how and why." Geoff sat heavily in his chair.

"When you were talking with Jack, I was still thinking of what happened to Mary. Then I started to wonder if Aunt Lilith could put a suggestion on Jack to make him think his Talents had been taken away."

"To which I wholeheartedly disagreed," Lilith interjected quickly.

"Yes, you did, but I convinced you to try. So, I baited him to get him to come closer and Aunt Lilith did the rest."

"And what about you?" Geoff rounded on David.

"Me? Lilith only told me to be ready. I had no idea what they were planning." He put his hands up in defence.

"There was no time to talk to you about it and I'm sorry we didn't, but I had to act. If we had all trooped out of that room to discuss it and then trooped back in, he would've known something was up. He isn't as stupid as he looks," Claire said. The clock chimed twelve and she looked at it. "Um, Uncle Geoff, do you want me to keep the Watchers bound up or do you want me to release them?"

"What?" Geoff asked shortly, his temper still up.

"The Watchers? I'm not sure if anyone will be checking on them soon or not, but they are still bound."

"Oh...them...yes, you'd better let them go." Still sulking on the events of the morning, he dismissed her with a wave of his hand as she left the house via the back door.

Once again, she started with the house across the street. She squeezed through the small gap in the cat door and flew into the living room. The Watcher was still in the same position— on his side and lying on the cot.

She hovered near his ear. "I do hope it didn't get too hot for you. Now this is what's gonna happen, Mr James. I'm going to release the bonds and you're going to remain exactly the way you are now for as long as the light is shining...got it? After that, you can do whatever you like. Nod if you understand."

He gave a small nod.

"Good." She flew to the ceiling and relaxed the ring of light that bound him. It slipped from his body but still hovered above his head. Mr James watched it with some trepidation.

Claire then left and made her way to the second house. She found the Watcher and told him the same thing. She was halfway through when a car pulled up and she saw Adam exit the vehicle and walk towards the door. She released the man behind her and extinguished the ball of light, pushing herself up into the corner.

"Tony, here's your lunch," Adam called out as he entered the back door.

Tony was just rising from the cot, but not reacting the same as Mr James had.

"Bugger lunch!" Tony said as he grabbed the keys that dangled loosely from Adam's hand and bolted for the door, leaving Adam looking confused and staring after him. Outside the car roared to life and tyres squealed as it peeled out of the driveway and down the street.

"What the hell?" Adam stood in the middle of the living room, staring out the window at the retreating car.

"I'm afraid I've been scaring your Watchers again," Claire said, increasing the volume of her voice so he could hear her. He looked around, trying to find the source of the voice. "It's me, Adam—Claire."

"I'm not sure I want to talk to you right now, Claire. I'm still angry at what you told me last night." He dumped the bag of food down on the cooler with a thump.

"I'm sorry. I needed you to know what was planned so that you could…oh, I don't know what you could to do with it. I just wanted to know if you were with us or your father, and I've totally screwed everything up! I'll leave you alone. Goodbye, Adam." She started to fly to the gap she'd entered by, but he called out.

"Claire, wait. Please, don't go. I miss you so much," he called out to her, still trying to find where she was.

She stopped in her tracks and turned back to him, hovering in another corner.

"I think there might be another way—other than killing your father," she told him.

"What is it?" he asked her, brightening a bit.

"We may be able to place a suggestion on him."

"Mind Touch?"

"Yes. We've used it successfully on someone else. We gave him a suggestion that his Talent was burnt out and that it cannot be used anymore."

"You burnt out his Talent?" Adam asked with some surprise.

"No. Just placed the suggestion. To him, his Talent was everything. I was thinking we could do the same to your dad," Claire replied.

"Was this someone Jack?" he asked but she didn't answer. "I take it from your silence that it was." He paced the room, thinking. "It is a better idea than killing him. How do we do it?"

"Well, you have Mind Touch, so surely you should know."

"To be quite honest, I only skimmed over the book Dad gave me—I studied the bits I was interested in," he said a little sheepishly.

"Dream Messaging being the main one?" Claire asked sarcastically.

"Yes, but I stumbled on that one by accident on my own." Adam finally sat down in the chair.

"How do you stumble on something like that?" Slowly she began to descend and now hovered somewhere halfway down the wall.

"I had a dream about you, and it just felt so real that I thought you were there. I could see you so clearly. I remember calling out and I thought you could almost hear me, but then that black smoke that hangs around you was there."

"Black smoke? What black smoke?" Claire was confused at this.

"You know, when we Dream Message, there is always a column of black smoke shape-looking thing. I'm not describing it very well, am I? Like last night when I messaged you to meet me, the smoke was right between us. Sometimes it's off to the side and other times it's right there."

"Oh, you see him as black smoke," Claire declared as comprehension loomed large in her mind.

"Him?"

"I don't know who he is, but in my dreams he's a man dressed all in black with a hood covering his face. I think he's there to protect me."

"You have a man who is in your dreams, and you think he is there to protect you? I think you should see someone about that." Adam gave a little chuckle.

"I have. My Aunt Lilith. She checked it out and told me that he is not there to hurt me but to protect me."

"This is stupid, Claire! Can't you just show yourself to me and we can talk properly?" Adam turned his head as he sat, trying to locate the spot her voice was coming from, but Claire moved again—always keeping her distance.

"I don't think that's a good idea, Adam—not just yet. Since all this started, I'm having a few trust issues with you. It has to do with the fact I've been lied to for quite some time. I take it you were aware of the Talents while we were in the city?"

"Well, yes, but I didn't know you had them as well. Dad only told me about them when he discovered I could get people to do what I wanted with a touch."

"I know you used Charm on me, but did you ever use Mind Touch?"

"Never! Not ever! I swear to you that I have not. I swear on my…my own life. I was going to say my father's, but I didn't think that would go down too well," he said with a slight smile.

Claire giggled in return.

"I've missed that laugh," he said softly. "I do want to stop him, Claire. But you have to understand something. He is my father. He's the only family I've ever known. And I was only recently told that I had an older brother." He paused and looked at his feet. "Can you tell me about my mother? Is she still here in the village?"

"She has left to keep her boys safe."

"Boys? So, I have younger brothers?" he asked brightly, his head coming up.

"Yes, two. They're nice kids," she told him.

"She's married, then?"

"Yes."

"Who to?" Adam sounded eager for the information.

"I'm not sure that's my place to tell you, Adam," Claire said calmly.

"Getting information from you is like pulling teeth! I could Charm it out of you, you know," he quipped.

"No, you need to see me to focus that Talent—hence why I am staying invisible. And it doesn't work on me anymore. I can tell when you're using it."

"Argh, you're no fun!" He laughed at that. "Well, is she nice? At least tell me what she's like."

"She can be a bit prickly, but I think that's changing. Underneath was a woman who was scared her secrets would come out and because of that, she held herself so tightly that she couldn't love properly. Does that make sense?"

"Sort of."

"Well, now her secret is out, she has discovered that the world isn't dissolving around her, and she has people who love her very much."

Adam was quiet for a while before he spoke again. "Do you think she will want to meet me?"

"I'm sure of it, Adam," Claire told him tenderly. "She said that there hasn't been a day that she didn't think of you."

Silence descended between them, and Claire's stomach started to growl as she watched him mull over what she had told him.

"Claire, when this is all over, do you think that we can be friends again?"

"I hope so, Adam. I really do hope so. I miss us," she told him frankly as she could feel the pain of that statement welling up inside herself. "I have to go now. They'll be worried about me."

"Don't go just yet! Can't you stay a little bit longer?" he asked, getting to his feet.

"No. I can't."

"Why were you here in the first place?" he asked her.

"Scaring the Watchers. See ya, Adam." With that, she left without waiting for him to say it in return.

Back home, Claire shed her invisibility and returned to her normal size. The hunger pangs were now growing quite painful, and she grabbed not one but two apples from the bowl and headed toward the lounge.

"I don't know what it was that you did to him, but the Watcher across the street just came tearing out of the house and ran down the road," David said, smiling at her as she entered the living room. Claire saw that Lilith was still laid out on the couch but was now asleep. Geoff was nowhere to be seen.

"Well, it was your fault!" she said while taking a huge bite from the apple.

"My fault? How did you come to that conclusion??"

"When I was practicing on you and I got angry, the binding became hot, remember, so I made it that if they struggled…"

"Their bindings would get hot," David finished for her.

"Yep. Where's Uncle Geoff?" Claire asked, finishing off the first apple.

"I think he's in his study. Is there something I can help with?"

"I'll talk to you all over lunch. I'm starving," she said, grabbing her sides as she felt the hunger pangs biting deep. "These apples are just not doing it," Claire complained.

"Come on. Let's leave sleeping beauty to her rest and we'll go whip something up." He steered her out of the room and into the kitchen.

The whole time they were together, Claire was quiet as David kept giving her sideways looks. He noticed that she stared out of the window a lot but said nothing. He knew her well enough now to know that she would talk in her own time.

Lunch was called, and Claire gently woke her great-aunt up.

"You must think me a foolish old woman," Lilith said, immediately patting her hair to make sure it was still meticulously in place.

"Not at all, Aunt Lilith. I think you were very brave today. I'm sorry I asked you to do it."

"It needed to be done," Lilith said, waving her away. "We couldn't have left him like that, or Mary, for that matter."

They sat at the table and were quickly joined by Geoff. Claire started to eat immediately and did not stop until her plate was cleared. She sat nibbling on a piece of bread while she waited for her elders to finish their lunches.

"So, are you going to tell us what happened?" David prompted her. Geoff looked up from his food and gave Claire a quizzical look.

"I let the Watchers go, but when I got to the second house, I was interrupted when Adam turned up. I released the Watcher, and he ran out of the house and took off in the car."

"And...?" Geoff asked.

"And I talked to Adam. He says he's on our side. I asked him outright, but he still wasn't happy about the plan—that was, until I mentioned that we could possibly use a Mind Touch suggestion."

"Claire, I am not sure it will work on Marcus. Yes, it worked on Jack, but his mind was suggestible to start with. I don't know about Marcus, he could be a lot stronger," Lilith told her.

"It's worth a try, though, isn't it? I mean, I don't want to kill him at all, as the thought of having to do what I might have to is giving me the willies." Claire shivered at the idea.

"We don't want you to either," David told her gently.

"All right, we will try the Mind Touch way first, and if I can't manage it, then you're going have to have the Light on standby," Lilith told Claire as they all looked at her. "What? Who else is going to do it?"

"Me—for a start," Claire said. "I don't want you risking your life, Aunt Lilith. I don't want to risk anyone else's life except mine."

"Well, you aren't going up there alone, young lady," David said emphatically.

"Definitely not!" Geoff chimed in.

"So, you are stuck with us," Lilith declared.

"No, I agree with Claire on your involvement, Lil," Geoff told his sister. "We have only just started talking again and there is no way I'm putting you in harm's way." She started to protest but he cut her off. "Malcolm would kill me if you got hurt."

"Aunt Lil, can you teach me how to Mind Touch in the way I need to?" Claire asked quietly, hoping to defuse the conversation.

"If that's the only role offered to me, then I will. But you'd better be careful—I may be too old to be of service." She shot a look at her younger brother.

"Not old, dear sister—just too precious," Geoff said, taking her hand.

"Get off me, you fool," Lilith ordered as she swatted his hand away.

"So, what else did you talk about?" David asked Claire.

"He wanted to know about his mother," Claire told him, breaking the bread into little pieces.

"What did you say?"

"I told him that she's nice—that she wasn't in the village at the moment and that he had two younger half-brothers. I told him how now that her secret was out, she was shedding her fears. I thought he can wait to find out any more information, as I didn't think he needed to know that his mother is my aunt."

David nodded at that. "Very wise!"

Claire and Lilith spent that afternoon up in Claire's bedroom, as her aunt helped her come to grips with Mind Touch and placing a suggestion on someone.

"Before we begin, I have to tell you that your mind is like a sponge, it soaks up new information, and then transform that information into action very quickly. But with Mind Touch, you must go carefully. You don't want to go stomping in boots and all, but touch the mind like a feather. I want you to first observe with all your senses and not just the common five. All right? We will begin."

Lilith sat opposite Claire and almost in benediction, she gently touched her head. In turn, Claire opened herself up to her great-aunt, but Lilith pulled back away from her.

"Too much, Claire. You offer too much up—never be that open with anyone."

Claire nodded and apologised as they started again. She could feel her aunt's touch, not just on top of her head but somehow inside. She could feel her moving around and sorting through thoughts and feelings, delving deeper into her mind and subconscious.

"Hello, Lil," his deep voice called through her mind. "Why are you teaching her this?"

Claire could feel her aunt jump both physically and mentally at the voice and the question, and as a result, she pulled out of Claire's mind a lot quicker than she'd intended. Claire wobbled at the lost connection and soon righted herself.

"Well, there's a turnup for the books," Lilith exclaimed.

"He called you Lil," Claire stated, her eyebrows knitting together.

"Yes, and there are only three people who have ever called me that—one is my twin, and one is Geoff."

"And the other?"

"Was your father." Lilith backed up and sat in the soft chair that now made Claire's room home.

"Dad?" she questioned, and Lilith nodded. "So, the man in black is...is my father?" The visions all became clear, and she realised she'd seen his face many times in her dreams, but she still didn't know why his name and face had been hidden in the first place. "I don't understand!"

"I don't know myself." She stared at Claire with utter confusion written on her face.

"Can you contact him again?" Claire asked her eagerly.

"Do you want me to?"

"Yes, of course. Please, Aunt Lilith," she begged.

The older woman nodded and moved to sit by Claire on the bed. Once again, she placed a light hand on the girl's head and began to search through her mind. Claire felt the tentative touch, and once again he was there.

"Lil," her father greeted Lilith a little darkly.

It was a strange feeling for Claire. There was a conversation going on in her mind that she had nothing to do with and no control over. She almost laughed at the maddening thought.

"John, how are you here in Claire's mind?" Lilith asked him.

"Jess did it. She's here with me—only weaker—and I'm not sure why. She can't tell me, either. As I understand it, it's not us fully, only a semblance of us. Just a small piece to watch over our daughter."

"That is *very* advanced. Not even I could attempt that!" Lilith said with awe in her voice.

"Now, I would like you to answer my question. Why are you teaching our daughter to Mind Touch?" John's voice sounded firm and demanding.

"Because she needs to learn it to not only protect herself but also those around her who love her. How much are you aware of the outside world?" Lilith asked him.

"We are aware more in her dreams, and we aren't happy about the boy who keeps visiting her there. We got the feeling that Claire's scared of him."

"He wants to help Claire. She only felt scared because she thought she couldn't trust him."

"Little Adam...we remember him. But he's still Marcus's son."

"John, please protect her in her dreams," Lilith requested.

"We will. Jess is tired and must rest." With that, his voice trailed away and faded back into her subconscious.

Lilith broke the connection slowly and put her hand over her mouth. Tears stood out in her eyes before tumbling down her cheeks.

"Oh, my dear," she said as she bundled Claire up in a hug.

"I don't understand. How is this possible, Aunty Lilith?" Claire asked, still trying to process what she had witnessed.

"I don't know. I've never heard of it actually being done before. I would have no idea how to go about it, but they are there. I could only just feel your mother's presence, but your father's comes through very strong." She broke the embrace and wiped her eyes. "I'm such a silly old woman," she said, giving a small derisive laugh. "But I miss them so much."

Claire wasn't sure how to react to this. It was almost an out-of-body experience, as if she'd eavesdropped on a private conversation. She waited for her aunt to collect herself. She wondered why she hadn't even been aware of her mother and said as much to Lilith.

"She was there. Your father was like black smoke—thick and dark—but your mother was a thin, wispy white mist." Lilith dabbed her eyes dry on a white handkerchief and then tucked it back in her pocket.

"There's always a white mist around in my dreams, especially Dream Messaging. Are you saying the mist is my mother?"

"Yes, dear. That is exactly what I am saying."

"Last night the mist was like a fog. A thick, heavy, almost cotton wool fog. I had trouble getting through it."

"Really? Hmm, I wonder…" Lilith said, trailing away her thoughts before coming back to herself. "This is going to take some thinking. But it's not getting us anywhere with what we're supposed to be doing. Shall we get back to work?"

So, they did, and Lilith was increasingly impressed by the speed she picked things up. Then Claire surprised her with a question she didn't even think of.

"How do I block someone trying to use Mind Touch on me?"

"Why do you ask? Do you want to stop me giving you sneaky suggestions?" Lilith smiled at her.

"Yes!" Claire laughed softly with her aunt. "Adam has Mind Touch, so I just want to be able to protect myself."

"Do you still have suspicions about his loyalty?"

"No, but yes. Does that make sense? What I'm trying to say is that he has abused my trust in him, and I don't know if it'll ever come back," she said sadly.

"Oh, I know that feeling. It will take a while, but it will get better. I know that Geoff has told you what happened when we were younger—and it took me a long time to not only trust him again but also to forgive him. What took me longer was swallowing my pride and trying to repair the rift. Forgiveness is the key. The answer to your original question is yes, I can. I'll give you the tools so that you can protect yourself if you need to."

Lilith was once again in Claire's mind, showing her what to do and what walls she could put up for protection. It was in one of these moments that Claire suddenly felt a shock of pain across her back and then again across her chest. She cried out in anguish. Inside her mind, images were swirling—blurred faces, voices calling and shouting—until there was only one: Adam's.

"Claire, Claire! Help me. Please come, help me."

Swirling around her were a mix of black, white, and pale blue. Adam's voice still shouted her name while pain hit her body repeatedly until she felt herself being lifted by the colour and dumped right back out into the real world. Her head was spinning, and she felt like she was going to be sick, but the pain was fading slowly, and she opened her eyes. Her aunt was looking at her as shock and worry chased each other across her face.

"What was that?" Lilith asked in a small voice.

"That was Adam. He's in trouble," Claire said breathlessly.

Lilith looked down at Claire's arm and noticed a red welt forming, so she grabbed her niece to have a closer look.

"How did you get this?"

"I don't know. I felt pain. Sharp pain hitting me over and over." Claire lifted her shirt and saw similar marks on her stomach and chest. She then turned, and Lilith confirmed they were on her back as well.

"What is going on, Claire?" Lilith asked in fright.

"We have to go now." She jumped up and started to look for shoes and her bag. "His father is not happy. He's being beaten. Oh, Aunty Lil, he is in so much pain." She started to sob but carried on trying and get things together.

Claire raced down the stairs, searching for her uncles. She found them in Geoff's study. The sight of the red welts and the fast-developing bruise on her exposed skin brought them to their feet.

"What's happened to you? How did you get hurt?" Geoff demanded, crossing the distance between them.

"Don't worry about me. It's Adam who needs help. Marcus is angry at him and is hurting him. Uncle Geoff, we need to get to the cabin now!"

"Calm down, Claire. Tell me what happened."

"But we have to go now! I'll tell you in the car." Claire flung her words at him. She was already pulling away and heading to the door, then stopped when she realised they weren't following. "Uncle Geoff, please."

Geoff looked toward his sister, who was in the doorway looking tired and shocked. She nodded to him that what Claire had said was true.

"You better do as she says, there is no time to waste," Lilith told him urgently. But still Geoff stood staring between the pair. "Geoff, now!"

Her words were enough to break him out of his stunned silence and into action.

"Okay, we knew we'd have to work fast when the time came, and it looks like that time is now." Geoff turned to David. "Grab what you need from the farm when you drive past, and we'll meet you at the access road. Lil, can you ring Mal and Bob and let them know what is going on? Tell them that we're going to Truman's cabin and that we're taking the access road. They've both been hunting up there enough times to get there themselves." He then looked at Claire. "Are you ready for this, Kid?"

"I think so," she said, following him out of the room while her Aunt Lilith called out behind them.

"You better keep her safe, Geoffrey Brown, otherwise I'll tan your hide!"

Chapter Twenty-Seven

The drive into the hills seemed to take no time at all, especially with Geoff speeding along the country roads. They reached the access track with time to spare, and they sat on the side of the road—partially hidden by shrubs and trees—waiting for David to arrive. The silence was punctuated by the calls of birds around them, but Claire was blocking them out, preparing her mind. Once again, a pleading and desperate Adam had managed to punch through to her conscious. She gasped at the pain he was in and could feel the broken bones and cuts just as deeply as he did.

Over and over, Claire repeated to Adam that they were coming. Begging him to hang on and telling him they would be there soon, until he slipped away from her like water through cracks in the earth. She came to and felt the fresh, angry welts appear on her skin.

"I'm fine," she reassured her uncle after seeing his concerned face.

Behind them, the distinctive roar of a diesel engine could be heard. They saw David's Ute race around the bend and hurtle towards them. He turned down onto the access track and stopped so that Geoff and Claire could climb in beside him. He then carried on driving down the rutted narrow trail.

They sat in silence while Geoff's knuckles were white on the dashboard as David came close several times to trees on the side of the track. But no one spoke a word until they reached the pull-in. As they got out of the cab, Geoff stood up and looked out into the forest with that faraway look in his eye. "I can sorta get a hint of them in that direction," he said, pointing the way.

"It's all right, Geoff, I know the way. The question is this: what will we do when we get there?" David asked, a backpack hung from his hand as he pocketed the keys into his jeans.

"Well, that's a very good question. I don't know; any ideas?" He looked at them and shrugged his shoulders.

"Really? You hadn't thought about how we were going to get access to Marcus? No plans tucked away somewhere?" David asked him in surprise. When Geoff shook his head, David took charge. "How about I take out that Richard guy, because I have a hankering to beat the living crap out of him!" When he spoke, it was with just a touch too much enthusiasm for Claire's taste. "Geoff, you disable the cars, and Claire— well, you know what you have to do. And here, you might need this." He pulled out a first aid kit from his backpack and handed it to her. She placed it in her own bag slung across her chest, and then changed on the spot.

Claire followed David through the forest, noting the noise behind them that Geoff was making as he crashed through the undergrowth. They reached the large tree they'd used a few days before and looked out at the cabin.

"Well, we won't have any problems luring Richard out with all the noise you make," David told Geoff, with a teasing grin.

"Sorry...I got Seek, not Stealth. I find, you track!" he replied, slightly out of breath. "Plus, I'm not as young as you."

"Excuses, excuses." David gave a little chuckle.

"Remember, you only want to maim and incapacitate—not murder," Geoff said seriously, placing a hand on David's shoulder, to which he nodded impatiently at the reminder.

"Right! You go that way and circle around to the drive. I'll go this way and see if I can have a catch-up with Dicky Boy. Claire, you still here?" David asked quietly into the air.

"Yes."

"I don't want you entering until I have him out of the way, understand? And watch out for any other of Marcus' goons. If you see any, let us know how many and where."

"Yes, Uncle David."

"Okay, then. Let's go."

They moved out and as Claire neared the cabin, she could hear Geoff trying to go quietly off to her left, but he wasn't too successful with it. As David had predicted, the noise Geoff was making did lure Richard out into the open and he followed the noise around the cabin. Meanwhile, Claire circled just under the eaves of the second floor, waiting for her uncle's signal.

Hearing more than seeing it, she was glad she didn't witness it. The distinctive sound of wood slamming into a human body, hard was sickening. Trying not to think about what he was doing, Claire swooped down and into an open window in the top story. It was quiet in the house, and she paused to listen but did not hear a thing. Moving from room to room, Claire expected to see the beaten remains of Adam at any time, but there was no one upstairs. Carefully, she inched herself down the stairs, keeping to the scotias. The kitchen bench came into view first and then the kitchen itself, but it was empty. She peered around the corner of the wall that encapsulated the stairs and looked out over the dining and living areas. Still no one. Creeping further in, she checked the only bedroom downstairs, and it was empty—except for a few bags on unoccupied and unslept-in bunks.

Hiding herself behind the flue of the potbelly stove, Claire tried to puzzle it out until she saw the open door that sat in the stair cavity.

"There's a cellar?" she asked herself, wanting to find David for confirmation.

Claire found David crouched over the inert body of Richard, checking for a pulse. He sat back on his heels and put his head in his hand.

"Uncle David?" He spun around, in his hands a large log of wood, which he gripped tightly. "It's me," she told him. "Is he…?" She left the question hanging.

"No, he's still alive. Did you find Adam?" David asked, coming to his feet but not releasing the log.

"No. There's no one in there that I could see. Is there a cellar?"

"I don't know. Why?"

"There's an open door under the stairs and I think it leads down."

"Let me just make sure this guy isn't going anywhere and then we'll look." David looked down at the inert and bleeding body of Richard. "I remember him from school. He was in our class."

David quickly used some zip ties he had produced from his backpack to bind Richard's hands and feet. They then turned back to the cabin. As they reached the French doors, Geoff came from around the house, wiping his hands on his jeans and leaving black streaks. Claire entered first and went to the open door under the stairs, peering inside. Her heart was racing, and she could feel herself start to sweat. She entered the narrow, dark space and sure enough, there were steps leading down. She took a quick look behind her to see her two uncles following and then went down. It had the musty smell of any space that is locked up for too long, but there was also another sharper odour. An almost metallic smell that cut over the top of the stale one. It wasn't until she was almost in the room that she realised what the smell was. Blood. She could hear breathing coming in ragged spurts, heavy and laboured.

Claire turned back and whispered softly for David to stop. In the dimness, Geoff almost walked into the back of David, scuffing his feet on the concrete steps.

"Richard, will you stop being a total sap and get down here? I need him woken up!" Marcus had mistaken Geoff's noisy movements for his lackey. "Richard! I won't call you again!" They could hear the footsteps get closer to the bottom of the stairs and Claire reacted without thought.

As Marcus came into view at the bottom of the stairs, he was hit full on the chest by a giant ball of sparking Light coming from Claire. The force with which it slammed into him sent him flying back, and he fell to the ground with a thud as his head hit the hard concrete floor. With a single leap, David cleared the rest of the steps and was on top of the man before Marcus could react. He flipped him over and bound his hands behind him.

Claire entered the dimly lit space and saw Adam tied to a chair, his head resting on his bare chest. Blood dripped from multiple wounds. Large contusions laced his entire body, many of which matched the ones that had appeared on Claire. She changed back to her normal size and knelt in front of him.

"Adam. Adam, I'm here," she called to him, trying to lift his head. His face was swollen and distorted from the beating he had received.

Geoff grabbed a knife that was lying on a table nearby, cut the bindings on Adam's hands and feet, and the young man then fell forward into Claire's arms.

"Adam! Wake up! I'm here, I came for you," she begged, holding onto him tightly so he didn't fall.

Geoff helped him to the ground and started to check him over.

From above them, they could hear footsteps. Geoff looked at David and he held up two and then four fingers. While watching over Marcus, David indicated to Geoff to take his place and then he mounted the stairs to peek at who had entered the cabin.

"Boy! Am I glad to see you!!" he exclaimed. "Charlie, we could use your help down here." Within moments, the space under the cabin was brimming with people. Bob, Malcolm, Ben, and Charlie stood huddled at the bottom of the stairs, taking in the scene before Charlie took charge and began to give out orders.

"I need a light," Charlie said as she started to examine Adam. Claire produced a bright white Light and suspended it over Adam's prone body.

"Thank you." Charlie ran her eyes over the mess that was Adam. "Open my bag and pass me some gloves."

Claire did as she was instructed and watched as Charlie put them on and then ran her hands over his body without touching him.

"Okay. There are a few broken bones, but first we need to clean him up a bit. Can you get out the saline and swabs, please?" She looked up at Claire's concerned and frightened stare. "He's going to be okay, Claire." Claire nodded and dived once more into the medical bag.

After Charlie had cleaned most of the blood off him, the fast-developing bruises stood out against his pale skin as she started to place her hand over the open wounds. When she took her hands away, the wound was closed but still angry-looking. Charlie worked her Healing Talent over his body on the worst of his injuries and then concentrated on the bones.

"These are always a bit tricky." She took a deep breath, placing her hands on either side of his rib cage. She breathed out slowly and carefully, nodding when she was done. She looked at his head and passed a hand over his hair a couple of times, closing the cuts she found there.

"There's not much I can do with the nose right now. I would prefer to work on it later, once I've checked him properly in the hospital," Charlie said as she sat back on her heels.

For now, she declared him fit to be moved upstairs and she watched over David and Ben as they heaved the boy between them, carrying him up. Once in the living room, they laid Adam on a couch and Claire sat down on the floor beside him. The anger she felt towards Marcus for what he did to his own son swelled up inside her and she felt murderous, looking around for him.

"Where is he?" she asked her grandfather Malcolm.

"Not yet, Kid," she heard Geoff say as he came over to kneel beside her. "There is plenty of time for dealing with him. Are you okay?" Geoff asked, concerned only for her welfare.

"I'm fine," she said as she turned to Charlie. "Why isn't Adam waking up?"

"Give him time, Claire. He sustained quite a few blows to the head. I've dealt with most of it, but he still has some bruising." She looked up at her husband. "Can you go get Claire a wet cloth, sweetheart? I think she might want to clean up a bit."

"Sure." Ben was back in a flash and handed Claire a wet washcloth. She looked up at him, puzzled as to why he had given it to her.

"You have Adam's blood on your face and hands," he told her gently.

Claire looked down at her t-shirt and arms, noticing for the first time the dark smears that covered her. The blood was already starting to dry and crust up as she wiped at it with the white cloth, but only managed to smear it in more. Charlie saw her feeble attempts and guided her to the bathroom to make a better job of it. Once inside, Claire looked at herself in the mirror and was shocked at her pale reflection. Her hair was coming loose, and she was alarmed at how much of Adam's blood was on her.

With shaking hands, Claire fumbled with the fabric as she tried to tug the shirt over her head before successfully throwing it in her bag. The sink soon ran red as she rinsed out the cloth and cleaned herself up. And when Charlie returned to the bloody scene, she handed her a singlet to wear, but Claire didn't ask—nor care—where it even came from.

Clean and tidy once more, Claire made her way back out to the lounge and sat on the floor beside Adam, taking his limp hand in hers. Her uncles were talking together, but she didn't take any notice of what they were saying. Instead, she sent out her thoughts, searching for any awareness of him.

"Adam! Can you hear me?" she called to him.

"Yes. Where are you? Everything's black!" he replied. There was a touch of panic edging into his voice.

Claire directed her thoughts to where she thought he was, and his voice became clearer. To her, the area was laced in white, and her father was nowhere to be seen. A figure became more distinct as she got closer to his voice and she found him, bathed in black.

"Dad!" she called out as the blackness dissipated and reformed into his shape.

"Dad?" Adam asked, confused.

"It's a long story—one for later on. Are you all right?" she asked, still keeping her distance and fighting the urge to hug him close.

"I don't know. I think I am. All I could feel was pain and wanting you. I didn't know if you heard me."

"I heard. I am with you now—right beside you," she told him comfortingly. She took a step closer, giving into her impulse, and her father stepped between them.

"Dad, please. He needs me."

"Not like this, Claire. You're there in body. You do not need to give your spirit to him as well."

The mist at her feet swirled around her and rose into a column, enveloping the girl. She felt peace as a whisper was carried to her. "My beautiful daughter." And then it was gone.

"Claire, you have to listen to me. It is not your time yet to be bonded to anyone, you are much too young," John pleaded. She lowered her head and nodded. He stood to one side, still watching.

"What just happened?" Adam asked her.

"Couldn't you hear them?" Claire asked.

"Them? Who?"

"My parents."

"All I can see is black smoke and white mist."

"That's them. The black is my father and the white my mother. Even my Aunty Lil can't explain it," she told him with a shake of her head.

"Okay, then, we'll leave that explanation for later," he told her, his look slightly sceptical before changing to one of dread. "What happened? Is Dad dead?"

"No, he's still alive. I'm not sure where he's being kept, as they won't let me near him yet. Adam, there's something you should know..." she started.

"You shouldn't tell him," her father spoke up quickly.

"Dad, *please* trust me." He backed off again as she turned back to Adam.

"Adam, I'm a Chameleon."

"A what?" he asked, clearly confused.

"A Chameleon. Your father didn't give you any information on other Talents?"

"Not really—I learned mostly on my own, but there were a few hints about other Talents in the book he gave me."

"Right...well, a Chameleon's a person who's able to take on and use Talents other than their dominant one."

"Funny, I thought a Chameleon was a small, strange creature from Madagascar." He laughed.

"Ha ha, very funny," Claire retorted.

"Sorry. I couldn't resist it."

"My dominant Talents are Flying and Hiding, but I soon learnt how to Recall, and the other Talents all sort of snowballed on top."

"So, what else can you do?"

"Mind Touch is the latest one, and the only other is Light."

"Light?"

"Yes."

"So, it's you? You're going to kill my father? I can't believe it, Claire. After our conversation this morning, I thought we had agreed." Adam took a step back, looking horrified at the thought.

"We did. I am not going to kill your father, Adam. Believe me when I say this: I find the thought just as sick as you do. Do you really think I would want to murder someone? Don't you know me at all, Adam?" Her voice was reaching a very high level, and he backed away from her a little more.

"I'm sorry. Yes, I do know you. I'm sorry I doubted you, Claire." He stared at her for a moment and then said, "So is it your aunt who will be performing the Mind Touch?"

"No. Aunty Lil isn't here. I'll be doing it." He was silent for a while.

"What suggestion are you going to give him?" he asked, and Claire could see he was still unsure and dubious.

"That his Talents have been burnt from him." She could see Adam was thinking this over, and she turned to her father.

"Do you really believe you can trust him?" he asked her in a low voice.

"I know the pain he went through and the fear that I felt coming from him. I believe him, Dad."

"That's not what I asked. Do you trust him?" John asked again.

"It'll take a lot to rebuild the trust I thought we had, but I forgive him. Isn't that the first step?"

"Yes, it is." John nodded with a slight smile.

"Claire, I can't let you do it," Adam interrupted.

"What?" It was Claire's turn to be confused.

"I can't let you do it," he said more emphatically as he walked over to her. "It has to be me, Claire. I couldn't live with the thought that it was you who messed with my father's mind. He was never really a good father, but he's the only one I've got. It has to be me."

"Adam, are you sure? You're too close to him, and especially after what he put you through?"

"I know him better than anyone else. I know his weaknesses and his strengths. His Charm means the world to him. Before I developed my Talents, he wasn't a great father, but we had our moments. After, he stopped touching me. He'd always make sure there was at least two metres between us, so I didn't use Mind Touch on him. He may have used me, but he was frightened of what I could possibly do to him. Claire, it has to be me. I want to have back what we used to have before, if not even more."

She was silent as the hurt poured out of him like a tangible presence. What was it with this man who couldn't love his sons? Or anybody except for himself? She didn't want to put Adam through this, but she knew she had no other choice.

"Claire, I trust you and I love you. Please trust me on this," Adam pleaded.

Claire felt outwards to see if he was using Charm on her, but there was nothing. His use of the word *love* was not lost on her.

"All right. But I supervise. Do you even know what it is you're supposed to do?" she asked him quickly.

"I know how to do a basic suggestion, but I've always used my Charm with it."

"Okay. I think I know a way to help. I'm going to have to leave. I have to find something out. Are you gonna be okay?" she asked, reaching out to him involuntarily before checking herself.

"Yeah, I'll be all right. And thank you, Claire." His image dissolved in front of her, leaving Claire standing there.

"Claire, what is it?" Her father was at her side.

"Why is Mum not as strong as you in my dreams?" she asked suddenly.

"She put so much effort into me that she left little strength for herself."

"How'd she do it?"

"I can't tell you that, Claire, because I don't know. She told me that she could, and I trusted her." Claire raised an eyebrow at that. "This was different. We were already bonded by our love for each other and by you." He reached up and stroked her face. "We are so proud of you—so very proud of the young woman you have become." She leaned into his touch and looked into his blue eyes as he hugged her. Claire remembered his hugs, his whiskers tickling her face, and the feeling of being safe and secure. She missed them both so much it hurt.

Reluctantly, Claire pulled away. "I've gotta go, Dad. I have to wake up."

"Yes, you do. Good luck." Engulfing her with the feeling of love, the white mist swirled up yet again as she awoke.

Chapter Twenty-Eight

Claire became aware of the voices around her but couldn't decipher what it was they were saying when she slowly opened her eyes. With her hand still cupping Adam's, she watched him breathing—slow and steady—and then her own body sent out some signals of its own. Both of her legs were cramped underneath her, and she moved, stretching them out one at a time. Her stomach growled loudly and persistently as she tried to ignore it. She hooked a finger on the strap of her discarded bag and pulled it closer to her, reaching in and retrieving the book that she had stashed inside before they'd left the house. She opened a page and started to skim over it.

"Here, eat this, you must be starving by now!" A plate was thrust in front of her with a large sandwich on it as David towered over the top of her and she stared at it blankly. "Don't tell me you aren't hungry?"

"Starving!" she said with a grin while taking the plate from him. "Thanks."

"How are you?" David sat down on the floor beside her.

"I'm all right. I've just had a conversation with Adam." David raised his eyebrows. "In here," she added through a mouthful of food and pointing at her head.

"And what did he have to say for himself?"

"He wants to be the one who puts the suggestion on Marcus."

"Do you think that's a good idea?"

"You sound just like Dad," she said before thinking.

"What do you mean by that?" She swallowed another large mouthful quickly and then related to him what had happened before Adam's first urgent call. He sat back against the coffee table. "There's a part of John in your brain?"

"Yes."

"Do you know how mad that sounds?" he asked quietly.

"Yes, but Aunty Lil can confirm it. It was really weird sitting there while they had a conversation in my mind." She took another bite and waited until she'd finished before adding, "Mum's there as well, but not as strong as Dad. He told me that she spent so much energy on him, she had only a little left for herself." He just sat there, trying to comprehend what it was that she told him.

"Jess? My Jess?"

"Yes," she said softly, seeing his reaction. As he got up and walked outside, she watched him leave and felt sad that she had given him pain.

Claire continued to read but only managed to get hints of what she wanted to find out. Pulling her phone out of her pocket, she quickly dialled a number and waited, but nobody answered, so she tried number after number until one picked up.

"Hello?" a small and weak voice answered.

"Grandma!" Claire cried out in some relief.

"Claire, oh, Claire! Is everything okay?" Grace asked on the other end.

"Yes, it's all fine—we're all fine—is Aunty Lil there? I need to talk to her! It's urgent."

"Of course. I'll just get her." The other end went quiet until Lilith spoke.

"Claire, what is it? Are you all right?" Lilith echoed her sister-in-law.

"We're fine. We're all okay. But I need to ask you a question."

"What is it?"

Claire spent the next five minutes telling Lilith exactly what it was she wanted to do. And together, they nutted out a solution that would fit the circumstance she had found herself in. When she finally hung up, she had the information that she needed, but now she had to put it into practice. The new knowledge went around and around in her mind as she put the pieces into place, reminding herself that she had to go carefully and not just throw the information at Adam. She tweaked and changed the details until she was satisfied and had it all formulated the way it had to be. Then she sat and thought. Different scenarios came springing into view in her mind. *What ifs* chased them, and she knew this time she couldn't just wait and see what happened—she'd need to be ready for anything.

"Are you ready, Claire?" Geoff asked breaking into her thoughts. Her head shot up and she looked at him. "I think we'd better do this soon."

"Umm, no. Not just yet. Please."

"Okay. Let us know when you're ready." He left her sitting beside Adam. She closed her eyes and contacted him again.

"You have to wake up now—they want me to do it soon," she told him.

"I'm trying, but it's hard," he replied with some effort.

She opened her eyes and tried not to be noticed, especially by Charlie. She slowly reached into his head with her mind and found the area that was stopping him from waking up. She moved it to one side as she felt his consciousness awaken. His eyes began to flutter until they finally opened a little.

"Hi," he said quietly to her as she looked into his green eyes.

"Hi back." She removed her hand and sat back. "Charlie," she called, and her aunt quickly walked over.

"Good. You're awake. How are you feeling?" she asked, crouching down to see him closer.

"Like a train has run over me. I hurt everywhere," Adam replied.

"You'll hurt everywhere, but I have healed the broken bones—except for the nose. Sorry. I'm not messing with that one. The open wounds have been closed, but the bruising's going to have to take its own time, I'm afraid." He looked at her, not really comprehending what she'd just told him. "I'm Charlie, by the way, Claire's aunt. I'm a Healer. How's the head feeling? Do you have a headache?"

"Yes, but not bad—just a dull ache."

"I recommend that you get a lot of rest and let your body heal naturally." He nodded as she moved away to sit at the table with her husband.

Adam struggled to sit up a bit and Claire helped him. "Have you figured out how you're going to help me?" Adam asked her quietly as he struggled to sit up. Claire placed her hand under his arm and helped him up.

"I think so," Claire answered in the same manner.

He looked around at all the people talking to each other. "Who are these people?" He looked around the room at the strangers that he found himself amidst.

"They're my family. Charlie and Ben are married. Ben's my Dad's younger brother and they're sitting with my Granddad Malcolm—who is my dad's father. You know Uncle Geoff, and he's talking to Granddad Bob, who is Mum's dad and outside is Uncle David, my mum's twin brother."

"So many people..." he trailed off.

"You didn't think I'd come alone, did you?"

"No. It's not that, it's just...they came to help me?" he asked in wonder.

"Of course. Did you honestly think that they'd leave you to the hands of your father?"

"I don't know what I thought." He shook his head and rubbed his neck with his hand.

"I can't believe your father did this to you. What happened?"

"Well, for starters, it wasn't my father. Richard did this." He indicated his body. "Dad never gets his hands dirty. I told you, he never even gets close enough to me. As for why, I was the one who was supposed to keep the Watchers in line, but they kept running off and he blamed me. So, this was his punishment."

"Sorry, that was my fault. Has he done this to you before?" she asked.

"Not to this extent." He fell silent and she sat beside him for a time just holding his hand, neither really realising that she was.

After a while, Geoff came back to them. "Claire, we must get on with it. I don't want to rush you. I know how hard it's going to be for you to do this."

"There's been a slight change of plan, Uncle Geoff. Adam's going to put the suggestion on Marcus—not me."

"Do you think that's wise?" he asked them both, sitting on the coffee table and resting his elbows on his knees.

"I know you don't trust me, Mr Brown, but I promise that I'll do nothing but make things right. My father has been making life difficult for a lot of people for a long time, so I think it is high time that he was stopped."

"Until someone else changes him back?" Geoff asked.

"That won't happen," Claire chimed in. "The suggestion that Adam will put on him cannot be reversed. I talked to Aunty Lil, and we worked it out together."

"I'm sorry, Adam, but I have to ask Claire this. Do you really trust him?" he asked.

"I trust him to do the right thing," Claire replied. It seemed like everyone was asking the same question.

"That isn't what I'm asking you, Claire."

"I know. Adam needs to earn my trust back, and that's why I'm trusting him to do the right thing today." She looked at Adam and he smiled back.

"Okay, so shall we get on with it?" He stood up and looked down at the teenagers.

"You're not going to argue some more?" Claire asked in surprise.

"No. I trust you've got a handle on it, Kid," he told her plainly and left them alone.

"Right. What do I have to do?" Adam inquired, sitting forward.

"Sit still and don't fight me."

"What?"

"Just shut up." Claire placed her hands on his head and closed her eyes. He continued to look at her with a small smile on his face before emulating her and closing his own. After a few minutes, she pulled her hands away and looked at him.

"Do you understand?"

"Yeah, I do. How'd you do that?" he asked, his eyes going wide with amazement.

"We'll have lots of time to talk about it later, but we've got to get this done. Are you ready?"

"Yes," he said gravely. Tentatively, he stood with a little difficulty and stretched himself to get moving.

"Uncle Geoff, we're ready." Geoff looked around and motioned them to the bunk room off the living area.

Claire went to the door and opened it. They found Marcus in the middle of the room, strapped securely to a chair with zip ties. He looked up as they stepped into the room.

"Claire! So nice to see you again! I would stand up, but unfortunately I am a little tied up at the moment, as you can see." Claire could feel the Charm crash into her even harder than it had a couple days before. She could feel the desperation coming from him as he tried to bend her to his will. Claire reinforced her walls.

"I'm afraid your Charm is a wasted effort on me, Mr Ryder," she stated flatly.

"So, is it you who has the Light Talent?" he asked conversationally. "You've been busy since you left the city. Such a pity that you didn't let us know you were leaving, we missed you this summer, didn't we, Adam?" he asked, now turning to his son.

"I'm touched," she told him.

"Son, are you going to just stand there and let her kill me?" Marcus turned his hard and demanding look on Adam.

"I'm not going to kill you, Mr Ryder," Claire interjected before Adam could answer.

"Marcus, please, Claire. I think we've known each other long enough for you to call me by my Christian name now."

"Dad, she's not going to do anything to you. I am." For a split second, fear glowed in Marcus's eyes. "Shall we get on with it? I don't want to spend another minute talking to him." Adam looked at Claire, and the dark bruising around his eyes didn't distract from the mental pain he was feeling.

"Adam, please!" Marcus begged his son, but Adam ignored him as he walked up behind his father and rubbed his hands together.

"Just as I showed you. I'll place my hands on yours—to make sure everything's working properly—and I'll not interfere unless I think it's necessary, okay?" Claire said to him sympathetically.

Adam nodded to her and then placed his shaking hands on his father's head. Marcus reacted by trying to move away from his son, but Adam only held on firmer, pulling his head back and holding it tightly in place. Marcus grunted as Adam's fingers dug into his scalp. Claire then placed one of her own smaller hands over the top and they both closed their eyes. Marcus jerked in his seat, trying to release their hold and stop them from what they were about to do. None too gently Claire clapped her free hand on his shoulder, mentally forcing him to sit still and his movements calmed down.

"Just the way I showed you, Adam," she said quietly, when she was satisfied Marcus would not interrupt them again. She felt him tentatively find the area in his father's mind he was looking for and steeling himself to act.

Within his mind, Marcus tried to rebel against the suggestion, trying to block with rapid thoughts and images, trying to hide from them in his mind. She also felt Adam pull all his concentration, ignoring the throbbing headache he still had and releasing the suggestion onto his father without hesitation, forcing it upon him with all his will. Marcus screamed.

Claire's walls slammed up as he did this, and she pulled away mentally as she watched Adam work—ready to react to anything. Adam still struggled against his father, his mental energy forcing the change he so desperately desired. Encompassing his will with even more force than was required. When he faltered a little, Claire added her own energy to his to reinforce the suggestion. Marcus stopped struggling. She then directed Adam to the Charm Talent.

The Talent loomed large before them, as a mirror-surfaced orb, which pulsated and threw back images that were meant to appease them. Images of father and son embracing warmly. Another of Marcus standing behind both Adam and Claire, as if he were giving them his blessing. Claire could feel Adam's reaction to those images, and felt the Charm almost entice him to give up his plans. Then she saw his eyes harden, his resolve intensifying as he shook of the illusionary tricks. The orb reacted to this and shrank, the surface dulling and the images fading as they lost their power.

Together the pair bound the Talent tightly. Blanketing it in the conjoined efforts to supress it so Marcus could not use it again. With one final effort Adam mentally pulled tighter on the bindings until it could not be seen. Breathing heavily, Marcus slumped in his chair even as Adam finished. He removed his hands from his father's head and looked at them shake before turning to Claire. She put her hands up and stared at Adam.

"What've I done?" he whispered with tears streaming down his face.

"Adam." Not letting her guard down, she walked into his arms and hugged him. Sobbing, he clung onto her as she gave comfort as best she could. His sobbing eased, and she guided him to one of the bunks and made him sit down. "I'm going to check on Marcus."

Adam nodded, and Claire moved back to his father. Her defences were still well and truly up when she laid a hand on his head. She searched for the suggestion that Adam had placed on him and found it easily enough. It sat in Marcus' mind, still raw and not quite as binding as she would have liked. Carefully, she made sure that it was fully in place and taking hold before adding a little refinement of her own. A slight change that she hoped the one who would receive the benefit of would appreciate, even though her mind told her that he probably wouldn't.

"You thought I'd trick you?" Adam asked suddenly when she retreated from Marcus. "You thought I wouldn't make the suggestion and I'd turn it on you! Didn't you?" He lifted his face and turned it to her. Pain, disappointment, and worse—loneliness—etched around his eyes.

"No, I..." Claire began, but he cut over the top of her words.

"You did. Please don't lie to me. I felt the walls. I know when you're readying yourself for something dangerous. I've been watching you for years taking on riskier and riskier stunts—I can feel it in my bones."

"Yes, I did have my defences up," Claire told him truthfully as she sat down beside him on the bed. "I am sorry, Adam, but I did explain it to you earlier. Trust is going to take a while to come back. I trusted you to do the right thing, but that doesn't mean that I shouldn't have taken every necessary step to protect myself. Adam, you mean a great deal to me and I'm not willing to walk away from our..." She paused for a moment, finishing with, "...friendship."

"It's more than a friendship that I feel for you, Claire," he whispered, grabbing her hands and holding them in his own.

"I know. Me too." She nodded and blushed.

Adam was bending down to kiss her when the door opened, and they broke apart.

"Ah," David said as he walked in and saw them. "Um…are you finished?" he asked, looking uncomfortable.

"We are," Claire told him as she stood up quickly. "It's all in place."

"Good. I'll go get Charlie to check him over, then." He then left the room. Claire turned back to Adam, who gave her a small smile.

Charlie entered the room and gave the pair a quick glance.

"Did it go okay?" She started to check Marcus over as Claire nodded. "Can we release these bonds?" she asked of Geoff who had just entered the room.

"Sure." He produced a pocketknife from his jeans and handed it to her. She made short work of the restraints and together—with the help of Adam and Geoff—they made Marcus more comfortable on one of the bunk beds. Adam stood beside his father, watching him sleep.

"How heavy was the suggestion that you put on him?" Charlie asked Adam.

"I'm sorry. I don't know what you mean," he told her, looking a bit startled.

"You didn't know what you were doing?" Charlie looked shocked at the thought.

"Adam's education in his Talent was missing some bits," Claire quickly told her. "I gave him the knowledge he needed to do the job and I was there to make sure it was done right." She peeked at Adam and looked back to Charlie.

"Why didn't you do it in the first place?" she demanded.

"I asked her not to," Adam informed her. "He's my father and if anyone had the right to do what we've just done, it was my right as his son."

"Well said, Adam," Geoff said, cutting in before Charlie could say another word.

"What's with all the noise? Can't a man get any sleep?" Marcus moaned from the bed.

"Dad!" Adam knelt down beside his father.

"Adam, what are you doing here?" he asked, clearly confused.

"What can you remember, Dad?"

"I went down to the cellar for something. I can't remember. What happened?" Marcus went to sit up and his hand found the lump on the back of his head.

"You had a fall, Dad! And hit your head. I found you," Adam lied.

"Who are these people?" Marcus asked, looking around at the three others in the room.

"You remember Claire, Dad—we go to school together—and Mr Brown, her uncle."

Marcus nodded but still looked confused.

"And this is my nephew's wife Charlotte—she's a doctor," Geoff told him.

"I want you to take it easy, Mr Ryder. You have had a very nasty bump to the head," Charlie notified as she checked him over. "Now, for the next few days to weeks, you may feel nauseous and dizzy. If it doesn't get any better by next week, I want you to go and see your GP. But for now, get plenty of rest and keep things quiet, okay? I'll leave you all in peace," Charlotte said with a kind smile before leaving the room.

"Let's leave Adam and his father for a while," Geoff suggested, taking her arm. Claire agreed and followed him out of the room, but not before giving one last smile to Adam, which he returned.

As she left the room, she heard Marcus say, "Adam, what have you done to your face?"

"You know me, Dad, I'm always getting into scrapes." She closed the door on the pair and still prayed her trust wasn't wasted.

Chapter Twenty-Nine

The next day, Claire woke and stretched out in bed. The sun was well and truly up over the hills, and it promised to be another beautiful summer's day in the village. The sleep she had just woken from was the best night's rest she'd had in a very long time, and it was the result of a suggestion from her great-aunt. Lying there tucked up under the covers, she wondered what her life would be like now, after having had her world turned completely upside down. How could she go back to the city and carry on like nothing had changed? And did she really want to go back there, anyway?

The city girl who enjoyed the thrills and excitement that a large place like that could give her, suddenly found she enjoyed the country. The people were friendlier, and she finally had family around her. But would she have more freedom? Now that everything was over, could she honestly envisage a life here?

Claire was still pondering these thoughts and questions when she slowly made it into the kitchen for breakfast. It was only when she looked around that she realised she hadn't heard her uncle up at any point that morning. And he wasn't sitting in his normal chair, drinking a coffee, and reading the paper like usual. Dismayed, she went to search for him.

The door to his study was slightly ajar, and Claire paused before she knocked. She could hear him in there moving papers around. Pushing the door open as she knocked, she saw him quickly shutting some files and placing them in his desk drawer.

"Claire, good morning!" Geoff greeted her. "Did you sleep well?"

"I did, thank you, Uncle Geoff. Have you had breakfast yet?" she asked.

"Hours ago. You've slept in. But if you quickly grab yourself something, you'll have plenty of time to eat it before we have to go." He pulled out a key from his pocket and locked the drawer, then carefully tucked it back away.

"Go where?" she asked.

"A village meeting has been called. The Elders are demanding answers about what happened yesterday, and we must go to give them." He stood up and buttoned the blazer he had on. Claire noticed he wasn't wearing his usual polo shirt and jeans, but dress pants and a neatly ironed white shirt with a tie, as if he was about to enter court. "Come on, Kid, get a move on." He hurried her out of the room and back to the kitchen.

Shortly after, they were walking down the road together, the morning sun warming them as they went. The questions still rattled around Claire's mind, and she finally spoke one to her uncle.

"Uncle Geoff, do we have to go back to the city?" she asked him slowly.

Her question surprised Geoff, and he stopped in his tracks to look at her.

"Are you serious? You don't want to go back to your old life?"

"I'm not sure. I was just wondering what life would be like here in the village with all of my family."

"It is something to think about." He carried on walking. "Wouldn't you miss your friends and school?"

"Friends? I really didn't have that many that I was close to, apart from Adam. And as for school, well, one's pretty much as dull as the next, isn't it?"

"Before I bite into that large bit of bait you just dangled in front of me, I just want to say you need to really think about this, Claire. I can set up shop anywhere. There's always a need for a solicitor in any town. But you're coming to the end of your schooling this year, and you need to think about what it is that you want to do with your life. You are book smart—there's no doubt about that—but what is it that you want to do? What's your passion? And please don't say free running."

"Yes, I love free running...and you know some people make a very good living out of it!" she teased while laughing at the face he made. "But honestly, I haven't thought about what it is I want to do."

"Think about it properly and we can talk about it when you're ready."

The roads around the village were like a parking lot, and the hall was packed with people, even more than the night her grandmothers had held a welcome-home party for her when she first arrived. Claire didn't realise there were so many in the village.

Geoff, seeing her amazement, chuckled a bit and then whispered, "They've all heard what happened and have come from near and far."

This made Claire feel shy as she leaned up against the back wall, hoping that no one would take notice of her. But unfortunately, Grace saw them enter and called out to them. With her hand waving frantically in the air, she gestured to them to come and sit in the seats she'd saved specifically for them. Claire rolled her eyes at her uncle, and he then led her up to the front of the packed crowd. She quickly became aware of how many other sets of eyes were on her.

The meeting was called to order and the facts and history leading up to the events of the day before were laid out to everyone there. The Elders each took a turn to tell everyone their views or anecdotes of their own dealings with Marcus—all except Mary, who was noticeably absent. When it came time to relate what had occurred, the Elders called on Geoff to speak. He rose from his seat and climbed the stairs to stand in front of the large audience on the little stage.

Claire sunk lower in her chair as he began to tell them what happened. His deep and melodious voice carried right to the back of the hall, as his tone was that of a well-respected solicitor who was used to talking and getting the facts across to a hostile jury. She watched him pace the floor as he spoke, using the space and his movements to engage everyone there. When she looked, all eyes were on him, and she felt proud to be his niece.

Questions came next from the floor, and Geoff stayed up on the stage to answer them as best he could. One person from the back called out over the top of many other voices.

"Are we going to hear from Claire?"

She spun in her seat and could see Jack standing there, staring at her. Other people started to turn to look at her as well and she started to blush, automatically beginning to disappear. A collective gasp went up from those who were sitting around her and her family, but she stayed sitting where she was.

"I think that gave you your answer, Jack. Claire will not be speaking here today. Her role in this matter has already been laid out for everyone, and I beg you all to give her the space and respect to let her deal with what has happened in her own time."

A few people nodded their agreement and some others even clapped, supporting the request. Claire slowly came back to herself, and Grace put a protective arm around her.

The time had come to decide what exactly The Community would do with Marcus. The Elders didn't mention Adam—Claire so astutely noticed—and for that, she was grateful. Suggestions came from the floor as well as the stage, and all were discussed in a civilised manner. Eventually there was no permanent decision given for everyone to vote on. It was agreed that he could stay in the village for the meantime but that he must have Watchers on him day and night, until the Elders were sure that the suggestion that had been placed on him was truly set and working. With that decision, the meeting broke up.

The scraping of chairs as everyone stood was deafening in the echoic hall, their voices all clambering against each other as they tried to make themselves heard while chairs were stacked, and the community filed out. Claire and her family remained seated until everyone was gone, and it was just themselves and the Elders left.

They descended the stairs, and each came up to Claire to thank her individually, taking her hand in theirs to shake. Claire blushed at the attention, but her family stood around her with pride in their hearts. This lost girl of The Community had come home and proven herself to be well and truly one of them, helping to heal many rifts in the process.

"Right," Lynnette said, forcefully taking charge. "Back to ours for a bit of celebration. What do you think, Claire?" She took Claire's hands in her own and pulled her up out of her seat.

"That sounds great, Grandma." Claire smiled at her mother's mother.

"Good. Grace and I worked up a storm in the kitchen yesterday while we were worrying what was going on. So, we can't let it go to waste!" She claimed one arm and Grace claimed the other, and together they escorted their granddaughter out of the hall.

Outside, people were still milling about, talking in small groups. As they passed them, both Grace and Lynnette invited people along. They were stopped at one point by a group of old ladies, wanting to know if they could bring anything. Claire left her grandmothers to it and carried on down the road, not going too far, when someone suddenly stepped out in front of her.

"Jack. You scared me!" Claire said, quickly backing away.

"Sorry," he apologized insincerely. "You know, the taking away of my Talent doesn't change a thing, Claire. My mother's visions have never been wrong — not ever." He insisted, taking a step closer to her as he said this, and she moved back further.

"Your mother admitted she hadn't had a good vision for over a year, Jack."

"See! More lies. I don't know why you'd lie to me, Claire. And I don't think Father will be too happy when I tell him what his precious little boy Adam did to him. I'm sure we can find someone who can undo what it was that he did," Jack told her.

"You can't. I made sure that the suggestion could never be reversed. I made sure that he could never go back to the way he was — back to being a narcissistic, unloving man. I did that so both you and Adam could actually have a *proper* relationship with him as father and sons should."

There was a moment when hope flickered across his face and Claire thought she'd gotten through to him, but it was gone all too soon as he sneered at her.

"You're just an untried girl who thinks she has all the answers." He moved towards her aggressively.

Just as fast, Claire was being pulled back and two others stood in her place. David and Ben both loomed over Jack, who halted in his tracks, looking up at the pair. Both her uncles had very nasty looks on their faces, and both emitted an aura of protection and anger. Jack took a step back from them, cringing slightly.

"I hope, Jack, that you aren't threatening our niece," Ben said in a voice that was much like his brother's.

"Because if you are, we are just going to have to imprint it on you very carefully that that's not a good idea," David finished.

"I was just talking to her!" Jack told them hurriedly, still taking small steps backwards.

"Oh, there you are, Jack. I've been looking for you everywhere." Mary came bustling up from behind Claire and took his arm. "Hello, David, nice to see you again. And Benjamin! It has been so long since you have been back for a visit. I take it the business is going well in the city? And your wife Charlotte is doing well, I hear?"

"Yes. Thank you, Mary. We are both doing well," Ben replied pleasantly.

"Good, good. David, can you tell your mother we would've loved to come around for a cup of tea today, but we have so much to do at home! And we are going to be visiting Jack's father later. He's come to the village for a visit. You know it's been such a long time since he was last here and he can't wait to get to know his boy," she said beaming at her son. "Goodbye!" she called out, steering her son past them.

"I think we're going to have to keep a close watch on that one," David told Ben as he watched them go.

"I don't know. Once he sees how his father is towards him, I have a feeling that he'll settle down," Claire hypothesized. They looked at her as if she had two heads and she laughed. "Jack is just a little lost boy who wants his daddy to notice him," she told them in simple terms. "The extra suggestion that I put on Marcus will see that both Jack and Adam get the notice that they deserve."

Comprehension dawned on her uncles, and they stood with her as her protectors until the rest of the family joined them. Claire was regretting the need for them, but she was grateful that they had stepped in when they did, as she felt closer again to her small family.

The rest of that week was busy for Claire since she spent as much time as she could with her grandparents and cousins. At first, she found the twins and Hunter a very big handful, but with the help of Jasper, they kept them entertained. She taught them how to tumble properly, and even how to do backflips. But that backfired one afternoon when Oliver fell badly and broke his arm. Claire made sure he had it secured to himself and rushed him to his mother's side.

"Well, it's off to the hospital for you, young man. You're going to need a cast put on that," Charlie announced to her son.

"But Mum, can't you just...you know, make it all better?" he begged her.

"It is a rite of passage for every young person that they experience the boredom and horridness of an emergency room and the nuisance of a cast. This is your time and now you must bear it," she told him grandly, bundling him into the car.

"I'm sorry, Charlie, so very sorry! I didn't mean for him to get hurt!" Claire apologised profusely before Charlie could leave.

"If it wasn't trying to do backflips, it would have been jumping from a tree or even an accident on his bike. Claire, it's all right. I'm not angry with you." Charlie hugged her. "He's a boy. He was going to get hurt eventually! This way, I can scare the bejeebers out of him and hopefully he'll learn his lesson," she said, smiling.

Claire decided that the boys had had enough of that activity for the day. And so, with the help of Jasper, they gave them a light show until it was time to go home.

While walking home, she decided to go the long way, travelling one block further down than she needed to and then circling back. Bound and determined, Claire just wanted to see the place Adam and his father were staying.

The drab house finally came into view. Dusk had settled over the village and lights started to go on in windows, shining out to the world like beacons. She stared at the rather ordinary-looking house for a while until a figure came to stand at a window and stare back at her. Marcus gave her a very strange smile and Claire shuddered slightly. She didn't know if it was because she was so used to being on her guard whenever he was near, or something about the way he was currently looking at her. But either way, it felt odd and eerie. Quickly, she moved on without crossing the street to see Adam, as she had originally intended.

No one had specifically said to her that she couldn't see or talk to Adam, but they hadn't said she could either. And to her, it seemed that every time she even thought of trying to contact him, someone would find her something to do. Time was marching on, though, as there was only one more week before school started again and she didn't know what to do. To go back to the city or stay in the village—that's what she wanted to talk with Adam about. This was something they would have worked out together in the past, but now it seemed there was a wall between them—a very large and unsurmountable wall.

That wall was the fact she had not trusted him to perform the suggestion fully. But her own little addendum didn't help, either. He didn't know about that one and she felt guilty she hadn't confessed to him what she had done. Again, with secrets. Secrets, lies and cover-ups—that was what the whole mess had been about.

The secret plans ate away at her as she made her way home, and just as she was entering the house, she decided what it was that she needed to do.

Later that night as she lay on her bed, Claire collected her thoughts and calmed her mind. So easily did she now slip into the dream state that she could not decide where consciousness ended and dreaming began. But the development of the white mist swirling around her gave her a good indication of where she was. This time she welcomed the mist, knowing who it was as it danced around in a circle.

"Mum," Claire said simply. The mist rose in an embrace-like manner and then dropped away again to reveal her father. "Hello, Dad."

"Claire, my girl." He hugged her tightly. "We are so proud of you."

"Thank you, Mum and Dad," she called out to the mist.

"So why are you here? The last week you have been sleeping so peacefully, and…" He drifted off for a moment as if listening to someone. "Ahh, I think you might be right, Jess. It's about Adam, isn't it?"

Claire nodded, sitting down on the ground so she could be closer to her mother. John sat down beside her as well.

The world around them began to coalesce into a scene. Before, the surroundings had been dark and blurry, only hinting at forms and shapes. Now she could see it was a park, set sometime in the autumn months, with bare trees slowly swaying in a non-existent wind. Under her was a blanket, and she remembered the one her parents would use when they took her on picnics. She was almost certain it was the same blanket and the same park they used to take her to.

There was one difference in the serene scene that she was immersed in. On the slight rise from where the path wound its way down, sat a group of stones standing tall and silhouetted against the sky. They were arranged in a circle, seven in all, and they looked so out of place, but somehow so familiar

"What is it that you want help with?" John asked gently, breaking through her thoughts.

"I want your advice. I want to know if I should tell him what I did to Marcus."

"Do you think that it'll help with things between you two?"

"I don't know. In one way, it will just show him that I didn't trust him fully, and in another, I think he might be grateful. But I can't decide which it will be and it's confusing me," she told him with a worried frown.

"Claire, one way or another, you are going to have to tell him. If not for his sake, then for your own. It will hang between you forever if you don't. And he will know you are keeping something from him but won't understand what it is. We think you should tell him and then deal with the consequences of your actions—whatever they may be. You're still young and finding your way in the world, and you will find that there will be a lot more of these decisions to be made, both big and small. It is how you own up to them that will define you."

"Thank you. I think you've helped a great deal." She stood and started to call out to Adam.

"Claire, you aren't going to tell him here, are you?" John was at her side, looking concerned.

"No, I wasn't. I wouldn't be that cowardly. I was just going to try to get him to meet me—somewhere where we wouldn't be interrupted by everyone else."

"Everyone else?" he asked.

"Yes. It's been so frustrating. Every time I turn around, they are there smiling and asking me to do things, making sure I'm fully occupied so I don't have any alone time with Adam. I haven't even talked to him since it all happened!"

"Just be careful. Sometimes the apple doesn't fall far from the tree," he told her with a little smile as he drifted back.

Claire watched him for a moment and then gathered her will to send out a message. It built up inside her until she felt the need to release it to the world, and a response was soon received. Walking out of the mist, Adam smiled at her.

"I wondered when you'd call," he said.

"You could've contacted me just as easily," she replied.

"No, I couldn't. In no uncertain terms, I was told not to contact you until you were ready to contact me."

Claire felt confused and then smiled.

"I smell the work of Uncle Geoff here," she said, her confusion slipping away to realisation. "The sly old…. he tells you not to talk to me and then keeps me so busy that I don't contact you. Wait till I see him in the morning!"

"That doesn't matter now. You called and I answered, isn't that enough for now?"

"It is. Adam, I've wanted to talk to you every day since, you know. There's something really important that I have to tell you."

"What is it? You know you can tell me anything," Adam reassured her.

"I know, but not like this. I need to tell you to your face...while you're standing in front of me." Adam looked down at his own body and then back up at her. "I mean for real. Not in a dream."

"Oh. It's that important, then?" he said, frowning.

"Yes, it is. Will you meet me tomorrow morning?"

"Where? You name it and I'll be there; I promise." He crossed over his heart with a finger.

"I go for a run every day. A few kilometres out of town is a white fence that keeps in a grey horse. Can you meet me there?" she asked hopefully.

"What time?"

"Early—about six-thirty early."

"Claire, I'll be there. I will find the horse and I will meet you," he promised.

"Good," Claire said with a satisfied nod. Before he could say anything else to her, she cut the connection.

"You're doing the right thing. We love you," John told her as his voice and vision faded from hers and she fell into a true dream.

The next morning, Claire was up and out of the house even earlier than she had planned. There was no way she was going to give her Uncle Geoff even the remotest chance of either delaying or stopping the meeting she'd carefully organised. And just to make sure, she made herself invisible and flew out of her bedroom window, keeping herself concealed until she reached the main road, before landing gently.

The road disappeared so fast under her feet, but there was no exhilaration or feeling of freedom in this run—only trepidation and fear. The reaction she had been dreading was looming closer and closer with each step, and that feeling was commuted to her feet as she felt herself slow down.

Janie's paddock came into view in what seemed like a very short time, and the horse was at the fence by the time she reached it. Janie bobbed her head in greeting to Claire and gave her a soft neigh that seemed to suggest that she was being told off for not being around so often. Claire pulled out a big red apple from her backpack and gave it to her.

"See, just as I promised," she told the horse, who greedily took the apple from her hand.

"That is a beautiful horse!" a voice said behind her. Claire knew that voice and turned with a smile.

"She's very friendly. Come and say hello. I didn't know you were behind me."

Adam walked up cautiously to the horse and stroked its long nose, standing on the other side from Claire.

"I could tell you were in the zone, and I could wait a bit longer. Plus, you were going too fast for me to keep up. What's its name?" he asked, looking down at her, his green eyes smiling.

"Janie. She's my Uncle David's horse." She fell silent again and leaned her head against its neck. His gaze was so intense, and she wanted to hide the blush that it was invoking.

"Claire, what did you want to tell me? It sounded important, and I'd rather you just told me straight." Once again, he proved that he knew her so well. She nodded and came out with her secret.

"When I checked on your father after you had placed the suggestion on him, I placed one on him as well," she admitted.

"Oh, yes, and what was that suggestion?" he asked, his voice a little strained.

"The suggestion was that he be a bit nicer and kinder to his sons. I'm sorry that I kept it from you."

"I did wonder." He moved around to the same side as Claire and gathered her up in his arms. "I didn't think his miraculous change of heart was all down to simply accepting that his Talents had gone. I thank you, and also thank you on behalf of my older half-brother—who also seems to have changed a bit."

"That was Aunt Lil's doing, not mine."

"But from what I gather, it was your idea."

"It was. Has he really changed that much? Jack, I mean. The last time I saw him, he wasn't very happy with me. Or you, for that matter," she told him, her arms now wrapped around his waist, liking how their bodies fit together.

"Yes, he was huffy. But there was a moment when Dad hugged him—I mean, where he truly hugged him—and apologised for not being much of a father. Then he told both of us that it was all going to change."

"Maybe I overdid it a bit," Claire said, looking up into his beautiful eyes.

"Nah, I think you did it just right. Jack was blubbering like a five-year-old by the end of it. It was pretty embarrassing really. But you'll be happy to hear he still thinks the same as he always has about me!" He laughed and smiled at her.

Adam bent his head and kissed Claire tenderly. Always hinted at but never spoken aloud, their love for each other was finally acknowledged, and Claire was enjoying herself immensely—until the horse nudged Adam's back, searching for more apples. They laughed together and enjoyed the moment.

"Are you two going to stand there all day? Or do you not want breakfast?" David had crept up on them, and now he laughed at having made the pair.

"Are we ever gonna get a moment alone?" Adam asked her quietly.

"Probably not. Especially if I have anything to do with it," David answered for her and then waited for them to join him.

"Oh, and Claire, I really enjoy the early morning phone calls from Geoff whenever you do one of your disappearing tricks. So next time, tell him where you're going, please."

"Yes, Uncle David!" She blushed.

"And as for you, young man," David said, turning his attention to Adam. "I think it's about time you met your mother. You've both been putting it off all week, and I'm tired of walking on eggshells. Quite literally, as she keeps dropping the eggs, she's in such a state."

"You haven't met Beth yet?" Claire rounded on Adam.

"No. I've been busy with Dad, and I—"

"Adam, that is no excuse." She slapped him lightly on the arm. "Come on. She makes the best French toast!" Claire grabbed Adam's hand as they followed David to the farmhouse.

To Be Continued…

The One True Child saga continues…

Six years have passed since Claire's uncle spirited her away to protect her. Embracing her ancestors, Claire heads to the university to study archaeology. There she is given a chance to join a dig in Scotland. Claire finds that the past has caught up with her she as she not only discovers past society, but also the world of her ancestors.

GUARDIANS

Book 4 of the One True Child Series

Claire Brown sat on the floor of her bedroom amidst piles of clothing, toiletries, shoes, books, and bags. She stared around her at the posters and bookshelves that lined the walls and wondered again at what she was doing. Was she really going to give up all her creature comforts to live rough on a hillside in the middle of Scotland for three months? Yes, she was, and she was very much looking forward to it.

Having gained her bachelor's degree in arts and science, Claire was now in the final stages of her honours in archaeology, and this dig in Scotland was going to be the trip of a lifetime. Her professor and mentor, Maggie Hallaran, had picked Claire to join her on this new excavation. She had been on other smaller expeditions around the country and a couple in Australia, but never had she been so far away from her family and the security they gave her.

Pulling a pile of clothes towards her, she started to sort them and remembered the other reason why this was an important trip. In some ways Claire was running away, but for a very good reason. It was a painful one and one that still cut deeply at her heart—the raw and explosive breakup of her five-year relationship with Adam Ryder. He had been her childhood best friend, her confidant, her boyfriend. Up until six months ago, that is, when she had caught him cheating on her with a very beautiful redhead.

She flicked her blond hair from her face with some irritation at her thoughts and shoved the clothing into the bag with a bit more force than she should have. The anger stemmed from the fact that he would not let up trying to get back together with her—calling, messaging, and never giving her a wink of sleep with his constant attempts to contact her. Claire was getting very tired of it all and wished he would just find someone else.

"I would pack some warmer clothing if I were you," a soft but deep voice said from the doorway, making Claire jump. Geoff was leaning on the door frame, watching his great-niece as she was miles away in her thoughts. His kind brown eyes twinkled down at her along with his cheeky smile.

"Uncle Geoff, you scared me," she told him as she laid out the shirt she had been holding. "I didn't hear you come in."

"That is because you were somewhere else and not employing your Talents. What's on your mind?" he asked, tiptoeing around the mess on the floor to sit on her bed.

"Stuff, I suppose. Just thinking about my life and everyone since I moved back to the apartment." Claire dropped her head and looked at her hands.

"I miss her, too," Geoff told her quietly and placed one of his big hands on her shoulder. "But I know what Lil would say to you right now. She would tell you to stop being silly and just get on with your life."

"I know, it's just…I'm going to be so far away from you all and I'm scared—" Claire's voice trailed away, not wanting to say the words.

"You are scared of losing more of us. But it happens to everyone at some stage, Claire, and we can't stop it. Your field of work should remind you of that. But look at us; we are all healthy and happy. There's nothing to worry about."

"I'm just being stupid, I guess."

"No, not stupid; just caring." He paused for a moment, then broke the somber mood. "Now, how is the packing going?"

Claire looked around the room at the mess she had made. There were jeans and shorts, shirts and hats, shoes, socks, and underwear all scattered around in badly combined piles. "I have no idea what to take. Have you got any idea what a Scottish summer is like?"

"Maybe. When we had built up the business a bit, Katy and I took a flying visit to England, Ireland, and Scotland. I wish now that it had been longer. Katy had heard about some historical site in the highlands from a small B&B we were staying at, and we drove up to see it. I swear we had four seasons in one day! By the time we hiked up to it, we were soaking wet and shivering, and then the drive back was glorious sunshine. I've got the photos somewhere." Geoff smiled at the memory.

"So that means…what? Make sure I have a raincoat and some rain boots?"

"Both, plus plenty of jumpers and warm socks."

Claire looked around again and sighed. "I am never going to get packed at this rate." She looked at her watch. "I only have 20 hours left!"

"Hang in there, Kid." He leaned on her shoulder as he stood up and used his long legs to get back across the room. "What you don't have, you can always buy when you get there. Anyway, I wouldn't leave it too long, otherwise Grace and Lynnie will do it for you. Everyone will be here soon." He left the room and headed out to the lounge.

She watched him leave and then went back to packing. Grabbing her rucksack she had been using for field trips, Claire started to throw clothing and other items in, then pulled open one of her drawers and started to stuff a couple of jumpers and other warm things in after. She pulled the drawstring closed and clipped the cover shut, then pushed it to the end of her bed.

This party was not her idea; she had hoped just to leave the city with Maggie and start their journey without any fuss. But her grandmothers, Lynnette and Grace, had insisted that everyone travel to the city and give her a good send-off. She loved them dearly, but they did fuss, and she marveled at the strength her grandfather Malcolm had. Her maternal grandfather, Bob, had been gone for three years now, and with the recent loss of her Great-Aunt Lilith, it hurt a bit more. She had only just met them all six years ago.

"Claire, come and help, please. You've changed everything around, and I can't find a damned thing anymore," Geoff yelled from somewhere in the apartment.

The apartment was where Claire had lived from the age of ten after her parents were killed. Geoff Brown was her guardian and great-uncle, and she had come to love him as a father. When she started university, he had let her live in the apartment rent-free while she was in the city. And when she turned twenty-one, he had made the deed over to her and handed her a portfolio of shares he had invested on her behalf. Claire was now in the very enviable position of being young and financially stable.

"Where are your serving platters?" he called again. "Claire, are you even listening to me?"

"Coming, Uncle Geoff." She untangled her legs and went out to help. The décor she had changed as soon as she possibly could. Out went the old green leather bachelor couches and in came a more practical and comfortable suite. The colours on the walls no longer resembled those of a gentleman's club but were now bright and softly coloured with tasteful artwork.

The doorbell rang and she went to answer it. In flowed a troop of people, young and old and some in the middle. All were family, and she greeted each with love and kisses. Her grandmothers immediately took over the arrangement of food, and her aunts and uncles made themselves at home. Her cousins made for the spare room to set up whatever game console they had brought with them, and her grandfather Malcolm came and gave her a bear hug.

"Your parents would have been so proud of you, Claire. We all are," he whispered to her, and Claire detected a slight catch to his voice. Not one to show much emotion, Malcolm had always been strong—he had to be, with Grace as his wife.

Geoff came and shook his hand as he handed his older brother a bottle of beer. Claire left them to talk and went to the kitchen, but she was soon banished as being useless. That was the way it had always been around her grandmothers. They liked to be in charge and busy, and Claire liked to indulge them.

In the lounge, her aunts and uncles were catching up. David Fuller—her mother's surviving twin—and his wife Beth had made the long journey from the village with their two boys, Jasper and Hunter. But Ben Brown—her father's younger brother—and his wife Charlie and their twins, Oliver and Owen, lived in the city. They were not like aunts and uncles to Claire, but more like much older siblings.

"We are thinking we might make the move at the end of the last term, just in time for Christmas," Ben was telling David.

"What's this?" Claire asked as she sat in between them.

"Charlie and I are moving to the village," Ben replied.

"I've been asked to head up the little hospital. So, we're jumping at the chance to get out of the city and have a bit of quality family time in the village," Charlie told her with a big smile.

"That is really great. I'm so happy for you. Let me know when and I'll help with the move."

"You probably won't be here. No, you will be off on some adventurous archaeology dig, finding some important artefact that will change the world. Like that chick in that movie—you know the one, the curvy one with big lips," David said with a cheeky grin.

"No, not even. It's all dirt, dust, mud, and grime in a dig." She dug her elbow into his ribs.

"Dinner! Come and get it while it's hot. Claire, will you go tell the boys?" Lynnette asked her. "They won't have heard me over the noise of that thing."

"Sure." Claire walked to the spare room and ducked her head in. "You lot, dinner—and you better have not messed around with Uncle Geoff's things, or he will kill you." She dropped her voice menacingly.

"Get real, Claire! As if," Hunter told her as he filed out with Owen and Oliver. Jasper came last, now much taller than her and filling out to be the same build as his father.

"Claire, wait. Adam wanted to know if he could come over." Jasper had his phone in his hand. "What do I tell him?"

"Tell your half-brother that using you as a messenger is not cool. And that if he turns up tonight, I will not be happy."

"I'm sorry it didn't work out for you guys. I really did think you would get married."

"What, so you could claim that not only are we cousins, but brother- and sister-in-law? I don't think so. Now get before they come looking."

What she had told him would have been true, but all completely honest. Adam was her Aunt Beth's child; she had given birth to him before she had married David, so technically they were not related.

With dinner over and done with and the dishes having been cleaned by the boys, they were now gathered in the living room waiting for Geoff to speak. This always seemed to take a while; his old, ingrained habits as a lawyer were hard to break. He stood and waited for them to be quiet.

"Right," Geoff began, taking charge of the room. "I'll only keep this short, because I know Claire hates being the centre of attention." There was a small bit of laughter at this, as everyone knew that Geoff did not really keep speeches short. "Tonight we are here to farewell Claire as she embarks on a great adventure. She leaves her family, whom she has only just got to know, to go in search of people who have long since disappeared. So if you would all raise your glasses, I would like you to toast our Claire."

The shortness of the speech surprised her, and she went and hugged him. And then she thanked everyone for coming and told them that they shouldn't have. She was still blushing when the doorbell sounded through the apartment. Claire was there before anyone else could answer, but when she opened the door, she wished someone else had.

"Claire, please; I just want to talk." Adam—tall and just as good-looking as ever—stood there pleading with her.

"Adam, no. I told you and I know Jasper had sent you a message not to come." She looked back into the lounge. "I'll be back in a minute," she told her family, then turned back to join Adam on the steps outside.

"I'm sorry I came; I know you have the family over, but I wanted to talk to you before you left. I wanted to let you know I still love you."

"Well, you had a funny way of showing it. How many others were there, Adam?"

"She was the only one, I swear. I was so drunk that night, I didn't know what I was doing."

"Oh, it looked like you knew exactly what you were doing. Now I want you to leave and not talk to me for a very, very long time. And stop the other thing too—I can't sleep properly." She eyed a man over Adam's shoulder as he walked past them, watching them argue. He had a cap pulled down over his face and a dark jacket with the collar turned up.

"I'll try; sometimes it's just automatic."

"Try harder, Adam." Claire turned and walked back into the building, leaving him standing on the steps.

"I'm sorry, Claire. I did tell him not to come tonight, and I thought he had agreed not to." Beth was there waiting for her.

"It's not your fault, Beth, if he can't get the message. I'm sorry for having you stuck in the middle of it."

"It is a bit difficult, but I'm sure he will calm down soon. You going away will help, I hope."

"We can but hope, Beth," Claire told her aunt and then went back to join her family.

The looks they sent her way did not go unnoticed by Claire, and she wished that they would forget that Adam had ever been in her life. Of course she couldn't, having been her first boyfriend. Her Aunt Lilith had warned her that first loves were the hardest, and she had been right. It was at times like these that she missed her most.

After moving to the village, Claire had spent a lot of time with Lilith, especially after school, poring over the archives of The Community and helping to sort them. That is where her love of history and discovery came from, and it was her aunt who had suggested she go to university and study history—from there, she discovered archaeology.

The evening started to wind down and the goodbyes and *good lucks* were said. There were lots of hugs and tears from Grace, and once they were all gone, there was peace and silence once more. Geoff started to clean up the coffee mugs, rinsing them and putting them upside down on the draining board, while Claire took the rubbish out.

Heading out the front door and down the steps, then turning to a little alcove at the side of the building, she dumped the bag of rubbish in the bin that was hidden there. As she walked back to the door, she was bumped by a man.

"Sorry," he said as he put his hands out to steady her.

"It's fine." Automatically, Claire put up her defenses and stepped back from him.

The man kept on walking and moved off down the road; Claire watched him go as she climbed the steps to her front door. He had a cap and a dark jacket on, and she was sure she had seen him before. Shutting the door and locking it behind her, she relaxed and felt calmer.

"Cup of tea?" Geoff asked her as she entered the lounge.

"No, I don't think I could drink another drop," she said, collapsing into the couch and putting her head back. "I love them all, but they are hard work. I didn't realise how much they talked over the top of each other."

Geoff chuckled. "Yes, they do that, but then so do you, Kid." No matter how old she got, Claire thought he would always call her Kid, and she didn't mind one bit. "Penny for them?" he asked her.

"Nothing, really; just how much I am going to miss them all. To tell you the truth, I'm a little bit scared of what is to come."

"You've been overseas before—this shouldn't be any different."

"There is a bit of difference between jumping the ditch to Australia and going halfway across the world to Scotland, Uncle Geoff. There will be no backup support."

"You'll have Maggie with you."

Claire laughed quietly. "You mean I will be babysitting Maggie the whole way to make sure we don't miss our connecting flights. I love that woman, but she has no sense of time or where she is."

"Don't be mean; she's lovely," he told her off.

"Do I detect a little bit of romance in the air?" Claire asked with a cheeky smile.

"Just because I compliment a woman does not mean I like her, Claire."

"I wish you would. You need someone."

"I had my one love and I lost her. I don't have enough time left to train another to the way I like things," he joked. "Besides, I'm still looking out for you."

Claire got up and placed a kiss on his forehead. "Thank you for looking out for me, but you can stop now. In case you hadn't noticed, I'm all grown up." She placed a hand on his shoulder and he patted it.

"Never. You will always be the Kid. Now get to bed; you have a big day tomorrow."

"Yes, Uncle Geoff. Good night," she said and walked to her bedroom.

"Night. Sleep well." Geoff sat there for a few more minutes reflecting on how he had come to be the guardian of this special girl.

Guardians available June 2022
PREORDER NOW FROM ALL MAJOR BOOKSELLERS

Loraine Conn grew up on the outskirts of Upper Hutt, New Zealand. Her backyard encompassed the surrounding farmland, river, hills, and mountains which she wandered with her brothers and fed her imagination. After discovering a love for writing in English class at the age of eight, she continued to write in secret. It was not until much later in life that Loraine turned what she thought was a hobby, and something fun to do, into her first completed novel. Now married, Loraine moved from New Zealand to Perth, Western Australia in 2008, and became a stay-at-home mum. While caring for her family and after battling breast cancer, a series was born from a kernel of a dream. Loraine has now published the seven book fantasy series, The One True Child Series, and Realm of Dragons, Fight for the Crown. Both the series and book have been released with the American based indie publishing company Between the Lines Publishing, under their Liminal Books branch, using the pen name L.C. Conn. She continues her career with many more stories waiting in the wings to be released, and even more ideas to be written.

CONNECT WITH L.C. CONN

Email: raindropc1970@gmail.com
Facebook: http://www.facebook.com/LCConn
Twitter: https://twitter.com/ConnLoraine
Instagram: https//www.instagram.com/l.c.conn
Web Page: https//lcconnwriter.wordpress.com/